LETHAL RESPONSE

BY THE SAME AUTHOR
TRASHED

PRAISE FOR TRASHED

Recipient of a 'Chill with a Book' award 2019
"A dynamic story that is never still for long and keeps you turning the pages."

"Well researched and written and it held my attention from the start… he clearly has the skill to develop the main character to become as well known as the Jack Reacher character. Just on this first story line I look forward to more stories…"
P L Humphreys (Amazon)

"One hell of an exciting read. I think we have found, in Norman Townsend, a new and very important voice in crime thriller fiction writing." *ThatsBooks.blogspot.com*

"Fast-paced and gripping, sometimes gruesome, but its kept me on the edge of my seat throughout… an excellent thriller, exciting and entertaining."
Joan Clapham (NetGalley)

"The plot is very thrilling and events are realistic. Roll in book number two. Great work."
Clare Jenkins (Amazon)

LETHAL RESPONSE

NORMAN TOWNSEND

Copyright © 2021 Norman Townsend

The moral right of the author has been asserted.

Apart from any fair dealing for the purposes of research or private study, or criticism or review, as permitted under the Copyright, Designs and Patents Act 1988, this publication may only be reproduced, stored or transmitted, in any form or by any means, with the prior permission in writing of the publishers, or in the case of reprographic reproduction in accordance with the terms of licences issued by the Copyright Licensing Agency. Enquiries concerning reproduction outside those terms should be sent to the publishers.

Matador
9 Priory Business Park,
Wistow Road, Kibworth Beauchamp,
Leicestershire. LE8 0RX
Tel: 0116 279 2299
Email: books@troubador.co.uk
Web: www.troubador.co.uk/matador
Twitter: @matadorbooks

This book is a work of fiction. Names, characters, places and incidents are either the product of the author's imagination or are used fictitiously and any resemblance to actual persons living or dead, business establishments, places of work, events or locales is entirely coincidental or used for fictitious effect.

ISBN 978 1800463 141

British Library Cataloguing in Publication Data.
A catalogue record for this book is available from the British Library.

Printed and bound in Great Britain by 4edge Limited
Typeset in 11pt Adobe Garamond Pro by Troubador Publishing Ltd, Leicester, UK

Matador is an imprint of Troubador Publishing Ltd

FOR AMY, MARC AND STANLEY.

My sincere thanks to all who helped get this book to press, namely; Jerry Lucas, Anne Kimber, Ann Lofthouse, Elvis Wiltshire, Jill Todd, and Marc Blackman.

My thanks too, to the Andover Writer's Circle, for their help and support, and to Jenny Cooling for constant encouragement.

CHAPTER 1

Media helicopters clattered deafeningly above the criminals' Weyhill compound. Police had cordoned off the whole area and were patrolling the perimeter with dogs. Smoke billowing from a smouldering building drifted around the site, smoky whirlwinds being created by the choppers' down draughts. Charred timbers protruded from a massive pile of brick rubble, the remains of a bungalow. TV crews and newspaper reporters were pushed back behind the cordon. Others were climbing trees, sitting on walls trying to get a view; all the time shouting questions. Social media bloggers with long lenses, trying to get pictures, resorted to screaming abuse at anyone refusing to face them.

Major Paul Stafford and his right-hand man, Captain Ryan Peters, were in danger of becoming national celebrities. Not good considering they usually worked covertly for HM Government. Dishevelled and dirty appearance; sporting scruffy black leather bomber jackets, torn and bloodied jeans, appeared to be no barrier. Peters, slim, blond haired, marginally taller than Stafford at six three, had a number three crew cut and blue eyes. He didn't look like a fighting man; this had worked to his advantage on many occasions.

Stafford, brown hair, same number three crew cut, bigger, broader, rugged and capable, did.

Acting Detective Sergeant Nicole Martin and her Aldershot Police Station colleague PC Lee Gibson had been seconded to work alongside the covert E Squadron's Major Stafford. The media discovered Gibson had been caught in the explosion that had brought the bungalow crashing down, breaking both his legs. They began to hound hospitals within twenty-five miles of the tiny Weyhill village to find out where he was being treated. But once they spotted Nicole Martin, they were in a frenzy to get pictures of her. Though scruffy and dirty with wild, short cropped brown hair framing her heart shaped face… She was stunning. Maybe five feet seven inches tall, lithe and sleek; a testament to her fitness regime.

Stafford's team, like law enforcement everywhere, had a love-hate relationship with the media. Sometimes you needed them to get the word out, sometimes they leaked information, putting the criminals on the front foot. Stafford knew it was time to leave; his job done, for now. The crooks had been rounded up and taken away. Immigration Enforcement, Armed Response Units and ambulances had long since left. Here, he could achieve nothing more; the clean-up now in the hands of professionals. The site would be heaving with activity for the foreseeable future as forensic teams picked it over in minute detail. They would report their findings to him as SIO.

The takedown had been spectacular, with a gun battle, three huge explosions, the discovery of a drug factory and a dozen and a half illegal immigrants; little wonder it had made national news. Apart from numerous cuts, scrapes and bruises, the away team had done well, with Lee Gibson the worst casualty.

The Royal Logistic Corps had deployed a group from their Explosive Ordnance Disposal Regiment to hunt for and clear any improvised explosive devices. Police had brought in Human Remains Detection dogs, and they added to the cacophony of sound, barking with fury at each gruesome find. Ground Penetrating Radar teams were finding recent graves. Graves containing the bodies of illegal immigrants, male and female. Many of them missing fingers and toes. Some had been decapitated, others had limbs severed, bones broken and damaged.

Blagging a lift in a Royal Logistics nine-tonne truck, Stafford, Peters and Martin were taken the half-mile to where they'd parked their silver Vauxhall Vectra Sri prior to the takedown. Stafford clambered into the driver's seat, Nicole Martin jumped in beside him. Ryan Peters dived almost headlong into the back as Stafford gunned the engine, anxious to avoid the gaggle of reporters and photographers chasing up the hill towards them. As Stafford screeched out of the service road, Martin said, 'Christ almighty, they look more scary than the scumbags we've just busted.'

Stafford grunted in response and headed at speed to the A303. He knew that the Sri's enhanced spec would outrun just about anything they were likely to encounter.

The chasing paparazzi ground to a halt, shouting and waving their arms at the departing car. Settling back,

Martin switched on the radio; the airwaves were full of it. The Police Commissioner and high-ranking officers were happy to take the plaudits, claiming sweeping successes in closing down a major drug factory and people-smuggling operation. She switched from station to station. They all told a similar story: '*This is a great victory, a victory over a massive and powerful syndicate of international criminals. At last we have the upper hand...*'

Stafford slammed his fist on the steering wheel and said, 'Why can't they see this is only the beginning? This lot we've busted are the foot soldiers, the real bad guys will be regrouping as we speak. What do I have to do to make these people listen?'

Martin and Peters, surprised at the outburst, said nothing. Stafford, eyes directly ahead; if he thought anything, thought his colleagues were too exhausted to respond. They had been on the go for over thirty hours, no let-up at all, not even for grub, apart from when he let the paramedics patch his scraped and blast-damaged legs. But he knew if they could get through the next two or three hours and finish this job, then maybe he could take a break from working for HMG. Get back to his apparent day job, running five recycling centres for Hampshire County Council.

II

Stafford and Peters were long-term military men. Both had, in their late thirties, been cut loose from Fort Monckton, the training centre near Portsmouth for the Secret Intelligence Service AKA MI6, Special Boat Service, and MI5 or the Security Service. Though 'officially' retired, they worked for MI6's clandestine E Squadron, a not-so-well-kept government secret. E Squadron personnel were an ad hoc group of highly trained elite force soldiers, selected for their 'special' skills. They were called upon by HMG through the covert office of Stafford's long-time, often irascible boss and occasional mentor, known only as the Colonel. They undertook tasks thought too small for the SAS or SBS, or when local knowledge was paramount. But more often than not, for deniability. Mostly they operated outside the system. They called it black ops. Call it what they will, there were no medals for what they did.

Stafford's involvement in taking down international terrorists and putting away gangs bringing into the UK huge numbers of illegal immigrants and drugs had seen him co-opted as Senior Investigating Officer to Hampshire Police Force's Major Crime Team. Stafford guessed he'd got this job because no one else wanted it. It had certainly been the case with the recycling centres, where he'd been tasked to clear out the trade in illegal immigrants, drugs and slave labour. But with Peters and Garfield Lewis alongside him, and the backing, when needed, of HMG, the Home Office and the MOD, he had achieved some spectacular results. Stafford was used to delving into people's minds. Helping them sort out jumbled memories. He'd been a 'pal' to thugs, bullied the traumatised and trapped the dangerous. He proceeded with thoroughness and cunning, earning him respect and hatred in equal measure. Stafford and his chosen few did the spade work; police hierarchy and the CPS tidied up.

The three of them stopped off at a burger bar in Winchester. After a cursory wash and brush-up in the toilets, they had cheeseburgers and coffees all round.

'So did Lee tell you how what's-her-name just happened to turn up at the boat and almost bugger up the whole operation?' asked Martin.

'Sort of, he was a bit groggy when I saw him. They had to put him under to sort the breaks in his legs,' said Stafford. 'But he said he'd split up from his wife and started living in a grotty bedsit, so rather than sleeping there, he took to staying with the secretary girl.'

'Classic case of pillow talk, then. I guessed he fancied her when we interviewed her, but I never dreamed he'd been shagging her,' said Peters.

'I know, and apart from screwing each other, they nearly screwed up the whole takedown,' said Stafford with a rueful grin. 'Mind you, we've got so much evidence against the whole of the Egyptian's gang I doubt we'll even need what we found on the boat to convict them… Something else is puzzling me, though. It may be nothing, but what did you make of those vinyl signs and bins dumped in the Transit van? What was it? Southern Washroom Services? Or something similar?'

'I thought they'd either nicked or bought the van, and hadn't got rid of the stuff inside yet,' said Peters.

'Never gave it a thought,' said Martin, fishing around in her handbag and pulling out an A5 notepad before jotting down some details.

Stafford nodded at her. 'Yeah, good, Nicole, guess it's another question to ask the scumbags we've banged up, including Kapusniak and that little scrote Winstone. Anyhow, let's move on; DCI Talbot is organising more warrants and interviews from their Eastleigh HQ and Aldershot nick is arranging a forensic search of the flat some of them used in North Lane. What we need to do now is go down to the safe house and try to get Marva and the kids back home to some sort of normality, so this is what I want to do…' Stafford outlined his plan.

'Excellent, said Martin. 'Then maybe she can settle down and arrange the sort of funeral her husband deserves.'

Stafford nodded, 'Yeah, needs doing, I've been putting off talking to her about it. I know Garfield wouldn't want a massive send-off, but the guys from the unit will want to pay their respects.'

He shook his head as if trying to dismiss the thought, but he knew he'd never forget. Jamaican-born Garfield Lewis had been one of his longest-serving sergeants. They'd served together at trouble spots the world over. They'd learned to trust each other implicitly. Garfield had married Marva, a beautiful black woman, and they had two young boys. Earlier, at the start of the operation codenamed *Trashed*, Garfield and Nicole had been following a lead at Saxon Wharf in Southampton when he'd been horrifically killed by an assailant wielding a Very pistol. The distress flare buried itself deep in Lewis's chest, where it exploded, destroying his face and upper body. Staggering to the water's edge, he'd thrown himself in. He died within seconds.

They now had circumstantial evidence pointing to Lithuanian, Jan Kapusniak, right-hand man to the Egyptian, Runihura, as the likely killer. The criminals had continued to threaten Stafford and his crew, plus Marva and Nicole. Marva and her boys were in a safe house in Portsmouth; Nicole had refused sanctuary there. She had been keen to continue with the investigation, and, for her safety, she'd moved into a spare room in Stafford's house. Now it was time to get Marva and her boys back home.

Stafford came back to the moment, took out his mobile and said to Peters, 'You contact the house, Ry, I'm going to step outside and talk to our friend the Colonel, keep him up to speed.'

'Yeah, go ahead, boss,' said Peters with a grin. 'I mean, he very nearly pulled out all the stops for us on this one.'

Stafford glared at him, excused himself and walked outside. Martin looked questioningly at Peters.

'Ah, he's going to keep our governor and "friend" the Colonel in the loop. Me? I think the Colonel is just a crotchety old git, biding his time till he fades away, but Stafford rates him.' He called the safe house, said the password, then, 'It's Captain Peters. The situation's been rectified; we'll be down with you in about forty-five minutes to collect your charges.

'Ha! From what I heard on the media, "rectified" is somewhat understated,' said the agent.

Peters laughed. 'Yeah, it did end up well for us, but then, we are the good guys. Anyway, get them to start putting their gear together and we'll see you shortly.' Before ending the call he asked for two or three pieces of miniature surveillance equipment to be ready when they arrived.

Stafford returned and sat back down at the table. 'OK? All sorted?' Peters nodded; Stafford continued. 'Before we move out, I've been thinking about where we are with this whole thing. It's good we've put a few scoundrels away, but I think we've only dealt them a body blow.' He paused, gathering his thoughts. 'It's a big body blow, I grant you, but we don't have a clue about the head.'

Peters stopped mid-chew. Martin hesitated, before saying, 'But we smashed the whole bloody shooting match.'

Stafford gave her a half-smile and put up his hands to ward off more protests. 'Nic, I hope you're right, but I reckon we've caught this creature by its tail and we don't know what the head looks like. We need to do something to bring this bastard out in the open, then chop the fucker's head off.' Stafford could see his colleagues were still not convinced.

'All along I've felt: OK, there's money in drugs and people smuggling, for sure, but is it enough? Is there enough money to warrant the number of bodies we've seen so far?'

The other two were staring at him,

'Somehow I just don't see it,' he continued, 'You can't keep bringing in immigrants week after week without it becoming noticeable. You have to house them, feed them, put them to work. So what's happened to them? Where are they? They surely don't just let them go?'

They finished their burgers in thoughtful silence. Standing, Stafford pressed on. 'No, too risky. We're missing something here, something huge.' He shook his head in puzzlement. 'Perhaps it'll be clearer when we've had some rest.' Walking out to the car park, he said, 'I want to stop off at Saxon Wharf and collect the Volvo. Me and Nicole will take that, Ry, you shoot down to Portsmouth in the Vectra... but look, give some serious thought to what I've said, OK?'

His colleagues nodded agreement as they headed for the car and the M3.

CHAPTER 2

Solicitor Howard Neilson didn't like to lose. Late thirties, suited and booted, he walked away from Winchester Police Station in a daze. He knew he'd have to make the call, but, once made, the repercussions would be enormous. He wasn't worried about his calls being traced or hacked – Aksanov had ensured each of his top lieutenants had phones with EncroChat messaging software – he could talk without fear. But Pavel Aksanov paid him to solve problems, not bring them to him.

Neilson's dilemma started the moment he answered the phone call from that bloody Egyptian, Ayman Runihura. Neilson had represented him and other members of his crew in court numerous times. And Neilson was a winner. He looked like a winner, tanned and expensive, successful in getting them suspended sentences or fines. Neilson made a very good living defending scumbags like the Egyptian. He was always well paid by Pavel Aksanov, the Main Man as they mostly called him, although Aksanov also revelled in the nickname the Axe Man. Most thought this was just a play on words, others knew differently.

This time, Neilson could see no winning. Major Paul bloody Stafford had smashed the whole operation in

Southampton and Weyhill overnight. The operations had been worth millions. Neilson, head lowered into the breeze, reached his car without any recollection of the walk. He opened his white Mercedes-Benz E-Class, climbed in, smoothed down his light brown hair and began to think about his options. There was no defence, they'd been caught absolutely – he smiled to himself as he struggled for the old cliché – bang to rights. The list of charges against them verged on the unbelievable: at least half a dozen counts of murder, people and drug smuggling, manufacture and dealing of drugs, torture, slave labour, and they had an arsenal of weapons and ammunition, including hand grenades.

Neilson could see no suspended sentences for this lot. The trial would be a massive media draw, probably the trial of the decade. Sure he wanted part of it, but not on the losing side. Defending these arseholes would leave him with a very uncertain future, both in and outside the law. Pavel Aksanov would need to pay him a fortune to keep his name out of the proceedings. And Neilson's reputation as the go-to solicitor would be destroyed. He knew if he walked away, he might as well sign his own death warrant. But he wasn't unhappy. His mind raced with possibilities, adrenalin pumping through his veins at the ideas churning over in his brain. He could win, he thought. *Not only can I win, I can make an absolute fortune; I can be the gaffer, I can be top dog.*

He was sweating now, wired with the excitement of the challenge. Even with his ambition, he wasn't sure he'd have the courage for this battle. But opportunity, power and wealth were his for the taking. He could see it, smell it, touch it... Almost. He had to take Aksanov out of the equation; easier said than done. But it annoyed him immensely how Aksanov had messed about with Stafford – instead of killing the bastard, he'd ponced about trying to destroy him mentally by killing and hurting his friends and crew. Neilson regarded this as a fatal mistake, if anything, it had made Stafford stronger. Perhaps he should talk to Sweetman about it. His hands shook as he fired up the Mercedes. He determined not to make the phone call yet, he wanted more time to think things through. More time to plan his next move.

Turns out he needn't have stressed about making the call, Aksanov was aware of the disaster. All the news channels were full of it. Aksanov needed answers, and fast. He'd tried contacting Runihura and the rest of his crew, but no joy. Finally he called Howard Neilson. It went to voicemail. He threw the mobile onto his desk, got up and paced backwards and forwards across the expensively carpeted floor.

The office, like him, was large and impressive. Bigger than his office at the World Citizen Hotel, a manor house he owned on the southern outskirts of Basingstoke. This one was on the middle floor of his Whitelines nightclub, a three-storey ex-department store he'd purchased in central Basingstoke a few years earlier. He'd turned it into the south's go-to venue. He stopped pacing, took off his beautifully tailored dark grey jacket and slung it into an armchair. Returning to his handsome, Victorian, mahogany, double pedestal desk, he sank into the massive brown leather seat and swivelled from side to side. *Where were these men, why can't I contact them.* They were his men, men he had empowered to earn unbelievable sums of money. And now, when he needed to find out what was going on, they'd vanished.

Picking up the remote control from the black-hide writing surface, he pointed it at the huge wall-mounted TV at the far end of the room. Local stations interrupted programmes to give continuous updates of the operation, detailing the destruction of his businesses. Even the national companies were now promising further details. He slumped back in his chair and tried to calm down, to think his way through this. He pulled out a packet of cigarettes, lit one and drew in the smoke deeply.

On the surface he was a successful businessman, owning the five-star World Citizen Hotel, with casino, swimming pool and eighteen-hole golf course. He was extra proud of the golf course; he'd designed it himself. As well as Whitelines he owned Hurricanes, a nightclub catering exclusively for the young. All these venues were enormously popular. The hotel and Whitelines catered for people like him; people with huge disposable incomes and an appetite for good food, gambling and extreme sexual and head-fucking chemical experiences. He would often play rounds of golf or even a single hole with his business guests when massive sums of money were at stake. Even Hurricanes boasted queues to get in almost every night. These businesses he had built from scratch, and they looked viable and kosher from the outside.

He noticed the inch-long stem of ash on his cigarette and flicked it carefully into the ashtray, blowing out a stream of smoke at the same time. He knew the money from the dark web, porn, snuff DVDs, prostitutes, protection, and moneylending, the invisible side of his business, would continue unabated. But without the drugs, the cash flow and huge profits generated from his drug-manufacturing facility his whole empire would soon be under threat by other syndicate members. Or current franchisees and chancers, seeing opportunities to expand their territory. Worst of all, once word got out about his inability to supply the demand for drugs, he knew he would be attacked from all sides. Albanian, Lithuanian, Italian and even Russian gangs would fight each other and him to get their hands on his lucrative stamping ground. To rebuild, he urgently needed vast quantities of the whole alphabet of drugs, and syndicate money.

He crushed his cigarette into the half-full ashtray. His reputation was on the line like never before. According to the media, everything had been destroyed. But what did they know? He'd always been an innovator, quick to spot a market then exploit it to the nth degree. As soon as he'd been introduced to the dark web, he'd realised its potential. Business conducted away from prying eyes in the virtual world, opened up opportunities like never before. OK, it was slow and unpredictable, but once you understood its intricacies; Tor, cryptocurrencies, PGP encryption and the like, then you could buy and sell anything and everything. The contacts for the immigrants he smuggled in, his raw material, as he called it, came via the dark web. And when his raw material expired, as they so often did, the dark web offered new opportunities to cash in. Even a fresh cadaver could reap previously unimaginable rewards; donor organs being snapped up by eager private clinics. He'd always had a nose for sniffing out trouble, now he aimed to stop Stafford and Co from sniffing out his dark web operations and other secrets. Should he suspend the operation, or move it further underground? The ultimate decision wasn't his alone to make.

He had already put rebuilding plans in place – part of being successful and surviving in the underworld meant having a B and C strategy. He tried Neilson's number again. It went to voicemail. This time he left a message: 'Neilson, where the fuck are you? And where are my men? I need to know what the hell is going on, so get your arse over to my office in Whitelines *pronto!*' He slammed the mobile down and sat for a moment, reflecting on the events of the last few days. Ironically, he knew precisely where his fleet of Mercedes pickup trucks were; real-time tracking devices pinpointed every last one of them. The last movements on screen for the ones used at Weyhill showed they were in the police compound in Eastleigh. It was a disaster, but he vowed to rebuild his operations and at the same time crush Stafford, physically and mentally.

'Fucking Paul Stafford, you're gonna regret you crossed my sodding path. You needn't come looking for me, I'm gonna hunt you down, and hack you limb from fucking limb,' he said out loud.

His top lieutenants, including Runihura and Jan Kapusniak, must have been arrested. And a Polish lad, Matis Bockus, arrested days earlier on other drug-related charges, was now in a coma, in prison, having suffered a drug-induced cardiac arrest while awaiting trial. These men had been key to his people-and-drug-smuggling operations.

They often used a flat he owned in Aldershot and he needed it cleared of any evidence pointing to him. He picked up his mobile again and dialled. It was answered immediately; he said, 'Kurt, find Ray and get up here.'

Four minutes later, Kurt Edwards knocked once and walked in with Ray Cooper a pace behind. Both men were built like fighters. Edwards, the taller and heavier of the two; maybe a middleweight. And Cooper, slimmer, not muscle-bound, just wiry enough to be an effective welterweight. Both men wore dark grey suits, button-down white shirts, skinny neck ties; they too had the look; Ex-Army, Afghanistan, Iraq, men used to fighting.

Aksanov slid three sheets of paper across his desk.

'OK, I can't contact either the Egyptian or Kapusniak. I reckon they've been busted by Paul bloody Stafford. We put the squeeze on him a few days ago and he moved some of his people into a safe house in Portsmouth. I'm trusting he thinks Runihura was the top man and now they've busted him, Stafford'll think it safe to move his people back home. I want you to watch the Portsmouth house, see what's happening.'

Edwards, at six foot two, the taller of the pair by an inch, took the lead.

'If it's in Portsmouth it's likely Stafford will have Security Service guys from Fort Monckton watching over them.'.

'Well, I didn't ask you to fight them, I said I need you to watch them,' said Aksanov.

'Yep, I heard what you said. I'm just pointing out it isn't going be as easy as you civilians like to pretend. These guys are likely to be pros with all the latest security and surveillance gear, is all I'm saying.'

Aksanov bristled at the 'civilian' jibe. His face set like stone as he tried to contain himself, but he needed the job done and done now, so he sucked it up. He pulled out another cigarette, lit it and grinned as he thought, *the cocky wanker, if he screws this up he'll find out why they call me the Axe Man.* He was still smiling as he blew out smoke and said, 'Yeah, yeah, OK, I understand, but don't worry, you'll be well paid.'

'So you've got the address then, boss?' asked Edwards.

'Yeah, those are pictures of the house with the postcode, the others show the people they're keeping there.'

'Nice one. How'd you manage to get these?' said Edwards, folding them and slipping them into his inside pocket.

'I owned a Detective Inspector from Aldershot. He came up with the details then smashed himself into a bridge on the M3,' said Aksanov with a sneer.

'Oh, he was one of ours then, I hadn't realised,' said Cooper.

'He didn't want to be. He gambled too much – lost; took the easy way out,' mused Aksanov. 'Anyway, I need to know if these people are still there. If they are, I want you to watch the house, let me know the moment they look like moving out. Go in separate cars and follow them. I need to see if Stafford thinks his job is done or if he knows the battle is ongoing.'

'Gotta beat working the door, boss,' was Edwards' parting shot.

On their way out, Aksanov shouted one final instruction, 'Before you go, send up Jamie.'

While waiting for Jamie Sweetman to arrive, he wandered through to his en-suite bedroom selected a seven iron from his golf bag and, returning to the office, began to practise the delicate little chips he found often helped him to beat his opponents. He found the whole action therapeutic and relaxing.

Jamie Sweetman knocked once and walked in. His name belied his qualities; he was far from being a sweet man. Ex-armed forces, including a stint with the SAS, he stood just under five feet ten inches tall, maybe thirty-six, handsome, solid build, broad shoulders, blond hair, maybe number two cut, maybe 165 pounds. Jamie fixed things. And not just for Aksanov – he also had allegiance to a higher authority, denoted by the skull tattoo with the letters MNP displayed on his right forearm. The letters, in Russian script, laced through the eye sockets and nose hole, could be interpreted to mean 'peace' or 'world', but to most Russians it meant, 'one who will never be rehabilitated'. He didn't fix stuff like if the power went off or the CCTV packed up – Jamie did wet work, as in if an outsider tried to move in and sell drugs in their venues or on their patch, Jamie made sure they were unable to do it twice.

Aksanov put the golf club back in the bag, and returned to his desk. Sweetman sat facing him. Aksanov opened a drawer, hunted inside, found a key and handed it to Sweetman.

'It's for the flat in Aldershot, I need it checked out. The guys who used it have been banged up. I need it cleared of everything, and I don't mean the furniture. Everything. You know what I mean.'

Sweetman nodded, picked up the key and left.

CHAPTER 3

Kurt Edwards and Ray Cooper positioned their cars some fifty metres either side of the Portsmouth safe house, but on the opposite side of the road. After an hour or so of inactivity, Cooper decided to join Edwards in his car, wandering over he pulled open the passenger door and clambered in. Edwards turned, eyes widening in disbelief.

'You fuckin' dinlo, what d'you think you're doin'?' he shouted.

Loosening his tie and settling into the passenger seat, Cooper said, 'I was beginning to drift off, so I thought I'd keep you company – better chance of staying awake. So who are these people we're watching?'

Edwards shook his head in despair. 'For Christ's sake, Coop, two blokes sat in a car – don't you see how bleedin' obvious...' He shook his head again. Too late to whinge.

'Well, the black beauty is Marva Lewis, she's with her two kids. Her old man was the geezer killed down at the marina in Southampton the other week.'

'Oh yeah, I heard about that,' said Cooper.

'Yeah, well, he was a buddy of Paul Stafford, the geezer who blew Aksanov's boat out of the water and smashed his drug factory. Christ, it's all over the news.'

'I know, but why are they in a safe house?' asked Cooper.

'Stafford is Security Forces or some such and Aksanov's been putting the squeeze on him by scaring the shit out of this lot.'

'So Stafford's lot are special forces then?'

'Him and Ryan Peters and the guy who got killed are, the rest are just cops. But he's got friends in high places, that's for sure,' said Edwards.

'So if these geezers have smashed up half of Aksanov's business, why the fuck doesn't he put a price on Stafford's head? How the hell is he going to keep goin'? We'll be out of a job.'

'Nah, you're looking at it all wrong, mate. Aksanov's been making millions for years, especially since he set up the drug factory. But, from what I hear, Runihura, Kapusniak and all the others involved in the manufacturing side of the operation are either banged up or dead. Aksanov's lieutenants are fucked, mate, leaving a gap two smart doormen like us can fill,' said Edwards, adding with a grin, 'if you're up for it?'

'We ain't got enough money between us to set up a gig like that.'

'But a lot of Whitelines' customers do – eh up, looks like we've got some action,' said Edwards picking up his mobile. They both slid further down in their seats.

As they peered over the window edge, a silver Vauxhall Vectra SRi pulled up across the driveway to the house.

Edwards had clipped a zoom lens attachment onto his mobile phone and took pictures of the driver as he got out. As the driver looked up and down the road, an old green Volvo estate rolled to a stop behind the Vectra. Cooper hissed, 'Christ, don't they drive shit cars?' They weren't to know, both cars were top spec, supercharged and with the latest gizmos, sat-nav, Bluetooth, dash-cam. Edwards ignored him, and clicked away as the Volvo driver, dressed in a black leather bomber jacket, torn, dirty jeans, walked towards the similarly dressed Vectra driver. Both men stood around six foot tall. They were met on the pavement by the passenger from the green Volvo, a good-looking woman with short brown hair. Dressed in scruffy clothes like the men, she still somehow managed to look stunning and she carried herself with confidence. After a brief conversation, they walked up the driveway to the house.

'Fuck, she's a looker, wouldn't mind her doing a full body search,' said Cooper. Then, 'See what I mean, though? We could easy take them out, *boom*, end of.'

'Yeah, but Aksanov likes to play mind games – death by a thousand cuts kinda stuff. Anyways, I think she's one of the cops they've got working with them, so I guess the geezers are Stafford and Peters. But I'll send some pictures to the boss, just to be sure.' Moments later, Aksanov confirmed their identities: Stafford, Peters and Nicole Martin.

Edwards couldn't see the front door, but he didn't dare risk getting out of the car or moving it closer, instead, he adjusted the rear-view mirror. They settled down to wait again.

Ten minutes later, Paul Stafford walked out to the Volvo carrying a suitcase, which he put in the car. He was followed by Peters, who also put a suitcase in the Volvo before returning to the Vectra. Edwards and Cooper slid further down in their seats, relying on the rear-view mirror and the limited vision of electronically adjustable wing mirrors. Moments later the black woman, Marva Lewis, and her two children walked out to the Volvo, a blond-haired, grey-suited, younger man with a military buzz cut behind them. As Stafford opened the passenger doors, Buzz Cut stood on the pavement, right hand across his chest, inside his jacket, and kept a watchful eye up and down the road. With the passengers in the Volvo, Peters, with Martin in the passenger seat, drove the Vectra away. Stafford shook hands with Buzz Cut, got into the Volvo and took off. Buzz Cut stayed on the pavement, watching until the car was out of sight.

'Bollocks,' said Edwards. 'See, should've seen that coming, you can't get back to your car till he fucks off. So I might lose Stafford, you bloody cretin.'

'Bollocks, you know where she lives, they'll be going there,' said Cooper. Edwards looked at him and shook his head in disbelief. On the opposite pavement, Buzz Cut walked slowly back up the driveway. As Cooper scrambled out of the car, Edwards hissed at him, 'Phone Aksanov, tell him we're on the move', and with his foot to the floor, he raced after the old green Volvo.

'Fucking dinlo,' Cooper said under his breath.

CHAPTER 4

DCI Talbot, head honcho at Eastleigh Police HQ, had worked with Stafford before. At Stafford's request, he'd organised warrants and a forensic team to meet PCs from Aldershot nick at the North Lane flat used by Ayman Runihura, and other criminals now in police custody. Tony Hawkins, a tall, calm fifty-year-old sergeant at Aldershot, had sent two uniformed constables to meet the forensic techs at the first-floor flat. Rolling up in their Fiesta patrol car, they parked alongside the cast-iron staircase, that looked like a fire escape. Two techs arrived in a small white van; together they were the only vehicles in the parking area. The forensic guys had keys taken from the men under arrest, the coppers had their battering-ram enforcer, although it wasn't needed – the techs found the correct key, separated it from the bunch and labelled it. Before going in, the techs handed the constables a lightweight, hooded, forensic suit, booties and gloves. They decided who would go inside with the techs and who would stay on watch outside. The cop left on guard tied blue and white police tape across the staircase and stuck a *Crime Scene – Do Not Enter,* sign to the flat's front door. He stood with his back against the side rail surveying the view. The whole area had been neglected for the best part of two generations. The red-brick houses were originally built as cheap rental homes. They'd long since been converted into flats in order to billet an overspill of married soldiers.

Suitably attired, the other constable opened the door and shouted, 'Police, police!' Getting no response, he found and turned on the light switch. A long narrow hallway led past three doors in the left-hand wall into a living room. The cop screwed up his face, assaulted by the smell of male occupation: perspiration, cigarettes and sweaty trainers. He checked out the three bedrooms on the left while the techs continued through the living room to the kitchen and bathroom. There was no one home. The forensic techs started in the living room and were immediately rewarded, finding seventeen passports in a sideboard drawer. All had different female names and nationalities. A second batch of passports, driving licences and ID cards, found in another drawer, had men's names. Knowing a number of foreign nationals had been detained in the takedown at Southampton and Weyhill, they hoped these would help identify some.

Carpets were pulled up, backs of sofas and armchairs ripped open, the bath panel was removed. They tapped walls, climbed into the loft space, and found nothing of interest.

'This doesn't feel right,' said one of the techs. 'We know at least four men used this place and they were all tied in with drugs and weapons, yet there's no trace of either.'

'I know, but for now, photograph the passports and email them to Major Stafford. I'll call in a K9 team, see what they can find,' said the second tech.

'You'll be lucky, haven't you heard? The clever sods in charge made cuts, we lost fifteen Hampshire K9 units, so it could take a month of bloody Sundays.'

'Ah well, won't hurt to give it a try.' The tech took out his mobile and called DCI Talbot at Eastleigh Police HQ. The DCI agreed to arrange a Dog Support Unit as soon as possible, but as they needed dogs trained to sniff out drugs and explosives, he was unsure when it could be deployed. They decided that as the flat was now uninhabited, it wasn't a priority. The forensic team did a final walk-through, then left.

But they were being watched. Jamie Sweetman was slumped down in the driver's seat of his car. It wasn't easy to be inconspicuous on a street like this, but Sweetman wanted to park his black Mercedes X-Class pickup close to the property and luck was on his side, rewarding his vigilance. And a guy as vigilant as Sweetman gets more luck than average. He slotted in between two cars parked just seventy metres away on the opposite side of the road. From there he had a good view of the target property. He snapped on a pair of surgical gloves, settled down in his seat and waited. He watched as the patrol car and white van left, then didn't hesitate. He bailed out of the Merc carrying a backpack and an empty cricket bag, reached the iron staircase, ducked under the police tape and entered the flat using the key from Aksanov. Locking the door behind him, he slid the two security bolts into place.

Not only was Sweetman vigilant, he was shrewd. In his line of work, he knew the importance of keeping schtum.

And with a ruthless gangster like Aksanov, he knew that one day he'd need an exit strategy. He'd already kept from Aksanov his friendship with Jan Kapusniak and had failed to mention some previous and current employers. His exit strategy though, was simple: working for Aksanov, he always drove one of the black Mercedes-Benz X-Class pickup trucks they used as company vehicles, but he had his own motor – a metallic black four-year-old two-litre Audi A3 TDI Sports Saloon, which he parked a few streets away from his home. He'd also failed to tell Aksanov he'd been in this flat before, neither had he mentioned the go-bag Kapusniak kept hidden there. It was the go-bag he was after now, and knew he'd find it in the kitchen.

He opened the doors to a double floor unit, dragged out the pots and pans, chucking them on the floor behind him. When the cupboard was clear, he took a knife from one of the drawers, slipped the blade between the base and the central front pillar. As he levered the blade in, the base panel lifted sufficiently to get his fingers underneath and tip it all the way back. The cavity was originally the depth of the plinth, but the floorboards had been cut away, creating a space some fifteen inches deep. Sweetman reached in and pulled out a camouflaged duffel bag that fitted into his cricket bag. He pulled a torch from his backpack and shone it into the cavity. Reaching in, he found two packs roughly the size of house bricks wrapped in brown waxed paper and a larger pack wrapped in clear polythene. He grinned to himself as he stuffed these into his backpack; he'd collected the ideal go-bag. Well, ideal for people like him. He refitted the base and returned the pots and pans. Closing the cupboard, he picked up his bags, walked to the front door, slid back the bolts and opened the door an inch or two. Seeing nothing to faze him, he walked calmly down the iron staircase and over to his pickup. The whole exercise had taken less than five minutes. He put the cricket bag on the rear seat and his backpack on the passenger seat. He texted Aksanov, the message was short: *Flat clear*. He didn't mention the cops got there first.

--- II ---

Earlier, Aksanov had put pressure on Stafford, trying to regain control of the lucrative waste tips, which had acted as a front for his drug running and other nefarious activities. Now he knew he'd never control the tips again, but he was determined to wreak revenge on Stafford for wresting them away. And he would never settle until he'd evened the score. He was determined to crush Stafford. Many of the people who worked for him, were like Sweetman, ex-army; any one of them could take him out. A bomb under his car, a single shot to the back of the head. But that would be too easy on Stafford; he wanted him to feel grief, guilt, devastation. He needed to show his men and the competition he would not be fucked with. Blowing his brains out was not enough; killing or maiming his friends had to be the key. But hurting Stafford's wingman, Ryan Peters, wouldn't hack it – as he was military too, Stafford would rationalise it as a casualty of battle. Hurting the woman Marva Lewis or her kids would make Stafford suffer, and suffer for the rest of his life. He tried to stop this train of thought, tried to concentrate on planning his way out of his current difficulties. But revenge was a strong motivator. He realised these were tactics his father would have used – brutal tactics had kept the Russian Bratva, or brotherhood, in control of criminality throughout Europe for a couple of centuries. He had kept his businesses free from Brotherhood involvement; their total ruthlessness, he thought, had outlived its usefulness in a first-world country like Britain. Maybe this was at odds with his own methods, but the Bratva didn't worry about killing civilians. The people he'd destroyed were all players. And players knew the score. But now with his business in jeopardy, he knew he'd do what ever it took.

He had been persuaded by his Albanian business partner, Shpresa Berisha, or Third Floor Sheila as they called her, to invite two members from a Birmingham syndicate and two of his late father's colleagues from London to come and discuss how to finance a rebuilding plan. Third Floor Sheila, among other things, ran the top floor of his Whitelines nightclub. She also ran the basement, where, as a little sideline, they made porn DVDs and snuff movies, as the illegals occasionally died on film through abuse or as a result of overdosing on the drugs they were forced into using. Both his father's colleagues were members of the Brotherhood and now he was questioning the decision to invite them. Fuck, he shouldn't have allowed TFS to persuade him this was the quickest and safest route to go, but he had an idea to put her back in her place, show her who was boss.

Since she'd brought the dark web into play she'd been getting ideas above her station, and he planned to cut her down to size, and soon. But it was tricky, he needed her tech savvy. It was TFS who had persuaded him to spend a small fortune on giving their top lieutenants mobile phones with EncroChat, so they could talk without being hacked or tracked by the law or other crime gangs. And it worked, but he was worried about her organising a coup. He'd been pacing around his office. Now he sat at his desk, took out a cigarette, lit it and thought about his options. He knew his imminent visitors would see the loss of his factory and control of the tips as a weakness, but trusted they would approve and support his tactics for rebuilding *and* revenge. Surely they would – after all, he'd known these men since he was a boy; they'd watched as he grew within the business and he'd never asked them for help before. He'd put great profits into the syndicate's coffers, surely they wouldn't let him down now?

Howard Neilson parked up near the rear doors of Whitelines. He punched in the entry code and wandered through the dimly lit storage area to the rear stairs, made his way to Aksanov's office, knocked once and walked in.

''Bout fucking time,' said Aksanov. 'Why don't you answer your sodding phone? What the hell do you think I'm paying you for?' Neilson strolled noiselessly across the thick carpet and settled down in one of the office chairs facing Aksanov across his desk. He adjusted the creases in his suit trousers and crossed his legs.

'You pay me to keep you out of trouble, Pavel. And you'd do well to remember it.'

Aksanov shot to his feet, leaned forward, both hands on the desk, eyes wide, mouth open. Neilson stayed seated, calm. Aksanov blinked, closed his mouth and sat back down. He stared at Neilson for a long moment.

'So what's the situation?' he said, when he'd regained control.

'They pulled the plug on the Polish lad, Matis Bockus, in Winchester Prison.'

'At least he went out on a high,' said Aksanov with a sneer. 'Little bastard was nicking powder from us, and he fucked up about the boat.'

'The whole Weyhill crew were arrested, but most of them only knew about their end of the operation. And they're not likely to get a deal, there's too much evidence against them.'

'What about Miller?'

'He was arrested, but no one knows where he is. He went off with Anne Borley, the duty solicitor at Eastleigh. But the others know he shopped the lot of them, so wherever he surfaces, he's a dead man.'

'Get the word out; five grand to the guy who pops him.'

'No, don't worry, Pavel, it'll get done for free.'

'Yeah I know, but I want him to know about it. I want him to know someone's out there. I want him looking over his shoulder. I want him shitting himself every waking moment – then I want him dead.'

'Borley will know where he is and if I can't find out from her, Stafford and Peters will know. But I'll try and find out from her first. I need some sort of leverage, something I can use to persuade her to tell me.'

'You're both on the same fucking side, Neilson. You're defending, Runihura, and the others, so it shouldn't be too hard.'

'There's no real defence for them, so I'm aiming for damage limitation. But Runihura's put out a contract on Stafford and Miller.'

'Well, you better make sure Stafford ain't hit until the black woman gets sorted; he'll want to die then anyway.'

'I can't see him pulling his contract now...'

'Fuck's sake, Neilson, I pay you to get things done, not come up with bloody excuses.'

Neilson allowed several seconds to elapse. 'If you've got enough money, you can sit behind your big desk, or practise your golf swing, then bark out orders to get people killed and maimed. When the money runs out, Pavel, what are you going to do then? Three months, Pavel, three months and you'll be desperate for people to back you up, and you know what? There'll be no one there.' Neilson looking relaxed, uncrossed his legs and made a thing of smoothing out the creases in his trousers again, setting himself should Aksanov decide to take action.

Aksanov was a bear of a man. He was once very handsome with a head of thick black hair. But life away from the front line had taken its toll. Maybe a 230-pound toll. Even his hair was now salt and pepper. Neilson knew he would be slow and ponderous, he knew he hadn't seen any significant action for years, apart from the occasional round of golf. And when he smashed someone, they were held or tethered.

But it pays to be ready, and Neilson was ready. Aksanov hesitated for a second, reached for a cigarette and said as he lit it, 'Don't you think I've been out on the streets? Don't you think I've done the hard yards? How d'you think we got this big, huh? And if you think this'll be gone in three months,' he waved his arms expansively, 'then it shows how little you know about the set-up. So if you think you can fuck with me, my friend, you've made a big mistake.'

Aksanov's mobile broke the uneasy quiet. It took him three or four seconds to pull his eyes away from Neilson. When he did, he checked his mobile's screen; he'd been sent three pictures. The caller was Edwards. Aksanov put the mobile to his ear, and after listening briefly said, 'Yep, Peters with the blond hair, Stafford's the other one, she's Nicole Martin. Stick with it. Make sure they're taking her home. Look, there's an extra ten K if you grab any one of them today.' He ended the call. Neilson raised an eyebrow at Aksanov. 'Stafford's picked up the black woman and her kids. Looks like he's taking them home.'

'Looks as though Stafford does think he's got the top man then,' said Neilson.

The two men looked at each other; like pre-fight boxers. 'Look,' said Aksanov in a conciliatory tone, 'I'm having a pretty bad day already. And I know it's not your fault, but I'll just say this, you would be well advised not to make it worse. So tread carefully, my friend.'

Neilson said nothing more, but left Aksanov's office with a calmness he didn't feel. He'd taken Aksanov's rebuke without comment. Grim-faced, he walked slowly back through the silent nightclub. He couldn't clear his head of thoughts of slapping Aksanov down, killing him even. He was aware of all of Aksanov's businesses; he knew the darker secrets of the nightclubs and the hotel. He knew where the bodies were buried, literally. He also knew, sometimes too much knowledge is a dangerous thing.

By the time he reached his car his mind was settled. He would talk to Jamie Sweetman.

CHAPTER 5

Ryan Peters had gone ahead of Stafford to check out the situation at Marva Lewis's Farnborough home. Rolling to a stop two or three hundred metres from the rear of her semi-detached house, Peters got out and Martin took over the driver's seat. He skirted through an alleyway leading to a block of sixteen garages, eight on each side of a service road. In the middle of each eight, a pathway. One led to the back gates of the houses in Marva's stretch of road. Finding the gate to Marva's house unlocked, he opened it, peered round and edged into the back garden. Seeing nothing untoward, he walked down the garden path, checking right and left. He checked the rear windows and the half-glazed kitchen door. All were secure and showed no sign of forced entry. He walked back around the block to the front of the house. Marva's Zafira was still parked in the driveway and the house looked peaceful and quiet. He squeezed past the car to the little storm porch and tried the door. It was secure. Examining the front windows he found no indication of attempted entry. Satisfied all was in order, he called Stafford.

'All quiet on the western front, boss.'

Moments later, Stafford parked his green Volvo across Marva's driveway. He'd briefed Marva and her children on their next move: she unclipped her boy's seat-belts and they climbed out. The three of them walked to the porch while Stafford brought up the cases. Marva opened the porch door, took two steps in and opened the main front door. As Stafford took the cases through to the living room, she relocked both doors behind them. When she returned, Stafford and the boys were waiting at the open kitchen door leading to the back garden.

'All clear out here,' said Stafford. Closing the door behind them, they moved swiftly through the garden to the back gate. Both boys with massive smiles were enjoying the game. Stafford put the suitcases down and opened the gate. Peering around it, he could see the passageway was clear.

'OK, quick as you can, round to the garages.'

They reached the garages where Ryan Peters was waiting with the boot of the Vectra open. Stafford put the cases in as Marva strapped the boys into the back seats then jumped in beside them. Peters climbed into the passenger seat. Stafford walked to the T-junction at the end of the service road and signalled all clear. Martin pulled out, turned right onto the road leading away from Marva's front door and headed towards Peters' Aldershot home. Stafford went back to the house and in through the back door, locking it behind him.

On a shelf used for cookbooks and kitchen paraphernalia, he set up one of the sub-miniature motion-activated surveillance cameras he'd got from the team at the safe house. Turning it on, he flicked to the relevant app on his mobile, returned to the kitchen door and walked through the camera's field of vision. Satisfied with the resulting video, he went to the front door and removed the little spy glass, replacing it with another sub-miniature surveillance camera, once again checking the video on his mobile. He hid the original spy glass in a kitchen drawer and called Ryan Peters.

'We're up and running my end, see what you've got and text me,' said Stafford.

All good pinged up on screen; Stafford walked into the storm porch, turned and faced the camera. Seconds later he received an identical text.

Satisfied, he wandered round the house, opening curtains and the little window in the upstairs bathroom. He stayed for a further forty minutes, then, checking the bolt was set on the front door's Yale lock, left the house with a wave and a shouted goodbye.

Some time later, Stafford drove into his own gateway and swung the car round to face the road, in time to see a black Mercedes X-Class pickup drive slowly by. In time to see the driver's face change from anticipation to shock as he leaned across the passenger's side then realised he was staring directly at a grim-faced Paul Stafford. The Mercedes lurched forwards and almost crunched parked cars in the driver's effort to retain control and accelerate away. Stafford pulled out behind, making a mental note of the registration number. The black motor raced away, turned left then right, tyres squealing as it lurched around narrow streets and side roads with scant regard for other traffic. Realising it was pointless to give chase, Stafford pulled up. Even as he wrote down the registration number, he guessed a DVLA search would show the vehicle as being owned by Whitelines Entertainment Ltd, with no details of the driver. Stafford had already come across Whitelines Entertainment Ltd and found it impossible to untangle the web of shell companies used to create chaos.

Calling Peters he said, 'Looks like the battle continues. A black Merc pickup followed me from Marva's, so get over to mine soonest and we'll work out our next moves.'

--- II ---

Kurt Edwards drove slowly past Marva's house. The old green Volvo was outside. Two hundred metres further down, he turned round and came to a stop some distance away from the neat semi-detached house.

Moments later Ray Cooper drove into the street, Edwards flashed his lights and Cooper rolled to a stop fifty metres away from the other side of the house.

Cooper's mobile buzzed and Edwards said, 'We'll wait till Stafford comes out, see what he does, then report back to Aksanov.'

'Aksanov says we get ten grand if we snatch any one of 'em today.'

'Got to be worth a go. We'll suss it out when Stafford buggers off,' said Edwards, ending the call. They slumped down in their seats to wait. Forty minutes later, noticing Stafford leaving the house, Edwards called Cooper.

'You follow him, I'll check out the house.'

'Wouldn't it be better if I came with you, to grab one of 'em?' Cooper asked before turning on his ignition.

'Fuck me, Coop, don't you think I can manage a woman and a couple of kids on me own?' Edwards laughed.

'OK, mate, up to you, but I still expect half the ten grand."

'And you'll get it, don't worry. Just find out where Stafford's going.'

Cooper pulled away, following Stafford's Volvo. Edwards waited for ten minutes. Nothing moved in the house. He climbed out of his pickup and walked purposefully up the driveway. Squeezing past the Zafira, he knocked on the storm porch door. Getting no response, he tried the door handle. It was unlocked. Stepping inside he spotted the spy glass and put his eye to it. He could only see black. *Must have a back cover so people like me can't look in*, he thought, smiling. He knocked on the door again and waited. Impatient, he moved backwards and forwards, side to side in the small space. He knocked once more: no answer. He dropped down on one knee and peered through the letterbox. He could see no movement and he could hear nothing. *Bloody unlikely with two kids in the house.* He didn't move. Not right away. He didn't want to. He had a terrible sinking feeling. Stafford had tricked them. Slowly he climbed to his feet, hit the door with his fist, once, twice, and then kicked it.

'Is anyone in this fucking house? Hey, Marva, if you or one of your brats can hear me, when I get you, I'll fuck you so fucking hard—' Realising he was wasting his breath, he turned, strode out of the porch and jogged down to the next street where the service road led to the garages and central alleyway to the row of back gates.

'Fuckin' tricky bastards,' he said out loud and ran back to his car. Climbing in, he found his mobile and called Cooper. 'Bastards have given us…give me a minute, mate… to catch me breath…the bloody slip, there's a bleedin' back gate. They're away with the wind, mate.'

'Maybe a bit of good news, then – Stafford led me to his place. He spotted me though, chased me for a bit – took a few streets, but I lost him.'

'Can you find his place again?'

'Yeah, no problem, I know Farnborough pretty well.'

'OK, get back there and park up close by, then text me the street name. I'll meet you as soon as I can,' said Edwards and ended the call. Five minutes or so later his mobile buzzed with a text showing the street name. He entered it into the satnav and fifteen minutes later stopped behind Cooper's Merc. He got into Cooper's passenger seat.

'Is he still inside?'

'Well, his car's still in the drive, but he may have nipped out the back gate,' said Cooper with a laugh.

'This ain't fuckin' funny, you dinlo, Aksanov will go apeshit if we've lost the whole bleeding lot of 'em.'

'Yeah? So what we going to do now?'

'Only thing we can do, mate, beat the living shit out of Stafford till he tells us where he took the black bastards,' said Edwards, opening the door and climbing out of the Mercedes. As they walked to Stafford's front door, both men loosened their ties, and undid the top buttons on their shirts.

CHAPTER 6

Jimi Hendrix's "The Wind Cries Mary" played on the stereo. Stafford, determined to stay awake waiting for them, despite the exertions of the last few days, wandered across to the fridge and took out a beer. He pulled the tab, walked back through to the living room and settled into one of the mismatched sofas, and reflected on the last thirty or so hours. It had been a tough couple of days, but his encounter with the driver of the black Mercedes showed that perhaps he was right. The battle was over but the war was not yet won. He shook his head. *No downtime just yet, then. Well, as soon as Nicole and Ryan turned up they would work out their next move.* He began to drift off – exhaustion coupled with Hendrix's lilting music.

He was startled semi-awake by a loud knock at the front door. His first thought was that Nicole must have lost her key in the chaos of the last few days. He was tempted to stay on the sofa. He knew she was with Ryan and he grinned to himself as the stereo clicked off and he thought, I'll stay here, see how long it will be before Ryan uses his lock picks to get in. Another loud knock. Bollocks, he thought, heaving himself off the sofa and wandering, yawning and unsteady, through the hallway to the front door. As he twisted the latch, the door crashed open, smashing into his hand and slamming him back against the wall.

'You crazy fuck,' he shouted, 'Ryan, what do you—'.

Before he could regain his senses, Kurt Edwards grabbed his left arm, dragged him from behind the door and into the open porch. The momentum caused Stafford to stumble headlong down the three steps where Ray Cooper smashed his knee into the side of his face. Stafford crashed sideways and rolled with the blow onto his back. Cooper, standing to one side of the doorway, swung a kick at Stafford's head. Stafford caught the foot with both hands and pushed with all his strength. Cooper staggered backwards, arms wheeling, desperately trying to stay upright. Badly dazed, Stafford struggled to his feet; Edwards lunged wildly at him and tried to land a roundhouse right. Stafford ducked and charged, head down, crashing into his midriff and smacking him up against the wall.

The Vectra SRi with Ryan Peters at the wheel drove through the gateway. Instantly assessing the situation, Peters drove straight at Edwards, who bolted towards the road. Martin leapt out of the car before it came to a stop and ran at Cooper. She stopped a few feet away and looked at him, her big brown eyes wide. She smiled.

She looked scruffy, but gorgeous. Cooper, unsure what to do next, stared at her, as though mesmerised. Still smiling, she took a pace forward and kicked him smack in the crotch. He screamed in agony and dropped to his knees, retching and clutching his groin. Rushing up to the car, Edwards hit the driver's door just as Peters was clambering out. There was an almighty crack as the door hit Peter's right shin. Though he gave a bellow of anger, the pain didn't prevent him from lurching after his assailant.

As Martin went to help Stafford, Cooper managed to stagger to the roadway. Peters limped after them, but by the time he reached the gateway, the two men were gone, so he also turned back to the house.

Stafford tried a rueful grin and winced with pain.

'Fuck,' he said, hand to his rapidly swelling cheek. 'Bloody good timing, though.'

Martin pulled his hand away, prodded his swollen and reddening cheek, and said, 'Ooh, that's going to need some ice.'

Stafford winced again. 'So don't keep prodding it then, and I don't want any smart-arsed comments from either of you,' he said as he led them to his kitchen-cum-office.

Martin said, 'Don't worry, Staf, you still look handsome, but only from the right-hand side.'

Peters chuckled, looked at Martin, winked, then said, 'Yo, Staf, you been having another fallout with the Mormons again?'

Stafford was silent for a moment, then said, 'One of them was the thug watching at Marva's house; bastard followed me here.'

'You sure? Did you ask them for ID? You don't see many thugs wearing collar and ties these days. What d'you think, Nic?'

'Defo could have been Mormons, but isn't he like this with the Plymouth Brethren as well?'

'I blame his mum, he's like it with all these religious types.'

'I did say I don't want any smart-arsed comments from you two, and you've said nothing smart yet,' said Stafford as he opened the fridge and pulled out a beer. He walked to the nearest sofa and flopped into it. As he settled, he rolled the ice-cold can up and down his left cheek. 'As it happens, the Mormon, fuck, moron who hit your car door is the one who peered through the spy hole at Marva's, so we've got his picture on the phone video.'

Peters pulled out his mobile, found the app and ran the ten-second clip. Not recognising the man, he switched to another app and sent the image to the printer in Stafford's home office. He collected the prints and gave one each to Stafford and Martin. Neither recognised him. Peters grabbed a brown folder from Stafford's desk, slipped in one of the prints.

Meanwhile, Stafford opened his laptop, checking his emails, he clicked on one with the subject line: *Passports found in 10a North Lane.* There were twenty-four pictures, which Stafford sent to his printer, saying, 'Bloody hell, guys, this little lot should help the police identify some of the illegals picked up from the bust last night, but I'm too knackered to do anything now. I think we'll start again in the morning.'

Peters and Martin looked through the pile of prints and agreed there was little they could do right now. Martin settled in another armchair as Peters waved the brown folder and said, 'Right, I'm going to shoot off home, make sure Marva's OK. But before I do, I'll call in the Aldershot nick and catch up with Hawkins, see if he recognises our man.' As he spoke, he realised the efforts of the last couple of days had at last caught up with Stafford. He had fallen asleep against the arm of the sofa, beer can still pressed against his cheek. Turning to Martin he said, 'Yeah, I think sleep is the best thing you can do too, so I'll see you both in the morning.'

'I'll put some ice in a towel or something, and put the beer back in the fridge, can't be very cold now. And yep, we'll meet up again tomorrow,' she said, getting up and walking with him to the front door.

Peters kissed her lightly on the cheek. 'Good night, Nicole, and really well done just now and over the last couple of days. You've done bloody well, I'll make sure your guv knows it.'

'You did good yourself, Ry. Take care now, and watch out for black Mercedes pickups,' she said with a grin as she closed the door quietly behind him. Back in the kitchen, she found a bag of peas in the freezer, wrapped a tea towel around it, and then carefully exchanged it for the beer can she pulled from Stafford's hand. Thinking it was pointless to walk the beer all the way back to the kitchen, she flopped into another of Stafford's recycled sofas, kicked off her shoes and popped the tab.

Stafford was unable to go into a deep sleep, the ache in his cheek causing him to drift between sleep and wakefulness. His mind wandered back to the first time he'd known what it was like to be hit and hurt by someone. He remembered he was maybe eleven or twelve years old, and he wasn't a big lad. He knew what conflict was – his parents argued constantly, his father had been in the army, his mother had been a nurse, had found God and thought everyone else should too. His parents never came to blows, though, and she taught Paul, their only child, to be gentle, conciliatory, to turn the other cheek. Something his father knew through experience was only good in theory; in practice, people believed you were scared and weak.

It soon became known that Paul Stafford never hit back and he became a prime target for the school bullies. His teachers stood by in despair as, week in week out, he would take a beating, sometimes verbally, most times physically as well.

One Friday, one of Stafford's friends dashed into the school from the playground, and screamed through tears, 'It's Stafford, sir, you need to get an ambulance, it's Stafford.' The teacher called for an ambulance, grabbed a first aid kit and rushed out to the playground to find Stafford standing in the centre of a group of boys. Many of them were shouting, laughing and patting him on the back.

As the teacher approached, the group parted and became quiet. On the floor, crying and spluttering blood, sat two of Stafford's known tormentors. A third was standing close by, cautiously dabbing a handkerchief to his bleeding nose. The ambulance arrived; the paramedics cleaned up the blood from split lips, grazed knees and busted noses, then took the boys to hospital to make absolutely sure no major damage had been inflicted on them. Their parents were called; they insisted on calling the police. The police interviewed teachers and boys alike. All gave the same tale: the three injured boys were indeed the school bullies. They had picked on Paul Stafford constantly because of his passive nature. On this particular day, Paul had decided enough was enough. There was no red mist, no anger; he simply determined whatever punishment he took, he would keep getting up until he was the only one left standing.

For the first time, at the headmaster's request, his mother collected him from school. He told her they were proud of her son for standing up for himself at long last. Paul got a beating from her when he got home for daring to disobey her. Out of her earshot, he got a *well done, son*, and a pat on the back from his father. This episode had a dramatic impact not only on his future, but also on his parents' relationship and his relationship with them. When he returned to school the following Monday morning, he was surprised to hear that the biggest of the bullies had been expelled. This episode was the catalyst for his interest in the military. He became close to his father, they spent hours talking about what it was like to be a soldier. He became fascinated by the science of fighting. Not the science of warfare or killing people, but the science of fighting for self-defence. How lightness and speed of movement could overcome physical size and muscle. He read, researched and practised, often with his father, all forms of hand-to-hand combat and disabling techniques. At fifteen years and eight months old, with both his parents' consent on the forms somehow, he joined one of the army's Junior Leader Regiments.

As a rookie soldier, Stafford's quiet leadership skills and intelligence coupled with his outstanding hand-to-hand combat ability singled him out from his peers. And it was through this that he gained some of his closest friends, Ryan Peters and the late Garfield Lewis among them. After a string of successful operational tours, he was selected for a commission. He reached the field rank of major by thirty-seven. But he soon found, as for any person with an outstanding talent or ability, whatever the endeavour, that someone was always waiting for the opportunity to prove themselves against you, to take you down. Paul Stafford had gained a lot of dangerous enemies.

--- II ---

He woke up with a start barely twenty minutes later, still cradling the bag of peas against his cheek. He looked questioningly at the peas then noticed Nicole had crashed out on one of the other mismatched sofas. As he realised she must have swapped the can of beer for the peas, he grinned and immediately regretted it as the pain raged through his jaw again. Wincing, he got up and crossed the room to a large mirror mounted above the open fireplace. He leaned in close, peered at his face and was somewhat disappointed when he saw it looked nowhere near as bad as it felt, although it was still swollen. Another bag of peas should do it, he thought. As he went back into the room Nicole stirred fractionally. Again he looked at her, taking care not to grin. Even dishevelled after the events of the last few days, he thought she was still a remarkably beautiful woman. He leaned over her and slipped his arms under her arms and knees and lifted her. He was surprised how light she was, not even 120 pounds, he guessed. She kept her eyes shut tight, but appeared to snuggle against him. He pushed the door open with his foot and walked through to the hallway. Carefully he placed his feet as he climbed the stairs. He knew exactly where the creaks were. She still hadn't stirred when he pushed open the door to the bedroom she had chosen just a week or so before. Stooping down with her still in his arms, he managed to grab the edge of the duvet and pull it back. Gently he laid her on the bed and pulled the duvet over her legs. Undisturbed, she curled into a little ball. Trying hard not to smile, he brushed her cheek gently with the back of his fingers, then silently backed out of the room and went downstairs, avoiding the creaky steps. He retrieved the now empty beer can and bag of peas and took them through to the kitchen, put the can in the recycling, the peas back in the freezer. Checking the shelves, he decided in the absence of another bag of peas, mixed vegetables would do just as well. He wrapped another tea towel around the veg and went, reluctantly, to his own bed.

CHAPTER 7

Ryan Peters parked up at the Aldershot Police Station, picked up his folder and wandered through to the desk sergeant, who signed him in and gave him an ID card dangling from a blue and white striped lanyard, then phoned through to Sergeant Hawkins' office.

'I've got Captain Peters here, he wants to see you – OK, will do,' he said into the phone, then to Peters, 'Yep, just go on up.'

Peters nodded his thanks and headed towards the sergeant's office. Slowly he climbed the stairs to the first floor, the effort of the last thirty hours now beginning to take their toll. Hawkins' office door was open, Peters tapped and walked in. Hawkins rose from behind his desk, hand outstretched.

'Bloody hell, you look a mess!' he said as the two shook hands. Peters grinned and dumped himself in the chair facing Hawkins. 'Mind you, great result on both the ops, brilliant outcome all round, I'm told.'

'Got to say, we're well chuffed, got a few injuries but no life-threatening ones, so a good result. Worst was your PC, Lee Gibson; got both his legs busted, but they reckon he'll make a full recovery.'

'Getting injured in the line of duty may be just enough to save his job after he nearly wrecked the whole sodding operation, shagging one of the witnesses.'

'But have you seen her?' said Peters. 'She's gorgeous, almost worth losing your job over. I hope your lot will go easy on him because he genuinely was effective during the investigation and, don't forget, he risked his life to dive in the river to save bloody Kapusniak. So he did play a huge part in this.'

'Huh, I'd have let the bastard drown, but we'll wait till we see the whole report,' said Sergeant Hawkins, smiling.

'Young Nicole Martin was brilliant, though, she stopped Ayman Runihura in his tracks.'

'You know she's passed her sergeant's exams? And with the reshuffle since the death of our former DI, I reckon the hierarchy will confirm her DS status any day.'

'Good, I'm really chuffed for her.'

'So,' said Hawkins, 'what did you really want to see me about?'

Peters opened his brown folder and slid the A4 pic of their recent assailant across the desk.

'We need to find out who this is – I wondered if he was known to you?'

'Can't say I recognise him. What's he done?'

'He must be part of this same battle. He followed us up from the safe house to Marva Lewis's place. This picture was taken of him while he was in her porch.'

'Christ, there's no let-up in this is there?'

'Not yet, there isn't. And another one followed Staf back to his house. He got a good look at him, mind, and noted his reg number. They like to drive black Mercedes-Benz

X-Class pickups, but they're all bound to be registered to the mass of shell companies under the banner of Whitelines. Frankly, it'll take a genius to untangle the sophisticated web they've created there.'

'OK, we'll bung this picture into the system, see if we get any results, but this Whitelines aspect gets me. Don't you remember? It was our not so dearly departed DI who flagged up Whitelines. So perhaps he got a bit too close to finding out who the real boss men are.'

They left it hanging for a while as Hawkins logged into the Police National Database and scanned in the A4 picture. They realised they might get zero results, but the PND gods were kind and spewed out forty-three possibilities. Peters wandered round behind Hawkins and peered over his shoulder at the pictures on the monitor. Most of the images were mugshots, custody pictures, most taken soon after the men had been charged. They looked tired, unshaven, aggressive and defiant. But there was one probable match, a Kurt Charles Edwards. Last known address was Aldershot, 10a North Lane.

'Bugger,' said Peters, 'they've already cleared the place out, no one's living there now.'

Sergeant Hawkins pushed a few buttons on his keyboard and a printer began to chunter away in a corner of the tiny office. Peters picked up the prints, handed a set to Hawkins and kept one for himself.

'Thanks for this,' said Peters waving the prints. 'We'll follow it up in the morning.'

Hawkins nodded, then said, 'Look, before you go dashing off, just sit down for one minute and hear me out.' Peters looked at him quizzically but returned to his seat.

The sergeant leaned forward, placed his arms on the desk. 'I said earlier, this battle, investigation, whatever you wanna call it, is never-ending. OK, so you put away some of the scoundrels, but then you've got new faces like this arsehole whose picture we just found carrying the fight to you with hardly a hiccup.'

'Yeah, so what are you getting at?'

'I'm thinking perhaps it isn't the Egyptian who's been running the show. Maybe there's at least another layer above him, and now they've started to pull the strings. They've had to become more involved, more visible at the sharp end. So I've been thinking about our old DI… He got in so deep, he ended up, uh, well, frying himself, I guess,' he said with a frown, remembering how the DI ended up in a fireball, crashing his car into a concrete bridge on the M3 motorway.

'Yes, wasn't he following up on enquiries with the five-star hotel on the outskirts of Basingstoke as well?'

'Yeah, my point entirely – something happened during his investigations, something spooked him so badly he decided to end it all.'

'It's certainly got to be worth another look, then. Thanks for the reminder, Sergeant,' said Peters.

'Keep me informed,' Hawkins said as Peters left the office.

CHAPTER 8

Edwards and Cooper shared a rented two-bedroom first-floor flat in Basingstoke. The flat was in a converted 1940s semi-detached house in the older part of the town. The front garden had been paved to enable four cars to be parked there. Edwards arrived first, pushed open the front door and dashed up the steep flight of stairs to their flat. Pulling off his jacket and tie, he threw them into an armchair as he made his way through to the small kitchen-diner. He grabbed two cans of beer from the fridge, threw one at Cooper, who had walked in behind him, pulled the tab on the other, took a swig and dumped himself down in the brown faux leather settee. Cooper chucked Edwards' jacket and tie onto a dining chair and slumped in the armchair.

'So what's the plan now?' he said as he cradled his can, unwilling to open it; knowing it would spray beer all over him.

Edwards wasn't ready to face Aksanov yet. Didn't want to admit that not only had they lost their quarry, but both of them were now on Stafford's radar. He needed time to come up with a new plan.

'One thing's for sure,' said Edwards, 'Aksanov wanted to know if Stafford thinks the job's over. Well, it's obvious he knows he ain't won the war, just a bloody skirmish.'

'I guess you're right, but I was thinking on the way back here—'

'Fuck, I'm surprised you can think at all after she kicked you in the bollocks, mate,' said Edwards, laughing.

'Yeah, copper bitch, took me by surprise.'

'Surprise? Took you by surprise? You didn't think someone as fuckable as her could hurt you! You just stood there with your mouth open, drooling like a dinlo.'

'Yeah? Well it's one thing she's gonna regret,' said Cooper. 'Cracking my nuts. I'll make sure the bitch squeals next time we meet, you can bank on it.'

'Yeah, yeah, we'll see. Anyway, what was this bright idea you were thinking about?'

'OK. Aksanov has pictures of the black bitch's house in Farnborough and the safe house in Portsmouth. We know where Stafford lives and I think he said they took pictures of where the bitch whore who kicked me lives. It's pretty certain Stafford knows we know about those places. Well, what about the other two – Peters and the other cop, the one who got his legs busted down in Andover? Maybe they're hiding the black kids and their old lady at one of their houses?'

Edwards thought about it for a moment or two before replying, 'Fuck me, Coop, maybe she kicked some sense into you after all.'

At nine the following morning, Edwards was drinking black coffee in their kitchen-diner when he received a text message from Aksanov: *hotel 10.30*. Edwards was feeling happier about facing Aksanov now, having spoken to Third Floor Sheila and worked out a plan he hoped would get them back in Aksanov's good books. He bashed on Cooper's bedroom door.

'Move your arse, Coop, Aksanov wants to see us at the hotel. We've got just over an hour, and we've still got to collect the gear for this next job from Sheila.'

———————————— II ————————————

The World Citizen Hotel was on the southern outskirts of Basingstoke. Set in gentle rural environs, it was surrounded on three sides by country lanes and farmland. On the fourth side was the golf course. The hotel was Aksanov and the syndicate's crown jewel. It catered for people like him – white-collar criminals who liked to present themselves as entrepreneurs. Money poured into the casino and came out a whole lot cleaner than it went in. It offered top-quality dining with a choice of food from France, Italy and England. It also offered a wide range of extras for those with pockets deep enough to pay. The casino and restaurant were packed most nights and you had to book tables two or three weeks in advance.

The office in Aksanov's first-floor suite was maybe twenty-five feet by eighteen, with a high ceiling. Two large windows on the left-hand wall looked out over the rear car park and onto mature trees and shrubs marking the edge of the third tee of the golf course. The vertical blinds at the windows were open; the morning sun streamed through. Like his office in Whitelines, it featured a luxuriously thick pile carpet, a massive, mahogany, reproduction double pedestal, Regency desk and, behind it, a deluxe brown leather executive chair. Halfway down the right-hand wall was a door opening into an en suite bedroom, which he used when kept late at a business meeting. Or, more often, when he was in the casino until the early hours; two or three times a week.

Aksanov knew their mega supplies of booze would not be affected by the events of the last day or so. But having lost the factory and drug-making facility in Andover, he knew their entire range of drugs, their most profitable commodity, would soon run out. He needed to replace supplies immediately or his empire would become a battle ground. Drug barons from far and wide would try to muscle in on the action in Hampshire. It was an area he had managed to control for years with a mixture of business savvy and ruthlessness.

At 10.30 a.m. precisely, Edwards knocked on Aksanov's door and walked in, Cooper a pace or two behind. They nodded to Aksanov and he indicated the two chairs in front of his massive desk.

'So what news do you have for me? It better be good, I don't need another day like yesterday.'

'Not so good, boss, I'm afraid. They tricked us.'

Aksanov, face reddening, said nothing, and waited for Edwards to continue.

'We followed them from the safe house to the black bitch's house in Farnborough,' he said, then proceeded to explain the sorry outcome.

Aksanov, stony-faced but livid, said, 'So you lost the whole fucking lot of them. Fuck me, why the fuck do I—'

'B-b-but we've got a plan that'll put us on the front foot again,' said Edwards.

Aksanov raised his eyebrows, leaned back in his chair, folded his arms across his barrel chest and waited.

'Look, it's obvious Stafford knew more was to come. He'd got this planned to find out if anyone was following them. Give us a couple of days, boss, we'll have Stafford eating out of our hands. Trust me on this.'

'Trust you? Trust you on this— Fuck's sake, just fuck the fuck off. Don't come back here till it's sorted. I'm warning you, your next screw-up will be your last, understand?... I said, do you understand?'

Both men nodded as they backed out of the room. Edwards felt a wave of relief as he closed the door. But he knew from now on they would have to keep a watchful eye over their shoulders. They knew Aksanov did not tolerate failure, this plan had to work. They had already picked up the gear from Third Floor Sheila at the Whitelines club. And he knew by doing this, they would make Paul Stafford regret he'd ever crossed the Axe Man. Outside the hotel, they climbed into their black Mercedes pickup and drove to the M3, heading south to Winchester.

II

The Royal Hampshire County Hospital in Winchester was easy to find. They parked up and wandered through the outdoor maze of paths and walkways, following the signs directing them to the main entrance. Edwards told Cooper to try and steal a porter's outfit from the laundry, a store room or a locker room where porters would change clothes. They arranged to meet in forty-five minutes in the car park. Leaving him to it, Edwards found a convenience store, and bought a bunch of grapes and a get-well-soon card. He paid cash. Taking the card out of its cellophane sleeve, he wandered across to the reception desk. He laid the grapes on top of the desk and held up the card.

'Oh, hi, love, can you tell me what ward Lee Gibson's in, so I can take these up to him?'

'Hold on a moment, love, I'll see what I can find for you. Lee Gibson you say?'

'Yes, the copper- er, policeman brought in from Andover with broken legs.'

'Ah yes, I see it now. I'm afraid he's not allowed visitors at the moment.'

'I thought perhaps he wouldn't be up to it yet, but if you give me the name of his ward, I'll take these up and leave them at the nurses' station for him,' he said with a broad smile as he picked a pen from a selection in a mug.

'No problem,' she said, returning the smile. 'It's Bartlett Ward, Level D in the Nightingale Wing. Easy enough to find, it's signposted all the way.'

Edwards wrote the details on the envelope and smiled at her. 'Brilliant, love, thank you very much.'

Picking up the card and grapes, he looked around and spotted a sign for Nightingale Wing, which he found easily. Level D was in fact the fourth floor. He found a waste bin and dumped the card and grapes then took the stairs. At the top of the stairs, he saw a sign for Bartlett Ward. Pushing the swing doors open, he walked in, immediately spotting the nurses' station. Two women wearing different uniforms were discussing a patient's notes and adding details into the computer. Edwards waited until they'd finished. The older of the two women, who was wearing a badge that said *Sister*, looked up at him, smiled and said, 'Sorry, my love, but it's out of visiting—'

Edwards smiled. 'Oh yeah, sorry, I know, Sister, but I'm just about to go on shift at the nick, and I won't be able to get in later. I thought I'd pop in and get a quick update on young Lee, y'know, Lee Gibson? The copper? So I can tell them at work, you know?'

'Oh, OK, I see, well he's still asleep at present. He had his op last night. You should be able to see him tomorrow.'

'Nah, can't make it tomorrow. But how's his wife, she bearing up OK? She hasn't answered our messages today.'

'I think she's trying to get someone to look after their children so she can get in later this morning.'

'Oh good, well, when you see her tell her the lads at the station wish him a speedy recovery, and if she needs anything, tell her to give us a shout, OK?'

'Yes, will do,' said the sister.

Edwards, who had started to walk away, looked back and said, 'Would it be OK if I came back in a while and waited in the Relatives Room? The lads have had a bit of a collection, you know, for emergencies, childcare, taxis and stuff – be good to give it to her.'

'Oh, how sweet of you, I'm sure she'll appreciate it. Yes, the room's on your right as you go out.'

A smiling Edwards said thanks and walked back through the swing doors into the corridor. Opening the door to the Relatives Room, he glanced around – no one was there, so he wandered in. The room had five or six Formica-topped coffee tables, each surrounded by a number of padded seats. It had a small kitchen area with a sink and a kettle and various pots labelled *Tea*, *Coffee* and *Sugar*. Edwards sat down at one of the tables, took out his mobile and called Cooper. While waiting for him to answer, he flipped through the various magazines on the table. Seeing nothing of interest, he moved to another table. Cooper answered.

'Did you find anything?' said Edwards.

'Yeah, managed to nick a porter's shirt and kecks.'

'Stash 'em in the car for now and stay with the motor. I'm going to hang on here a while… His missus is due in later, so I'll try and get her to come out to the car when she's been in to see him.'

'Fuck, d'you think that's wise? She'll be able to identify you.'

'Dinlo, think about it, it ain't going to matter much, is it? Besides, can't wear a balaclava in here now, can I?' he laughed.

'You could try, I suppose,' said Cooper, laughing even though he was pissed off with Edwards calling him a dinlo again. He ended the call.

CHAPTER 9

The following morning at just before nine, and forty-five miles south-west of Farnborough, Howard Neilson was keeping tabs on Anne Borley. He was sitting in his car on Eastleigh High Street, fifty metres or so away from the offices of the firm of solicitors she worked for. Although he had seen her in passing at both Winchester and Eastleigh police stations, and once or twice at Winchester Prison, they'd never met. He had an A4 picture of her printed from her company's *meet the team* web page. He guessed she would park in the nearby multi-storey car park and walk the short distance to her office.

A black Ford Focus pulled up and parked in front of him. To his surprise, Anne Borley stepped out of the car, grabbed a couple of folders off the rear seats and dashed across the road to her employer's offices. Neilson slid down in his seat. He liked to think things through, scope things out in his mind. He knew Brandon Miller, arrested at Weyhill, hadn't yet been charged. The police wouldn't want to keep him in the remand unit as he would be a prime target. They hadn't let him go home either; he'd checked his address earlier. As Borley had parked in a restricted area, he guessed she must be leaving soon, possibly to visit Brandon Miller. Most likely to visit Brandon Miller.

If he stayed where he was, would she spot his car? Recognise him? Maybe it would be safer if he drove round the one-way system and parked up further behind her. It was risky; she could come out again and drive off while he was going round the block. Worth the risk though, as she would surely still be in the one-way system and he'd be able to catch up. His luck was in. The Ford Focus was still parked there as he completed the circuit. He pulled into a space some twenty-five metres behind it and waited. Moments later, Borley returned to her car. Neilson switched on the ignition. Borley pulled away from the kerb and Neilson let two cars pass before he pulled into the traffic. The Ford Focus headed towards Southampton, past the railway station and the airport. At the motorway roundabout, Borley headed up the slip road towards Portsmouth on the M27. Neilson shook his head in disbelief.

'What? How stupid?' he said out loud. 'Surely they wouldn't use the same safe house?'

Neilson knew Stafford had arranged for Marva Lewis and her two children to be placed in a safe house in Portsmouth, to prevent the possibility of further reprisals. No way should they use the same house, it would be plain madness.

Traffic was heavy, but moving at close to the speed limit. Neilson had to concentrate hard to stay in touch, yet invisible to Borley. Normally the twenty-mile journey would take around thirty minutes to Portsmouth and fifteen minutes to the safe house he knew about. During the drive, he convinced himself Anne Borley and her team wouldn't make such a stupid mistake and they must have a number of safe addresses they could use in this sprawling city or outlying area. But when she pulled off at Junction 12 and headed in a direction he knew, he realised with glee that his opponents had made a huge mistake by stashing the whistle-blowing Brandon Miller in the same safe house.

Neilson was stunned; stunned but excited as Anne Borley pulled up outside the very house Marva Lewis and her kids had been holed up in. He drove on, thinking it unnecessary to stop to try to get a glimpse of Miller. He was certain now; this was where Miller was. Certain this would be Miller's final address. Neilson could hardly wait to tell Aksanov about this glaring miscalculation by his legal adversaries. Heading back to the M27, he was confident his next meeting with Aksanov would see him back in favour. As he drove, his thoughts were coming thick and fast. *No, it can't be right; she'd not be so stupid ... surely? Someone in their team or one of the coppers would twig, wouldn't they? Someone had to think it was a crazy idea! They can't all be this blind and stupid, can they?* A few miles further on, a new thought struck him. *What if it's a bluff? What if they're sat there all tooled up, just waiting for a reaction from those Miller had shat on? Could be another bloodbath if Aksanov's men went in mob-handed. But if they chucked a grenade or two through a window, they'd very likely kill Miller anyhow.* He pondered ideas for a few more miles, then... *But fuck it, what if it's a double bluff? What if Miller's not there? What if they want us to think he is, to see who reacts?* A mile or two further on, he laughed out loud and said, 'What am I worrying about? What do I care? It won't be me chucking in the hand grenades. I'll just tell Aksanov what I've seen and leave the decision to him.'

When Anne Borley pulled up outside the safe house, she switched off the ignition, but didn't get out of the car. Instead she made sure the dash cam was working then looked in her rear-view mirror. She saw the white Mercedes closing in behind her and was certain it had been behind her from the moment she'd left Eastleigh. As it got closer, she switched to looking in her offside wing mirror. The Mercedes slowed considerably as it approached, then sped up as it cruised by. She was able to clock the registration number, but didn't need to remember it; the dash cam had done it for her.

In its hands-free cradle, she tapped her mobile.

'You were right, Major Stafford, a white Mercedes saloon car, reg number WM17HOO followed me all the way from Eastleigh and has just driven past me outside the safe house in Portsmouth.'

Over the car's speakers, Stafford's voice said: 'Yep, it's your colleague Neilson's motor all right. I'm guessing you're going to press on to the other house and check on Miller? Meanwhile I'll put wheels in motion to get surveillance where you are. It'll be interesting to see who takes the bait, but I don't want to alert Neilson, so can we keep this between us?'

'Oh God, yes! No problem, I want to see how far he's shifted to the dark side.'

Stafford laughed with little humour. 'Good, thanks, but sadly for him, once you cross the line, there's no way back. Nevertheless, Ms Borley, whatever you do from now on, stay vigilant; these guys don't muck about.'

'Don't worry about me, Major, I can take care of myself. Oh, and call me Anne.'

'OK, Anne. Good, and most people call me Staf. But no, I mean it, stay vigilant.' He cut the connection.

Anne Borley sat with the mobile in her hand for a long moment, contemplating the call. Then shaking her head just once and with a small smile she put the mobile away, started the motor and continued to her meeting with Miller.

―――――――― II ――――――――

Call ended, Stafford hesitated for just a moment, then dialled the Colonel's number, hitting the speaker button. He needed extra bodies to mount immediate twenty-four hour surveillance on the Portsmouth safe house. The house was stuffed full of the latest digital surveillance gear, inside and out. What he needed was a mobile unit, a van equipped with monitors and data-receiving equipment, an extra bod to drive the motor and set up the systems, and two more men to be deployed around and about the house.

The Colonel outranked Stafford, of course, but as head of E Squadron he sanctioned Stafford's frequent clandestine operations. He was obligated to assist Stafford in bringing the enemy to book, whatever their race, creed, colour or nefarious speciality might be. But most of all, he tried to ensure Stafford got the job done, help or no help. Stafford was never certain he'd get the help he needed when he needed it. When the Colonel answered and the niceties, such as they were, were over, he said, 'Tough subject to talk about, Staf, but some of the men down here have been asking about Garfield's funeral. What's happening on that front?'

'Nothing yet, Colonel. We're hoping once we get Marva back home we can help her set it up.'

'If she needs anything from us, just let me know and we'll get it done, OK?'

'Thank you, Colonel, I know she'll appreciate it,' said Stafford. Both men reflected for a moment, and then Stafford outlined the situation with the safe house and explained what he needed. He suggested when the operation was set up they should use the codename *Rehashed*.

The Colonel gave it some thought, then said, 'So you lose one of your men in a marina car park, another of your workers dies alongside a civilian in a tip, and a policeman gets both legs broken. What's going on, Stafford? Do you think I can just pull more people out, like rabbits from a hat?'

Stafford stayed silent, waiting. He knew the Colonel was still there; he could hear him breathing. The Colonel broke the awkward quiet with a sigh.

'So when is this supposed to start?'

'It'd be good to get it in place today, sir. Though I can't see them taking action just yet, especially in daylight hours. And in all honesty I have no idea how long we're going to need them, but could we say three days, and see how we go? Peters and I will get down to them and sort out a roster as soon as we tidy up here.'

'Oh, so you do intend to be part of the op then, Staf? You're not just leaving it for us to sort out?' said the Colonel and ended the call.

Stafford put his mobile away and grimaced. *Well, Colonel, one thing's for sure, when Marva does go back home, you're not getting your two agents back in a hurry. I can find plenty to keep them busy.*

CHAPTER 10

Jamie Sweetman parked the black Mercedes, picked up his backpack, pulled his cricket bag from the back seat and carried them up the short front garden path to the door of his mid-terrace home. The house, in a resurgent part of Basingstoke's old town, had been built in the 1920s and, though it had a narrow frontage, it boasted three good-sized bedrooms and a rear garden. Sweetman's chosen area of expertise and grateful bosses had helped him start climbing the ladder of success. He carried the bags through to the living room. Dumping the backpack on the floor, he placed the cricket bag across the arms of a modern armchair, opened it and took out the camo duffel bag. He sat down on his sofa, put the bag on the floor in front of him and opened it. He laughed out loud as he took stock of the contents. His opinion of Jan Kapusniak had gone up ten points and he thought, *fucking hell, Jan, why stash this lot away for a rainy day if you ain't got it with you when the monsoon hits?*

He took out each item and examined them carefully. First was a Beretta 93 machine pistol. Sweetman knew this was the weapon of choice for the military, police forces and criminals worldwide. And this one came with a full magazine, two fully loaded spares and a metal, extending, detachable stock. Under the gun was a khaki towel wrapped around a polythene bag of white power. He guessed the powder wasn't for doing his laundry. He held the bag in his right palm and waggled his forearm up and down trying to estimate the weight. A good half kilo, he thought. Putting it to one side, he reached back into the bag. The final two items amazed even Sweetman. As he hauled them out, he knew what they were, but had never seen them in the flesh until now. First, a taser. In fact, the Taser X26C, complete with six cartridges, spare batteries and a practice target. The other item didn't need a practice target; for it to work you just had to be up close and cosy, tight enough to jam the spikes into any part of your enemy's anatomy. Then the vicious Vipertek VTS-989 stun gun would blast fifty million volts and pulverise the nervous system, temporarily at least. And yet it looked just like an ordinary torch – handy.

'Fuck me, Jan,' he said out loud, 'where did you get this stuff from? And when the hell did you expect to use it?' Kapusniak had put together a top escape kit; the powder alone was worth about twenty K, but when he needed it most the silly sod was banged up fifty fucking miles away. Sweetman laughed. 'Perhaps I'll get the chance to thank him when his case comes to court, because he won't be needing this for a while.' Kapusniak had gone down nine points in his estimation.

As he replaced the Beretta, he noticed a small burgundy wallet in the bottom of the bag. It was a Lithuanian passport, the photo obviously Kapusniak, but who the hell was Stephan Modrić, he wondered. Before he put the white powder back, he slid open the Ziploc, sucked the tip of his index finger and dipped it in, and then rubbed his teeth and gums with the finger. After a few seconds he closed the bag, grinned to himself and said another silent thank you to Kapusniak. It was undoubtedly the good stuff, 60 per cent pure he guessed, and Sweetman knew just the crew to move it on. Then he remembered he'd put more packets into his backpack. Putting the camo bag to one side, he reached across and pulled the backpack closer. He unfastened the large zipper and pulled out three packets. As he unfolded the ends of the two packs wrapped in brown paper he discovered he'd got one pack of compressed heroin and one of compressed cocaine. Even with his track record and experience, Sweetman's hands were shaking as he pulled the polythene wrapping from the final pack. As he opened out the layers, he revealed ten packs of £20 pound notes each neatly bound with a red and white paper band stating: £1,000.

'Jesus Christ, Jan, what a fucking dickhead you are. You could have retired on this,' said Sweetman out loud, shaking his head. But he had no intention of taking his own advice, or handing this stuff over to Aksanov. This stash, he knew, would propel him into the big time.

CHAPTER 11

Lee Gibson was feeling groggy. He'd had his operation and was still suffering from the effects of the anaesthetic. He was also feeling nervous; he knew his wife was coming to visit and he guessed by now she would have learned the sordid details of his torrid affair with the secretary of a Hampshire Council executive. The executive had been brutally murdered by the same men who had put him in hospital. And now he might be kicked out of the police force, all because one boozy night he'd told his mistress, who had also been shagging the executive, they'd found the boat her boss's killer used for smuggling immigrants and they were staking it out. The murdered man's widow turned up at the boat, set fire to it, putting the rest of the operation in jeopardy. Lee's mistress later admitted telling the woman about the boat, simply to get her off the doorstep, when she'd arrived to berated her about the affair with her husband.

He turned over the various scenarios in his mind. *Surely it was Sophie's fault.* If she hadn't decided she needed some time apart, her own space, he would still be living at home. And he wouldn't now be in the only shitty bedsit he could afford after he'd given her most of his monthly salary. If they'd carried on living together, he would never have thought about having an affair, probably. So in effect, it was definitely her fault. He knew she wouldn't see it quite the same. Mind you, his mistress: *what a looker, what a body; she really is something else*. Could I go back to the wife now? Do I want to? I know I'll miss the kids, but then it was her who wanted me out. I guess I'll just have to play it by ear, but one thing's for sure, I don't want to stay in that shitty bedsit much longer.

In reality, he knew the decision was not in his hands. The job was at the back of all their problems. Lots of women married to coppers, military men or men with hugely stressful jobs found it difficult to cope with the demands the job put on them as a family. Now the job had put him in hospital he knew she would use it against him. He was not looking forward to this visit.

Neither was Sophie Gibson. Her mind was in turmoil. She was devastated to learn of her husband's injuries, but furious a married man with two children would put himself in such a life-threatening position. He'd been a beat cop when they first started going out together. She'd loved the thought he was doing something worthwhile, and for the community. And she thought he looked lovely in his uniform. A thought soon swept away and replaced with fierce determination. Yes, they'd been happy at first, the hours unsociable, but bearable, and Aldershot was hardly the centre of the criminal underworld. She had never worried he might get stabbed or shot.

Then the kids came along and everything changed. She knew if she hadn't been so… *No, sod it, I've practically had to bring up these kids on my own. They hardly ever saw him when they were little. When he was home, it was always the kids, the kids. Never a thought about me being knackered looking after them all day. Then when I told him I'd had enough, he couldn't get out the door quick enough. I guessed he's been seeing some tart all the while. I will go and see him, but only to tell him that when he's able to walk he can collect the rest of his gear and stay out of my life.* Even as she drove to the hospital she couldn't stop thinking about the children. Should she have brought them? They wanted to see him, but she knew she couldn't say what she needed to say with them around, so she had left them with her parents. Her mind was churning and she drove on autopilot thinking about the situation. Jeez. Major Stafford – I mean, what the bloody hell was Lee doing with them? How the hell could he go from an ordinary, steady beat cop to some sort of gung-ho cowboy almost overnight? Mucking about with the security forces, of all people, trying to be like James frigging Bond, for Christ's sake. Didn't think about me or the kids when he decided to throw in with them, did he? The selfish prick!

By the time she arrived at the hospital, she was fired up and ready to face anyone or anything standing in her way. Finding a place to park and having to pay for it; pay for the privilege of seeing her cheating husband, did nothing to help her mood. As she gazed at the ticket machine, she noticed that if she stayed less than half an hour, her parking would be free. She could do what she needed to do and say what she wanted to say in less than two minutes, she thought, with a wry grin. She pulled the wheeled suitcase she'd packed with his clean clothes from the back seat and walked across the car park. She followed signs to the Nightingale Wing then the Bartlett Ward, where she found the nurses' station. A student nurse walked with her to Lee's bed and pulled the blue plastic curtains around for a little privacy. Lee Gibson pretended to be asleep, propped up on pillows leaning against the metal headboard. He opened his eyes at the sound of the curtains being pulled across. He waited till the nurse had finished and gone, before saying, 'Hello, love, all right?' It was all he could think of to say.

'Oh yeah, never better, Lee! How do you think I am?'

'Yeah, I know, sorry, love,' he said, in the little hangdog way she once found so endearing.

'Yeah? Sorry? Sorry for yourself. Sorry you got your legs broken and sorry I found out what a cheating bastard you are.'

'Oh come on love, Sophie. It was you wanted me out of the house. Can't we talk about this?'

'What's there to talk about, Lee? First opportunity you get, you're off shagging some tart or other.'

'It wasn't like— She's not a— Well, you obviously didn't want me. What did you expect? Did you want me to join a monastery? You pushed me out of the bloody house, pushed me away completely. Didn't want anything to do with me, maybe *you* had someone else. How do I know what you've been doing?'

'Don't you put this on me, Lee. I just needed some time apart to sort out our priorities.'

'Yeah, and your priorities didn't include me, did they?'

'And your only priority was work, not me or the kids.'

'And what did I get every time I walked in the door, eh? Just whinge, whinge, bloody whinge.'

'And you haven't even asked about the kids since I've been here.'

Neither spoke for a moment or two. She pushed the suitcase towards the bed.

'Collect the rest of your stuff when you can walk,' she said, then turned away. Lee opened his mouth to speak, but realised whatever he wanted to say, it was way too late. Sophie stormed through the curtains and marched out into the ward. As she approached the nurses' station, one of the nurses called out.

It was a second or two before Sophie registered she was being spoken to. She hesitated, blinked back tears and looked towards the nurse.

The nurse smiled, realised Sophie was close to tears and said comfortingly, 'Don't worry, Mrs Gibson, he's going to be fine, you know.' When Sophie nodded and walked across to her, the nurse continued, 'A little while ago one of Lee's colleagues came in and I think he has something for you, something the lads all collected for you.' She smiled encouragingly at her. 'I think he's still waiting in the Relatives Room.'

Sophie perked up a little; maybe it would be Major bloody Stafford. She thanked the nurse and stalked off, keen to give whoever it was a piece of her mind. As she pushed open the door to the Relatives Room, Kurt Edwards rose from his seat. Before he could speak, Sophie launched straight into the attack.

'If you're Major Stafford or any one of those bloody cowboys—'

CHAPTER 12

At six the following morning, Stafford awoke. Startled to find the right side of his face lying on a cold, soaking wet tea towel wrapped around a soggy plastic bag of mixed veg. He flung the bag and towel to the floor and laid his head back down on the pillow. It too was soaking wet. Now wide awake and mildly annoyed, he sat on the edge of the bed, pulled on a pair of boxer shorts and wandered into the bathroom, slowly wriggling his jaw from side to side. He peered into the mirror above the sink. His jaw cracked and ached a bit as he moved it from side to side and when he opened his mouth to yawn, but the swelling had gone down considerably. He washed and dressed in a pair of clean jeans and short-sleeved shirt, then changed the wet bed linen. As he picked up the bag of soggy veg, he heard Nicole make her way to the bathroom and shouted 'Tea?' as he wandered downstairs.

'Yes please,' was shouted back. A few moments later, wearing an outfit similar to Stafford's shirt and blue jeans, looking refreshed and sensational, she joined him in the kitchen. As Stafford added milk to the two mugs of tea, she asked him how his face was. He didn't answer, he was deep in thought, preoccupied with Lee Gibson, still in hospital. He knew Gibson's job was on the line. He'd almost blown their last operation wide apart for the sake of a shag or two. Stafford decided he would put into his report the woman's interference in the takedown at Shamrock Quay, but emphasise how useful and brave Gibson had been throughout the whole investigation, even dragging the injured Kapusniak out of the river.

He knew Gibson would not be relishing the thought of his wife's visit later in the day, and Stafford was not going to get involved in their domestic affairs.

He turned his mind to Marva Lewis and her two boys – he felt so sorry for her. First her husband had been murdered, his head, face, hair and eyes burned to an unrecognisable cinder, and now she'd been hounded out of her own home, not once, but twice by the bastards still trying for vengeance over him. Stafford knew these criminals could easily kill him, but they didn't want him to die easily; they wanted him to know his friends were dead because of him. Dead, because he refused to cooperate.

He called Ryan Peters to get an update on the situation with Marva, and agreed to meet at Ryan's place within the hour. Marva and her two boys had settled into their temporary home, and the Security Service agents from the Portsmouth safe house were in close attendance. Peters' house had been selected for this move because of the earlier threats posted to Stafford using pictures of Marva's house and Nicole's apartment. The criminals knew where Stafford lived; bizarrely, they seemed unaware of Peters' home address.

ll

As Stafford and Martin rolled to a halt outside Peters' house, a security service agent came out to meet them.

'All's quiet, sir. No sign of any suspicious activity,' he said, as he shook Stafford's hand.

'Good, we'll give it another few days, then reassess where we go from here.'

Marva and Peters were in the kitchen, Marva making coffee. After handshakes and hugs all round, they settled in the living room.

Stafford said to Peters, 'Looks like this address is safe, then.'

Before Ryan could answer, Marva brought the coffee over to the table.

'You should know, Staf, these lowlife crooks are beginning to piss me right off. I want to get back to my place. Try to get some semblance of order back into our lives, for the kids' sake. It's bad enough they've lost their father, but with all this on top, it's just so unsettling for them.'

Stafford, unsure what to say, pondered for a moment.

'Look, Marva, I reckon just a few more days and you'll be back home. They're so badly damaged, it's likely they'll disappear up their own arse holes and feel lucky they escaped further retribution.' There were a few amused looks around the table as the image took hold.

'Oh, come on, Staf, you can't expect me to believe that. These guys don't give a toss, they even attacked you in your own front garden, for Christ's sake. They aren't just going to stop, are they? They want their business back. Too much money to just give up.'

Stafford held up his hands, palms out. 'OK, Marva, you're right. Look, I'm sorry, but I hate to see you and your boys mucked about like this. I want to get you back home and settled, just as soon as possible.'

'I know, Staf, but you don't have to bullshit me, just tell it like it is and let me decide where and when me and the kids go from here. OK?'

'Point taken,' said Stafford with a sheepish grin, 'and to be honest, I do think you're in the clear. I reckon the main men will take a couple of days to assess the situation, then try to regroup and pick up the pieces of their business. They'll be too busy fending off marauders to worry about us.'

'Yes, I think you're right, boss,' said Peters, 'and we need to talk about it now. Are we going proactive? Do we go looking for them, or wait, see what happens?'

'Well, judging by the size of their lab in Weyhill, I'm guessing a huge amount of income was generated through drugs. So they'll need to bring in new supplies, probably across county lines, until they set up another lab – that should present some opportunities for us. And I think they'll be concentrating on rebuilding, rather than hurting Marva or the boys.'

'OK. Staf, here's how I'm thinking,' said Marva, 'we'll stay here with Ryan until the end of this week. If nothing bad happens here, we go back home on Monday.'

CHAPTER 13

Sophie didn't manage to say any more. Edwards, with a huge grin on his face, said, 'Whoa, whoa, no, I'm not Major Stafford, I'm a copper, Kurt, one of Lee's mates. And don't worry, we all feel the same about his lot as you do.'

Sophie could feel herself going red. Unsure what to say, she held out her hand. 'Oh, oh my God. I'm so sorry, forgive me, but I'm so wound up by all this… I'm Sophie, Sophie Gibson.'

Edwards took her hand and said with a smile, 'Well, Mrs Gibson, me and the lads had a bit of a whip-round at the station, and if you'll give me a minute to call my mate Ray, to bring the car round the front, I'll walk you downstairs and get it for you, OK?'

Sophie smiled and blinked back tears. Feeling stupid she said, 'Yes, of course it's fine, sorry about the outburst.'

Edwards smiled again. 'Nothing to apologise for. Now, just give me a sec,' he said as he pulled out his mobile. Hitting a speed dial button, he waited a second or two, then, 'Coop, yeah, it's me, I'm with Mrs Gibson now, will you bring the car round to the main entrance? Then we can give her what we've collected… Yeah, good, see you in about ten minutes then.' Call ended, he looked at Sophie. 'Right, Mrs G, let's go and get your stuff, I hope you'll be pleased.'

Sophie, now even more embarrassed, said coyly, 'You know, this is really sweet of you, and please, call me Sophie.'

As they walked together through the busy corridors and down the three flights of stairs, Sophie began to unwind. She found him easy to talk to, and talked about how it was really nice, you know, the way policemen had the camaraderie to do this sort of thing. She felt relieved to have someone, an adult, to talk to about her situation. As they walked, she turned her head surreptitiously to look at him. She liked what she saw. Edwards was a big man, not particularly tall but broad across the shoulders. He was good-looking in a rugged sort of way. There was a hint of danger about him, and it sent a little shiver through her. She was surprised it was a shiver of excitement, not fear. She wasn't surprised to see that, like Lee, he was constantly watchful. Head, eyes, turning, moving often, always. She smiled inwardly; a copper's trait.

After a moment, she asked, 'Did you know Lee and me have separated?'

Edwards hesitated mid-stride, then grinned as he carried on.

'What? No. What a dinlo, he sure kept that quiet. So where's he living now?'

'Oh, he's got himself a bedsit in Aldershot, but I gather he's found another bed to share, with some tart in Winchester.'

Edwards chuckled. 'Dirty little git. Mind you, we always thought he was punching well above his weight with you.'

Sophie squirmed a little with pleasure, and gave him a demure half-smile, hoping he hadn't said it to make her feel better. Hoping he meant it.

They were now close to the front entrance, where the automatic doors hissed open as they walked out to the drop-off area. Edwards saw the Mercedes some fifty metres away. He took hold of Sophie's left arm, and said 'Ah, look, there he is, let's wander over, make it easier for him to park up for a minute or two.'

She had no idea that he simply wanted to move away from the CCTV cameras covering the drop-off point. Cooper pulled up. They walked to the Mercedes and as Edwards pulled open the rear door, he said to Sophie, with a smile, 'There, look, love, it's on the back seat, I'll get it for you.' He nodded at her encouragingly, hand on her arm gently guiding her to the rear door space. Cooper had left the engine running. He peered over his left shoulder, a friendly grin on his face. Sophie returned the smile. Edwards turned to her and said, 'Bugger, can't quite reach it, hang on a sec.' He slid onto the rear seat.

Sophie moved around the car door and started to speak, 'You know, this is really nice of—'

Edwards, who had reached down behind the driver's seat, spun round to face her. At the last minute, too late to react, Sophie noticed he was now wearing gloves and holding a glass jar. He swung his arm, the jar hit her high on the chest. The contents spewed out, covering throat, chin, mouth, her whole face. Running down her neck, inside her clothes, onto her breasts, down her back. Stunned motionless for a split second, she heard Edwards yell, 'Go, go, go!' and the roar of the engine as the car sped away.

Then screaming in agony, she crashed to the ground, her hands tearing at her face, pulling and scraping at her eyes as she tried to stop the trail of liquid fire. Shock and terror shattered any control over her body's functions. She defecated and urinated before darkness set in and her body shut down.

As Cooper headed for the M3, Edwards threw the Kilner jar onto the back seat, pulled off his gloves, took out his mobile and called Aksanov.

'You wanted Stafford back in the game, we just ensured he will be,' said Edwards, outlining the events at the hospital. 'Yep, yep, we'll see you shortly.' He ended the call.

--- 11 ---

Aksanov was out of his chair, pacing up and down the office. 'I'd have preferred it to be the black woman, but this'll screw with Stafford's brain, for damn sure,' he said out loud, smiling to himself. Satisfied his vendetta with Stafford was back in play, he needed to get back to the real business of the day. Four of the syndicate's top men, two from London and two from Birmingham, were due to arrive within the hour. He knew his future in the syndicate was on the line – fuck, his whole future was on the line. He needed these guys to provide him with a continuous supply of the whole alphabet of drugs. The London guys were both Russian and had links with the Aksanov family going back to their struggles to survive poverty in the Mother Country. They had other links too, Brotherhood links, but he was sure they'd support and help him until he was able to re-establish his drug-manufacturing facility. After all, it was he who had introduced them to the dark web and cryptocurrency and he who had built the drug factory in Weyhill, not to mention developing their growing spare parts trade. And all this had brought them massive financial rewards. However, he needed their agreement to use syndicate funds to buy isolated farm buildings or a warehouse to set up anew.

He guessed he might have a problem with the two from Birmingham. They were Asian, and would have no idea his business model was the reason for their success.

Most owners of hotels and nightclubs thought that with the right location, lots of publicity, advertising and luck, they would eventually make a profit. Aksanov, however, created the right locations by ensuring the customers came back day after day. He offered them the chemical thrills they wanted. He controlled the supply of drugs, bringing vast quantities cheaply across the English Channel, and by using the dark web he'd cut out many of the middlemen. He'd set up the rural factory to manufacture, process and supply crack cocaine, MDMA, E and marijuana, and then set up lines of distribution, selling franchises to other club owners and dealers rather than have them set up in competition.

While using a boat to smuggle drugs into the country, he brought in illegal, paying immigrants. They were used as cheap labour: manufacturing and distributing the drugs; stripping precious metals from scrap electronics; prostitution. Aksanov realised technology offered so many new and lucrative business opportunities, but as he was not tech-savvy, he brought in someone who was: his Albanian business partner, Third Floor Sheila. Both Aksanov and TFS knew that a drug-addicted workforce was a loyal workforce. Their sole aim, the next fix. Some even sold their body parts for the next fix. Others weren't given the choice. So yes, the Russians would back him. The Brummies? It didn't matter, he had other plans for them.

Aksanov returned to his desk, lit a cigarette and switched on the monitor. He selected the icon for CCTV pictures, the screen split into eight sections, each showing live colour pictures of areas around the hotel's interior and car parks. Clicking onto the main car-park views, the picture filled the screen. The car park was two-thirds full, but he couldn't see the two cars he was looking for. He knew the Russians would arrive in a white Range Rover Evoque; the Asian pair from the Midlands in something more flashy; more osten-bloody-tatious. He'd even heard rumours of a Porsche 718 Cayman coupe in metallic jet black.

'Stupid fucks are just asking to be pulled over by the filth,' he said out loud.

CHAPTER 14

Stafford and Martin said their goodbyes at Peters' house and made their way back to Staf's Farnborough home. He said little, concentrating on driving. Martin settled back in her seat and waited. She knew he would open up, share his thoughts... When he was ready.

Stafford was mulling over Marva's situation. None of this was her fault, yet here she was in limbo with her two boys. And it was because of him. He and Garfield had known each other for ten or twelve years. They'd fought together, side by side with Captain Ryan Peters, in trouble spots all over the world. Sometimes in uniform, sometimes undercover as part of the E Squadron. They'd had their fair share of close calls and near misses; they all bore scars to prove it. But they'd survived. And now back in Blighty, Garfield was dead, and not a medal or citation to show for it. You don't get medals for doing the stuff they did. Their only reward was knowing they'd put away another crook. But back on home territory, you don't expect to have some two-bit Lithuanian no-mark burn your face off with a flare gun.

Martin looked across at him. She sensed his exasperation, but couldn't define the cause. 'D'you want to talk?' she said.

'Not sure, can't sort things out in my head yet. I dragged Garfield into this and now Marva and the boys are paying the price.'

'Staf, you dragged no one into this. Garfield and the rest of us are involved because we want to be. We all had – have – the option to drop out. He was doing what he wanted, working to take down the bandits.'

'Not sure I can explain. I mean, look at the guy I promoted to manage the Winchester tip. I promoted him to his death, signed his death warrant, as good as. Now I can't help feeling this whole thing with Garfield and Marva… You know he'd been alongside me for years? And now he's dead because of it.' Stafford paused for a long moment, then continued, 'And she's had no time to grieve, because her life is still being pulled around by these crooked bastards – because of me.' Turning the Volvo into his driveway, he switched off the ignition. Neither spoke or moved for a moment or two. 'Don't you see, anyone who hangs around me for any length of time ends up dead? And I have this nasty feeling things are going to get a lot worse before they get better.' He stepped out of the car, Martin following a pace behind. He opened the front door and they wandered through into the huge kitchen-cum-office.

Martin picked up the kettle. 'Coffee?'

Stafford nodded absentmindedly. 'OK, so we've managed to bust a few villains and I expect the whole bunch will go down for a long spell in prison. But most of all I want the fucker who put Garfield down, Jan Kapusniak. But we have no proof, no witness to the killing, nothing. It's all circumstantial. Oh yeah, we can get him on the other stuff, possession of a firearm, drug dealing and maybe even attempted murder, but a smart-arse lawyer will see the gaps in our case. And trust me, Nicole, Howard Neilson is a smart-arse lawyer and he won't be too far away from this.'

She finished making the coffee and pushed a mug across the table to Stafford. 'Yeah, and if I'd stayed with Garfield at Shamrock Quay—'

Stafford cut her off. 'This isn't your fault. You both did what was right at the time.'

'Yes, but if—'

'No, there's nothing you could have done. So now we need to get a full confession out of Kapusniak or get one of the others to grass him up. Then we go after his governor.'

Again there was silence between them.

'I can't see Kapusniak or any of the others confessing, but from what we know, I reckon Winstone was another regular in their band of brothers, and I think he's got to be the weakest link,' said Martin.

Stafford's mobile vibrated in his pocket. He checked the caller ID. *Talbot*.

As head of Hampshire's Special Branch, DCI Talbot had been invaluable, organising men and equipment for Stafford's most recent, and still ongoing, investigation. Stafford took the call.

Talbot said, 'Thought you should know, Floyd Winstone is going to be released on bail.' Stafford said nothing and the DCI continued, 'The Crown Prosecution Service have decided, in their wisdom, that because the charges against him are as an accessory and not as the main perpetrator, and because his earlier convictions are for fairly minor offences, he poses no flight risk. Nor is he thought to be a risk to the public. They'll soon be discharging him from the hospital, so he'll be free on bail pending further investigation.'

Stafford pursed his lips and shook his head in disbelief, even though Talbot couldn't see it.

'What's the matter with these people? They don't appear to live in the same world as the rest of us. How would they feel if it was one of their family or friends put to the sword this way?'

'I know how you feel, Staf, but as you well know it's a risk we always face. At least we have an address for him, vouched for by his legal chap, Howard Neilson.'

'Neilson, eh? I knew he'd be at the front of this. What's the chances of putting surveillance on Winstone?'

'I don't think we'll be able to justify it, let alone spare the manpower – you know we've still got a large team at the Weyhill site. . . But why? Do you think he'll be up to more skulduggery?'

'No – quite the reverse, in fact. We reckon he's the weakest link in their crew, and our best chance to get decent evidence against the two lieutenants. And if we think he's a weak link, so will his masters. I reckon the CPS just signed his death warrant.' As he let Talbot process this information, Stafford asked, 'So he's not been discharged from hospital yet?'

'No, maybe later on today, but the doctors were good enough to give us the heads-up.'

'So what's the address he's given re his bail conditions, then?'

'He gave the Aldershot flat at 10a North Lane, the address on his driving licence. I'm trying to get a K9 team in there, but we don't have a team local at the moment, we're being stretched too far. But what's worse: Howard Neilson is trying to swing bail for Kapusniak.'

'What? Surely not?'

'The CPS thinks the case against him for killing Garfield Lewis is too weak. We have the probable weapon, but only circumstantial evidence. Howard Neilson is jumping up and down saying he's hasn't any priors against him in the UK or anywhere else, so he's pushing for bail as soon as he's well enough to leave hospital.'

'Jeez, makes you wonder why we do this, doesn't it? The law is never on the side of the victim. And I can't believe Kapusniak's got no form anywhere. I mean, you don't just rock up in a new country and decide you want to be a criminal. He has to have form somewhere, it's just a matter of finding it.'

Call ended, Stafford said to Martin, 'It looks like I'm not going to be able to take a break from HMG anytime soon, so I'll use the rest of today doing the rounds of the five recycling sites, make sure the managers are good to carry on running the show for a bit longer.'

When Stafford, Peters and Lewis had been cut loose from Fort Monckton, it was rumoured they were working for HMG as part of the unquantifiable E Squadron. Investigative journalists began to delve, to google it, but getting a lead on it was like stacking eels. They'd been tasked with investigating and destroying what appeared to be a terrorist-led drug-manufacturing and distribution network. It was operated by criminals employing illegal immigrants as slave labour, using the recycling centres for cover.

Stafford took over the contract for the five sites in question. They successfully sorted out the five sites. He realised the full business potential of the tips and enjoyed the thrill of discovering interesting and collectible items dumped in the waste. The tips were now producing good profits and his staff were geared up to put aside any items that might be considered interesting, or anything retro, vintage or antique, whatever the condition. These were collected by his site supervisor, who would take anything undamaged to local auction houses. Articles in need of restoration would be taken to the double garage at Stafford's home. Stafford, in his limited spare time, loved to work on these objects and make them whole again.

'Before I go, I'll talk to Ryan and get him to follow up on Winstone's address and keep an eye on him for a while. At least till we can put him under pressure to talk to us.'

'So what do you want from me, boss?' said Martin.

He thought about his answer, then said, 'You can ship Kapusniak's mugshot and the original e-fit picture of him into Interpol's database and request a search, see if their facial recognition system comes up with anything. And check if they've issued an international alert for him. If not, get them to ask the Secretariat to issue a Red Notice, using Kapusniak or any name their system throws up. OK?'

'Yep, no problem, though if they'd issued a Red Notice, surely we'd have seen it when his name cropped up originally?'

'Yes, you're right, but they might have just filed a Diffusion and it'll only have been sent out to two or three countries where they think he's most likely to run to. You know, somewhere the suspect speaks the same language.'

'Let's just hope the system has more facial images than before, then.'

'I'm more confident now – Interpol have partnered up with a hi-tech biometric and security company, so fingers crossed.'

Stafford called Ryan Peters and told him about Winstone's imminent release. Peters knew the flat in Aldershot, having been there during their last operation. He confirmed the staff at his Aldershot recycling centre would be able to cope without him and agreed to watch the North Lane flat, but not make contact unless it was obvious Winstone was going to do a runner or be abducted by his former colleagues.

Stafford left the house and headed for the M3. He'd decided to start the site visits at the Basingstoke tip. The half-hour drive would give him chance to scope out the next move, chance to sort things through in his mind. He slid a Jimi Hendrix CD into the player and put his mind in cruise; his tried-and-tested method of busting through a log jam.

Martin settled in front of the computer and found the mugshot and e-fit pictures of Jan Kapusniak. Logging into the UK's National Central Bureau, she requested an international facial recognition search. Having satisfied the various checks and balances, she shipped Kapusniak's pictures into the system. Bam! There they were, on screen; seventeen faces. Each one of them a long-haired, thin-faced likeness of Kapusniak. She shivered with excitement as she leaned forward to examine them. The passport they held in his name showed his country of origin as Lithuania. There was certainly a Lithuanian lookalike, but the name under the image and on the arrest warrant was Stephan Modrić. A Stephan Modrić was also the subject of an arrest warrant issued in Bosnia and three more warrants outstanding from Slovakia, Moldova and Romania.

'Looks like the evil bastard got wise to the art of hiding in plain sight when he came here,' she said out loud. She printed off the pictures of Modrić, along with the arrest warrants detailing the crimes he was suspected of. She leaned back in her chair, took a deep breath and began to read these through, in chronological order. As she read, it was as though she was reading a work of fiction: dark fiction.

Crimes of violence, murder and all manner of sexual abuse against men, women and children. His crimes crisscrossed Eastern Europe. Martin could see Kapusniak's atrocities became more deviant, more perverted as he moved from country to country, as though taunting his pursuers; his crimes funded and fuelled by drug dealing. Kapusniak, or Modrić, whoever he was, liked prepubescent girls. He found ways to lure them away from their parents, then plied them with drugs in order to molest, abuse and rape them. When he killed them, he disposed of their broken bodies by dismembering them and dumping their remains in different locations; rubbish dumps, recycling centres and landfill sites. He was the prime suspect in the deaths of five girls all under the age of thirteen. He was also wanted in connection with the deaths of three women and a man, all of whom were the parent, guardian or older sibling of the murdered girls.

These crimes were finally linked by a senior detective in

the Romanian capital Bucharest. It was linked by chance; a civilian security guard shot a vixen dragging a black sack containing large chunks of raw meat from a landfill site to her cubs. Forensic examination showed it to be the bottom half of a young female torso. DNA tests proved this to be a missing twelve-year-old Romanian girl and a match to Kapusniak/Modrić's DNA was found in semen traces within the torso.

Martin listed the details in her notebook, folded the various A4 prints and put them together with her written notes. As she worked, the bile rose in her throat, she was so nauseated and disgusted by the depravities of this man. At least now, she thought, there was no way this evil man would be released. She clicked off the computer and closed her notebook, wondering if the UK had an extradition arrangement with Lithuania.

CHAPTER 15

For most of the last couple of years, Floyd Winstone had all but lived at the syndicate's compound in Weyhill. This compound also housed other syndicate men and illegal immigrants. Winstone made bail when the Royal Hampshire County Hospital in Winchester discharged him. He had been arrested fleeing a burning boat on the River Itchen. Evidence of anything more serious than being in possession of Class A drugs and an involvement in people smuggling at the Southampton and Weyhill operations was flimsy. The CPS were adamant: they needed more.

He was relieved to be out of hospital, albeit with limited use of both hands. His right hand had been smashed some weeks earlier, and his left had suffered burns as he was escaping the boat where he was arrested. He had arranged to be picked up from the hospital by Tony Amos, who had also been rescued from the burning boat and arrested then released on bail pending further enquiries. Amos arrived driving a battered old white pickup truck and, as Winstone had one arm in a sling and bandages on his other hand, he leaned across the passenger seat to open the door for him. Winstone climbed into the front seat. Neither man said anything as they headed for the M3.

'I guess you want to go to Aldershot, then,' said Amos eventually.

Winstone nodded. 'No alternative, mate. I wanted to talk to Aksanov, but fuckin' Howard Neilson warned me off.'

Amos shot a glance at him. 'Yeah, me too. I think I'll have to in the end, though, I don't wanna be looking over my shoulder for the rest of my life.'

'Mark my words, you'd be well advised to keep away from him after your fuck-up on the boat.' Again there was an uneasy quiet between them. This time it went on for a few miles. Amos picked a packet of cigarettes from the top of the dashboard and lit one. Taking a deep drag, he said, 'Well, bloody Runihura, he pushed me into doing the job when he knew I had a bird lined up.'

'So you decided to down a whole bottle of fuckin' vodka instead of keeping watch?'

Blowing out a stream of smoke, Amos said, 'Fuck you, Floyd. Turns out they'd been watching us for ages, they were gonna bust us anyway. They just waited till we got the immigrants into the van. We were fucked from the time that mad bastard Kapusniak killed the black geezer.'

'Yeah, maybe you could try explaining it, but I doubt Aksanov will see it that way,' said Winstone. 'And don't I know it – why do you think I wanna get to the flat? Kapusniak told me where he hid his escape bag: reckon it's the only chance I got.'

'Yeah? When we find it, we're gonna split it, mate, because my need is just as great as yours.' Amos took one last drag and threw his cigarette out of the window. They finished the journey in silence. When they arrived at the flat, the blue and white police tape was fluttering in the breeze like leftover bunting. Amos ripped it from the railings, screwed it into a ball and ripped the crime scene sign from the door.

'Wankers,' was his only comment as he turned the key and let them in. The flat was a shambles, furniture pushed into corners, sofas upturned, backs and bottoms ripped open. Winstone didn't seem to notice, wandering through the hall to the kitchen, and kneeling down by a kitchen unit, he opened the cupboard doors. Reaching in, he put his arms around the contents, and dragged the lot out onto the floor, wincing as pain shot through his damaged hands. Sweeping the pots and pans to one side, he tried to lift up the cabinet base, but couldn't get a grip. He shouted to Amos to find him a knife or screwdriver. Amos opened a couple of drawers before he found a dinner knife, which he handed to Winstone. Though he could hold the knife, his damaged hands meant that every time he tried to lever up the base, his fingers weren't sufficiently healed to cope with the pressure and he kept dropping it.

'For Christ's sake, get out the bloody way and let me do it,' said Amos, pushing Winstone's shoulders. Winstone hauled himself to his feet and gave the knife to Amos, who dropped to his knees, peered inside the cupboard and slipped the blade into the gap between the front of the cupboard and the base panel, levering gently. As the base started to rise, he put his fingers underneath the panel and propped it against the rear of the cupboard. Peering into the bottom of the unit, Winstone knelt beside him, almost pushing him out of the way.

'So what we got then?' he said.

Amos scraped his hand around the bottom of the space, reached out his hand, placed it on Winstone's shoulder and pushed himself upright.

'Absolutely fuck all, mate, absolutely fuckin' nothin'.'

In disbelief, Winstone leaned forward and almost fell into the cupboard, his arms deep in the cavity trying to find something.

He got out, sat back on his haunches, chin on his chest. Amos chucked the flat keys on the floor beside him and left the flat. *I'll have to talk to Aksanov now, it's my only chance*, thought Winstone.

CHAPTER 16

Sophie Gibson staggered backwards and crashed to the ground, her hands covering her face. She lay on her right side, her unconscious body thrashing around, legs twitching in shock. The hospital entrance was busy. A number of people slowed to look at the prone figure, but moved swiftly on; most happy to let others deal with the situation. One or two did seek out the professionals to tell them about the injured woman on their doorstep.

The first doctor to Sophie's side tried to take her hands away from her face. But the skin from her hands had dissolved or melted and was now welded to the skin on her face. In seconds, porters appeared with a gurney. As they lifted her onto it, the doctor inserted an IV line of saline solution and rushed her to the nearest examination room. Inside the confined space, fumes from the liquid soaking her caused their eyes to start streaming.

The doctor shouted, 'It's acid… No smell, almost certainly sulphuric, protective glasses and masks *now*!' She pushed the gurney to the examination table and, pulling out the flexi hose and tap, began to hose, carefully, Sophie's face, hands, neck and shoulders with cold water. At the same time, one of the nurses fitted her with protective glasses and a mask to cover her own nose and mouth.

'Right. I want shears, a nurse with a pair of surgical shears each side of her. Then start cutting the clothes off her top half, starting at her wrists. And don't try pulling the clothes off, fold them out so we can hose her down.' That done, they cut through the middle of her blouse and bra, folding the material back to expose her breasts.

As Sophie lay half-naked and motionless, the damage to her face, neck, shoulders and top half of her breasts showed in sharp contrast to her pale, blemish-free lower body. They lifted her clear of her damaged clothing and placed her on the examination bed. The doctor began to properly assess the damage.

The hospital's security chief had been notified, he called the police, then got porters to cordon off the area where the attack had taken place. Local police arrived and, after discovering Sophie was the wife of one of their own, began to backtrack her movements, using CCTV footage. Starting from the time she was found, they traced her footsteps back to the moment she entered the hospital, confirming that she had visited her husband in the Bartlett Ward. It was obvious they needed to find – and find urgently – the unknown man who'd escorted her from the ward to the front entrance. From the CCTV, they discovered a second, similarly dressed man just a pace or two behind him, and they followed his movements too.

While one officer continued to search the CCTV pictures and transfer them onto discs, another logged onto the Police National Database and found Major Paul Stafford listed as lead investigator for recent events involving PC Gibson, and how he ended up in hospital. He called him.

Stafford's day had so far been rewarding and enjoyable. He was feeling buoyant; the sites were all looking good and one had managed to find him a couple of unusual antique pieces of furniture, which, after a little restoration, would do well at auction. His managers were happy that things were now quietening down and they were back to the business of making money. What pleased him most, though, was coming up with an idea to move the investigation forwards. An idea to create more chaos and disruption to the criminal's syndicate and further limit their financial capability. And he knew he could do it without calling in help from the Colonel or DCI Talbot. All he needed was a bit of time. Time to clear up the constant obstacles these scumbags kept throwing in the way and time to find more evidence to bring the top guys down. And with the help of Immigration Enforcement, he could get it done. He knew just the man to talk to, but needed convincing evidence to get the ball rolling. He was heading south on the M3, Led Zep in the player, head moving in time to the music. The song cut out as Bluetooth cut in and a voice came over the car's speakers.

'Major Stafford?'

'Yep.'

'There's been an incident at Winchester hospital. PC Gibson's wife Sophie has been attacked, and badly hurt.'

Stafford said, 'I'll be there in twenty minutes. How bad is it?'

'It's bad, Major, real bad. Doctors are assessing her now. Apparently some sort of chemical, probably acid, was involved.'

Stafford had never met Sophie Gibson, but he knew instinctively this attack was designed to ensure he stayed in the fray. Earlier, they'd wanted him to give way to their demands and work with them. Now it was different. There were no demands. They could easily take him out. The two guys he'd fought with at his house could have shot him or placed a bomb under his car, but it was obvious they wanted to screw with his mind. Someone wanted him to suffer the pain of knowing his colleagues and friends were being targeted because of him. They knew the attack on an innocent like Sophie Gibson would haunt him forever. Normally calm and level-headed, Stafford found himself full of fury. He crashed his hands onto the steering wheel and vowed he would find the scum who did this and bring them to justice. Not the CPS kind of justice, his kind of justice. Justice with no compromise. Immigration Enforcement would have to be put on hold for now.

He pulled off the motorway and headed for the Royal Hampshire County Hospital. The area around the main entrance was a hive of activity. Areas had been cordoned off with police tape and forensic techs were searching for evidence. He showed his ID to a uniformed constable; as he waited, he noticed the gaggle of reporters busy filming and talking to bystanders and the forensic team. ID checked, he was directed to the security chief's office.

As he strode through the hospital, a wheelchair-bound Lee Gibson was being pushed by a porter down the main corridor. One fully plastered leg sticking rigidly out in front, the other was plastered from the knee down. Gibson, eyes red and puffy, spotted Stafford.

'Stafford! Hey, Stafford, you sneaky bastard, don't you fucking think you can slope off and ignore me,' he shouted. 'Have you seen her? Have you seen what they've fucking done to her? This is your fault, Stafford,' he screamed, arms flailing.

Stafford strode up to the copper.

'Pull yourself together, Gibson, this is no more my fault than yours. And no, I haven't seen her, but rest assured we will find whoever did this.'

Gibson hung his head, trying to control his tears.

'Will you do it, Staf? Will you find these fuckers?'

'I won't stop until we do, Lee, I promise you.' As he walked away, Stafford wondered if he should warn Gibson about talking to the media. He decided not to mention it – Gibson would likely as not go against anything he said.

Gibson gripped the wheels of his chair so the porter couldn't move him away. He held still for a second or two, watching Stafford disappear into the distance, then said quietly to himself, 'If you don't, Stafford, I fucking well will.'

Stafford entered the security office and sat down at the table with the two investigating constables, who talked Stafford through their findings so far. They passed across a number of A4 prints they had extracted from the CCTV footage. The first picture showed a smiling Sophie Gibson, walking and talking to a smartly dressed man in the corridor outside the Bartlett Ward. Though the pictures weren't great quality, Stafford recognised the man; the suit, the collar and tie. It was the man who'd been trying to peer through Marva's front door; the man he'd fought in his front garden not twenty-four hours ago.

'Jesus Christ! Yeah, I recognise him. I had a bust-up

with the bastard just yesterday,' said Stafford, throwing the prints down and resisting smashing his fist onto the table. Face red with fury, he shouted, 'Jeez, why the hell didn't I take him out yesterday?'

'Yeah, a pity you didn't bust him a bit harder,' said one of the coppers ruefully, adding, 'when the guy you're looking at came into the hospital, there was another bloke behind him. We're not sure if they were together, but they were dressed in a similar way, both in suits and wearing ties. So we tracked his movements too. See what you make of this…'

Stafford pulled up the office chair so he could view the monitor. The security chief pressed a button, ejected a DVD and inserted another one. The flickering picture showed a view of the hospital entrance from the inside, just as Suspect No. 2 walked through the doors. Stafford asked if he could halt the film. The security chief pushed a button, the image froze.

'They're poor pictures,' Stafford said, leaning in close, 'but I'm certain he's the guy my colleague booted in the nuts during the ruckus in my front drive.'

The image was jerking around as they continued to play the film, following the man from camera to camera. The security chief explained, 'He seemed to be wandering aimlessly about, so I chopped out the bits in between… Now this, I think, you'll find interesting.'

The film showed Suspect No. 2 stopping to read signs at a junction of corridors and then taking a left turn. As he walked, he was looking left and right, seemingly for a specific location. There were no wards in this area, just a number of gurneys and wheeled containers; one of the service areas. Suspect No. 2 disappeared into a side room; moments later he came out carrying a bundle of clothes under his arm.

'Looks like he's just nicked a porter's uniform,' said the security chief, as the film continued to follow Suspect No. 2 back to the front entrance and out, pulling out a mobile phone and putting it to his ear as he went.

Shaking his head in consternation, Stafford said, 'My oppo, Ryan Peters, has been trying to find out who the first guy is, I hope he's got the bastard's name.' As he spoke, he took out his mobile to call Peters; asking the security chief to leave the room. Putting Peters on speaker, he said when Peters picked up, 'Have you found our strong-arm peeping tom?'

'Yeah, yeah, he came up on the PND as Kurt Charles Edwards, ex-army. Last known address was North Lane, but we know that's been empty for a while. Got a bit of form going back some, but he's been off the radar for eighteen months or so.'

'Sod it, bit of a dead end then, but at least we've got a name. What about his current employment?'

'Seems he's been working as a club doorman. His last brush with the law shows him working security at a club in Slough. So why the urgent interest?'

'The cowardly bastard threw a pot of acid over Sophie Gibson when she went to visit Lee earlier. I'm at the hospital now.'

Stunned, Peters said nothing for a moment. Then, 'Jesus, how bad is it?'

'I've not been able to see her, she's been airlifted to a specialist burns unit in Salisbury, but the people here tell me the damage is catastrophic. So, mate, we need a break here, we have to find this bastard before he does any more damage. I'm going through the CCTV footage, see if there's any more we can glean from it. Meanwhile, you got any thoughts on how we can find this scumbag?'

'He was working the doors for a number of clubs in Slough – I can't see him changing his work habits too much.' Peters paused for a moment or two, then said, 'And Sergeant Hawkins reminded me – the dodgy DI at Aldershot was spending loads of money in a Basingstoke nightclub, and claimed expenses for visits to the World Citizen Hotel – you know, the one on the outskirts of Basingstoke? How about I start nosing around there?'

'Bloody hell, good thought, Ry! Yes, it sort of went off the radar a bit after we tidied up in Weyhill. But we've had nothing from the guys we've arrested to link Weyhill to the nightclubs or the hotel. So we need to find something, anything to link the two. So, yeah, good shout. What do you think? This time of day, start with the hotel, shake the tree a bit, see what falls out?'

'I've not seen anyone turn up here. I mean, there is a chance he's inside right now, of course, but without knocking on the door, I've got no way of telling. So yeah, I'll do a bit of tree-shaking, no sweat. Do you want me to pick up Nicole on the way or get her to cover me here?'

Stafford, without hesitation, said, 'No, leave her for now. I need to talk to you about her, but don't want her involved just yet, we don't need her to end up like Sophie. And we can always pull Winstone in again later if we need to.'

'OK, Staf, you're the boss. So I'll catch up with you

later,' said Peters. Then, 'How's Lee, by the way? I guess he knows about the attack?'

'Yeah, Jeez, he's torn apart. Although they were separated, he was absolutely incandescent at what they did to her... Blamed me at first. Bit worried about him, actually, I think he's about to– well, I don't know, both legs in plaster, he's a bit stymied, but I think he's ready to blow, getting close to being a loose cannon.'

'Can't say I blame him,' said Peters, 'I'd want revenge too. And I hope we'll help him get it.'

'It'll happen, Ryan, one way or another, it'll happen,' said Stafford as he ended the call.

As he watched the rest of the CCTV footage, he was still brooding on the bastards who had killed his colleagues and destroyed the lives of PC Lee Gibson and his wife. Though the office was cool, he could feel the sweat running down his arms and soaking into his shirt. Beads of sweat formed on his forehead. He had to find a way to protect his friends and end the torment. Had to get Nicole out of harm's way, but that was easier said than done. Even the thought of pushing her away hit him hard. He felt exhausted, spent, done.

For some time, he was unable to break his gloom. And the fact his jaw still ached didn't help. Slowly, piece by piece, anger grew inside him. Now he'd be forced to put some distance between himself and Nicole, just when he thought they'd have the time to get to know each other better. It fuelled his sense of outrage. Even on the battlefields, he'd never had this sort of hatred for the enemy. In battle, they too were under orders – kill or be killed. Here in Civvy Street, it seemed the enemy had no boundaries. He'd made it a rule never to take a case personally. Now, with the attacks on his friends, he'd have to tear up his own rulebook.

CHAPTER 17

Pavel Aksanov was unique for a crook with Russian heritage. There was his love of golf for a start, but at heart he was an old-fashioned, honest-to-goodness criminal. He was in it for the money, plain and simple. His fellow countrymen, the members of the syndicate arriving today, were a different breed. A breed apart. They were government-backed – Putin's government. Their goals were on a different level entirely. They wished to destroy the country from within. To weaken it financially. Destabilise it by creating a land of drug-addicted no-hopers. They wanted to create mayhem by instilling fear into a population currently disillusioned and feeling its political classes had lost the plot. Fear induced by random acts of violence. Internally, they used ruthless brutality and torture to keep their foot soldiers in line. But they weren't averse to public displays of unimaginable violence to stop interference from outsiders. The police never found any witnesses. These men wanted to create a working class of incompetent druggies who believed they were governed by drug-addled and corrupt buffoons.

His Russian colleagues would see the collapse of half his organisation at the hands of Paul Stafford as a sign of weakness. He could not afford to show further frailty. But he had a plan: in return for their help in rebuilding the empire, he was going to offer them total control of the Birmingham operation, currently governed by the Asian pair soon to arrive. They were coming to the meeting expecting to expand their business by making up Aksanov's shortfall. Aksanov was prepared to show he too could be brutal and ruthless. He glanced again at the monitor and, though he would never admit it, his stomach lurched. He reached for a cigarette and, as he lit it, began to wish he'd never let Third Floor Sheila persuade him to invite them. As he watched, a white Range Rover rolled slowly by the faux Grecian portico, the hotel's front entrance. The Russians stepped out of the vehicle and handed the key to the bellboy who had dashed down the steps to meet them. Aksanov switched the monitor off, took a deep drag on his cigarette, stubbed it out and tried to settle as he waited for his guests to arrive. The door to his office opened and the two elderly Russians walked purposefully into the room. Aksanov came from behind his desk and greeted both men with a handshake, followed by a full-on bear hug.

'It's been too long, *tovarisch*,' he said, patting both men on their shoulders. 'Come, sit down. What would you like to drink?'

'Well, *brat*,' said the older of the two smartly dressed visitors, as they sat in the two comfortable chairs Aksanov had arranged in front of his desk. 'We will have tea.'

Aksanov noted the use of the Russian word for brother, and trusted it was a good sign. Picking up his desk phone, he called room service. 'Bring tea for our guests and for me; yes, to my office.'

The older man glanced at the lack of chairs and said, 'I thought more were coming, they should be here by now – they're being disrespectful.'

Aksanov waved a hand dismissively. 'Yes, but they're just Asian punks, *kozel*, no class.'

'But still willing to bail you out, Pavel,' said the younger of the suited visitors with a snide look. He was smaller than his colleague, not as fat, and shorter, darker-skinned, but with the same greying light brown hair.

'You're wrong there, my friend. They're coming here to help you out, but they don't know it yet. They're driving down from Birmingham in a motor designed to attract attention wherever it goes. They have no idea how to keep a low profile. Even their buyers are beginning to complain about how their money is being spent. And if *they* collapse, then the whole operation in the Midlands and further north is in jeopardy. I'm sorting that problem out today; before it happens.'

'Pity you didn't do the same in Andover, Pavel,' said the older man.

'Do you see the police knocking on my door, *tovarisch*? No, because I keep a tight rein, not like the shambles your lot created in Salisbury. The whole operation in Weyhill, everything on the site was leased to the Egyptian, Ayman Runihura. No comeback on me, and no one, not even you, my friend, can legislate for trigger-happy foreign psychos, and that's what started this off.'

Aksanov's mobile buzzed. He glanced at it, and missed the icy look his visitors exchanged. He pressed a button on his mobile, and selected the app for the hotel's CCTV pictures. Ensuring his monitor had the same pictures as his mobile, he swung it round for his visitors to see. As they watched, a high-performance metallic jet-black Porsche 718 Cayman rolled into the hotel's car park. It paused for a moment, before parking alongside the Russians' white Range Rover, a vehicle recovery truck pulled up next to it. Aksanov's guests appeared bemused and looked at him questioningly. Aksanov nodded in a 'keep watching' sort of way. Two Asian men got out of the Porsche and stretched. They exchanged words across the top of the car and began to make their way to the hotel's front entrance. Aksanov pressed a button on his mobile and the screens on the mobile and monitor split into two pictures. One showed the original view with the Porsche, the other showed the two men walking across the car park. Both looked as though they'd been pumping iron since they were kids, and both wore Nike tracksuits and trainers.

'What is this, Pavel? We came here to do business, not watch films and play silly games,' the older Russian man said.

'Trust me, *tovarisch*. This is no game, this is live, happening now. Just watch,' said Aksanov icily.

As they watched, the recovery truck driver was swinging the vehicle's Hyva crane over the Porsche. A chain dangled from each corner of a rectangular metal frame and each chain was fitted with what looked like grappling hooks. As he lowered the frame carefully, the hooks came to rest on the tarmac close to the Porsche's wheels. The driver fitted the hooks around each wheel and was preparing to raise the vehicle when the Asians became aware of something happening behind them, and, as they turned to look, a hooded man started striding towards them.

The silence in Aksanov's office was total. On screen, one

of the Asians took a pace towards the hooded man before – arms flailing, legs performing an uncoordinated jig – he crashed to the ground; thrashed around for a few seconds and lay still. The hooded man indicated for the second Asian to kneel down next to his friend, then handed him a long industrial cable tie to bind the now semiconscious man's hands together behind his back.

The hooded figure bent down and with gloved hands removed the taser barbs from the incapacitated man, rewound the wires and pocketed the weapon. Reaching into another pocket, he pulled out what looked like a torch and pointed it at the second man, who nodded, his face etched with fear. Together, they pulled the bound and helpless man to his feet and walked him to a black Mercedes pickup truck, where they bundled him into the back seats. Hoody pushed the other man in through the back door and jabbed the torch-like stun gun into his neck. The man convulsed once, his mouth opened wide. It was obvious to the watchers that he was screaming in pain.

In the office, no one moved or spoke. Aksanov noted his visitors had leaned forward for a better view, both sets of eyes intent on the screen, both pairs of hands resting on their knees. For the first time, both men were smiling. Aksanov hoped this show of strength was going to work. Doing this would actually cost him a good deal of money, and the wrath of Third Floor Sheila. She had often bemoaned that the small number of Asian and black immigrants they brought into the country fell far short of requests via the dark web for donor organs. And now here he was, sacrificing the opportunity to make a few thousand bucks, firstly in the hope the Russians would see this as a gesture of goodwill, and secondly, in the hope that the Asians' disappearance and subsequent discovery would send Stafford on yet another resource-consuming investigation.

He couldn't resist a slight smile at his thoughts. *Sheila's right, though, it's an area I should pursue, maybe with a new boat? And if I can persuade the Russians to take over the Birmingham operation, perhaps they could ship us a few home-grown ones.* He put the thought out of his mind, it was for the future.

Surreptitiously he looked across at his guests and for the first time he noticed the faded, fuzzy blue-black outlines of crown tattoos on their left hands. He said a silent prayer to a God he didn't believe in. There was a knock on the door and a waiter walked in with the tea. Aksanov told him to leave it on the desk and waved him away.

On screen, Hoody pulled out another cable tie, and bound the second man's hands behind his back before slamming the rear door. In the background, the recovery truck drove out of the car park with the Porsche on the back. Aksanov smiled as he watched the hooded Sweetman put the stun gun back into his coat pocket, climb into the Mercedes and drive away. He switched off the monitor; the two Russians sat stony-faced. It was seconds before anyone spoke.

In an accent much thicker than earlier, the older Russian said, 'And you say this is for our benefit?'

'The removal of the Porsche now winging its way to a customer in Bosnia means thirty-five K I won't have to take from the syndicate's coffers to re-establish my manufacturing facility. I want you to provide me with the merchandise I need to cover my current shortfall. Those two in a Porsche

Cayman? They were bound to attract the attention of the police soon enough. The important thing is, they run operations in and around Birmingham. I've just opened the door for you to take over the Midlands operation. You came down here hoping to expand your territory, now I've given you the opportunity, so don't try taking my operation apart, *ponyat*, comrades?'

CHAPTER 18

As Ryan Peters pulled away from North Lane and out onto the main road headed for the M3, a battered white pickup truck trundled around the corner towards him. In his rear-view mirror he watched, cursing, as it pulled into the flat's parking area. Traffic was heavy, heavier than usual. Forty minutes later, as he got close, he turned on his dash cam. He drove through the large open entrance in the walls surrounding the hotel, then past the faux Grecian portico main entrance. Driving into the large car park at the rear, he had to stop to allow a recovery truck with a black performance car on the back to complete its manoeuvre. While he waited, he glimpsed out of the corner of his eye a hooded man pushing something into the back seat of a black Mercedes pickup. He watched as the sports car was hauled away, shortly followed by the Mercedes pickup, which pulled out of the car park at speed. Realising the impatient driver would get stuck behind the recovery truck for some miles before he could overtake, Peters couldn't help but smile.

Further into the car park he noticed numerous CCTV cameras high up on the hotel walls.

Judging by the Mercedes, BMWs and Porsches in the car park, the patrons were well heeled. Not one car was more than three years old. In first gear, he cruised in a large, slow circle and was interested to see parked there four black Mercedes X-Class pickup trucks. Not proof, not confirmation, but the bad guys they'd arrested in the earlier operation had a penchant for the same motor and a number of them had been seized. It was likely these were company vehicles and indicated that the two operations were probably linked. All they had to do was prove it. Peters decided to raise a few eyebrows and questions in the CCTV control room. He did another circuit, ensuring he managed to film the registration plates of the four Mercedes pickups, and then drove back out onto the country roads surrounding the hotel. He smiled as he imagined the consternation of the men watching the monitors. Had they clocked his car? Had they clocked him? Should they follow or should they play it cool and leave the next move to him?

He'd been a watcher many times himself, knew what they were thinking; he laughed as he drove further into the countryside. After a few miles, he pulled over into a muddy lay-by. Opening the glove compartment he found a biro and notepad. He called Nicole Martin and, while waiting for her to answer, flipped down the screen on the dash cam. He replayed the film with the Mercedes pickups and jotted down their registration numbers. He was amazed to see he had also caught the plate of the speeding Mercedes pickup as it raced out, as well as the recovery truck and the Porsche it was carrying. They were blurred, but he thought he could make them out, and he knew they could enhance the images later if needed.

Martin finally answered and Peters brought her up to speed, telling her of the horrific attack on Sophie Gibson.

The phone was quiet for long seconds. Peters was beginning to think he'd lost connection, when Nicole said, 'Jeez, there's no bloody let-up is there? Poor girl, poor Lee; is she going to be OK?' They talked about it for a few minutes and then, desperate to change the subject, Peters told her the rest of the day's events, shipping her the dash-cam film and asking her to find out who the vehicles were registered to. Just as Martin was confirming that she'd get back to him with the details, Peters noticed a black Mercedes pickup drive slowly by.

He ended the call, turned the car around and drove back to the hotel; this time reversing into a space where he had a good view of the remaining three Mercs. Turning the dash cam on again, he slumped down in his seat and waited. Within moments the missing Merc returned and parked in the gap it had occupied earlier. The door opened and the driver clambered out, slamming the door behind him. In two paces he was at the rear of the truck, heading for the hotel entrance when he stopped, did a double-take at Peters' motor and began to walk slowly towards it. He was halfway across the car park when Peters got out and sauntered towards the main entrance. Peters could now see the Mercedes driver was a well-built, blond-haired man in his early thirties, wearing an ill-fitting company suit, white shirt and tie. Embroidered on the breast pocket of his jacket were the words *World Citizen Hotel Security*. He stopped, shuffled a pace or two towards the entrance, then turned and shuffled a pace or two towards Peters. Peters continued walking, clocking the guy's uncertainty. He almost felt sorry for him. They knew they were being watched on CCTV and Mr Security would be judged by his peers and bosses for what he did next.

He looked at Peters and said, 'Help you, sir?'

Peters stopped and said, 'I reckon you need more help than me. Did you forget something?'

'What d'ya mean?' said the guard as he fell in step alongside Peters. 'It was just we were wondering what you were doing, you know, driving round in circles in our car park. So the boss asked me to see if I could help.'

'Oh, what? Like following me? So what spooked the boss, then?'

'Nothing spooked him, it's, well, some of our customers drive very expensive motors, always a target…'

Peters' mobile vibrated and buzzed in his pocket.

'Excuse me, I need to get this,' he said as he checked the screen, a text from Martin: *All five Mercs registered to Whitelines Entertainment Ltd.*

'Sorry about that,' he said to the security detail, 'just my mate apologising, said he won't be able to make it today, after all. So what were you saying?'

'The boss was concerned when you drove in and out; thought you were casing the place.'

Peters looked at him, laughed and said, 'What, like in the movies, casing the joint?'

'Look around you,' said the security guard as they walked on, 'there's some very expensive motors parked in here. Our clients wouldn't be very happy to see them stolen or broken into, we do have our reputation to think of.'

'Point taken. I saw you had a Porsche Cayman pulled out of here earlier…what happened there then?'

'Oh, bloody hell; too clever by half these cars today, electronics buggered up, being sent for repair.'

'Yeah? Seems a bit drastic, you'd think they'd send

someone out to sort it,' said Peters and shrugged. 'Whatever... I drove round the car park and out, because I didn't see my mate's motor, then a mile or two up the road I had a phone call and I pulled over to take it, in case it was him saying he was on his way. It wasn't, then I thought sod it, I'll go back and see if I can get a bit of lunch. So nothing to get spooked about. And I hope you can swing it for me to get some food, this late in the afternoon?'

Peters grinned at the security guard as he spoke. Together they walked to the main entrance, climbed the impressive steps and walked past the huge open wooden doors to the rather smaller, but still imposing pair of automatic glass doors. With a gentle hiss, the glass doors slid open as they approached.

'The bar is through there,' said the guard, pointing. 'It's your best bet to get something to eat. You'll get nothing in the restaurant, you need to book a couple of weeks in advance to eat in there.'

'I hadn't realised this place was so grand,' said Peters, waving his hands expansively and looking around the opulent foyer. 'So who's the governor?'

The security guard turned to walk away, but stopped, hesitated for a moment, then said, 'The hotel is run by Mr Aksanov, Pavel Aksanov. Why, what's it to you?'

'No, nothing, I had a feeling it wouldn't be owned by an Englishman,' said Peters smiling.

'Ah, I said it was run by Mr Aksanov, I don't know if he owns it. And he's English, just has Russian ancestors, I think.' He walked away leaving Peters to find his way to the bar.

He strolled through the foyer, making no noise as he

walked, the luxuriously thick pile of the carpet cushioning every step. Even the signs directing patrons to the amenities – *Bar*, *Restaurant*, *Casino* and *Swimming Pool* – were tastefully designed and exuded quality. Much money had been lavished on this place, thought Peters, and judging by the number of well-dressed people wandering around, it had been money well spent. As he walked up to the bar, a young barman approached, also wearing a company suit with *World Citizen Hotel* embroidered on the breast pocket, and a bow tie.

'I know it's a bit late in the day,' said Peters, 'but I was hoping I could get a bite to eat – what have you got in the way of food?'

The barman handed over a leather-bound menu, asking, 'Can I get you a drink while you check out the menu, sir?'

Peters ordered a half of bitter and asked the barman to select from the extensive choice. Turning his attention to the selection of sandwiches, he picked roasted chicken caprese. The barman handed him his drink and said, 'Shall I put it on your room, sir?'

'No, I'll pay by card. I'm not staying here, just stopped off to meet a friend, who didn't turn up,' he said, waving his card over the offered electronic payment device. He picked up his glass and found a table in a quiet corner that gave him a good view, not only of the people already in the bar, but of new customers wandering in. He settled down, took out his mobile and called Stafford.

'Jeez, boss, there's some money in this joint,' he said quietly into the phone, 'which might be why they're so hot on the CCTV – they followed me, asked me what I was up to. Not sure if they recognised me or the car, or if they're just being vigilant. Anyway, it seems they share a liking for black Mercedes-Benz X-Class pickups with the Weyhill crew. Four trucks were parked up when I drove in the car park, and a fifth one drove out, so I shipped Nicole some dash-cam pics and asked her to check 'em out and she's confirmed it: they're all registered to Whitelines Entertainment Ltd.'

Stafford agreed that gave them enough clout to get DCI Talbot to put the wheels in motion for search warrants for the hotel and Whitelines nightclub, and maybe get a Certified Fraud Examiner in to unravel the shell company tangle for definite proof.

Stafford also filled him in on Anne Borley's phone call from the safe house in Portsmouth, about how Neilson followed her all the way down there – in his white Mercedes. Peters spluttered a laugh, then said, 'Neilson was a bit of an idiot to get spotted – just shows what a cocky bastard he is... Anyway, I'm going to try and get a look at the governor here – I'll try not to wind anyone up too much, then I'll see you back at yours in a couple of hours.'

'So did you find out who the governor is, then?

'Yeah, English, apparently with Russian heritage, name of Pavel Aksanov.'

Several moments elapsed before Stafford said, 'I wonder if he's still got Eastern European connections... Fuck, Ryan, could be a whole different ball game if the Ruskies are involved. It's food for thought, I'll talk to the Colonel about it, see if he's got any intel. Take extra care and I'll see you back at mine.'

Peters ended the call to Stafford and phoned Martin immediately. 'Hiya, Nic, we're going to be with you in a couple of hours… Do me a favour meanwhile and check out a gent called Pavel Aksanov – yeah, yeah, you got it,' said Peters as she checked the spelling with him. Then, 'He's boss man of the World Citizen Hotel, d'you know the one? Yes, just outside Basingstoke. Staf's going to talk to the Colonel about it, too, see if he's got any intel on a possible Eastern European connection.'

As he disconnected, he thought, it's going to be really interesting to see what happens when I leave here. I guess by now they'll have figured out who I am. If they're going to do something it'll be out in the car park, they won't want to risk it in here. At least Stafford and Nicole know where I am if it all goes belly up.

CHAPTER 19

Finally passed the recovery truck, Jamie Sweetman settled back behind the wheel, pushed his hood back and looked in the rear-view mirror at the two Asian men, who were now fully conscious and struggling to get upright.

'Man, you fuckin' filthy English bastard, you don't realise what big trouble you in,' said the tasered man in a thick Brummie accent.

Sweetman laughed out loud and said, 'Hey, Mangosteen, are you thinking Ganesh gonna come to your rescue now then?'

'No, but my fuckin' boys will hunt you down and kill you and all you fuckin' FEBs.'

'Oh, trust me on this, Mangosteen, you'll need more than boys to stop me.'

Sweetman wasn't laughing now. He turned off the motorway and headed for North Lane. He pulled up alongside the iron staircase leading to the first-floor flat, climbed out of the motor and pressed the key fob, locking all the doors. He ran up the stairs and let himself into the flat.

Stepping into the hallway and towards the kitchen, he shouted, 'Winstone, hey Winstone, give us a hand here!

Now!' He couldn't help but chuckle as he remembered Winstone's broken, burnt and bandaged hands.

Winstone came rushing into the kitchen and said, 'Fuck me, Jamie, you frightened the life outa me. Thought it was the law bustin' in again.'

'So what's with all the shambles, mate? Couldn't find the right size pan? Or just bad feng shui?' said Sweetman, nodding at the pots and pans littering the floor.

Winstone looked blank for a second or two, then said, 'Nah, I was told I could get Kapusniak's stash from here, I was gonna piss off till things calm down a bit, but the fuckers have screwed me again. There was bugger all in there.'

Sweetman grinned, looked around at the mess and said, 'Look on the bright side, mate, I've got some new housemates for you, just need a hand getting them in here. I could stun them, but then we'd have to carry the bastards up.'

'Christ, mate, how many have you got?'

Sweetman laughed again, 'Only the two. You won't even know they're here, they're so quiet. And they won't trouble you for long,' he shouted as he went back down the iron staircase, Winstone following him. At the bottom, Sweetman noticed Winstone had removed the bandages from his left hand. It looked a mess, but functional enough for what he needed to do.

Sweetman told him to stand close to the far side rear passenger door and stop the men trying to get out. Then he opened the other rear door and dragged out tasered man, relocked the car and called Winstone over to help get him into the flat. They bundled him up the stairs and into the living room, where Sweetman ordered him to lie face down on the floor. The Asian spat at him; the phlegm fell short and landed on the filthy carpet. Sweetman responded with a thudding right hand to his midriff. The Asian sagged at the knees and bent almost double. Sweetman grabbed the man's thickly gelled black hair, pulled him upright, then landed another right hand punch smack on his nose, spreading it messily and noisily across his face. Grabbing the man's hair again, he dragged him to where the gob of phlegm had landed and rubbed his face in it.

'Believe me, Mangosteen, that's the last time you spit at a FEB,' he said quietly to the Asian as he bound his ankles with a couple more industrial cable ties. Standing, he grinned at Winstone and said, 'Right, one down, one to go.'

They walked through the hallway and back down to the car. They could hear muffled shouts coming from it. Sweetman looked disparagingly around. Several of the area's buildings had been boarded up, many of the businesses closed down. Those operating, no kind of respectable; quite a step from the wealthier suburbs. Noise wasn't a problem round here. Someone being dragged screaming from a car? *Just a domestic, close the blinds, it's their problem.* Satisfied no one was about to respond to the guy's cry for help, Sweetman ordered Winstone to the far passenger door and unlocked the car. He opened the door nearest to the steps and said to Winstone, 'OK, open your door, get in and push him towards me.' A look of consternation crossed Winstone's face. Sweetman grinned, 'Fuck's sake, it's all right, his hands are tied.' Winstone nodded, did as he was told. The man, unhelpfully, keeled over sideways.

Sweetman grabbed his right arm and dragged him bodily across the seats; Winstone dashed around to help. Together, they got him, screaming and shouting, up the stairs and into the living room.

With Winstone holding the Asian's left arm, Sweetman released his grip and walked in front of them. He looked at the Asian, grinned, winked, then said to Winstone, 'Oh, you know Kapusniak's stash? Well, there was ten grand in cash, a pile of weapons and a brick of H and C, mate, and I don't mean hot and cold – and I got to it first.'

Winstone's mouth opened a second before Sweetman's fist smashed into his face. He was unconscious as he crashed to the floor. Sweetman pushed the Asian man into an armchair, and walked across to his prone colleague. Kneeling beside him, he gripped each side of the man's head, moved his hands backwards and forwards a few times, grinned with satisfaction as he found the right spot. He looked at the man in the chair, grinned again and said, 'See? It's so fucking easy, from this life to the next.'

Tears ran down the seated Asian's face. Sweetman's hands a blur; a simple twist to the right. They both heard the crack as the dislocated vertebrae tore through the spinal cord. Using the dead man's head for leverage he pushed himself to his feet. His face screwed up in disgust as he looked at his palms; then attempted to remove the Asian's hair gel by wiping his hands on the back of another chair. He turned back to the man in the armchair, dragged him into a standing position, cut off the cable tie and pushed him, shaking, towards the unconscious Winstone. He said, 'Now, this is where you get some payback, kicking the shit out of a white man. Your chance to get even for all the shit we give you lot. Like this,' he said, aiming half a dozen kicks into Winstone's ribs as the Asian man stood, watching. 'Fuck me, don't you wanna do it? Get a bit of payback?' Sweetman, now losing patience, said, 'Just do it, else I'll put you down with them.'

The Asian man swung a tentative left foot at Winstone.

'Yeah, attaboy, give it some welly, kick him in the head. Now you got it.' Sweetman watched as the Pakistani started getting into a rhythm; almost enjoying himself – so engrossed, he didn't see Sweetman's knife till it was deep in his gut. Sweetman twisted the knife upwards and ripped it out, violently. He jumped back at the first gush of blood, then as the flow subsided, took a pace forward and pushed the man back into the armchair.

Sweetman knelt beside Winstone and rolled him onto his back. He wiped the handle of the knife on Winstone's shirt and, holding it carefully by the edges of the blade, put it into Winstone's left hand. Reaching into his inside jacket pocket, he pulled out a Glock 26 handgun. Placing the gun in the dying Asian's right hand, he lifted up his arm, took careful aim and shot Winstone where he assumed his heart would be. Deciding not to leave the gun, he took it out of the Asian's hand, grinning at the at the confusion the missing gun would cause.

He moved to the rear of the chair and slid his hand into the dying man's tracksuit top, pulled out a wallet and mobile phone. He switched it on and wasn't surprised to see it had the EncroChat system. He went through his other pockets and found a small bunch of house keys. Moving to the Asian man on the floor, carefully avoiding the congealing blood, he knelt and hunted inside his top until he found his wallet. He found a similar mobile phone and a bunch of keys in his tracksuit bottoms.

He looked around the room – at first glance, it looked like three criminals had had a massive and fatal falling-out.

Putting the wallets on the table he searched through them. Each had a few hundred pounds in fifties and twenties, which he stuffed into his own wallet. He pocketed the empty wallets and the two mobiles, then took a slow walk around the flat assessing his handy work. He wasn't too bothered about leaving some traces; after all, it was a flat of multiple occupancy. As he watched, the seated man coughed, blood spewed down his chest, his last breath. Satisfied, Sweetman decided to go. He didn't go home, he had more work to do; delivering the keys and driving licences to a higher authority. He was certain they would be worth a buck or two to the Ruskies.

CHAPTER 20

The security guard at the World Citizen Hotel who had spoken to Peters wandered back to the security office, knocked once and walked in. The office was large, maybe twenty by thirty feet, with a small windowless room at the far end. On the worktop against one wall were eight monitors. On another wall were a further two rows of six monitors. All showing in real time views of the hotel's car park, grounds, reception area, inside corridors and staircases. Two men using keyboards and joysticks were so focused on their screens they ignored the incomer completely, as did two operatives at the centre table, rolling their wheeled office chairs from side to side checking screens. On the opposite side of the table, two more men worked four monitors, the screens divided into six separate pictures, each of these showing a different guest's bedroom or bathroom, the views and angles changing as the operatives tapped keyboards and waggled their joysticks.

The men seemed to be in their early thirties, the oldest of them by far, the man they called Guv or Governor, wore a badge stating: *Head of Security. World Citizen Hotel.* He got up, belly hanging over his company trousers, and said, as he pushed a wheeled chair towards the incoming security guard, 'So what was that all about? What did you learn?'

The guard stopped the chair's forward motion, sat down on it and wheeled himself expertly to the monitor his boss had just left. 'To be honest, Guv, I'm not sure what I learned,' he said, moving the joystick and studying the screen. 'He reckoned he was here to meet a friend for lunch. Said he drove round the car park looking for the friend's car, then drove out because he didn't see it.'

'So how come he came back?' asked the Guv.

'He was in a lay-by a couple of miles down the road. Said he was taking a call from his friend, who said he wasn't going to make it. Then he thought, I'll go back and have lunch there anyhow.'

'He's not stopping here, then?'

'No, just going to have some lunch. Seemed a bit odd, though – I mean neither him nor his friend had booked a table. In the end, I pointed him to the bar and said he could get a snack there, because he wouldn't get served in the restaurant without a reservation.'

'So he might still be in the bar?'

'Yeah, I'm looking for him now.' An experienced hand on the joystick, he soon found the SRi driver, eating lunch. He increased the picture to fill the screen and his boss leaned over to check it out.

'Fuck, yeah, he's one of the guys who busted the Weyhill lot. Get in close as you can, get some head shots, then clock his motor and print off a couple of each.'

The Guv walked into his tiny office and phoned upstairs. 'Thought you should know, Mr Aksanov,' he said, 'one of the men who busted Weyhill is in the bar. Looks like Ryan

Peters to me, Stafford's right hand man. You can get him live on camera B61.'

The Guv winced and pulled the phone away from his ear as two loud plastic thuds echoed down the line. He could hear the muted sounds of a keyboard being tapped, then Aksanov said, 'Check your email,' and terminated the call.

Opening his encrypted internal email account, the head of security read the most recent message: *Yeah, it's Peters all right. Get him into one of our special suites downstairs, but I don't want you to take him in the bar. Get Edwards and Cooper and at least two more with you. Trust me, with this prick, you're going to need it – he might look like a fucking pansy, but he's lethal. And get rid of the car. I'll get back to you when my guests are gone.*

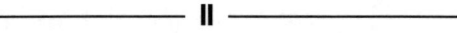

A starving Howard Neilson drove into the car park of the World Citizen Hotel and parked up. He strode up the steps and decided he'd grab something to eat before catching up with Aksanov. As he made his way to the bar, he spotted Ryan Peters just finishing a sandwich. Neilson ordered a cappuccino and a sandwich, and sat at the bar. Peters wandered over, held out his hand and said, 'Must be working hard if this is a late lunch, Howard.'

Neilson hesitated for only an instance before shaking Peters' hand, and replying, 'Yes, always working; just checking the place out actually – I've an important client coming up, need to impress. Thought I might bring them here for lunch, I hear they do great food. You know how it is.'

'Yeah, looks pretty good to me, and their security is good; cameras everywhere. It'll cost you an arm and a leg, though. But hey, you've just landed a couple of wealthy drug dealers as clients, so at least you'll be able to afford it,' said Peters, patting him on the arm as he walked away chuckling. Neilson took out his mobile and dialled Aksanov's number.

Ryan Peters reached the huge front doors and practically skipped down the steps. At the bottom he couldn't help smiling again. After over twenty years of soldiering, he knew complacency, when up close and personal was usually his enemy's biggest mistake. If they were going to do anything they should have organised their retaliation first. Got their people strategically placed in the car park, but there was no one. He set off across the tarmac and had almost reached his car when someone shouted from behind.

'Leaving so soon, Mr Peters? Our hospitality not to your liking?' Peters turned, five men were coming towards him.

For an E Squadron man, situational awareness is as necessary as eating. Peters took in the details without a second glance, ruling out three as non-contenders: the overweight older head of security and his two underlings, including the one Peters had met earlier. The other two were different; in their mid thirties, with the look and bearing of experienced fighters; ex-armed forces, no doubt, both dressed in dark suits with collar and ties. He recognised both men from the punch up in Stafford's front garden. He would need to be wary of these two. He realised too, that one was their peeping Tom, the man they had identified as

Kurt Charles Edwards. The man who had destroyed Sophie Gibson's lovely face. Peters was tempted to get in the car and drive at them. Did they really think this was the way to attack him, to hurt him? It would certainly teach them a lesson about future strategy. But he knew if he managed nothing else he wanted to beat to a pulp the cowardly Kurt Charles Edwards.

It was the fat Governor who had spoken. Peters addressed him first.

'Do yourself a favour, old man,' Peters said, 'and take your two kids back to the crèche. You don't need to get hurt.'

The Governor took a step forward, pointed a finger. 'You're gonna regret you said that, pretty boy.'

Peters shook his head despairingly. 'Decision's yours, old man,' he said, then pointed at Edwards. 'But as for you, you cowardly prick. Yeah, I'm talking to you, Kurt Charles Edwards. You and your fuckin' boyfriend, you are gonna get some serious damage.'

Edwards frowned and looked as though he was about to speak, but said nothing. The red-faced Guv was now close enough to take a swing at Peters, and lunged forward with a roundhouse right hand. Peters moved towards the punch, took half a turn to the left and caught the man's fist in his right hand, his left elbow now perfectly positioned to crash into the right side of the onrushing man's face. Though Peters softened the blow, he went down like a sack of shit. Guv's two oppos came at him together. Peters, right hand now free, smashed his fist into the side of the first security guard's head. The guard's eyes widened in surprise, then instantly glazed over as he staggered back two steps before crashing to the floor.

The second guard, realising he was being watched on CCTV, was bouncing up and down on the balls of his feet, hands to his face, making like a boxer. This was the guard Peters had spoken to earlier.

Peters smiled at him and said quietly, 'Look, son, I'll make you look good for the cameras, but when I put you down, grab the fat man and your mate and get the hell out, OK?' The young man nodded, then rushed forward, pumping out straight left jabs, eyes closed as he anticipated the incoming blows. Peters smothered a few head shots with his arms, and then doubled the guy over with an uppercut to the solar plexus. The guard staggered and Peters caught him with a second uppercut directly on the point of the chin. He was out cold before he hit the deck. 'Sorry, sonny,' said Peters, 'but I did have my fingers crossed when I said I'd make you look good.'

Edwards and his suited friend had stayed behind the action, allowing Peters to move back between his car and the next. They could only get to him one at a time. It was a mistake, giving Peters an edge. Edwards' colleague moved around to Peters' left, a car or two further down, trying to get behind him. But it was a tremendous disadvantage, trying to clamber over the rear ends of vehicles parked there. In effect, Edwards was now alone, but too canny to approach Peters as the others had. Peters wanted to draw him in. Taking out his car key he clicked the fob, unlocking the doors. Edwards didn't move; Peters opened the door. Now Edwards made his move – but it was the wrong move. Peters had no intention of driving away, yet. Edwards reached the door and with his left arm, lashed out trying to hit Peters before he got into the driver's seat. Peters slammed the door on Edwards' arm and, pushing on the door with all his strength, smashed his right fist repeatedly into Edwards' face. Within seconds, his nose was a bloody mess; snot and gristle spread wide. Both eyes were closing and his forehead had flesh flapping some half an inch away from where it should be. Peters' fist was covered in blood, most of it Edwards', but some was his, where broken teeth had cut and split his knuckles. The thug's mouth and lips were split and swelling, and his blood flowed like a stream, soaking his shirt.

As Edwards' colleague climbed over the Vectra's boot, Peters slid into the driver's seat. Edwards, too stunned to move his arm, was still trapped in the gap between the car and the door. Peters drove out into the car park dragging the man with him. Peters opened the door; Edwards splattered to the ground. Peters reversed at pace. The other suited man, on the back of the car, crashed to the tarmac. Slamming the door shut, Peters rammed the gear stick into first and lurched forward. Edwards tried to push himself up and out of the way. He was quick enough to pull his head out of the danger zone, but not quick enough to get his arms out from under the radial tyres fitted to the Vectra SRi. Inside the car, Edwards' screams were so muffled by the revving engine, Peters was tempted to throw the car into reverse and go again, but realised it would be seen as over the top; especially as the CCTV cameras would be rolling.

As he drove out, he pulled a handkerchief from his trouser pocket and wrapped it as best he could around his bleeding hand. He called the emergency services. They responded quickly. Peters said, 'Ambulance and police. Accident at the World Citizen Hotel, Basingstoke, one man, busted arms and busted nose, two or three others with minor injuries. I'm Captain Ryan Peters, from the Security Services E Squadron, can you patch me through to the police? One of the injured men is the subject of an arrest warrant issued by DCI Talbot from Hampshire HQ.' Peters gave them his code word and was patched through; he gave them the details and ended the call. As he drove, he thumped the steering wheel with his good hand and shouted, 'That was for you, Sophie!'

CHAPTER 21

Before starting the forty-five-minute drive home, Stafford called DCI Talbot and told him about the five black Mercedes trucks at the World Citizen Hotel and how they could link the business to the goings-on at Weyhill. Talbot ummed and ahhed, but agreed to try and obtain search warrants for both the hotel and Whitelines nightclub. He went on to give Stafford more bad news: the techs had said the mobiles taken from Kapusniak, Runihura and some of the others arrested had the latest in encrypted messaging software, and no one – not even the French, who'd first found the system– had been able to crack the codes or hack into the system yet.

'So even if we had other phone numbers, we couldn't triangulate to pinpoint them?' Stafford mused. 'Christ, no wonder they always seem one step ahead.'

Usually with a good loud band like Roxy Music to accompany him on a drive like this, Stafford would clear his mind, feel refreshed. But fifty minutes later when he turned into the driveway of his Farnborough home, he was still feeling anger, grief and fear. Anger at those trying to hurt him, by harming and destroying his friends. Grief for those dead or damaged by the same hands. And fear, not for himself, but for the people close to him, his colleagues, his friends. Nicole could be next in their sights, but if he could get her back to normal police duties she'd likely be safer. He stepped out of the car, not relishing what he had to do next.

During the drive home, he'd made one other call, to Sergeant Hawkins, at the Aldershot police station. He'd asked if he would organise an immediate recall for her and get her back on normal police duties. He said, 'She's been a tremendous asset, but after the attack on Gibson's wife, she could well be their next target.' Hawkins, delighted to get her back, had agreed, and now Stafford needed to tell her she would no longer be working with him. Both he and Hawkins knew she was going take it badly, like a slap in the face, so Hawkins said he'd phone her and tell her the top brass had sanctioned her promotion and wanted her back asap.

'I'll leave the other bit to you, OK?' It was the "other bit" Stafford didn't relish.

Stafford took the three steps to his front door one at a time. Slowly he turned the key in the lock. He'd always kept his work and relationships with women separate. But recently, because of a threatened grenade attack on her flat, Nicole had stayed at his house, using a spare bedroom. Trouble was, she wasn't just smart, she was beautiful and funny and brave and… Stafford pushed these thoughts to the back of his mind as he walked through the hall. Before he opened the door to the kitchen-cum-office, he checked in his coat pocket for the hundredth time; the prints were still there. He didn't want to show them to her, but if it came to it, he would. As he opened the door to the kitchen,

Nicole stopped what she'd been working on, grabbed her coffee mug and was out of her seat, heading for the kettle.

'Guessed it was you. Coffee?' she said, sounding slightly subdued.

Stafford nodded and grunted, 'Please.'

Nicole frowned momentarily, filled the kettle and switched it on. Stafford sat at the large kitchen table and said, 'You've had the call from Hawkins, then.' A statement, not a question.

Nicole, facing the window, back towards him, said, 'Yeah, apparently they want me back working out of Aldershot.'

'OK – did they say when?'

'I was told to clear up any loose ends here. Then I'm stood down for seven days, reporting back to Aldershot nick as their new sergeant afterwards.'

Stafford said nothing and the quiet in the room grew. The sound of the kettle warming the water and the click of the spoon seemed amplified as she prepared the coffee.

'I'm pleased for you. Well done, good on you for the promotion,' he said eventually. Then, 'OK, so give me a shout when you've finished packing and I'll give you a hand with your suitcases.'

Nicole turned, picked up his coffee mug and thrust it on the table in front of him. Steaming coffee sloshed onto the pine table. Stafford jumped, his chair shot back as he tried to avoid the hot liquid flowing over the edge of the table. She grabbed her notebook and rushed past him, her footsteps thudding on each step as she dashed up the stairs. He contemplated the spilt black coffee; trying hard to dismiss the thought: *she knows I take milk*. He walked to the kitchen sink and ripped a couple of sheets off the paper towel roll. Mopping up the spillage, he could hear Nicole thumping around in the bedroom.

Ten minutes later a door slammed, followed by a continuous thud, thud, thud, down the stairs. He walked into the hall, and watched as a puffy-eyed Nicole dumped a suitcase near the front door.

'I said I'd help you with those.'

She glared at him. 'No need, I'm not helpless… I can manage.'

Stafford looked away. He couldn't help but see the hurt in her eyes. He knew she didn't deserve this. He stood there for a few minutes, but then she brushed past him and thudded back up the stairs.

He returned to the kitchen. Sitting down at the table, he slumped in the chair, head down, both hands around the coffee mug.

Fuck, fuck, fuck, fuck, fuck, why didn't I tell her… Then he dismissed the idea. He knew she had to go. Staying with him, working with him, put her in severe danger. Garfield Lewis, the Winchester tip boss and at least three civilians had been killed by this gang. PC Gibson had busted legs, his wife, Sophie, was in God knows what state. Surely Nic could see if she continued to work alongside him, she too could end up maimed or dead? He knew if he spelled it out to her, she would argue and say she could look after herself. But as much as he wanted her alongside him, he knew he couldn't risk it. He had to push her away and she had to believe it was what he wanted. He screwed his knuckles into his eyes for a second or two, then drank his coffee, cursing inwardly as the effort exacerbated the ache in his jaw. He reached inside his coat pocket, pulled out the A4 prints and placed them on the table. Steeling himself to look at them again, he picked one up. It showed Sophie lying on her back outside the hospital, her hands covering her face, the effect the acid had on her hands visible. The next picture showed how her hands were welded to the skin on her face.

Stafford was in the process of mopping up the mess from the floor when Martin walked in. He scrambled to his feet, but was too late to stop her from picking up the photos. Slowly, she laid each one on the table and asked, 'Sophie Gibson?'

Stafford nodded, 'I didn't want you to see those.'

Nicole stared at him for a second or two, as he returned her gaze. 'You expecting a tender moment here?' he said.

'I'm not a child, Stafford, I'm not a fucking child.'

He opened his mouth to answer, but said nothing as she walked out of the room. He stood looking at the open doorway for a few moments before he returned to sit at the table. He shook his head sadly, toying with his mobile phone, pondering what had just happened, knowing he had to get back to work.

He hit a saved contact number, put the phone on speaker. The dialling tone stopped as the Colonel said, 'Yes, Staf, how can I help you this time?'

'Ryan mentioned one of the main players is of Russian stock – is there any intel about Russians in this area?'

'I'm guessing you mean Russian Based Organised Crime.'

'Yes, RBOC; and definitely Russians with a penchant for drugs, illegal immigrants and hurting people.'

'Well, my boy, I have to tell you there's no shortage of 'em out there, and current intel shows quite a lot of movement in and out since Salisbury.' The Colonel hesitated for a moment, then said, 'Look, Staf, this is dangerous stuff we're talking here, this goes right to the top, both here and throughout Europe… a lot of it lands up at Putin's door. Now if you're sitting comfortably, I'll tell it you as it is.'

Stafford nodded. 'OK, Colonel, fire away.'

'The tough law-and-order stance from Putin was simply rhetoric – for gangsters, it was business as usual, but with a twist. The state is the biggest gang, so never challenge it, and you work for it when told. The underworld soon caught on – tattoos were out, designer suits were in. The gangster-businessman had arrived. The Kremlin use them to undermine the West's unity. These so-called businessmen are pouring black money into the UK and we accept it greedily. Sadly, it doesn't flow into one cesspit we can block, it floods in via football clubs, investment property, casinos and so on, like a massive open sewer. It needs action from the very top to sort it and we're just going through the motions, if you'll excuse the pun.' Stafford silent, the Colonel continued, 'I hope you're hearing what I'm saying, Major – if the Russians are involved, this is going to get messy.'

'So have you heard anything specific about movement in our neck of the woods?'

'Frankly no, but then after Salisbury we thought we might get a period of quiet, but I'll start digging, see what we can come up with. Meanwhile, try not to lose any more men, stay vigilant. These bastards don't play by our rules,' he said ending the call.

Stafford sat tapping the mobile phone on his left palm, thinking through the conversation.

--- **||** ---

Nicole Martin, meanwhile, had brought her second suitcase downstairs and put it into the boot with the first. She stood beside the car, deciding whether to go back indoors and say goodbye properly. After all, it had been great; scary, but exciting and rewarding. But she was furious at the way he was treating her; didn't their time together mean anything to him?

'Arsehole,' she said out loud, scrambling into her car, desperately trying to stop the tears from flowing. She thought she knew him, but this was a side to him she'd not seen before. His attitude towards her was inexplicable, inexcusable… almost. If nothing more, she thought they were friends.

Thirty minutes later she pulled up in the parking area outside her Aldershot flat, having no recollection of the journey. She sat for a moment gathering her thoughts, then got out, opened the boot and dragged out both cases. One in each hand, she marched to the entrance. With suitcases still in hand she reached up to the entry pad and punched in the four-digit code. As the lock clicked open she barged through and pounded up the stairs to the door of her first-floor flat. Dumping the cases on the floor, she leaned her head against the door, and took a moment to catch her breath. She opened the door and booted her cases into the narrow hallway. The flat smelled unaired and musty; screwing up her face in distaste, she walked through to the little kitchenette and opened a couple of windows.

She grabbed a bottle of Pinot Grigio from the fridge, a half pint glass and headed back to the living room. She slumped into the two-seater sofa, poured the wine, raised the glass and said, 'Up yours, Major Paul bloody Stafford, see if I bloody care,' then took a very large swig. It didn't hit the spot.

CHAPTER 22

Aksanov and his Russian visitors had watched the altercation on the monitor. When Peters drove out, Aksanov called the security office from his desk phone.

'Listen, you fucking clowns, get that mess cleared up now! Before the cops arrive! And get rid of all the CCTV footage, this never happened, *comprendez*?' He slammed the receiver down. He picked up his mobile and called Sweetman. It went to voicemail. Aksanov said, 'Meet me at Whitelines in twenty-five minutes.'

Meanwhile the two Russians had been talking quietly to each other in their native tongue. Now they addressed him in English.

'Pavel, get us two rooms, we will stay a while – and maybe visit your cathedral, I think,' said the older man with the hint of a smile.

'And make sure they're rooms with no surveillance,' said the younger man.

He called the reception desk and arranged for a porter to take his guests to their rooms, and though he needed to get out before the police arrived, which they no doubt would, he lit up a cigarette and tried to assimilate the day's events. His mobile rang: Neilson. Walking out of his office, he took the call. Neilson asked if he was free to see him. Aksanov said he was heading to Whitelines, so Neilson outlined the details of his journey to Stafford's Portsmouth safe house. When Neilson had finished, Aksanov ended the call. Tapping the mobile against his left cheek, he contemplated his next move. Decision made, he hit a contact – *Cooper* – issued instructions and added, 'Liaise and collect the item from Sweetman later today and don't screw up this time.'

Call ended, Aksanov left the hotel through a rear exit, climbed into his favoured black Mercedes pickup and drove to the club. Parking behind the building, he walked across to the rear doors, punched in the four-digit security code. It was late afternoon, the club didn't open till 8 p.m. so it was quiet, with just a few staff members preparing for opening time. Some of the staff shouted a greeting as he walked through the ground floor to the stairway leading to his office. Knowing he couldn't afford to ignore them, or let them see he was rattled, he held his head high and waved as he strode by. Unlocking the door to his office, he crossed the thick pile carpet and threw his keys onto the desk. Sitting in his luxurious office chair, he leaned back, eyes closed, arms cushioned by the soft leather armrests. He tried to control his breathing; 'Slow and easy, slow and easy,' he said to himself, but it didn't work. In the pit of his stomach he felt an empty, sickening ache as the adrenalin subsided.

He lit a cigarette and tried to relax, telling himself he'd overcome worse. But his body was pulsing with involuntary ticks and twitches, limbs and head dead weights. He couldn't afford to lose control. He took a deep pull on his cigarette, shook his head and reached into the bottom drawer of the desk. He pulled out a cut-glass tumbler and a bottle of Jack

Daniel's and poured himself a good three-fingers' worth. As he sank it in one, he said out loud, 'And you can stuff your fucking shit vodka.' He shuddered as the warmth of the amber liquid began to kick in. He knew drink wasn't the answer, but it certainly helped to stop the jerking and twitching.

Now it was time to get to work, sort out Paul Stafford once and for all, and keep his Russian comrades in their place. He realised his visitors owed much to Britain's liberal attitude to immigration. Britain had got used to wealthy Russians setting out their stalls in the UK and didn't much care how they'd made their billions as long as she got some of it. Aksanov's guests would never acknowledge such a debt; they were not merely *shestyorka*, these were men with authority, with power over life and death. Men able to bring a city like Salisbury to its knees.

With the collapse of the Soviet Union, ex-KGB, Security Force and Secret Service personnel joined the Bratva and controlled much of Russia's economy. He and his father had had long discussions about the politicians who'd promised to destroy these criminal cartels and they'd laughed knowingly as politicians were bought. They'd had first-hand reports from so-called family members who had seen what happened to those who refused bribes. And Aksanov suspected his two visitors had been responsible for some of the online photos and videos showing the mutilation during and after the killing of politicians. Pictures circulated on social media as a warning to others. Aksanov had been told by his father how the Bratva hierarchy had used ex-KGB and Special Forces personnel to train hundreds of *shestyorka* in the fine art of close-quarter combat. The fast, quiet methods of killing, and bomb-making. These men were equal to SAS or Delta Force troops, but in ruthlessness and methods of torture, the Bratva were way ahead. These were men to be feared. The controlling cartels had such disregard for life, such brutality, Aksanov tried to distance himself from them, and now they were here, in his hotel. But by sorting out the Asian pair and giving their territory to the Russians, he was confident they would work with him, and perhaps help him deal with Stafford. He put the Jack Daniel's back in the drawer, stubbed out his cigarette, pulled out his mobile and called Jamie Sweetman. The ticks and twitching had stopped.

Once the Russians had settled into their rooms, the younger man knocked on the adjoining door and walked through. The older man put a couple of tumblers on the table and checked the mini-fridge. Finding no vodka, he pulled out two miniature bottles of Scotch whisky, shook his head with distaste and said, 'It seems Pavel needs to rethink some of his priorities.' He pulled out a pack of cigarettes and they sat on the upholstered bay window seat.

'So,' said the younger man, lighting up the offered cigarette, 'are we going to take on the Midlands area?'

'Of course, my friend. My first thought, coming here, was to take over Pavel's operations. But on reflection, it seems his problems are not all of his making, and I'm thinking the Midlands will be much more lucrative than Pavel's territory.'

'Ah, so are we not going to take over down here?'

'We will see what happens, my friend; perhaps we leave it until Pavel builds his new manufacturing facility. We let him do the work – leave it as it is for a while. After all, he has set up the Midlands for us and of course his business model manufacturing crack cocaine and the use of immigrants has been exemplary, a profitable example to us all. No, first we help him resolve his current difficulties, then we introduce ourselves to our new Midlands family.'

'*Tvajo zdarovje*,' they said in unison, clinking glasses, celebrating a lucrative and easy day.

The senior man downed the Scotch, pulled a face, and picked up the house phone. After a few seconds he said, 'Put me through to the security office, please.' As he waited, he opened the drawer in the phone table, took out a hotel notepad and pen, then said, 'Ah, yes, it's Room 182... I need the address for your Mr Jamie Sweetman.' There was some hesitation from the person who had answered; the Russian's conciliatory tone vanished. 'Because Mr Aksanov and I would like to send him a little bonus for his efforts today.' Seconds later and with a little smile, he wrote down the address. Before he put the telephone down, he said, almost kindly, 'And what is your name, may I ask?' Again he made a note, and ended the call.

He called room service. 'Room 182. Send up a bottle of vodka, and make sure it's Russian vodka – please.'

--- || ---

Peters pulled into the lay-by he had used earlier. He called Stafford and briefed him on his eventful lunch break, adding, 'So I reckon we've established there is a link between the hotel and Weyhill.' Stafford agreed to meet him at the hotel as soon as he could.

As Peters ended the call, two black Mercedes pickups raced by, rocking the Vectra as they passed. Immediately he dialled the emergency services. It was answered after half a ring. 'I'm Captain Peters from the security services.' He gave them his security code and continued, 'I need you to put out an all-points message, to car crews, ANPR and CCTV operators... we need to stop and apprehend drivers of two black Mercedes X-Class pickup trucks. Not sure of the numbers, but it'll be any two from this four.' He gave them the numbers and continued, 'I'm guessing they're headed for the M3 southbound. The occupants of both cars are fleeing a crime scene; one is believed to be needing hospital treatment. He's also wanted in connection with an acid attack earlier in Winchester.'

As Peters finished, he could hear emergency sirens in the distance. It was likely they would arrive to find no sign of the incident having taken place. He settled back in his seat and tended to the cuts and nicks on his hand. It was almost fifteen minutes before the first of three police cars tore down the road towards the hotel.

He pulled out from the lay-by and headed back the same way. The three police cars were parked haphazardly around the car park. Two uniformed police constables were leaning against one of the cars, chatting. Peters parked and walked over to them as an ambulance drove in. He winced as he pulled out his wallet and hoped he hadn't re-opened the cuts on his hand. He showed his ID to one of the two policemen while the second policeman walked over to the paramedics and said, 'Sorry, lads, but this looks like it's a hoax call.' The ambulance crew decided to check with the hotel staff and climbed the steps to the front doors. Peters followed them to the reception area where they were met by four police officers. Peters introduced himself to the senior officer and showed his ID. The officer, a sergeant, told him the hotel's head of security and two assistants had been attacked by an unknown lunch guest in the car park.

Peters grinned at the sergeant.

'What an interesting version of events. As it happens, I was the unknown lunch guest, hence my damaged hand –' he raised his fist, showing the blood-stained handkerchief wrapped around it – 'and when they came out into the car park, they not only knew my name, but my car as well. They came into the car park *for* me. And came mob-handed – there's no way I'd attack them. They have cameras all around the car park; have you asked to see the CCTV footage?'

'Yeah, we asked, but apparently the whole system has been down for most of the day, so they have no record of the guest – you – arriving or leaving, and importantly, none of the alleged altercation.'

Peters laughed. 'Amazing. So have you spoken to the Governor, you know, the head of security and his two minions?'

'It seems one of the guards was so traumatised, he needed to go home to recover. The other guard took the head of security to hospital, because he was apparently knocked out cold for a while.'

'And of course they weren't sure which hospital,' said Peters.

The sergeant grinned. 'You're right, but we've assumed they would go to the Basingstoke and North Hants, because it's nearest, so we've organised a crew to go there and check it out.'

Peters asked, 'Did they say what happened to Kurt Edwards, the guy with the broken arms?'

The sergeant hesitated, before saying, 'No one's mentioned that name, and they're adamant none of their staff suffered any broken bones. We thought it was just the three security staff guys. Are you saying there was more?'

'Yes, there were two other guys, both wearing dark suits, collar and ties. One of them was Kurt Edwards, who's wanted for questioning concerning an acid attack in Winchester this morning. I recognised the other suit, but I don't know who he is.'

'So you're saying the five of them came out after you? Why would they do that?'

Peters grimaced. 'It's a long story, Sergeant, but Edwards attacked me; tried to stop me getting into my car. He ended up trapped by his arm between my car door and the car body as I was driving out. He's got to be in dire need of medical attention, because it must have busted at least one of his arms.'

'According to the security staff and the hotel manager, it was just a minor altercation, no one on their payroll suffered anything more than bruises.'

One of the paramedics interrupted. 'OK, folks, seems like we're wasting our time here, so if it's all the same to you, we'll be on our way. Unless you want us to patch up your hand?'

'No, you press on, lads, it seems to have stopped bleeding now; sorry to have wasted your time like this.'

The sergeant too nodded his approval. As the paramedics left, Paul Stafford came striding through the foyer, spotted Peters and headed towards the group. Peters introduced him and brought him up to date. Stafford took his time to digest the information before saying to the police officers, 'So have you spoken to the hotel's managing director, Pavel Aksanov?'

'No, when I asked to speak to the boss, I was told the security manager was the most senior person here.'

'OK,' said Stafford. Turning to the receptionist, he said, 'Is Mr Aksanov in the hotel now?' She picked up a clipboard, flipped through a couple of pages and said, 'No, he was in first thing but left at, uh… 11.15 a.m.; I've put a note saying "no calls", as he's gone to a business meeting.'

'What about Mr Neilson, is he still here?' asked Peters.

'Ah, oh yes, the solicitor, yes, I saw him walk through to the bar earlier, but I haven't seen him come back out yet. Would you like me to put out a call?'

'Yes, please, if you would.' He took Stafford by the arm and steered him away from the reception desk, indicating for the three PCs and the sergeant to join them. They moved to a seating area where guests could wait for taxis and transfers. Peters asked one of the constables if he would check the car park for a white Mercedes-Benz E-Class saloon car, the constable nodded and beckoned to one of his colleagues to join him.

As the others sat down, an announcement on the Tannoy system said, *Would Mr Neilson, Mr Howard Neilson please come to reception.* Peters smiled.

'Yeah, I thought so. I met him in the bar earlier, told me he was checking the place out as he had an important client he wanted to impress. Yet not only does the receptionist know him, she knows his first name and his profession. Sounds like he's a regular to me.'

The reception phone rang, the woman on the desk flicked a switch to answer. Four sets of eyes turned towards her. The call lasted a few seconds. Realising the men in the waiting area were watching her, she ducked her head down. The group was silent for a moment.

Stafford nodded and said to the sergeant, 'Can you radio your men in the car park? If Neilson's car is still there and he comes out in the next few moments, ask them to ask him nicely to come back in to reception?'

'Yes, no problem; brief description?'

Stafford nodded to Peters, who said, 'Around six feet, light brown hair, tanned, clean shaven, smart suit.'

Moments after the sergeant had leaned forward and spoken quietly into his radio, Stafford and Peters looked up at the sound of the hiss as the glass doors opened. Howard Neilson walked through, closely followed by the police constables. Neilson was trying to look nonchalant as he sauntered through the foyer, right hand in his trouser pocket and a *what the fuck?* expression on his face. Stafford rose, stretched out his right hand. He noted Neilson's slight hesitation then the smile as he recovered and gave Stafford a slightly firmer than necessary handshake.

'Ah, thanks for joining us, Howard; here, take a seat.'

Neilson found a space on the banquettes. 'So, Major Stafford, what can I do for you?' he said, avoiding eye contact as he sat down. 'I'm not used to being dragged out of hotel car parks.'

The sergeant said, 'Firstly, I'm sure my officers didn't drag you anywhere, but merely asked you to come and answer a few questions. Isn't that so, gentlemen?' He looked at the constables for confirmation.

'Yes, Sergeant; we told Mr Neilson that you and Major Stafford wanted a few words with him.'

The sergeant nodded, looked at Neilson, and said, 'And secondly, if you'd used the customary exit instead of the tradesman's, we wouldn't have had to follow you into the car park. Regardless, you're here now. So thanks for joining us... over to you, Captain Peters.'

'Thank you, Sergeant,' said Peters, as the two cops backed off. 'Well, hello again, Howard. Now, when I left you in the bar earlier, did you become aware of an altercation in the car park?'

Neilson contemplated the question for a while, then he said, smirking at Peters, 'I have many talents, Captain Peters, but sadly I'm not clairvoyant and nor can I see through numerous brick walls.'

'Clairvoyance, eh? Interesting subject; I think the young woman behind the reception desk is clairvoyant,' said Peters.

Neilson stared at him, shaking his head. 'Good grief, man, what are you talking about? Could you please get to the point – I've got far better things to do than sit here listening to this nonsense.'

Peters beamed at him and asked, 'How often do you come here, Howard?'

Neilson thought for a second before saying, 'Like I told you in the bar, I'm giving the place the once-over. I need a dinner venue to impress a client.'

'But it wasn't the question I asked. I asked, how often do you come here?'

Neilson looked from Peters to Stafford, 'What's this nonsense about, Stafford? Why these ridiculous questions? What's all this bullshit about clairvoyance?'

'Well, may I remind you, it was you who brought up clairvoyance, and, also according to you, today is your first visit to this establishment, yet the young woman behind the desk not only knows your profession, she knows your Christian name as well,' said Stafford.

Neilson's head shot round to glance at the receptionist, but only the top of her head remained visible.

As he turned back, Peters said, 'And after only your first visit here, you knew how to, ah… how shall I say it? Escape? No, let's say *leave*, by the tradesman's exit.'

Neilson, unsure where to look, settled for Stafford.

'What on earth has it got to do with you how many times I've been here? And what the hell does this have to do with an altercation I've previously told you I didn't witness?'

'We assumed, as a lawyer, you wouldn't want to go away thinking you'd been caught out on such a stupid … shall we call it an *inconsistency*? And therefore you'd want to clarify the situation for us,' said Stafford.

'Just ask your questions, Major Stafford.'

Stafford smiled and nodded his appreciation.

'Very well… So are you Pavel Aksanov's lawyer?'

Neilson looked at him for half a dozen seconds, then at the others in turn. Standing up, he said, 'You'd best ask Mr Aksanov that question… I'm done here. Good afternoon, gentlemen.'

Stafford caught his arm before he could walk away. 'Listen, Neilson, next time you see Mr Aksanov, tell him from me: Kurt Edwards is just the beginning. He's going to need more than a couple of second-rate doormen and a hick town lawyer to hide behind. But it seems he hasn't got the guts to show his colours.'

Neilson wrenched his arm away, looked as though he

was going to reply, and walked away shaking his head. At three paces, he turned and said quietly, 'You're your own worst enemy, Stafford, that's why people around you are disappearing.'

Stafford, eyes ablaze, lunged forward, but Peters reached out, grabbed his shoulder.

'Not now, Staf – not here.'

Stafford and Peters settled back down on the banquettes, and sat quietly for a few moments. Stafford told Peters how Martin had left his and gone back to her own flat. Peters was about to respond when Stafford felt his phone vibrate in his pocket, he pulled it out. *Talbot.* He took the call.

'OK, Detective Chief Inspector, excellent timing – we've just about finished here, so we'll head out and meet the K9 unit at the Aldershot flat. Any news on the warrants yet, by the way?'

'That's a no, then?' said Peters, as Stafford disconnected the call.

'"I'm a DCI, Major, not a miracle worker",' whined Stafford in his best imitation of Talbot, as they strode out of the hotel to their cars.

CHAPTER 23

Cooper with the badly injured Edwards didn't head for a hospital. He knew turning up at a hospital with a guy so badly hurt would raise too many questions and the hospital staff would certainly involve the police. Once he with a couple of the security guards had managed to get Edwards lying down on the back seats of the Mercedes pickup they'd been using, Cooper headed out. Maybe just dump him somewhere? He dismissed the thought immediately; Kurt was a mate, he couldn't just leave him. But fear of Aksanov was the deciding factor, so he headed for home. He knew if the police got involved they would soon link the whole affair to the World Citizen Hotel, and then to Aksanov, and Aksanov's wrath would be more lethal than anything the police could throw at him. But even before he got home, Aksanov called telling him how he could redeem himself and he knew he'd have to do it.

Arriving at their flat, he dashed from the car, opened the street door and unlocked the door to their apartment. Getting Edwards up the stairs would be difficult. Not only was he a dead weight, but Cooper might hurt him more. He listened at his downstairs neighbour's door and heard nothing, but he couldn't afford to take chances. He ran up the stairs and into the kitchen-diner, opened a couple of drawers, found a roll of gaffer tape and a knife, and dashed back down to the car.

Edwards had slipped half off the rear seats, and was wedged by his shoulders against the front seats, making strange mewling noises, obviously in severe pain. Cooper cut off a short length of gaffer tape and stuck it over Edwards' mouth, saying, 'Sorry, mate, gotta do this, can't risk you waking up the whole fuckin' neighbourhood.' He ran to the far side of the car and opened the rear passenger door. Reaching under Edwards' shoulders, he lifted him back onto the seats. Slamming that door he ran back to the other side and began to pull his friend out by his legs, sliding him slowly across the seat. Edwards' trousers were torn from knee to ankle, and were covered with drying blood. The one shoe he still had on was scraped through at the toe, blood congealed on the shiny outside surface. On his other foot was the bloodstained remnant of a grey sock, from which poked out the bloody stumps of his toes. He got Edwards' feet on the ground, leaned forward and, putting both hands behind his neck, managed to haul him into the approximation of a sitting position.

'OK, mate, this is gonna hurt like fuck,' he said as he put one hand between his mate's legs and the other to his left shoulder, and heaved.

Eventually he had Edwards in what to all intents and purposes was a fireman's lift. Edwards' arms swung at odd angles; blood began to seep through his jacket sleeves. Edwards' body was cold, limp, and Cooper thought, *fuck you, Kurt, don't peg out on me now.* His knees buckled with the weight, but staggered the few paces to the front door.

Once inside he was able to use the handrail for leverage, and step by step managed to climb the first half dozen stairs. He collapsed to his knees, winded, breathless. It was fully five minutes before he felt able to continue. But he couldn't stop himself thinking, the last time he'd done something like this it had been with a drunk yet reasonably attractive girl, and at least he'd got a shag at the end of it.

'Fuck me, Kurt, you've got a lot to answer for when we get through this,' he whispered. Edwards made no response.

Cooper finally found the strength to haul them both up to the landing.

He staggered to the doorway into the living room, banging Edwards' head and left arm against the door jamb as he squeezed through.

'Whoops,' he said.

Reaching the settee, he put his left hand on the middle of the back for support and, as slowly and gently as he could, laid Edwards down, resting his head on the arm. He got his breath back then ran back downstairs to lock the truck and close the front door.

When he got back, Edwards hadn't moved. Cooper could see his chest moving rhythmically up and down, so he decided to leave the gaffer tape on while he thought of his next move. He slumped into one of the armchairs, then after a moment or two got up, walked through to the kitchen-diner and took a beer out of the fridge. Popping the tab, he took a deep swig, put the can down and lit a cigarette, all the time thinking, *what the fuck do I do next?*

He was halfway through his can of beer before he came to a decision. It was not a decision he was happy with, but, way out of his comfort zone, it was the best he could come up with. He looked at Edwards and shook his head. He was torn between sadness, panic and disgust. He looked away, face screwed into a grimace; disgust had won. Since driving away from the hotel he'd been running on adrenalin, now in the peace and quiet of their home he realised his friend had crapped himself; the smell was overpowering. He got up, stubbed out his cigarette, opened a window and took a few deep breaths of fresh air. Turning back to Edwards he said, 'Fuckin' hell, Kurt, this is worse than when you've been bingeing on Indian takeaways.'

With Edwards unconscious, this was a good time to clean him up. But first he phoned his sister; he'd put it off long enough. He could see no other way of helping his buddy. It was through his sister, Charlotte, that he'd got to know Edwards in the first place – surely, he thought, she couldn't turn him down in his time of desperate need? Some years earlier, Edwards had been going out with the recently divorced Charlotte, a nurse at the Basingstoke and North Hants Hospital, but in time she'd realised he was in fact a recidivistic crook and not the thrusting entrepreneur he'd made himself out to be. She dumped him soon after, but during their time together Cooper and Edwards had become partners in crime. Though Charlotte loved her brother, she had remained distant and single.

She answered. 'What trouble are you in now?'

'Oh, don't be like that, sis, it's not me in trouble, it's Kurt.'

She was silent for a very long moment, then, 'Ray, you arsehole, how bloody dare you? I want nothing—'

'Sis, listen a minute, I know you fell out with him, but

he's in a terrible state. Badly smashed up, broken arms... everything.'

'Well, get an ambulance then, get him to hospital. It's what normal people do.'

Cooper guessed she was about to hang up. 'Charlie, Charlie,' he said, his voice cracking and pleading, 'don't hang up, listen to me for a sec. I don't know what to do, I'm afraid he's gonna die.'

Charlotte loved her brother, but she often thought he'd been born a week late and never caught up. Even while she guessed she was making a mistake, instead of hanging up, she listened.

'Sis, he's unconscious in the flat. I can't take him to hospital because the law will get involved, then we'll have some right motherfuckers on our case.'

She could hear him struggling, trying hard to keep his shit together.

'Sis,' he whispered, 'I'm desperate here, he's my mate. I can't just leave him to die.'

There was a long, uneasy quiet on the line, before she sighed loudly and said, 'So what's wrong with him?'

'Poor sod's been run over by a car, his legs and feet are ripped open and both his arms are busted – maybe in more than one place.'

'And what the fuck do you think I can do? I'm just a bloody SRN, not Jesus fucking Christ.'

'I was hoping you'd be able to patch him up a bit, even plaster his arms... I don't know, but he's gonna die if we don't do nothin.'

'Oh, like you think I keep a bucket of plaster handy, do you?'

'Well, splints or bandages or summat, and something for the pain; poor bastard's been screaming for an hour,' he said with his fingers crossed.

She said nothing, but he could almost hear her thinking.

'OK,' she said, 'I'll see what I can do, but it's gonna be at least an hour before I get there.'

'Fuck, fuck, fuck, thanks Charlie, honest, I really do appreciate it.'

He put his mobile down on the coffee table, looked at Edwards again and, retching at the thought, decided it was time to start cleaning the poor sod up.

It was more than an hour before Charlotte Lesney, née Cooper, rang the bell to her brother's front door. Cooper ran down the stairs. He wrenched open the door and a look of surprise crossed his face; she was in her nurse's uniform. She had a carrier bag in each hand.

'Well, I haven't got long, I'm due in work later,' she said, pushing past him into the little hall.

He grabbed both bags and as he dashed back up the stairs, said, 'Christ, sis, so bloody good you came, I'm just about at my wits' end here.' She followed him up the stairs, walked into the living room and grimaced as the stench of excrement, vomit, cigarettes and lemon air freshener hit her. The grimace turned to obvious shock when she saw the unconscious Kurt Edwards. Cooper had stripped him; cleaned up the shit, much of which had managed to stay in his jockey-style underpants. But as he'd pulled him around to remove his clothes and clean up the mess, so he had reopened cuts, grazes and rips. Even his head and face had been scraped and torn during the fight in the hotel car park. Cooper had been unable to stop retching and puking as he'd cleaned up the mess. To clean the crap off the settee, he'd laid Edwards on the floor. He'd turned the cushioned seats over then put a sheet and towel over them to get a dry base for Edwards to lie on. For modesty's sake, he'd dressed him in a pair of boxer shorts. As he worked, he'd tried to mask the stench and taste of vomit and shit by swigging cans of beer. Half a dozen cans littered the floor of the living room. The soiled clothes, towels and sheets he'd used in the clean-up he'd stuffed in a black sack, and this he'd left marinating in the kitchen-diner.

Hand to her mouth, Charlotte walked towards the settee and knelt down, cursing immediately as the wet carpet soaked into her tights. 'Fuck's sake, Ray, can you put a few towels down while I see what I can do here?'

Cooper dropped her bags, ran into the bathroom and brought out a couple of greyish towels. She looked at them with distaste.

'Christ, I hope you cleaned him up with something more hygienic than this, poor sod could die of the plague,' she said as she laid them in front of the settee. 'Have you given him anything for the pain?'

Cooper shrugged. 'I tried paracetamol,' he lied, 'but it didn't work, so I used the gaffer tape.'

'Very fucking helpful.'

Cooper lowered his head, looked at the floor.

'Has he been unconscious all this time?'

'No, he's been drifting in and out.'

'OK, well, have you got any gear?'

'What? You mean like *gear*, gear?'

'Yeah, Ray, gear as in heroin, or H, if it's easier for you to understand?'

He wandered into Edwards' bedroom, saying, 'Yeah, could probably find a bit.'

She walked into the kitchen-diner and found a tablespoon. Taking out the contents from her bag she found the sealed syringe, which she tore open. Turning to her brother she said, 'Lighter.' He gave her a little bag of brown powder and pulled a lighter from his trouser pocket. She tipped a little of the powder into the spoon, then filled it with water. Taking the lighter she heated the bowl of the spoon, while rocking it gently back and forth. Putting the spoon on the work surface to cool, she picked up the syringe and expertly siphoned in the brown liquid. Letting it cool, she began to tend Edwards' open wounds. Maybe because of the pain or perhaps the tenderness, his eyes opened. He tried to speak, so she pulled the gaffer tape from his mouth as gently as she could.

'Charlie ... Charlie.'

'It's OK, Kurt, I'm gonna give you something for the pain.' Picking up the syringe she found a vein and gently squeezed in the pain-killing liquid. She watched as it began its work. His eyelids half closed, his face muscles relaxed, then a slight smile creased his face.

'OK, Ray, now get me a bowl of lukewarm water, the pack of ModRoc, the pack of tights, a pair of scissors and the bundle of newspapers.'

Cooper scurried to the kitchen-diner, returning with the bowl of water. It was another half an hour before Charlotte had patched up Edwards to her satisfaction and felt able to leave.

She walked down the stairs in front of her brother, and said, 'Ray, this is bloody stupid. You've got to get him to hospital. He'll need constant looking after for six weeks at least.'

Cooper, shaking his head, mumbled his thanks as she walked to her car.

CHAPTER 24

Nicole Martin woke up with a start, still on the sofa, still fully clothed. She glanced at the tumbler of wine on the coffee table, surprised to see it more than half full. Probably the last knockings of the bottle, she thought as she lifted the opened bottle. But it was three quarters full. Contemplating it for a few seconds, she found the cap and screwed it back on. Carrying the almost full glass and bottle through to the open plan kitchenette, she put the bottle back in the fridge and poured the stale contents of the tumbler down the drain, half-smiling as she thought about the wasted pleasure. She dumped the tumbler into the sink, and leaned against the sink unit. Automatically her arms folded across her chest as the memory of Paul Stafford's last words came flooding back. She shook her head in disbelief. Then in frustration and anger. Christ's sake, did he really not know how she felt?

She refused to pursue the thought, pushed herself off the sink unit and almost ran through to the bathroom. Seconds later, her clothes a heap on the floor, she stepped into the shower. Turning up the control as hot as she could bear it, she grabbed the shower gel and a flannel and tried to scrub thoughts of Stafford from her mind. Ten minutes later, she stepped out of the shower. By the time she'd finished towelling herself dry, scrabbling around for clean underwear and getting dressed in her usual jeans, shirt and trainers, her mind was made up. It didn't matter what time it was, she was going into Aldershot Police Station. She guessed that at this time of the evening Sergeant Hawkins would be the most senior cop there, but now they were the same rank, he wouldn't be a problem. Any constables around would stay well clear of a newly promoted female sergeant. Grabbing her black leather bomber jacket and stuffing her A5 notepad into her shoulder bag, she went out to her car. She flung the jacket and bag across to the passenger seat, lowered herself into the driver's seat, switched on the ignition and headed for Aldershot nick.

Stepping out of the car at the station, she slipped on her jacket, grabbed her bag, and strode across the car park and in through the front door. She nodded a hello to the constable on the front desk and rewarded him with a smile when he said, 'Congratulations, Sergeant Martin.' Dashing up the stairs to the incident room, she stopped by the open doorway and listened for signs of occupation. All she could hear was the slow, gentle taps of a computer keyboard. Guessing it was a lone cop typing up a report, she walked purposefully into the room. The tapping stopped as a uniformed constable peered over the top of his monitor.

'Oh, hi, Sergeant, what brings you in so late? And congratulations by the way, well done on the promotion.'

'Thank you. I got the order to come back here, so I thought I'd check a few things out before it gets too hectic.'

He peered over the top of the monitor, nodded and then, head down, started tapping away again. She found a desk with a computer and monitor, far enough away to give her time to change websites should he come across. She sat, fished around in her bag and pulled out her notebook and pen. Before logging into the system, she decided to make a coffee. She walked through to the little communal kitchen and was chuffed to see a pack of cheese and onion sandwiches in the vending machine. Coffee made, she got down to work. It took her a few moments to find the information she was looking for. She jotted down a few details, closed her notebook, ripped open the sandwiches and contemplated her next move as she ate. *Sod it, I've got a week off, I'll do my own thing. So stuff you, Major flamin' Stafford, stuff you.*

She discovered that a Pavel Aksanov owned a large, red-brick house in Dummer, a village just six miles southeast of Basingstoke. The village had around 200 homes. Martin checked out the house on Google Maps and was not surprised to see it was the largest in the village. The satellite view showed a huge swimming pool linked to the rear of the property by a large paved terrace. Open fields stretched out behind. Alongside the house was a long building with a slate roof; checking the street view she saw it was a single-storey three-car garage. She printed off a couple of pictures of the house. There weren't likely to be many Pavel Aksanovs living in the Basingstoke area, so she was certain this was the home of the man they were interested in. About to leave, she hesitated, went back to the computer, hit a few more keys and, relieved to see Stafford hadn't yet locked her out of the system, found a few pictures which she printed off and stuffed into a brown A4 envelope.

Clicking off the computer, she said to the constable, 'OK, that's me finished, I'm off. See you in a week – goodnight.'

It was almost nine o'clock and, though the light was fading, Nicole Martin didn't feel a bit like going home. She got into her car, chucked her bag and the envelope on the passenger seat, sat for a few moments, then started the car and, with her mobile's sat nav set for a postcode in Dummer, headed for the M3. Traffic was light and the journey took a little over half an hour. The house sat back from the road, surrounded by tall, evergreen bushes. The property itself was a handsome two-storey affair, fronted by a massive in-out driveway with heavy five-bar gates; both were open. Martin drove slowly past, found a field with a gateway and pulled off the road. She cut the engine and the headlamps, picked up the brown envelope, stepped out of the car and walked towards the house. She stuffed the envelope into her inside pocket. Her first thought had been to skirt around the outside of the property, but she now realised that Aksanov – either by good fortune or possibly by design – had got himself the ideal property. Ideal, if you don't want people snooping about. With open fields at the sides and back, and she guessed a couple of CCTV cameras covering the area, it was virtually impossible to get close to the house covertly. By the time she arrived at the nearest five-bar gate, she could see the whole driveway was loose gravel – it would be impossible for anyone to make a silent approach. She made up her mind. She'd just wander up to the house and knock on the door.

'Simples,' she said out loud. Turning into the driveway, she started to crunch her way across the gravel. There were no lights showing at the front of the house, but she could hear muffled music. There were CCTV cameras at each end of the house and one directly over the front door. Five paces in, she jerked to a halt. She could no longer hear music, but was aware of other noises. Out in the open with the breeze moving the branches of trees and leaves in nearby bushes, it was difficult to separate the sounds – She took another pace forward; head cocked and standing stock still, she tried to differentiate the noises. Perhaps it was just the wind… Could it be blowing traffic noise from the nearby motorway?

Not sure what she could hear and with heart racing, she ran back to the five-bar gates at the end of the drive and the hedgerow. The noise was getting louder, and now she was certain that it was the sound of an approaching vehicle. Seconds later, a faint glow began to light the dark evening sky, increasing at pace along with the sound of a car engine. Martin crouched down behind the nearest gate and backed into the hedge. The throaty purr of a quality car being driven at speed resounded in the quiet of the evening and she could see little flashes of light coming towards her through the hedgerow. Suddenly, she was hit full in the face by six thousand lumens of LED headlights as a car swung through the open gateway from the lane, momentarily blinding her. When the car hit the gravel, her senses were further assaulted; as the noise reached a crescendo, it was almost unbearable. The car passed the midway point along the drive and the whole area flooded with light as motion sensors kicked in. The car ground to a halt. Clouds of gravel dust rose from the tyres. It was a moment or two before Martin got her bearings; then she moved swiftly towards the leading edge of the gate, ready to flee. Although the evening was cloudy, there was enough moonlight filtering through for her to spot an almost invisible line of small circular paving slabs leading from behind the garage to the five-bar gates. She guessed it was a way to get from the house unseen by the CCTV cameras.

She stood for a moment and looked back towards the house. She still wanted to get inside, talk to these people, get some answers. But she knew in her heart of hearts it was a crazy and reckless thing to do. Standing there, she wondered why Aksanov hadn't put the car into the garage. Out here in the quiet of the countryside it must be a target for thieves, so maybe it wasn't him. She heard, rather than saw, the car door being shut. She realised it wasn't the black Mercedes pickup truck she'd expected to see, but a pale-coloured Mercedes saloon car. Could be silver, maybe white. The driver was obviously a man – a tall, well-built man. She watched as he walked to the front door, and was surprised when he didn't take out a key, but appeared to use the door knocker. Seconds later she cursed for not taking pictures of the car before the motion sensor lights went off. Leaning against the gate, she watched as the front door was opened by a woman, who moved forward to greet the visitor. Both figures were now silhouetted against the indoor light and they hugged before going inside. Martin was tempted to creep closer and check out the car's registration number, but decided against it. Instead she took out her mobile and took two or three pictures, then set it to video, and panned slowly backwards and forwards across the car, hoping she might get lucky with some usable pictures. Putting the phone away, Martin jogged back to her car. *What a bloody stupid thing to do, could've ended in disaster. But I'm glad I did it, because the only light-coloured Mercedes I've seen lately belongs to Howard Neilson, the slimy git. So I'd bet my bottom dollar Mrs A is knocking off her old man's solicitor. And what a useful snippet of information that could be.*

CHAPTER 25

Stafford and Peters made their way to their cars. As they walked, Stafford said, 'These bastards are definitely trying to do a job on us. They must know we know this whole thing is a massive cover-up.'

'I know, and they'd even managed to clear up the blood Edwards leaked around the car park,' said Peters with a smirk.

'I wonder where they've taken him? I mean, he's got to need medical attention.'

'One thing's for sure, he's not going to be throwing pots of acid around for a while,' said Peters as they reached Stafford's Volvo.

Stafford opened the door. 'I want to follow up on this with the head of security and the other two guys you put down. They have to be involved with the clear-up and the loss of CCTV pictures. And who the hell is the Porsche driver? And where is he? But I think we'll give it a day or so. Let them get complacent, then turn up; see if we can't ruffle a few more feathers.'

'OK, Staf, you're the boss. See you over in Aldershot,' said Peters, going to his Vectra.

Less than half an hour later, they were both parked up in North Lane, leaning against the iron external staircase leading to Flat 10a. The K9 team hadn't yet arrived, but only a few moments passed before a Ford Focus estate, emblazoned with *Police Dog Unit* and the familiar blue and yellow Battenberg paint job, pulled up onto the residents' parking area.

'Guess this is the K9 outfit then?' said Peters. 'Stealthy as ever.'

'Getting to be a rare breed now, these boys; got to spread the word best they can,' said Stafford, as he heaved himself off the staircase. The dog-handler got out of the car and walked across to them.

'Good to meet you,' said Stafford shaking hands.

'Hope you've got keys?' said Peters as he shook the man's hand. The dog-handler reached into his pocket, pulled out a bunch of keys and said, 'Yeah, no worries, the forensic lads passed them over; it's the first floor flat, then?'

'Yes, as far as we know it was unoccupied before the forensic team were here, so hopefully this shouldn't take too long,' said Stafford.

'Good. Look, you take the keys and I'll get Harley out of the motor.'

Stafford and Peters looked at each other, then at the dog-handler. 'Harley?' they said in unison.

'Yeah, I called him Harley because when he gets the scent, he growls and sounds just like a cruising Harley until he finds the target.'

He opened the rear door. Talking all the while to the black and white springer spaniel, he attached the lead, saying, 'Come on, Harley, time to go to work.' Harley jumped out of the vehicle and sat panting quietly, eyes alert, waiting for his cue, while his partner locked up the motor.

The handler gave an imperceptible signal and they walked towards Stafford and Peters.

They patted the dog and Stafford said, 'Good to meet you, Harley.' Harley sat; if there had been a cue for the action, Stafford and Peters didn't see it. Peters smiled, looked at Stafford, and shook his head. Stafford said, straight-faced, 'Team member, Ry, one of the good guys.' To the handler he said, 'We'll go up first, open up and leave you to it. We'll come in on your call.'

The dog-handler nodded. Stafford and Peters climbed the steps to the front door. Stafford tried the door; it was locked. The key was stiff at first, but then the latch bolt clicked back. He swung the door inwards. The smell of death was unmistakable.

Peters said quietly to Stafford, 'I have a bad feeling about this, boss.'

Harley and his handler followed them up the iron staircase. Halfway, Harley hesitated; a threatening growl starting deep in his throat as he continued. He stopped by Stafford and Peters at the threshold then, straining hard against the lead, padded into the dark hallway. It was a moment or two before the dog-handler's call came.

'Better get in here, guys, this isn't what we were expecting.'

Stafford and Peters stepped cautiously over the threshold and Peters elbowed the door shut. They joined Harley and his partner at the doorway to the living room. They glanced round the room, taking in the grisly scene. Stafford, as Senior Investigating Officer, took control. While he ascertained that the individuals were actually dead, Peters checked out the other rooms. There were no more victims, or suspects. Stafford pulled out his mobile phone and called DCI Talbot at Eastleigh Police HQ, outlined the situation, and requested a forensic team and pathologist.

He continued, 'Out of interest, one of the dead men is Floyd Winstone, so this is likely to be linked to the Weyhill takedown. I'm guessing this is clean-up time or payback. So that's got to be on the CPS. God knows where the two Asians fit in though.'

Talbot said, 'You're right; with Winstone and Matis Bockus, the other prisoner dead, looks like a clean-up job to me too. Just as well you requested a second safe house for Miller. Christ almighty, we're rapidly running out of witnesses, I'll have to redouble my efforts to keep Kapusniak in custody. Mind you, I don't think he'll talk.'

'And Runihura will be as much help as a block of concrete,' said Stafford.

The DCI promised to get Scene Of Crime Officers to him as soon as possible, then hung up.

Stafford called Sergeant Hawkins at the Aldershot nick and requested a couple of uniformed constables to guard the scene and run the entry log. Next, he switched his mobile phone to video and slowly panned around the room. Staying in the doorway, he took a few still pictures of the bloody tableau.

Harley's partner discontinued the drugs and weapons search, saying they would wait until the forensic team and pathologist had done their bit. Stafford and Peters went back to their cars and pulled out the go-bags they always carried. They put on their forensic suit packs, booties, gloves and skull caps. Stafford dug out a roll of blue and white police crime scene tape, which he tied to the rails at the bottom of the staircase. By the time they were ready to re-enter the flat, the dog-handler and Harley were outside.

'Looks like there was a stash of something underneath one of the base units in the kitchen. It didn't take the dog to find it – there are pots and pans all over the floor, the cupboard doors were open and the base was propped up inside – but he did get excited about the cavity, so there were drugs in there recently.'

'OK, so someone knew it was there. Now, could you and Harley stay here till the cops from Aldershot arrive? The pathologist and the SOCOs are on their way,' said Stafford, as he and Peters went back into the flat.

Stafford, avoiding the blood, moved behind the armchair. He reached over the seated man's shoulder and slid his hand into his tracksuit's inside pocket. He found nothing. He tried the other pockets and came out empty-handed. He looked over at Ryan Peters, who had knelt down beside the second Asian man, Peters nodded and went through the man's pockets.

'No ID here either, or anything else,' he said as he stood up.

'Best not jump to any conclusions,' said Stafford, 'so we'll carry on and search the rest of the flat. See if they've stashed wallets or stuff anywhere else, but why would they?'

'Buggered if I know, but it looks like someone is trying some serious misdirection here,' said Peters.

'Yeah, unless Winstone nicked their wallets and they had a hell of a bust-up about it.'

'Nah, can't see poor old Winstone taking on two guys like these. But bang goes our next line of questioning, thanks to the good old CPS,' said Peters.

Finding nothing of any use, they wandered out to the cast iron landing at the top of the staircase. As they leaned against the rails waiting for the forensic team, Ryan Peters said, 'Look around the car park, Staf. There's only the K9 motor and ours there. I can hazard a guess how Winstone got here, but how did the other two? Someone must have brought them, but why and from where?'

'And there's no way they wouldn't have had cards or money, driving licences probably, keys – and they would definitely have had mobiles,' said Stafford. 'I'll give the security guy at the County Hospital a ring, see if one of his lads can find out who picked up Winstone when he was discharged. With any luck, they'll have it on CCTV.'

--- || ---

As the security chief at Royal Hampshire County Hospital came off the call from Stafford, his mobile pinged with the arrival of a mugshot of Floyd Winstone. He touched an app on the mobile's screen and sent the picture to his printer. Seconds later he held an A4 colour print. He contacted the ward Winstone had been in; the ward sister gave him the date and time he was discharged. Settling in front of his monitor, he tapped on the keyboard and the screen showed different views of the front entrance, the corridor leading to it and outside views to the left and right. Tapping a few more keys, he found the film footage of the day in question and began to fast-forward. He realised he wouldn't get a great shot of Winstone's face, but knew he was looking for a man with both hands bandaged and plastered. The ward sister told him he'd left wearing the same clothes in which he was brought in and therefore wasn't carrying a bag or suitcase. She also mentioned his damaged right hand was wrapped in what looked like a blue plastic mitten and his left arm was in a light blue sling. He soon spotted his quarry heading towards the main doors. Pressing another key or two, the monitor showed a larger picture of Winstone, head down, walking slowly, closing in on the exit. Wandering through the glass doors and out to the drop-off point, he glanced right and left, then took a seat on one of the outside benches. Traffic was hectic, ambulances were moving in and out. Some were parked up, back doors open. Cars, too, moved cautiously in and out, all vying for a convenient spot to drop someone off or pick someone up. Winstone's back was now towards the camera, head forward, shoulders slumped. The security chief tapped a key repeatedly: Winstone stayed still, but the traffic sped up around him. After a few moments, the chief stopped tapping and the traffic moved by at normal speed. In the background a beaten-up white truck drove slowly past. Winstone's head rose and he looked towards the pickup. He put his right hand on the bench and began to get up, but pulled his hand away and, shaking his head, put his arm across his chest. The security chief laughed out loud as he realised Winstone had forgotten the damage to his right hand and tried to push himself up. The truck came back into the picture from the right-hand side of the screen and pulled up in front of Winstone. He made no attempt to open the door, but raised both arms to show the driver. The driver didn't get out of the vehicle so the chief reversed the film and inched it forward second by second. Sure enough, he could see the movement inside the truck as the driver leaned across, but the on-screen image showed only the top and side of the driver's head and, with light reflecting on the window, there wasn't enough to identify him. Slightly annoyed and with his face close to the screen, the chief inched the film forward. Within seconds he had a picture that showed the number plate of the truck. He stopped the film and enhanced the image as best he could, sent the image to the printer, then emailed it to Stafford.

CHAPTER 26

Jamie Sweetman was looking forward to a relaxing hour or two, when his mobile rang. He checked the screen: *Aksanov*.

'Got another job for you. I'm at Whitelines,' was all he said.

Sweetman sat for a few moments contemplating the call. OK, he'd earned a great deal of money working for the Axe Man, but the man showed no respect. Fuck, it was just the same in the army; get a couple or three stripes and they forget who does all the dirty stuff, who takes all the risks. He stood and put the Asian men's mobile phones and wallets into his pockets. Guessing he would need it he picked up his handgun, ejected the magazine to check it was fully loaded, and replaced it. He reached behind his back and slipped the gun into his waistband. Pulling on his black hoody, he was ready to go. As he put his hand on the latch, he paused for some seconds. Then he muttered, 'Perhaps it's time to teach him a lesson in respect.'

His visit to Whitelines was short. Aksanov handed him a bulky padded brown-paper package, and said, 'Take this to Cooper, he knows what to do with it, but remind him what'll happen if he fails again. OK? Then terminate Edwards' contract.'

Sweetman nodded, took the package and left. He parked up a short distance from the house his sat nav had directed him to. He watched as Cooper left the flat; he sounded the car horn, grabbed the package from the passenger seat and stepped out of the car. At the sound of the horn, Cooper turned, recognised Sweetman and walked a pace or two towards him. With his right hand, Sweetman, reached behind and patted the hand gun. He felt complete. Arrogantly he strode across the road to meet Cooper. He held out the package and said, 'Aksanov said you know what you're doing with this, yeah?'

Cooper took it and said, 'Yeah, I get all the great fucking jobs.'

'Shouldn't keep fucking up then, should you? He also said to remind you what'll happen if you do cock up again.'

'Great, thanks for bugger all,' said Cooper.

'How is he then – Edwards?'

Cooper, ready to walk away, replied, 'Hmm, not fucking great.'

'So were both his arms busted?'

'Yeah, poor sod's pretty well smashed-up.'

'How's he managing with busted arms then?'

Cooper, who didn't want to chat, said as he was walking away, 'My sister came over – she's a nurse, patched him up some.'

Without another glance at Sweetman, he got in his motor and drove away. Sweetman stood and watched the black Mercedes disappear from sight. He walked back to his own vehicle, climbed in and waited, in case Cooper decided to return. After five minutes, he was ready to get the job done. He knew Cooper and Edwards lived on the first floor. As there was no outside staircase, he guessed the street door would be left on the latch.

He sauntered across the road and pushed the door with his shoulder. It opened onto a small dark hallway; there was a staircase on the right and the door on the left was obviously to the ground-floor flat. He shouldered the street door closed, moved towards the downstairs flat and leaned his head up against the door, listening. Nothing. Searching in his pockets, he pulled out a pair of latex gloves and snapped them on. He climbed the stairs two at a time. Reaching the front door of the first-floor flat, he leaned up against it and could hear muffled noises. Sussing it was a television, he pushed the door – it too was on the latch.

He walked through and shouted, 'Anyone at home?' Even as he spoke he began to shake with laughter. He followed the sound of the TV and pushed open the door to the living room. Edwards was slumped, half-lying, half-sitting on a three-seater settee, wearing a black towelling dressing gown. The sleeves had been cut off about three inches from the shoulders. His arms had been roughly plastered: the left, from elbow to wrist, the right, from shoulder to just below the elbow. Sweetman could see it was a good amateur attempt. Blobs of white plaster littered the floor and sofa; the dressing gown too was crusted white in places where Edwards had rested his arms as the plaster dried. A torn white sheet lay draped over one of the settee's arms – it had been torn into strips to use as bandages.

Edwards stayed motionless as Sweetman moved in front of him.

'Fuck's sake, look at you. Call yourself a soldier? Failed SAS? Failed fuckin' Boy Scout more like,' he said. He looked around the room, a smoke-blackened spoon with a sticky brown substance lay next to a syringe on the floor, a testament to Cooper's pain control. A packet of cigarettes, a lighter and a poly bag with a small quantity of brown powder sat next to an ashtray on a nearby coffee table.

'Ah, I see Coop's been playing nursey then,' said Sweetman with a grin. Then, 'Well, my son, I'm gonna save you six weeks of anguish.' Sweetman sat down on the arm of the sofa, pulled out a packet of cigarettes and offered Edwards the pack. 'Oh, you've given up now then, Kurt?' he said as Edwards remained still. Sweetman pulled out a cigarette, reached across, picked up the lighter from the coffee table and lit it. He stood and blew out a stream of smoke. 'You know, I was going to make this real quick and just pop you one with this,' he said, removing the Glock 26 from his waistband. 'Nothing personal you understand? It's just, well, you and Ray, you've both worked at the nightclubs and the hotel, but you've both fucked up, and you've seen too much. The Axe Man needs you useful or dead and you're neither. But I see you've got a new hobby,' he said, glancing at the drug paraphernalia. 'I think I'll let you go out on a real high, for a change.'

Edwards didn't move, then his eyelids drooped and tears began to roll down his cheeks. Sweetman looked at him in disgust, put the cigarette in his mouth, raised the pistol and fired. The noise didn't bother him, he knew he'd be long gone before anyone responded. He put his cigarette in the ashtray and shaking his head in distaste said, 'Fuck, man, you shouldn't have done that, but then, you always were a bullying, cowardly bastard.'

He got out the wallets and mobile phones he'd taken from the Asian pair, wandered through to one of the bedrooms and placed them in a chest of drawers. Job done, he left the flat.

CHAPTER 27

Having arranged shifts of uniformed officers to guard the crime scene until further notice, Stafford and Peters had done all they could at the flat. They walked back down the iron staircase to the parking area. They thanked the dog-handler and patted Harley goodbye.

Press and media organisations had got wind of the police presence. TV crews were setting up cameras and presenters were checking make-up and preparing scripts. Stafford knew that hundreds of columns of newsprint would be filled. Much of it commenting on the almost invisible Security Service men rumoured to work for the worst kept of government secrets, the E Squadron, and of course the rising death toll.

Walking to their cars, they took off their forensic outfits and put them into a brown paper sack ready for disposal. As they prepared to leave, they were besieged by reporters and the paparazzi, all shouting out questions.

'How many dead?'

'Is Nicole getting involved in this one?'

Stafford waved them away. 'We'll call a press conference later,' he shouted. At that moment his mobile pinged with an email. As he checked it out, a puzzled look crossed his face – the sender was the County Hospital's security chief, and he was looking at a poor quality CCTV image of a vehicle's registration plate. Although heavily pixelated, it was enough to check the number out on the ANPR system. Stafford showed the image to Peters.

'I'm going to head over to Aldershot Police Station and see our friend Sergeant Hawkins. Trace this number, see what comes up. You press on down to the lads watching the Portsmouth safe house, and I'll catch up with you soon as I can,' said Stafford.

'You'd better hope Hawkins is the only sergeant you come across there,' said Peters.

Stafford thought for a second, then said, 'Should be OK, Hawkins said she's been stood down for a week.'

Peters response was a wry grin and a shake of his head as he went to get into his car.

'What?' said Stafford. 'What?'

Peters continued to shake his head as he got into the SRi. Stafford noted it was still shaking as he pulled away. He watched thoughtfully as the car disappeared, then got in his Volvo and headed for Aldershot nick.

His mood wasn't helped as he walked towards the front entrance of this drab, dismal-looking red-brick building. Stafford had been in and out of this and other local government buildings like it, all over the world. They were never pretty, always just about functional.

He went through to the constable behind the desk, signed in and received a visitor's ID card on a blue and white lanyard. He draped the ID round his neck as he went up to Hawkins' office. They shook hands and briefly discussed the deaths at 10a North Lane then Stafford asked if he could have access to a desk and computer.

The sergeant spread his arms wide. 'You know the set-up now. The hierarchy are all well aware of the situation, so the office is at your disposal. We might not be able to offer you any more manpower,' he said with a hint of amusement, 'but find yourself a spare workstation in the incident room and fill your boots. Oh, by the way, when I came in today the lad who was covering last night told me Detective Sergeant Martin came in late on. Apparently she settled herself out of the way behind one of the corner desks, told him she wanted to sort out a few bits before things got too hectic.'

'Odd… Thought you said she'd been stood down for a week?'

'Yes, she has. So I went to the desk she'd where been working,' said the sergeant, chucking an A5 pad across the desk to him. 'Not sure if she meant to leave it there or if she forgot to take it.'

Stafford flipped past the first few pages and stopped at the last used one. It showed a list of five vehicle registration numbers, linked by a bracket. Further to the right she had written *all registered to Whitelines Entertainment Ltd*. Below this she'd written a personalised number plate, then a name, which looked either Indian or Pakistani. Another note said *recovery vehicle* and she'd written a registration number next to it.

Stafford said, 'You did tell her she's not working with us? She's back to normal police duties?'

'Yeah, course; why?'

'To give her the benefit of the doubt, I suppose this could be what she'd sorted out for Ryan earlier. But I have to say, the address she's written down here worries me.'

Hawkins raised an eyebrow at him.

'I think this is the home address of Pavel Aksanov, the boss man of the World Citizen Hotel, and the guy we suspect masterminded the operation we've just smashed in Andover and Southampton. She's not taken it with her, so hopefully she's passed the info on to Ryan, but knowing Nicole, I bet she's put Aksanov's house details on her sat nav,' said Stafford, shaking his head.

'I tried phoning and messaging her, but the calls went to voicemail and she hasn't responded to texts or emails,' said Hawkins.

Stafford went on, 'Mind you, it looks as though she's solved one of our queries; I think she's given us the name of one of the dead Asian blokes. I'll have to follow up on the personalised number plate to get the address, but it's a start. So thanks, Sergeant, I'll leave you to it.'

Stafford slid the notebook across the desk, back to Hawkins, and walked through into the incident room. Half a dozen cops were there, some in civvies, some in uniform, all busy with reports or research. As Stafford looked around for an empty desk, a number of hands were raised in greeting and a few more shouted friendly comments about his crew's recent successful bust. Stafford acknowledged them all with a wave and said, 'Sadly, folks, it was only a battle… seems the war's still ongoing.'

Murmurs of reluctant agreement rippled around the room as Stafford found a desk and logged into the system. First, he checked the number plate County's security chief had texted him. It was an old white Ford pickup truck, owned by a Tony Amos from Southampton – a man they had previously arrested and bailed.

The personalised plate belonged to a metallic black

Porsche 718 Cayman, owned by Abduk Ravani, the name Nicole Martin had in her notebook. The address given was in a leafy suburb of Birmingham. He checked out the man's police record and discovered he had twenty-seven convictions for various offences, the latest all concerning drugs. Mr Ravani had served two prison terms, the last for three years – he'd served twenty months and hadn't appeared on the police radar since his release eighteen months ago. His bio also threw up the name Hakim Buzdar as a known associate. Stafford was willing to bet this was the second dead Asian bloke. He checked his address on Google Maps and found it was less than two miles from Ravani's.

Contacting the West Midlands Police HQ, he asked for the DI named in the online report. Introductions out of the way, Stafford said, 'It seems we've got a couple of your finest down here in Aldershot. Namely, Abduk Ravani and Hakim Buzdar.'

'Ha! I knew they'd turn up sooner or later, been off our radar for a while,' said the DI.

'They're not going to be lighting up your radar any more, that's for sure – they're both dead. In most unusual circumstances.'

'Bugger! I guessed it would happen sooner or later after Ravani treated himself to that Porsche. Any other vehicles involved?'

'No, this wasn't an RTC, this looks like murder. Three dead: your two and one from our patch. We're going to need someone to notify their next of kin. And to ID them.'

'Yes, we can do that. Are you going to send someone up here to check out their homes and work places, Major?'

'I think we'll have to, I've got to find out what they were doing down here on our turf. And how they connect with our crims.'

'Well, you can take it from me, it's going to be drug-related. These boys have done it all. They've come up through the ranks, and they're top bananas now. We haven't been able to pin anything on them for almost two years, but it's not because they've gone straight, it's because they dish out the orders and direct operations. If it is them, their demise is going to cause chaos up here, with their troops battling for top spots.'

'We'll try and keep their names out of the media for as long as we can, but you know how it is, these things always get out.'

The DI asked, 'So what about the car? The Porsche?'

'At the moment we haven't got a clue. We came across it quite by chance as part of another investigation. We managed to film it on the back of a recovery truck, some twenty-five miles from where their bodies were found.'

'What? Had the car been in an accident, then?'

'No, according to hotel security, where it was found, it had faulty electrics and was being taken to a Porsche dealer for repairs.'

'Sounds a bit dodgy; I'd have thought Porsche would send out a crew. Anyhow, at this end, I don't know if they have any live-in partners or family, but we'll go to their home addresses – if there's no one in, we'll gain access and suss out the situation from there.'

'Good, thanks for that, and I'll keep you posted on developments here,' said Stafford.

They exchanged email addresses and mobile numbers. The DI ended the call, saying he would let Stafford know when the next of kin had been notified and were ready to identify the bodies. As the call ended, both men knew this phone conversation would have devastating and far-reaching consequences. Across the country, many syndicates knew of each other. They had their demarcation lines, and these would have been battled over in the past and agreements reached. Apart from a few minor skirmishes, generally peace would reign among the criminal syndicates. Borders were understood and adhered to. Respect, the order of the day. Until, that is, someone decided to take the West Midlands' main men out of the game. Someone in Hampshire. Someone on Stafford's patch. It would take three or four days for the West Midlands syndicate to realise their lines had been, not so much breached, as eliminated. But it would take only twenty-four hours for them to find out who had crossed this unacceptable line. Stafford knew disrespect of this magnitude could not, and would not, be tolerated.

He sat contemplating the phone call with a sinking feeling. With Lee Gibson and Nicole Martin out of the picture, the situation was rapidly getting too much for him and Ryan Peters to cover all the angles. Now on top of everything, they'd have to go to the West Midlands to follow up on Ravani and Buzdar. They needed to find Tony Amos, investigate Pavel Aksanov, talk to the hotel security staff again, follow up on the recovery truck and keep a watchful eye on Howard Neilson. Not to mention maintain Brandon Miller's safety and track down Sophie Gibson's attackers. Stafford knew the evil bastards were throwing up these obstacles as a smokescreen, to stop him getting close to the top man. He had a sort of failsafe: hanging on to the two Security Service agents currently looking after Marva and her two boys. He remained reluctant to remove them until he knew the threat was over. Sergeant Hawkins had said he couldn't give him any extra manpower, but maybe the Colonel? No, perhaps not... Would DI Talbot down at Eastleigh lend him a couple of bods? Stafford also knew they'd say, *get DS Martin back on board*, he knew she'd be the obvious choice – she knew the whole set-up and the dangers. She'd proved herself, been a key member of the team.

As he posted the latest information on to the Police National Database, he began to regret letting her go. Almost. It took a while to get her out of his mind – her lovely face, the swing of her hips, the way she...

———————————— ‖ ————————————

Some time later, 137 miles away, and almost exactly due north, two Pakistani families were in mourning. Two families. Two wives, four sets of grandparents, two fathers, two mothers, and four young sons. A few brothers, aunts and uncles. But their grief, their mourning, was interrupted as they were unable to follow their normal Muslim traditions. The dead men should have been bathed, covered with white cotton and buried within two days of their death. Instead, the bodies of Abduk Ravani and Hakim Buzdar were lying in refrigerated drawers in a Basingstoke hospital morgue, awaiting formal identification. A partial post-mortem had been carried out to confirm – what to most people would seem fairly obvious – the cause of death. Both bodies' vital organs had been crudely replaced; the incisions stitched together with little care. Death had been deemed as unlawful killing in both instances. With the knife wound in one and a broken neck in the other determined as the root causes, the deceased were spared a cranial examination.

Both families had been visited by the West Midlands Police. Both families had only now been told a formal identification would be required, and were making arrangements for the journey.

CHAPTER 28

Ray Cooper wasn't knocking on Mensa's door, but he wasn't stupid either. He was streetwise and he'd seen how Aksanov worked, close up. It didn't fill him with confidence for his long-term future. An ex-soldier, he was used to obeying orders, but this mission didn't feel right. They'd earned good money on Aksanov's payroll, and Edwards seemed happy with the tasks he had been ordered to do. Cooper himself had laughed and joked with Edwards and some of Aksanov's other employees. They'd spent evenings drinking, smoking or shooting up, while watching homemade DVDs. The DVDs showed beatings, rape, both male and female…and worse. OK, the lighting wasn't great and the perpetrators kept their faces hidden, but when you'd worked and lived alongside these people, you could recognise body shapes, head shapes, rings on fingers, and so on. Cooper had committed his fair share of beatings, and as a soldier he'd killed people; he'd seen people blown apart, maimed. Had body parts crashing to the ground around him after an explosion, but only in the heat of battle. The stuff on the DVDs was for sport, for fun, and some of them showed a large man, armed with an axe, attacking unarmed and terrified people. Cooper was certain the large man was Aksanov; useful but dangerous info.

As he got closer, the feeling that he was being set up grew. If nothing else, he was realistic. He knew they regarded Edwards as the alpha male; so was he regarded as the weakest, a dinlo, as Kurt often called him? Dispensable? As he got closer, the feeling intensified. Why had Sweetman brought him the grenade to do the job? Usually it was the Egyptian bloke from Weyhill – *what the fuck was his name?* He reached the M27 and decided to stop at the next service station. He cruised past Junction 4 and spotted the sign for Rownhams Services. Pulling off the motorway, he rolled to a stop in the parking area. Uncertain what to do next, he slumped down in the seat, pulled out a pack of cigarettes, lit one and stayed there, contemplating his next move for five minutes. Deciding he needed a coffee, he climbed out, ground out the cigarette with his heel and strolled slowly across the concourse to the main rest area. Coffee in hand, he sat at a table and peered out of the window, totally unaware of the view. His mind raced, but one thought kept coming back. Up to now, he'd done some pretty bad stuff, but he'd not actually killed anyone in civilian life. If he carried out Aksanov's instructions and Brandon Miller was in the safe house, then Miller and a number of Security Service personnel would most certainly be killed or injured.

He realised he had three options. First, he could carry on down to the coast and the ferry terminals. Then spend the rest of his days trying to evade Aksanov and the authorities – but he knew he didn't have the finances or the cunning needed to survive for long. Second, he could go ahead and carry out his mission, throw the grenade in through the safe house window, kill Miller. If it wasn't a set-up he could escape and get away with it, but then he would be under Aksanov's control for ever. Third and final option: he could turn himself in. He'd serve time, but eight to ten was a damn sight better than life. And he could possibly do a deal, new ID, new location, bit of plastic surgery…

He began to think about Miller, his target. He knew only what he'd been told by Aksanov and some of the other crooks. That he thought of the others as crooks gave him pause for a laugh. They said Brandon Miller had rolled over and told the cops all he knew about the drug factory, people smuggling and the other operations in Andover and Southampton. Aksanov had so far escaped detection by creating layers of dispensable foot soldiers between the villainy and his respectable business front. But such is the way of life, he thought, people at the top barking out the orders, raking in the profits, safe in their bunkers, while people like him did all the work, took all the risks for… for what? However much he'd been paid, it wasn't enough to compensate for twenty-five years in jail. He took out his mobile phone and searched online for the number of Hampshire Police HQ. He added the number to his contacts and sat for a few more moments, finished his coffee and walked back towards the car. In his motor, he lit another cigarette, opened the offside window an inch, and pulled out his mobile. Hesitating for the merest fraction, he hit the new contact.

He stated his name, then said to the call handler, 'Listen, my friend, just listen – try to question me, and I hang up, do I make myself clear?'

The call handler: 'Take your time, speak clearly.'

Cooper almost laughed at the response, but said, 'Good, now I was involved in a bust-up at the World Citizen Hotel in Basingstoke. Your lot could be out searching for me now. I wanna talk to the guy in charge of this, and the other bust in Andover a few days ago – Major Stafford, Paul Stafford.' The call handler began to speak, but Cooper held his ground. 'Listen, dinlo, I did warn you, now you have this one chance. Tell Stafford: Brandon Miller is about to die – a grenade through the window. Tell him I want to meet him in half an hour –' he checked the information on Google Assistant – 'at Kingfisher Caravan Park in Browndown.'

He cut the connection, took one last drag on his cigarette, flicked it out of the window and drove back out onto the M27, heading for Browndown.

───────────── ‖ ─────────────

At Hampshire Police HQ, the call handler had patched the phone conversation through to his sergeant, who recognised Stafford as the link man in two recent high-profile take-downs. He contacted DCI Talbot, who listened to the recorded conversation and read the transcript as he phoned Stafford. Talbot outlined what Cooper had said.

'I have to agree, it does sound kosher,' said Stafford, 'But there's no way I can get there in thirty minutes. I'm still in Aldershot. Captain Peters, though, is on his way down to Portsmouth to meet up with the Security Service guys watching the safe house. I'll call him now and get him to head for the Kingfisher site. So thanks for the heads-up.'

Stafford disconnected and called Ryan Peters. 'Where are you?' he said, as Peters' Bluetooth kicked in.

'I'm about ten minutes away from the safe house. Why? What's up?'

'OK, did you see a caravan park in the last few miles?'

'Ye-eh, there's a big one, five minutes back in the other direction.'

'Great I want you to make your way back there asap. It's called, Kingfisher Caravan Park, out near Gosport. Seems your friend from the punch-up at the hotel, Edwards' mate, he's asked to meet me there in…' Stafford glanced at his watch, 'in, about twenty-two minutes. Apparently he's got info about an intended grenade attack on Miller at the safe house. He's called Ray Cooper.'

'Should I go and warn the guys at the safe house first?'

No, leave it with me – I'll contact the Colonel and Anne Borley, who's on her way to the other safe house to interview Miller. I'll also put a call in to the Royal Logistic Corps, get them to organise a Bomb Disposal Unit to make a silent approach to the caravan park, and stay somewhere out of the way until you call for them. You're going to have to try to take this Cooper in, so, if he comes nice and quietly, take him to Eastleigh Police HQ. I'll get to you as soon as I can, but it's gonna be at least an hour.'

'OK, boss, I'll do my best to keep it all quiet down here until then.'

'Good. Now listen, don't take any risks. If you think he's got a grenade or a bomb with him, get Bomb Disposal in. I'll text you the details, and we're using the code word *Rehashed*. Don't approach Cooper till you've received the text. I mean it, Captain Peters, this is back to business.'

Stafford ended the call with Peters. He clicked on the

Colonel's number then held the phone about twelve inches from his face.

'*What now*, Staf?'

Stafford couldn't help but smile. 'Thought you'd want to know, we've just had a call from one of the bandits, seems he has info concerning a grenade attack on the safe house. If you've managed to get men in place, you might want to alert them, just in case it's for real.' Stafford paused a second, then said, 'We're supposed to be meeting him at Kingfisher Caravan Park in Browndown in about eighteen minutes.'

'Good, so we might get this over with today? I take it you'll contact the Explosive Ordnance Disposal people?'

'Yes.'

'Fine, I'll take care of it down here,' said the Colonel.

'Thank you, sir, and I'll inform the agents at the other safe house in case it's a ploy to get us to take our eyes off the ball.'

Stafford called the Royal Logistic Corps operations centre, gave his codename and explained his need. They immediately put wheels in motion to get a bomb disposal team in place near Kingfisher Park and gave Stafford contact details, which he passed on to Peters. The bomb disposal team were told to text Peters the one-word code, *Rehashed*, once they were in place. Stafford needed to get moving; talking to a man with a grenade had to be number-one priority. But he had so much else on his plate. Blowing out his cheeks in exasperation, he walked through to Sergeant Hawkins' office, tapped on the open door and went in. He came straight to the point.

'Look, Sergeant, I need someone to make a few phone

calls to try and trace this recovery truck and driver,' he said, passing him three A4 prints, taken from Peters' dash-cam footage. 'I've got to go and talk to a Ray Cooper, who's got intel about a potential grenade attack on one of our witnesses, otherwise I'd do it myself.' He shook his head slowly, a resigned expression on his face.

'Have I got a choice, *Major*?'

'Don't be like that, Sergeant. It's all snowballing too fast, but trust me, we will get on top of it. Now I've got to go, I'm supposed to be in Eastleigh in about twenty minutes.'

Hawkins watched as Stafford left. Of course he knew Stafford worked for HMG and answered to a much higher authority. He could, if necessary, turn the whole nick over to this investigation. Hawkins picked up his mobile and said, 'OK, Major Stafford, I'll get you your help. You won't like it, but it's the best I can do.' He pulled up Nicole Martin's number and sent her a text.

CHAPTER 29

Ryan Peters was looking forward to seeing Ray Cooper again. They'd never met properly, but their paths had crossed twice now: in Stafford's driveway and at the hotel, and both times Cooper had come off second best. Maybe I should offer him the best of five, he thought. Up ahead he could see the site's gates and a large sign proclaiming *Kingfisher Caravan Park*. He indicated a right turn and pulled into the entrance. To his left he could see a large parking area. He guessed that during the summer season it would be chock-a-block, but today only one car, a black Mercedes pickup, was there. Driving slowly around, he stopped alongside it. Guessing it was Cooper's, he peered in through the windows. No one was inside. Glancing around, he spotted a signpost with arrows indicating *Camper van Parking, Shop, Restaurant, Pub* and *Shower Block*. Electing to wait, he parked up some ten metres from the Mercedes, facing the opposite direction. Walking over to the Merc, he bent down, head close to the radiator – there was no sound of the engine cooling and the bonnet was cool to the touch. He leaned up against the car's offside wing and looked in the direction of the pub, restaurant and shop.

He settled to wait and watch, as long as it took. In the army he'd seen lots of action, but waiting and watching, he soon learned, became a necessary skill. You learn that patience brings its own reward. Impatient early action was often a precursor to disaster.

Moments later, eyes squinting to distant focus, like sniper vision, he spotted a movement. A far-off figure, dark clothes, maybe a suit, head down, hands held in front. Peters noticed a bulge in the man's right jacket pocket, and it hung lower than the left side. A few paces closer confirmed it was Cooper. Ten paces on, Cooper had unwrapped a packet of cigarettes, looked around and then discarded the cellophane wrapper. As Peters watched, Cooper took out a cigarette, slipped the pack into his jacket pocket and, as he lifted his head preparing to light it, his eyes fixed on Peters. He stopped mid-stride, paused while he finished lighting the cigarette, then continued walking towards the cars, exhaling a cloud of smoke which billowed and dispersed behind him. Two paces from Peters, he stopped. Peters couldn't help thinking, bit late for a risk-to-benefit analysis now, but he said, 'Those things will kill you, you know.'

'I can think of worse ways to go,' said Cooper as he flicked the unfinished cigarette away.

'Like a grenade through a window?'

Cooper nodded and said, 'Yep; but me? I hurt people, I don't kill 'em. Anyway, where's Stafford? I asked for a meet with Stafford.'

'Yeah, but you said half an hour. He was over an hour away. I was closer, so I'm going to take you to him.'

'You reckon? I'm gonna need some guarantees first.'

'You think you're in a position to ask for guarantees?'

Cooper grinned, patted his bulging jacket pocket and said, 'Well, I'm the one with the grenade.'

Peters took a pace forward and said, 'And I'm the one who's going to take it from you – one way or another.'

Cooper stood motionless for several heartbeats, then put his hand into the bulging pocket and looked Peters in the eyes. 'So no chance of being patted down by the female cop who kicked me in the nuts, then?'

Peters smiled warmly. 'And the only chance you've got of not getting hurt again is to give me the grenade.'

Cooper nodded, blinked a couple of times. Then with his face screwed up in concentration, ripped his hand out of his pocket, threw the grenade at Peters and dived headlong to the far side of the Mercedes. Peters caught it with his right hand, instantly checked the pin was still in, and slipped it into the inside pocket of his jacket.

Leaning back against the car, he said, 'Yeah, really funny, Cooper. So when you're ready.'

It was a moment or two before a red-faced and grinning Cooper scrambled to his feet and brushed himself down.

'Oh, come on. You gotta have a laugh, ain'tcha?'

Peters grabbed him by the shoulders and slammed his face up against one of the windows of the black car.

'Tell that to Sophie Gibson, arsehole.' Peters patted him down, found the key to the Mercedes pickup, a house key and a packet of Rothmans cigarettes; nothing untoward. Pulling Cooper away, he opened the driver's door and indicated for him to get in. Peters reached into his inside pockets and pulled out two industrial cable ties.

'Don't even think about running, because I won't hesitate to pull the pin,' he said, patting the bulge in his jacket. 'Now put both hands on the wheel.'

Cooper complied. Peters, using the cable ties, secured Cooper's hands to the steering wheel. Peters backed out of the car and walked round to the passenger door, checking through the glove compartment and underneath the seats. On the back seat he found a pair of black, thick leather gloves wrapped in a long-sleeved green work shirt bearing the County Hospital's logo, and a pair of matching lightweight trousers, wrapped around a one-litre Kilner jar. He took out his phone and photographed them in situ, with a close-up of the logo. Moving to the back of the pickup, he lifted the cover to the load space, and peered inside: empty. He closed it then climbed into the passenger seat. His mobile phone buzzed, the screen lit up; he had a text, it said *rehashed,* and showed contact instructions. He complied, the call was answered almost immediately.

'The word is *Rehashed*. This is Captain Peters. We have a World War Two standard pineapple hand grenade. Black Mercedes-Benz X-Class pickup in the main car park.'

Within moments, the Bomb Disposal team's DAF truck rolled into the caravan park. As they pulled up, Peters climbed out and walked across to them, shook hands with the commander, then reached into his inside jacket pocket and pulled out the grenade. The commander studied it briefly, turned and threw it to one of his men, who caught it then stored it in the rear of the truck, ready for safe disposal. Peters nodded his thanks to the crew and watched as they drove out of the caravan park. He had come across guys like these many times before, in Iraq and Afghanistan.

He knew, despite their often flippant manner, these were hardened professionals who used humour to alleviate the constant pressure.

He returned to the Merc, climbed in, reached into Cooper's inside breast pocket and pulled out his wallet. Flipping through it, he found a driving licence.

'Is this your current address?'

Cooper nodded in response, then said, 'Is this gonna take long? Cos I could do with a fag.' He tugged at the cable ties as he spoke.

'I'm doing you a favour here, I told you, those things'll kill you,' said Peters, putting the wallet in his pocket. 'But don't worry, old son, just answer a few questions, and you'll be smoking in no time. What about your mate, Edwards? Where does he live?'

Cooper hesitated for a moment, then said, 'Same place, we share the flat.'

'So which hospital did you take him to?'

'I didn't, I just got him home and got some bird we know, who's a nurse, to patch him up a bit.'

'This bird looking after him now, then?'

'Nah, she plastered him up, then wanted nothin' more to do with it, so I've been looking after the poor sod… Fuck, man, you did a real job on him.'

'He deserves more, and I'll make sure he gets it. A couple of busted arms are mendable. What he did to Sophie Gibson is unforgivable. Jesus, she's not even a player, she's a civilian…' Shaking his head, he got out of the pickup and walked over to the SRi, opened the boot and leaned in, finding the go-bag he and Stafford and others like them kept ready and close. He selected an L109A1 hand grenade, weighed it a few times in his right hand. He was so tempted to chuck it in Cooper's car. He could say Cooper had somehow set it off accidentally, or had decided to take his own life in a moment of remorse. He stared at the Merc, then, shaking his head, reluctantly put the grenade back into the bag, taking out a clasp knife instead. As he did, he wondered why Cooper's governor had given him a World War Two grenade. All the weapons they'd collected from the Weyhill site had been fairly modern, certainly less than ten years old. Why a vintage grenade now? Christ, he thought, it might not even be operational. Could it be a bluff, a dummy? He knew the bomb disposal boys would check it out.

Taking out the clasp knife's blade, he returned to the Mercedes and opened the driver's door, knife in hand. Cooper shrank back, his face pale. Peters gave him a look of disdain and cut through the cable ties.

'You don't know it yet, Cooper, but this is your lucky day.' Pulling him out of the car, he folded the blade away, frogmarched him to the SRi and shoved him into the passenger seat. Peters walked round to the driver's side, leaned against the closed door and called DCI Talbot to organise the recovery of the Mercedes pickup for forensic examination. Call finished, he climbed in, said, 'Buckle up, Coop, I don't want you showing any signs of damage when we get to Eastleigh.'

'Only my friends call me Coop.'

Peters looked at him. 'You got friends?' he said.

CHAPTER 30

On his way to Eastleigh, Stafford shoved an ancient Spooky Tooth CD into the player and wound up the volume: his tried-and-tested method of helping him to think through difficult times. He realised with some consternation the growing size of the investigation. They were still tying up loose ends from operation *Trashed*; he was using a squad of men in Weyhill. Two agents were at Peters' house looking after Marva and her children, another two agents watched over Brandon Miller, more agents and van watching the empty safe house in Portsmouth, and now the Bomb Disposal Unit sitting outside a caravan park in Browndown.

Just as Spooky Tooth finished 'I Am The Walrus', Stafford's Bluetooth cut in. It was Ryan Peters. Stafford said, 'So was the grenade real?'

'Oh yes, boss, looked very real. A little gem, in fact a World War Two US cast-iron pineapple in very clean condition. But I can't understand why they gave Mr Cooper, who's here with me now, such a vintage grenade. I mean, how could they be sure it would work? The bomb disposal boys took it, so I'll check with them later, see what they made of it.'

'That is odd, considering the stuff they've used up to now has been top notch. Guess we'll find out in due course. Right, once you're done in Eastleigh, head over to Southampton to pick up Winstone's driver, who, it turns out was Tony Amos. You might have to try some gentle, I say again, gentle, persuasion for him to come back to Eastleigh to answer a few questions.'

'You're the boss. And as you know, gentle is my middle name,' said Peters, ending the call.

Hmm, Stafford mused. Ten minutes later he drove up to the security barrier at Hampshire Police HQ in Eastleigh, rolled to a halt, wound down the window and pushed the speaker button.

'Major Stafford to see DCI Talbot.'

The barrier rose, Stafford drove through and parked up. The reception desk was manned by a call handler who recognised him, buzzed through to Talbot's office and gave Stafford the usual ID lanyard. Stafford made his way to the second-floor office, where Talbot rose from behind his desk, stretched out his hand and said, 'Stafford, take a seat.' Stafford shook hands and sat as the DCI asked, 'So where are we now, then?'

'Captain Peters has picked up Ray Cooper – as you know, he was under orders to lob a grenade at the safe house where we've got Brandon Miller. We're expecting him to cooperate and name names. They're on their way here; the grenade is on its way to Bomb Disposal.'

'Cooper, Ray Cooper? Isn't he one of the scrotes suspected of the acid attack on Sophie Gibson?'

Yes, and I think I'll need to use that as leverage to get him to tell us what he knows about the bigger picture.'

'Compromise. Always the way I'm afraid, Staf; double-edged, but a useful tool.

'When they arrive, Peters is shooting off to Southampton to try and pick up Tony Amos. He's the driver who took Floyd Winstone from hospital to his death. When we've had a little chat with him, I need to get up to Birmingham, or at least see what I can find out about the two dead Asian guys. See what mischief they were up to down here.' He paused a moment, leaned back in his chair and shook his head. 'To be honest, at the moment it feels like I'm chasing shadows.'

Talbot's desk phone rang; he listened for a second or two, then said, 'Good, send him up.' Putting the receiver back, he said to Stafford, 'Peters is here. Cooper's been cautioned and put into a cell.'

Peters walked in, patted Stafford on the shoulder, and reached across and shook the DCI's hand. 'Good to see you, sir,' he said, grabbing a chair. 'I can't believe Cooper's attitude – he seems to be treating this grenade thing as some sort of joke. I don't think he realises what deep shit he's in. Or else he thinks he's got a get-out-of-jail-free card for talking to us. I don't know, just seems too cocky to me. And talking about deep shit, apparently he and Edwards share a flat in Basingstoke. Edwards can't go anywhere because of his busted arms... do you want me to ring Hawkins, see if he wants to pick him up?'

'Wow, too bloody right,' said Stafford. 'Lee Gibson's one of his, so he's bound to want to do it. As for Cooper; that's good for us, easier to get him to cooperate when I explain he's up to his eyeballs in it.'

Peters stood. 'Right, gentlemen, I'll phone Sergeant Hawkins, then go get Amos.'

Stafford said, 'Don't mention the two dead Asian guys or Winstone, just say we need a few more details about his involvement in Weyhill.'

'Roger that,' said Peters striding out of the room.

Stafford stood and said to the DCI, 'I'll press on and have a chat with Cooper; be interesting to see if he asks for our friend Neilson as his solicitor.'

CHAPTER 31

Nicole Martin had managed a few hours of undisturbed sleep. She completed her morning ablutions and was sitting in her tiny kitchenette drinking coffee, trying to enhance the pictures of the white Mercedes. She knew she could get some technical bod back at the station to sort it, but she didn't want to wait – she wanted to get ahead of the game. Her smartphone had a number of apps for this purpose, but while they were OK for daylight pictures, it was proving more difficult with pictures taken in the dark. After twenty minutes of trial and error, she had a soft focus, extremely pixelated image; still, it showed enough for her to write down the vehicle's registration number. She leaned back in her chair and took a swig of coffee, pleased to have confirmed her suspicions at least. While interviewing suspects they'd arrested during an earlier operation, she had seen enough of their solicitor, Howard Neilson, to know this was his car. *I wonder if he went to see Aksanov or the woman? I reckon it's got to be her, he could see Aksanov any time at his offices. It's a little piece of intel I can use to get some answers from one or the other of them.*

She grabbed her shoulder bag from a worktop and hunted through it for her notepad. Not finding it, she checked the bedroom and the living room, to no avail. *Where the hell was it?* She went out to her car and gave it the once-over with no joy. Returning to the kitchenette, she finished her now lukewarm coffee, trying to remember where she'd last had it. She cursed under her breath as she recalled having it at the police station the evening before. Bollocks, she thought, it's in the goddamn incident room. Guess I can pick it up later. Her mobile chirped and vibrated: a text from Sergeant Hawkins: *phone me soonest.* She sat with the phone in her hand, watching as the screen faded out. I wonder if he's found out about last night's jaunt, she thought, then; no, bollocks, I'm on leave, he can wait till I get back. Even as she thought it, she knew she wouldn't be able to stay away from the investigation or the station. With a sigh, she touched the screen and called him, putting the phone on loudspeaker on the worktop while she washed her mug in the sink.

He answered promptly. 'Ah, Sergeant, thanks for – no, never mind. Listen, I know you're on leave, but I also know you want to be part of this investigation.'

'Too right I do,' she said.

'I know Stafford moved you out thinking he's protecting you. And he's worried about getting other people involved because of what's happened to Sophie Gibson and the others.'

'Yeah, but I was involved in the whole shooting match, so I'm no more a target now than I was then.'

'And I think the same, so can I make a couple of suggestions?'

'Fire away, Sergeant, fire away.'

'OK. Well, Stafford needs a few things checking out, which you can do from the safety of this office. You need to get more evidence against those in custody, Kapusniak and Runihura. And to do that you need to follow up some of the stuff in your notebook.'

'Ah, you've found it, then?'

'And read most of it. And it's good stuff, worth following up. I don't see how Stafford can whinge at you following up on what you'd discovered earlier. So if you want, come in and we'll talk about what needs doing.'

'Hey, Sergeant, did I tell you – you're my favourite sergeant ever.'

'I can understand that. So when can I expect to see you?'

''Bout twenty minutes,' she said and ended the call.

Twenty-five minutes later she was in his office, sitting opposite him.

'First off, here's your notebook back. If you're sure you want to get involved in this again, Stafford wants a follow-up on the recovery vehicle. He wants to know who the driver is, why he picked up the Porsche and who instructed him to fetch it.'

'Yes, good thought,' she reluctantly agreed. 'I can do that, it may provide us with a useful link.'

'Talking about links, Stafford, like the rest of us, sees a link between Weyhill and the goings-on with our former DI at the nightclubs and World Citizen Hotel. Now in the depths of your notebook, you've made a note about Southern Washroom Services, check 'em out, see where it takes you.'

Martin looked sceptical, but said, 'Yeah, Stafford brought that up, we were going to ask Floyd Winstone about it; OK, I'll check it out.'

Picking up her notebook, she walked through to the incident room. She chose a desk and settled in. Reading her early notes, she came across jottings concerning Jan Kapusniak's international criminal history. As she read, she realised with horror that though they now had his fingerprints and DNA details from Romania and Lithuania, they hadn't checked them against fingerprints taken from him when he was first arrested. Nor had they checked them against the fingerprints taken from the Very flare gun. How the hell could we have missed that, she thought. Christ, if this all ties in, it could go a long way to proving Kapusniak killed Garfield Lewis. Even Howard Neilson won't be able to get him off this. But who to tell? Their new DI had been named as Thomas Masterson, but he hadn't yet got his feet under the table, so Stafford or Peters? Even they would have to get the techs to check it out. The answer, she thought, was obvious: DCI Talbot. OK, so Stafford might get a bit shirty, but then, he wanted her off the case, so she was just doing her job as a police officer. She picked up the receiver and called Talbot.

'Sergeant Martin? I thought you'd been stood down, awaiting a new assignment.'

'Yes, sir, that is the case, but I've come up with something I hope will help us to hang on to Jan Kapusniak and keep the bast—um…culprit in jail.'

'Ah. Have you reported this to Major Stafford?'

'No, sir. I'm no longer working alongside the Security Services, so I'm just doing my job, sir.'

'Good answer, Sergeant, good answer. So tell me what you've found.'

'So much has happened since we arrested Kapusniak and he went to hospital. I'm not sure if anyone followed up on the fingerprints found on the flare gun and flare box. I can't believe it would have been missed, but I think it's worth checking. You see, I've found details of his criminal history. It's now been posted up on the Police National Database and Interpol's National Criminal Bureau, but, in short, Kapusniak's real name is almost certainly Stephan Modrić, and he's wanted in at least four other countries as well as his home country of Lithuania for robbery, assault, rape and murder – perhaps even four or five counts of murder.' She paused for breath. 'He likes underage girls, so with fingerprint and DNA evidence we should be able to keep him locked up while we go through the extradition process. That's if they want him back – sir.'

She could hear the sound of keys being tapped and assumed that Talbot was logging into the PND. After a period of quiet she heard him calling out for other officers to get into his office, and then he got back to her. He explained that Kapusniak was due for release from hospital imminently and said he'd ensure the guard was increased until they could get him into a remand centre. Major Stafford would be told what was going on and DCI Talbot would tell him he wanted Martin back working alongside them as part of the Major Crime Team.

'Yes, thank you, sir, but…' Realising the phone was dead, she shook her head in exasperation and put down the receiver. It was a few moments before she contemplated her next task.

--- ‖ ---

'Right, I want the guard on Jan Kapusniak doubled as of now,' Talbot said to the officers he'd summoned. 'And I want him handcuffed to his hospital bed until such time as he's transferred to prison on remand, is that understood?'

'Yes, sir,' said the officers, leaving to carry out their orders.

Talbot picked up the phone to call Forensics and outline what was needed, stressing the urgency. Replacing the receiver, he used his mobile to call Stafford. 'When you've finished with Cooper, come to my office, please.'

Moments later, Stafford knocked on the DCI's office door. Talbot waved him in and pointed to a chair. Stafford sat down saying, 'Cooper's decided he needs to be represented and he's asked for the duty solicitor, Anne Borley, who's down in Portsmouth at the moment. So, Detective Chief Inspector, what can I do for you?'

The DCI leaned back in his chair, clasped his hands, then pulled his right hand away and pinched the bridge of his nose.

'Come on, DCI Talbot, out with it,' said Stafford.

'We appear to be a long way behind the curve here, Major.' Talbot was grim-faced, and Stafford didn't miss the change from Staf or Stafford, but said nothing. Talbot continued, 'The bodies are piling up and we seem to be no nearer to closing this out, and now I've discovered that there's been no follow-up on Kapusniak's status. It appears he has a criminal history through Eastern Europe a mile bloody long. For Christ's sake, man, what's going on? We almost let this guy out on bail.'

'As it happens I asked one of my team to research him after an earlier conversation with you about the CPS feeling the case against him was weak.'

'But she's not one of your team now, is she? You've decided to sideline her for some reason or other. I want her back on this investigation working alongside you as part of the murder team.'

'I sidelined her for her own safety. You talk about the body count, but can't you see that apart from the lowlifes killing each other, all the other people killed, injured or threatened either worked alongside me or were connected to me in some way?'

'In that case, Major, perhaps you're the one who should be removed.'

Stafford was silent for a long moment, then got to his feet and walked to the door. Turning back, he said, 'Don't you think I know that, DCI Talbot?' and strode out of the office.

CHAPTER 32

Sergeant Hawkins picked up his vibrating mobile: the screen showed *Peters*. He took the call on loudspeaker. 'What's occurring then, Captain Peters?'

'Thought you'd like to know we've picked up Ray Cooper. Apparently he shares a flat in Basingstoke with Kurt Edwards. But Edwards is stuffed, he can't go anywhere. Cooper says his arms are in plaster and his feet are fuck— ah, in a bad way too. He definitely needs hospital treatment, but I guessed you'd wanna be involved in getting him there.'

'That's great news, give me the address; I'll get an ambulance sorted and get right on it. Any news on Sophie, by the way?'

Peters gave him the address before saying, 'No, heard nothing more, I'm afraid. Anyhow, good luck with Edwards, and give him a few from me.'

'Bastard deserves more than a few,' said Hawkins as he disengaged. He swivelled from side to side in his chair; he wouldn't be picking up Edwards. *I'd likely add a few more injuries to the man*. He called Nicole.

'Just had a call from Peters, he's given me an address in Basingstoke where we'll find Kurt Edwards. How do you feel about making the arrest?'

'Wow, that's brilliant! Too right, Sergeant, be my pleasure – and by the way Talbot's put me back on the investigation.'

'That's great news; doubt if Stafford'll see it that way though. Regardless, Edwards needs to get to hospital. Now, are there any spare coppers in the incident room with you?'

'Yeah, a few writing up reports and things.'

'Right, grab one of 'em and go and pick him up, OK? I'll organise an ambulance to meet you there. And Nicole, for Christ's sake, take care, we know this guy is incapacitated, but he's a nasty bastard, so be on your guard… and Sergeant, call me Tony.'

'OK, Sarnt, uh, Tony.'

She looked around the incident room and spotted a copper she'd spoken to some evenings earlier. She walked across to his desk and asked what he was doing. He glanced up at her and she was amused to see he blushed before looking back at his monitor.

'Just finishing up a report on a stolen car, Sergeant.'

'How long?'

'Just a couple more minutes, Sarge.'

'Good, meet me in the car park in five, we're going to Basingstoke.' She made her way to the front desk and took the key for the Ford Fiesta squad car. Easing herself into the driver's seat, she drove to the front entrance. Within minutes she was joined by the young PC, who clambered awkwardly into the passenger seat. He immediately found the lever and shot the seat back as far as it would go; then strapped himself in.

'Comfortable now?' she asked.

The PC nodded, an apologetic look on his face. 'So what are we up to then, Sergeant Martin?' he asked.

Reading his shoulder number, she said, as she headed for the M3, 'First things first, PC 173, what's your name?'

'Ah, yes, I'm Harry, Harry Whitley, Sarge.'

'Right, PC Harry Whitley, we're off to Basingstoke to pick up a suspect called Kurt Edwards. He's wanted in connection with an assault, actually an acid attack on the wife of one of our own…'

'Oh, God, yeah. Lee Gibson's missus, Sophie.'

'Yep, that's the one. Do you know her?'

'No, but I know Lee, he's much older than me, he sort of took me under his wing when I first came here.'

'Not sure Lee would be happy with the "much older" tag,' she said smiling. 'So how old are you anyway, PC Whitley?'

Whitley, red in the face, looked not at her, but straight ahead.

'Twenty-four, Sergeant.'

Martin too looked straight ahead, hoping Whitley didn't spot the look of amusement on her face.

'Just us two, then?' he asked.

'Yeah, why? Don't you think we can handle it?'

'I was thinking, if he's wanted for assault, he might well kick off when we try to arrest him.'

'Don't worry, PC 173, I'll look after you,' she said, and then laughed out loud as a look of horror crossed his face.

'I, er, I didn't mean it like that, Sarge.'

'Don't worry, PC Whitley, I'm teasing you. Apparently a colleague had an altercation with him in a hotel car park. This left our man, Edwards, severely handicapped. That's according to his flatmate and partner in crime, Ray Cooper, who is now in custody. So it should be a doddle.' They remained silent for three or four miles. Nicole broke it. 'The only difficulty we may have is getting a pair of handcuffs on him.'

Whitley shot up in his seat and stared at her. 'I thought you said the arrest would be a doddle?'

'It will be, but getting the cuffs on a man with both arms in plaster could prove difficult,' she said, smiling.

'Guess we can manage, then,' said Whitley as he settled back in the seat.

She rolled to a halt outside the semi-detached property. No cars were parked on the paved front garden.

Martin leaned forward and peered out of the car window. 'I'm guessing these two aren't terribly successful criminals,' she said as she studied the downtrodden look of the area.

'How d'you want to play this, Sarge?'

'Apparently the house has been converted into two flats, and our man lives on the top floor, so I'm hoping the front door is open.' She paused for a moment. 'I'll go in first, you hang back by the open street door, we'll suss out how to get upstairs once we're inside.'

'OK; you're the governor,' said Whitley as he climbed out.

Martin stepped out, leaned her arms on the car roof and looked at the open first-floor window. Pushing off the car, she joined Whitley on the pavement. He walked to the dull and peeling black front door and pushed it firmly. It opened slowly. Martin moved past him into the hallway. It smelled damp, and the embossed wallpaper, peeling in places, appeared to have been painted a shade of nicotine. To her left, a single door; to the right a narrow staircase.

The hall and stairway had been carpeted, she estimated, some forty years earlier and by the look and feel, hadn't been cleaned since; forty years of dirty shoes and grubby hands had created the interior design. She took the stairs two at a time and waited on the dark little landing for Whitley to catch up.

Indicating for him to move to the far side of the doorway, she positioned herself by the nearside door jamb. She made eye contact with him, nodded and rapped the door with her knuckles, twice, hard. No response.

She rapped again, shouting, 'Police, police, open up, it's the police.' Again, no response. She pushed the door with her knuckles, it moved inwards. She pushed harder, it swung open. She shouted, 'Police! Police! Stay where you are, hands where we can see them.' Moving through the doorway, she wrinkled her nose at the smell of excrement, cigarettes, male sweat and lemon air freshener. They were in a clean, bright, short hallway. It had been recently decorated. She frowned, and moved towards the door ahead. It was ajar. Pausing, she called out again, 'Hello, anyone there? It's the police.' Getting no reply, she pushed the door with her foot, waiting a second before cautiously rolling around the doorframe into a living room.

She knew he was dead the second she saw him. The halo of red on the back of the sofa, stark contrast to the pale blue-grey of his face. She motioned to Whitley to stay in the doorway. Moving warily into the room, she walked carefully, quietly past the sofa to a door on the right-hand wall. She eased her head around the door, and pulled back.

She had an instant snapshot of the bedroom; certain no one was there, she moved into the room. Seeing nothing threatening, she checked under the bed. Again nothing, apart from a pile of porno mags. She backed out and indicated for Whitley to check out a room behind an open door on the left-hand wall. Whitley stopped, mouth wide open, eyes bulging as he stared at Edwards sprawled on the sofa.

Martin hissed at him and pointed to the open door. 'Check it out, now!'

It took a second or two for Whitley to react and move across the room to the doorway. Meanwhile Martin checked out the second bedroom.

Meeting up again in the room with the corpse, Harry told Nicole the small kitchen-diner was empty.

Now certain no one else was in the flat, Martin turned to Whitley and said with a wry grin, 'I think we can rule out suicide.'

Whitley managed a slight smile in return. Martin studied his pale, boyish face for a second, shook her head and called Sergeant Hawkins.

'We're at the flat. Edwards is dead, yeah, head shot, centre of the forehead. So you can call off the ambulance for now, and will you organise a couple of uniforms to run the entry log? I'll call Talbot to get the doc and SOCOs out and contact you when I find out more.'

As a fully fledged sergeant affiliated to the SIO, she was happy to take control. She disconnected and called the DCI. He agreed to get a SOCO team on their way in minutes. Call ended, she phoned Peters, putting him on speaker.

'Have you got Cooper in custody?' she said.

'He's in Eastleigh, waiting for the duty solicitor Anne Borley,' said Peters.

'Good, because we're at the flat to pick up Edwards and he's dead. Yes, murdered – head shot, dead centre between the eyes.'

Peters let that spin for a second or two before saying, 'Christ, it's never ending. We can't get after the main players, this shit keeps getting in the way. OK, I'm on my way to pick up Tony Amos, another bit player. I'll let Stafford know; he's about to interview Cooper and this'll put a totally different slant to it.'

'OK, thanks, I've been on to DCI Talbot to get forensics and the rest of the Murder Squad out here, I'll let you know the situation when we have more details.'

Call ended, she threw Whitley the key to the car, saying, 'In the boot, you'll find a roll of police tape, and bring up a couple of forensic coveralls and latex gloves. OK?'

He fumbled the catch and, red-faced, retrieved the key from the floor. He nodded, but didn't make eye contact as he rushed through the room and down the stairs. He returned, looking pale. Giving her the coveralls, he said, 'I've tied the tape right across the front of the parking area and the bottom of the staircase and I found a *Crime Scene – Do Not Enter* sign and put that on the stairs as well.' DS Martin nodded her approval.

Having put on protective clothing, she switched her phone to camera and took photos of the body. Some full length, some close-up head shots showing profile and full face. She also took pictures of the ripped sheets, blood and plaster splatters on the sofa and floor, as well as the mass of blood, hair, bone splinters and bloodied grey matter covering the back of the sofa, behind the dead man's head. She moved to the hall doorway and, facing the gory scene, set the camera to video and panned slowly around the room. Moving forwards she filmed across the corpse, and on to the coffee table, showing the open pack of cigarettes and ashtray. On the floor she filmed the drug paraphernalia.

As she looked at the items on the table, she noticed that the filter tips on the cigarettes in the pack seemed to be a slightly different colour to one of the cigarette butts in the ashtray. Leaning in closer and peering at the butt, there was just enough of the unburnt white paper to see the copperplate letters *Be*; definitely a different brand to the opened pack of Rothmans. Squatting down by the table, she looked again at the scene, and realised that, with his arms how they were, it would have been impossible for the dead man to smoke a cigarette alone. So had this lone cigarette butt been smoked by his flatmate, Ray Cooper, or had someone else been here? She stopped filming, and moved back into the hallway. She began emailing the pictures to DCI Talbot and Sergeant Hawkins, and finally to Stafford.

'Right, PC Whitley, go into the smaller bedroom and see if you can find anything that will help us determine what happened here. Any drawers, pull 'em out and check the bottoms – we've found all sorts of good stuff that way.'

Whitley nodded and walked across to the bedroom doorway, where he stood, taking in the room for a second or two, then moved towards a pine chest of drawer.

Martin said loudly, 'And look under the bed.'

The room was sparsely furnished. A double bed, a pine bedside cabinet, a freestanding wardrobe and the chest of drawers. Kneeling on the plain green carpet, he peered under the bed. A couple of pairs of shoes, but nothing of interest. He moved to the chest of drawers and opened the top drawer. On the right-hand side were socks, belts and an unopened pack of condoms. He rooted through the socks and found nothing. To the left-hand side, sitting on a stack of handkerchiefs, were two black leather wallets and two mobile phones. He picked up one of the wallets and flipped it open; there were six bank cards inside. He took one out, it was in the name of Abduk Ravani. Checking the second wallet, he found bank cards in the name of Hakim Buzdar.

'Hey, Sarge, I think we've got something.' Martin appeared, empty-handed. He pointed to the open drawer and said, 'I think these guys are muggers or pickpockets.'

Martin picked up a wallet, pulled out the bank cards and noted the name. She put the cards back and checked the second wallet; flipping through, she realised, with mounting excitement that these wallets and phones belonged to the Asian pair murdered in the North Lane flat. Putting the wallets back, she picked up one of the mobiles, a top-of-the-range Chinese phone. Switching it on was easy enough, getting further was not; it was password-protected. She put the phone back and took out her own mobile. She held it up to Whitley and pulled a face. 'Can't begin to think how much Messrs Buzdar and Ravani would have paid compared to this little beasty, and these phones have this new encryption system everyone's talking about. But these guys aren't muggers. And Edwards isn't a victim of a robbery, this was no opportunistic banditry, this is a "you're no use to me now" clear-out.'

Whitley nodded, but again Nicole noted the questioning look on his face.

'Out with it, Harry, out with it.'

'Can't believe how you only read those names two seconds ago, yet you remembered them straight away. I read them just before I heard you say them, and still I'm not sure what they were.'

Martin looked at him and smiled. 'I'd love to say it's because I've got a photographic memory, like some of these detectives you read about, but I came across Buzdar's name earlier. He was found murdered in the flat in North Lane, with another Asian man, who I guess will turn out to be Abduk Ravani.' As she spoke, she had been navigating various screens on her phone. She touched the screen again, and Sergeant Hawkins answered, on speakerphone for Whitley's benefit, 'So what's occurring now then, Sergeant Martin?'

'You won't believe this, Tony, but we've discovered the wallets, bank cards and phones belonging to our recently departed Asian guys."

'Jesus H Christ, that's brilliant. Stafford's going to love that, it all begins to fit into place. So we'll see you back here shortly, then?'

'Yes, we'll stay until forensics and the doc gets here, see if we can learn anything new, then get back and write it up, but to me, it looks like a cynical clear-out.' Call ended, she looked at Whitley, and almost laughed at his bemused expression. 'Sorry, Harry, but you've joined us right in the middle of some major happenings. Finding these wallets and phones is not just an isolated event, it's a bloody massive leap forward, linking a gang responsible for murder, drug dealing and manufacture, as well as illegal immigration and—'

'Fucking hell, Sarge! Excuse my French, but I thought we were just going to arrest a guy for alleged assault.'

'And?' said Nicole.

'And now... Well, this I why I became a copper, Sarge, not to sit writing reports on stolen cars or booking speeding motorists.'

'OK; so did you check the bottom of the drawers?'

'Yeah, course I did, nothin' there.'

'Did you check the space under the bottom drawer?' Whitley hesitated for a fraction of a second, turned and went back into the bedroom. She, meanwhile, put the wallets and phones into evidence bags. Moments later Whitley came out of the bedroom with half a dozen DVDs in plastic wallets, and sheepishly handed them to her.

'You can bet your bottom dollar that these aren't going to be reruns of *Only Fools And Horses*!' she said as she put them into an evidence bag for the forensic team.

She made one further phone call, bringing her new DI up to date with the situation and requested round-the-clock shifts of uniformed constables to protect the scene until further notice. As she ended the call, the pathologist, followed by the full forensic team, pulled into the parking area.

CHAPTER 33

Stafford, pissed off with Talbot and Nicole Martin, walked back to the incident room and found a vacant desk away from the others. He knew it would be some time before Peters arrived, with or without Amos. He was convinced Amos, Miller, Cooper and Edwards would now be desperate to save their own skins. The legendary loyalty among thieves was only true when things were going well. When the day of reckoning came, and it had surely come for this lot, it would be a contest to see who could squawk the loudest. But Stafford didn't want the loudest squawk, he wanted the most informative. Going to the nearest printer he pulled out a few A4 sheets and returned to the desk. He rooted around in the drawers till he found a biro, then wrote down the four names. Immediately, he crossed out the name Miller – they had interviewed him earlier, in the aftermath of Weyhill. He was an HGV lorry driver and had delivered bins of scrap electronics to the Weyhill site. He knew about the retrieval of precious metals at Weyhill as well as the Southampton smuggling operations of both people and drugs, and the drug manufacturing. And he had told Stafford and the police everything, grassing up everyone who worked at Weyhill. That was the price on his head, the reason for his being held in a safe house while he awaited trial. Stafford needed more information on the wider operation. They'd saved a number of immigrants in Southampton and discovered more at the Weyhill site. But what happened to the others who had been brought in earlier?

It was frustrating – so many lines of investigation to follow, and plenty of leads, but he couldn't seem to get on top of any of them. He needed to find the elusive connection from the operation at Weyhill to the syndicate hierarchy. Police top brass had said on the radio about busting a syndicate, but they had no real idea who the syndicate bosses were. Pavel Aksanov was the only name they had and, to make a move on his hotel or nightclubs, they would need much more than mere suspicion to obtain search warrants. Second on his list was Tony Amos – he could prove more useful, thought Stafford. Amos had fucked up big time, and would do anything to get Aksanov off his case. They had interviewed him before and much of his testimony revolved around the smuggling side of the operation: people, drugs and weapons. But now they had discovered Winstone's body and the two dead Asian blokes, perhaps they could put the fear of God into him, and use the threat of charging him with three murders to jog his memory and recollection of events.

Cooper and Edwards were not, as far as Stafford knew, involved in Southampton or Weyhill, but he thought they must be involved with the syndicate hierarchy, otherwise why the attack on Sophie Gibson, and why follow Marva from the safe house? So with Cooper now in custody, he was the obvious place to start. And when they caught up with Edwards, they could play them off, one against the other. *We need something to get our teeth into here, we keep getting bogged down with the red herrings they keep throwing our way*

Stafford's head was spinning with frustration, so he began to prepare a list of questions for Cooper. It was a second or two before he realised his mobile was vibrating; he'd received a text. It was Anne Borley, saying she'd arrived and was ready to sit in with Cooper for his interview. No sooner had he read the message, when the phone rang again – the screen showed *Hawkins*. Stafford put the call onto loudspeaker and said, 'Tony, what can I do for you?'

'Have you started interviewing Cooper yet?'

'No, we're just about to.'

'You may want to hang fire on that, Staf. Captain Peters called me saying that Edwards and Cooper share a flat in Basingstoke, so I sent a couple of officers to pick up Edwards, but someone got to him first.'

'*What?*'

'Yep, single bullet to the head, dead centre, between the eyes. No one else in the flat. Just waiting for forensics now.'

'Bastard, that was far too good for him. Who found him?' said Stafford. The delay in response told Stafford all he needed to know. 'You sent Nicole.'

'I didn't have any choice – as you know Talbot wanted her back on the team. But I'd have sent her to pick him up anyway, being mates with Lee Gibson. I thought she'd appreciate the chance to – well, you know.'

'Yeah, I know.'

Hawkins went on, 'What they found in their flat will interest you though…'

'Come on then, Tony, spit it out.'

'They found two top-of-the-range mobiles and two wallets. The wallets are complete with bank cards and it all appears to belong to our two dead Asian guys. Bank cards confirm both names.'

Adrenalin surged as Stafford thought of the implications. He'd spent the morning – wasted it, more like – waiting to interview Cooper and Amos. Now with this new information, he felt at last they were on the edge of something. A connection from the out-of-town syndicate men linking two Basingstoke thugs working at Aksanov's establishments to the Weyhill operation. Stafford was now sure this could be the link they were looking for.

'Bloody hell, Tony, that's excellent. Listen, I'm going to leave Cooper and Amos, when he gets here, stewing for an hour or two and come up to Aldershot. I'll organise the tech boys to come and analyse the phones and I'll be up with you as soon as.'

'Nicole's got that in hand. She says the phones have the EncroChat encryption system. Doubt if we'll get much, so get up here whenever you like.'

Stafford stayed silent for a moment. Finally, he said, 'Guess I'll need to be eating some humble pie, then?'

'Maybe, but if you want to keep her out of harm's way, you could always get her to go up to the West Midlands and see what she can find out up there.'

'It'll have to be done some time, so I'll give it some thought on the way up. See you soon, Tony.'

∥

Anne Borley strode into the incident room, looked around and headed towards Stafford. He stood and shook her outstretched hand. She pulled another chair across to the workstation, sat down and said, 'Flaming Brandon Miller gave me nothing more interesting than at our previous meeting. Bit of a wasted journey, actually.'

'Yes, I sort of anticipated it might be, but at least we got our tricky friend, Howard Neilson, to show his true colours.'

She nodded. 'Yes, I guess that's a bit of a bonus. So, are you ready to interview Cooper?'

Stafford looked sheepishly at her and said, 'Sorry, Anne, I was about to phone you – something massive has happened that needs my urgent attention in Aldershot. It impacts on the way I approach Cooper's interview, so I'm going to leave you to it for now. He's requested a solicitor anyhow, so it'll give you a chance to see what defence he comes up with.'

Anne shrugged and made to get up, saying, 'OK, not a problem. So at present he's being charged with the assault on Sophie Gibson and…'

'And possessing an offensive weapon; namely, a hand grenade, with intent to, etc, etc.'

'Fine. It'll be a blast, I'm sure.'

Stafford grinned, unsure if she meant the pun. 'And Ryan Peters is currently looking for Tony Amos, the guy who collected Winstone from hospital. Now, he's also going to need legal representation, so maybe you could have a chat with him too?'

She stood up and smiled. Christ, he thought, I'd forgotten how pretty she is.

'Gosh,' she said. 'I wish I'd met you before, Major Stafford.'

Caught off balance, he hesitated for a second, glancing at the desk, the clock on the wall, before looking at her questioningly.

'Turns out you've been extremely good for business since we met,' she said as she sashayed away.

It took an effort for him to move his gaze from the rear of the retreating solicitor. Snapping back to the moment, he gathered his bits and pieces together, put on his bomber jacket and, heading out of the incident room, called Ryan Peters. The call went to voicemail.

Stafford said, 'I need to get to Aldershot. If you bring Amos back to Eastleigh, get him booked in, Anne Borley's there to act for him, ready to do a deal, but he's got to start talking, give us something to get our teeth into. Otherwise he's in deep shit. So, meet me in Aldershot, soonest. I think we're on the move at last.'

Peters had located Tony Amos; he'd agreed to come in voluntarily and answer more questions. As they got into the SRi, Peters saw he had received a voicemail; he put it on speaker. It was Stafford telling him to drop Amos off at the Eastleigh nick and meet him in Aldershot.

Peters turned to Tony Amos and said, 'Well, you heard that. It means having to delay our interview for a while. But trust me on this; the duty solicitor at Eastleigh is Anne Borley. I'm telling you now, it's in your best interests to talk to her and get your story straight. If you try and bullshit your way through this, you may find the whole world comes crashing in on you – Tony, you need to believe me on this. I shouldn't be saying it, but we're going to be asking you about some pretty heavy stuff, so my advice is to tell it straight, don't try to be a smartarse.'

Amos, aghast, took out a packet of cigarettes and moved to the edge of his seat. 'But I ain't done nothin' since you lot busted me in Southampton, and then I told you all I know.'

'For your health's sake, mate, don't light that. And for your sake, I hope you are telling the truth, because the stakes have been raised.'

Amos's face paled as he put the cigarettes away. He sank back in his seat and mumbled, 'Fucking bastards, you never let go when you get your teeth in. Am I gonna need an alibi?'

'It would be a step in the right direction – have you got one?'

'Guess I could rustle one up if I had to,' he said, smiling thinly.

'Duh,' said Peters shaking his head, then, 'Tone, me ol' mate, you know what they say; if you can't take the heat, you shouldn't have stood so close to the fire.'

Amos glanced across at him, then straight ahead, and said, 'You're no mate of mine.'

CHAPTER 34

Nicole Martin and Harry Whitley stayed at the flat until the forensic team and pathologist arrived. Introductions out of the way and as the team donned their forensic outfits, Martin approached the head tech and said, 'When you go into the living room,' she paused as she saw the irony in that statement, 'you'll see an ashtray on the coffee table. There's a cigarette butt lying on one side. It looks like it wasn't stubbed out, but left to burn down. Well, it's a different brand to the pack on the table and you'll see when you get in there that the deceased could not have smoked a cigarette unaided, so can you get it bagged and shipped for DNA analysis pronto, please.'

'OK, Sergeant, I'll sort that out for you, no problem.'

'Great, thanks. But there's more. We've got two mobile phones, belonging – we think – to the dead Asian suspects from earlier. They're password-protected and have the new encryption software, but we need to get into them if we can.'

The tech frowned. 'OK, I'll see what I can do, but it'll be tough if they've got EncroChat.'

'Listen, you can only do your best. Anyhow, there's nothing more we can contribute here, so if it's all the same to you, we're going to shoot off back to the nick, but bell me if you find anything you think will move the investigation forward.'

'No worries, Sarge,' said the tech.

'And I'm going to take these half dozen DVDs. We need to view them soonest. They're booked out to me on the log. OK?'

Still frowning, the tech nodded and as they exchanged names and numbers Martin realised he wanted to get on with his work. She found PC Whitley, who had now got some colour back, and together they headed out. As she pulled away from the kerb, he said, 'Do you think his flatmate, er, what was his name? Cooper? Ray Cooper? Do you think he did this? Or could this be a gangland-style killing?'

Martin smiled, 'A gangland-style killing? Well, these two guys are a couple of turbo-charged scumbags, earning a buck or two, hurting people to order. It seems they've been working out of Whitelines nightclub, but they were also involved in a bust-up at the World Citizen Hotel near Basingstoke, so if we can establish they're doing the dirty work for the boss of those places, then this really is gang-related.'

PC Whitley's eyes grew wider as he settled down in the seat.

Arriving back at Aldershot nick, they found themselves a vacant desk in the incident room. Martin pulled out her notebook and said, 'So you're not working on anything specific at the moment then, Harry?'

'No, Sergeant, I cleared up all my outstanding stuff before we went to Basingstoke.'

'Right, good. Now what I need you to do is check this registration plate, it belongs to a recovery truck. We need to find out the name and whereabouts of the company and the driver.' As she spoke she gave him her notes, and then downloaded Ryan Peters' dash-cam footage of the recovery vehicle driving away with the Porsche Cayman on the back. PC Whitley whistled as he watched the playback.

'Beautiful motor,' he said.

'Yeah, well we need to find out why it was taken and where it was taken to. There are so many questions around it.' Whitley looked ready for more, so Nicole continued, 'Who ordered the truck and why?'

'Why? Wasn't it the owner then?'

'We don't know, but we don't think so. The guy who owned it came from the West Midlands, he parked up at the hotel and disappeared. Then he and a buddy end up dead in a grotty flat, twenty-five miles away.'

'Ah, the two Asian guys whose stuff we found.'

'Yep, they're the ones, and at some stage we're going to have to go to the West Midlands and liaise with the police up there. You know, see where they lived and, more importantly, how they earned their money. Anyway, first things first: check out that registration number.'

Martin, meanwhile, decided to look into Southern Washroom Services. Moving to another desk, she powered up the computer. Taking the easy option, she typed the name into the search engine. Lots of stuff came up but no Southern Washroom Services. She tried various social media and networking sites, to no avail. Cursing under her breath, she thought, have we got the right company name? God, why didn't we pay it more attention? Take a picture or something? Exasperated, she leaned back in her chair and looked up at the ceiling. Bloody hell, she thought, the answer is obvious; the SOCO boys and forensic techs are still down at the Weyhill site. She hesitated for a moment, as she didn't want to phone DCI Talbot again to ask him for contact numbers, then she remembered she'd just taken the phone number of one of the forensic guys in Basingstoke – he'll know who's down there, she thought, getting out her mobile to call him.

'Oh, hiya, it's Nicole Martin, DS Martin, we just met at the crime scene in Basingstoke… Listen, do you know if any of your team are still down at the Weyhill site? I need information regarding some signs we found in a van down there. Actually, what I need is a photo of some stick-on vinyl signs – I think the company was Southern Washroom Services – and also the phone number. So one picture showing both will do. They were just stacked in the Tranny van parked there.'

While she waited for the tech to contact the Weyhill team, she decided to search the internet for Howard Neilson. She got loads of hits. She skipped through the parts that told of his meteoric rise from law school to qualify as a solicitor. Reading between the lines, it seemed that, since qualifying, his quest for further success had somehow hit the buffers. Searching for more up-to-date posts, she found numerous newspaper articles, mainly provincial, but with the occasional tabloid mention. Local journalists seemed to love him, or at least love his style. He seemed to defend the indefensible. He appeared smart and charming. His style in court was to play ball – hardball. He tore into prosecutors, exposing each misstep, every ill-thought-out strategy. He pulled witnesses apart, destroying their testimony and evidence by creating so much doubt in its veracity that judges and jury felt almost bound to discount it. Definitely a winner, but still a big fish in a small pond. Surely, she thought, with his smarts he could have scaled the ladder, gone to the bigger cities to find more and better opportunities? Or maybe he'd found the pot of gold working with men like Pavel Aksanov. Taking a moment to process this, her thoughts were interrupted as Harry Whitley called across.

'Have you got a minute, Sarge?' She switched off her monitor and scooted in her chair across to his desk.

'What's up?' she said. He angled his screen towards her, pointing at it.

'The recovery truck is owned by Southampton Metal Recycling Ltd, based in—'

'Southampton,' Martin interrupted. 'The plot thickens.'

Whitley looked at her, frowning.

'It's another link, Harry,' she continued. 'We had a few dealings with that company in an earlier investigation. Some good, some bad, but it gave us more questions than answers, that's for sure.'

'The boss man is a guy called Francis Healey. Do you want me to call him?'

A few seconds passed while she mulled it over. Finally, she said, 'No, I don't think so. I'll talk to Captain Peters about it, but I think we're going to have to visit him in person.' She paused for a moment, leaned towards Whitley, excitement showing in her eyes, her face, as she said, 'And this, Harry, means we have another link from the operation in Southampton and Weyhill to our friends in Basingstoke.

And with these solid links we can now get the warrants, and then we can really rock 'n' roll. With luck and a following wind, this could mean we move in and tackle the syndicate's top boys.'

He beamed at her, eyes wide, sharing her excitement.

Her mobile buzzed. Scrabbling to pick it up, she saw she had received a text: a photo. The picture was of a sign lying in the back of a van, the sign advertising *Southern Washroom Services*, complete with a mobile contact number. She texted back, thanking whoever had sent it and logged the number into her contacts. She phoned the number on the sign: nothing. She tried again: nothing. She googled the number on her phone; it was out of commission.

'I think Southern Washroom Services have gone down the pan,' she said.

Ryan Peters signed in at Aldershot Police Station, collected his ID lanyard and made his way up to the incident room. Nicole Martin waved him over and, as he made his way between the desks, said, 'Surprised to see you here, I thought you were picking up Amos. I sort of anticipated Stafford might show his face.'

'Yeah, I picked up Amos, and Staf should be on his way.'

She hesitated a moment, then changed tack. 'You'll be pleased to know I've got us another pair of hands. Captain Peters, meet PC 173, AKA Harry Whitley. Harry, this is Captain Ryan Peters from the Security Service, who at the request of HMG, has, ah, how shall I put it…'

'I think it's probably best to say, we're on attachment from the Security Service, and we've been helping the police with this, and earlier investigations,' said Peters, smiling, and shaking the PC's hand. 'Good to meet you, Harry.'

'And good to meet you, sir,' said Harry.

'Ryan or Ry will do… So where are we with the late, barely lamented Kurt Charles Edwards?'

Martin brought him up to speed and went on to say, 'But best of all, Harry found wallets and phones, stashed away in a drawer, belonging to the two Asian guys. I've got the tech team trying to unlock the phones as we speak.'

'Christ, Nic, be interesting to see what comes out of that,' said Peters.

'Listen,' she said, 'when you brought in Cooper, did he seem distressed or agitated in any way?'

'No, quite the opposite. He tried to be amusing. Odd really, considering he was handing himself in while carrying a grenade and admitting to being under orders to bung it through the safe house window.'

Nicole managed to suppress a smile as PC Whitley crashed back in his seat, eyes wide.

'And thinking about it, he seemed so cocky, it was almost as if he felt he had the upper hand. It was all a bit odd,' said Peters.

'Does he smoke, do you know?'

'Yes he does, why?'

'Didn't happen to notice what brand?'

Peters, brow furrowed, said, 'Sod it, can't remember – when I patted him down, I found car keys, a house key and I'm sure I pulled out a packet of ciggies. Can't think what they were though. Why? Is it important?'

Nicole explained about the odd cigarette butt, and said, 'So if it's not the same brand as the two in the flat, it could be a third person who may be the killer.'

'OK. I'll let it be for a minute, it'll come to me. So, Stafford said he'd left a few things with Sergeant Hawkins, has he—'

'Yes,' interrupted Martin. 'He wanted us to follow up on that recovery truck and find out where it went, and what happened to the Porsche, et cetera, so long story short, it's Frank Healey's recovery truck, you know, from Southampton Metal Recycling. We were just saying, do we phone him or pay him a visit?'

Ryan's eyebrows shot up. 'We'll hang fire on that, I think; Stafford was down in Eastleigh, maybe I can get him to – er, no, not a such good idea at the moment.'

'Why not? If he's down that way?'

Peters shook his head and said, 'When I dropped off Amos, he was already on his way here. Trouble is, you know what he's like – if he thinks he's letting the side down, or if he thinks we've pulled a misstep by not asking him—'

Martin shrugged. 'I see your point, I suppose.' They pondered the situation for a while.

'*Rothmans!*' said Peters breaking the mood, 'That's what the cigarettes were, Rothmans.'

'Jeez, Ryan, frightened the life out of me. But no, that's brilliant, it means the one butt was smoked by a third party; we need to find out who. Now the other thing we followed up on was those washroom signs.'

CHAPTER 35

Anne Borley strode through Eastleigh Police Station to the little communal kitchen area at the rear of the ground floor and got two coffees from the vending machine. Grabbing a handful of sugar sachets, her work bag slung over her shoulder and a coffee in each hand, she was escorted to the interview room where Tony Amos was waiting. She hadn't met him before, but guessed by now he would be extremely pissed off, hence the coffee peace offering. She nodded her thanks as the police constable escort opened the door for her. As she walked into the drab windowless twelve-by-ten room, the lone occupant lifted his head from his arms on the table in front of him, peered blearily up at her, pushed himself away from the table and said, "Bout bloody time.'

'Yes, I know, sorry about that, Mr Amos, but I've bought you a coffee. Do you take sugar?' Amos nodded. Borley put the coffee in front of him, sat on the metal chair opposite and scrabbled around in her pocket for the sugar. Amos tore the sachets apart, and stirred vigorously with the wooden spatula she had placed on the table.

'So, Tony…is it OK if I call you Tony?' He nodded as he swallowed coffee, so she went on. 'Good, well, I'm

Anne Borley and I'm here as your solicitor. You're not under arrest, you're here voluntarily to answer some follow-up questions and you're at liberty to leave whenever you wish. Are you OK with that?' Another nod. 'Now, none of what you tell me will go back to the police, unless you expressly tell me there's something you want them to know. Do you understand?'

He stopped, coffee halfway to his mouth. 'Do I look thick?'

She glanced at him. He was wearing a grey hoody over a faded black T-shirt with a band logo she couldn't place. She guessed he was wearing tracksuit bottoms. His brown eyes were moving constantly. His shortish black hair was gelled into a peak down the middle, and looked out of place on this thirty-plus man.

'No,' she said, 'you don't look thick,' but, she thought, you look nervous and shifty as hell. 'OK, now I'll take a few notes as we go, if you don't mind? So let's get started.'

'Whatever,' he said.

'So tell me how you came to take Floyd Winstone from Winchester Hospital to the flat in Aldershot?'

A puzzled look crossed his face. 'Well, his hands were busted. Couldn't drive, see. So I got a call, sayin' would I pick 'im up. He's a mate, so I did.'

'Did you two have a row?'

His eyes cast down, flicked from side to side. The look seemed to say, how did you know? 'Nah, not a proper row; he had a bit of a go, because I got pissed on a job when his hands got burned, but he soon shut it. I reckoned he'd spilled his guts to the filth. Else why'd they let him walk free? Eh?'

'So what happened when you got to the flat?'

Amos frowned and shook his head. 'Well, nothin', we just went in an' got settled like... Wha's all this bollocks about, anyhow?'

'You didn't carry on arguing in the flat?'

'I told you, we 'ad a few words in the truck, that's all.'

'And how long did you stay in the flat?'

He thought for a second before saying, 'I don't know, maybe fifteen minutes. He had some idea that someone who stayed there had left some gear in a kitchen cupboard, but we didn't find nothin'. So I thought, bollocks, and went.'

'And there was no one else in the flat when you arrived?'

The frown and puzzled look returned. 'What the fuck is all this about, lady?'

'It's a simple question, Tony. Was anyone else in the flat while you were there?'

'Nah, like I said, just me and 'im.'

'And Winstone, was he all right when you left?'

'Yeah, course 'e was. Why, what's goin' on 'ere then?' Amos fidgeted in his seat, unable to keep still.

'OK, let's try this from another angle. Were you or Winstone expecting to meet anyone in the flat?'

'No, I fuckin' wasn't. Soon as I realised we weren't going to find Kapusniak's stash, I was off.'

'So you hadn't arranged to meet up with any Indian or Pakistani men there?'

'What? No way... Look, what's this all about, lady? Best start telling me what's going on, or I'm off. Savvy?'

Anne Borley said nothing. Seconds passed, then, 'Remember, Tony, everything you say to me is confidential.

I can't start to defend you unless you tell me the truth. Now, are you sure there's nothing you want to tell me about your visit to the flat?'

Amos went to stand up, and as he back-heeled the chair out of the way, it crashed to the floor.

'This is fuckin' ridiculous. I don't get what you expect me to say…' He started to sway from side to side, his breathing laboured. He clutched his chest.

Borley rushed over to him, pulled the chair upright, grabbed his shoulders and pushed him back into the chair.

'Stay there, don't move!' she said, rushing to the door. She dashed into the kitchen, picked up a plastic cup and filled it with cold water. Back in the interview room, she was relieved to see he was still there and upright. She held the cup to his lips and he drank noisily.

After a second or two, he turned sheepishly towards her and nodded. 'Thanks,' he said. 'Don't know what happened there.'

She smiled at him and put the cup down on the table. 'No need to apologise. I've seen it happen before, it's just a, uh, ah—' She paused, not wanting to say panic attack. 'It's an anxiety thing. Now would you like me to call the doctor, just to be on the safe side?'

'Nah, piss off. Oh sorry, no, I'm OK,' he said as he sat upright in the chair, pushing his chest out. 'No, let's get this done.'

'Well, if you're sure, but say if you need to stop. OK?' Another nod. 'Good. Look, Tony, believe it or not, I'm here to help you. I'm not trying to trap you, but if what you say happened at the flat is true, then you'd best prepare yourself for some bad news.'

Amos grabbed the coffee and took another swig. His hand trembled as he put it back on the table. She almost felt sorry for him. He slumped down in the chair and nodded, he was ready.

'I'm sorry to tell you, Tony, your friend Floyd is dead. He's been murdered.'

Amos stared at her, eyes and mouth wide in disbelief. He slumped forward onto the table, the plastic cup and the two empty coffee containers falling to the floor. His head rested on his arms, just as he'd been when she'd first walked in. She reached out to touch his arm, but he was beginning to sit back up. Eyes alert, agitated, he said, 'Jesus, I knew this would start fuckin' happening. They said Aksanov would look after us, but instead they're getting rid of us. Bastards lookin' after 'emselves. That's Floyd, Matis, me Polish mate in Winchester Prison and Christ knows what's happened to Miller. You see, it'll be me next.'

'What do you mean, Aksanov would look after you?'

Amos looked at the floor for a full minute. 'Said too much already.'

CHAPTER 36

Marva Lewis had no idea when or even if Ryan Peters returned home at night. She never heard him come in, but she never felt afraid or alone. Her two boys had spent much of the last few days either playing on their Xbox or listening, open mouthed, to the tall stories the Security Service agents told them. Now, they were beginning to suffer cabin fever. It was great to have time off school at first. But it's only OK if you are free to go where you want, do what you want. Marva and the boys were only allowed out in the back garden, and kicking a ball about with your mum or a distracted, constantly vigilant security officer was definitely losing its appeal. Marva knew it was time to move on. She spent part of Sunday evening packing the boys' suitcases and stuffed what little she had brought into her own case. She moved from room to room looking for one of the agents. She found the tall blond one playing Sniper Elite 4 with her sons. As she stood in the doorway, he stopped and looked up.

She walked a pace into the room. 'Sorry to disrupt your game, but I thought I'd better tell you; I'm going to organise a taxi to take us home in—'

'Ah, right. Mrs Lewis…er, Marva, that's not how we're going to do it. But don't you worry, it's all in hand, tomorrow my oppo will go ahead to your house and check it out. Make sure it's all OK. Meanwhile, we'll load up the second car with your things and as soon as we get the all-clear signal, then, and only then, will we leave.'

Marva's brow furrowed and her eyes narrowed as she readied to launch an attack on how she was pissed off with everyone else organising her life. She stopped, took a deep breath, then her face relaxed and she smiled broadly at the agent, then burst out laughing. The officer couldn't help but laugh back – it was the first time he'd seen her smile, let alone laugh.

That night she went to bed looking forward to tomorrow; the day she could start planning her life again. She slept fitfully; dreams getting in the way of reality. One moment she was planning Garfield's funeral, the next she saw him floating face down in Southampton waters.

She got up early and sat quietly with pen and paper, making lists. People to invite, letters to write, emails and phone calls to make. She knew Garfield wouldn't want a great fuss, but she knew his colleagues in arms would want to pay their respects. Maybe I'd better talk to Ryan and Staf, get their thoughts before I talk to the Colonel, she mused.

Peters came downstairs and into the kitchen where she was sitting.

'Hiya Marva, fancy a coffee?'

'Yeah, go on then,' she said.

'So, hopefully, today's the day when you get to go back home?' he said as he filled the kettle.

'Yep. Well, it's time. Time, I think, to get the kids back to a bit of normality. You know, don't you, that I appreciate all you've done? And all the love and support you've shown me and the boys. But once we get back home, we can start to move forward, you know, get on with our lives.'

Coffee made, Peters slid a mug across the table to her and sat facing her.

She nodded thanks and picked up the mug. 'I was hoping to get a chance to talk to you and Staf today. I need to start preparing Garfield's funeral, and I wondered if you had any thoughts on how many guys will want to come? Firstly to the service, and then after, at home, er, for the wake, I suppose you'd call it?'

Peters cupped both hands around his mug and stared intently at the contents. It was a while before he answered.

'Yes, it needs to be done. Have they said when they're releasing his, uh, Garfield to you?'

'No. Not yet, I'm expecting a call when I get back home. I can't see there's any reason to hold him any longer.'

Peters let that settle for a moment. 'If you want, I'll talk to the Colonel, see if he has any input?'

'Would you, Ryan? That'd be a great help, I always get tongue-tied talking to him, posh bastard – oops, shouldn't say that, he's been supportive too.'

Ryan's face creased with a smile. 'I know he comes across as a bit of an ogre, a hard-nosed bugger, but he's got a heart in there somewhere. At least that's what Stafford reckons.'

Marva smiled in return, and went upstairs to chivvy along the boys.

As he sipped his coffee, Peters felt his mobile phone vibrating. He checked the screen, frowned… he didn't recognise the number, but accepted the call anyway.

The caller said, 'I've been trying to contact Major Stafford, but I'm getting no response.'

'Who is this?' said Peters. 'I'm Ryan Peters, Major Stafford's number two.'

'Oh, sorry, I'm phoning from Basingstoke and North Hants Hospital mortuary. It's about the two Asian gentlemen we have with us currently.'

'OK,' said Peters, 'how can I help?'

'Well, we've been talking to the police in the West Midlands, and we've set up a meeting with their families for three o'clock today. They're coming down to the hospital to do the formal ID.'

'Ah, OK. Bit short notice, but thanks for the call, I'll make sure we have someone there.'

CHAPTER 37

Stafford walked past the Eastleigh front desk, handed in his lanyard ID and went out to the car park. As he settled into the Volvo, he felt his mobile vibrate. Cursing, he was tempted to ignore it and let it go to voicemail, but after a second's hesitation, he took it out and checked the screen. The caller ID showed an 01722 number, a Salisbury code.

'Stafford.'

'Ah, yes, Major Stafford, I'm calling from the Salisbury Burns Unit. We have you down as lead investigator in the assault on Sophie Gibson. Can you confirm that this is you?'

Stafford said, 'Yes, yes, of course.' He rattled off a number and asked, 'Why? What's—'

'We have now notified Sophie's husband Lee Gibson and he insisted we contact you. I have to advise you that Sophie tried to commit suicide earlier this afternoon. Sadly, she died later of her injuries, in intensive care.'

Stafford slumped in his seat. 'Oh Jeez, that's bloody awful, how on earth could that happen?'

The doctor, obviously nervous, said, 'We're not exactly sure.'

'What do you mean, you're not exactly sure? Was nobody looking after her? I thought she was in ICU to start with.' There was silence for a while.

'There will be an enquiry, of course… somehow she managed to get on a roof… we'll get you a copy of the results as soon as possible. Sorry to be the one to give you such bad news.'

It was a moment before Stafford realised the connection was dead. He sat there, phone in hand, dumbfounded. He battled inward turmoil as he thought; given the horrific extent of her injuries, maybe this was a— No, he would not allow his mind to venture there. He sat in stunned silence for five minutes before heading out to the M3. He couldn't get Sophie out of his mind. He'd never met her, but the burden of guilt weighed heavily; she'd died because the crooks wanted to screw with his mind. If Lee Gibson hadn't worked alongside him, Sophie would still be alive. Stafford pulled off the motorway and headed for the Royal Hampshire County Hospital.

He parked into the multi-storey car park, and ran all the way to the Nightingale Wing, where he paused for a moment to catch his breath. Getting to Level D and the Bartlett Ward, he walked up to the nurses' station and asked to be taken to Lee Gibson. When the nurse explained he wasn't seeing any visitors at present, Stafford took out his Security Service ID.

'I understand why you're saying that, but, please, show him this card, tell him I'm here. Let him make the decision.'

Taking the card, she read it and said, 'Oh, you're investigating the attack on his wife, aren't you?' Stafford could only nod. 'All right, Major Stafford, I'll see what he says,' and she walked to the far end of the ward. Stafford watched as she pulled the curtain around Gibson's bed aside. He watched and waited. After a couple of minutes, she came out, visibly shaken. Reaching Stafford, she handed back his card.

'Yes, he'll see you. Please don't stay too long, he's in shock, and has been given medication.'

Stafford nodded his thanks, and walked to the curtained-off bed. Gibson was lying, propped up with pillows, his head cast down. Stafford moved quietly forward and sat on the edge of the bed. He grasped Gibson's left hand and said, 'Lee, I'm truly sorry for this. I'm here, we're all here for you. And we'll do whatever it takes to get justice for Sophie.'

Gibson raised his head, his face gaunt and weary. He looked at Stafford with watery eyes and nodded; not able or not wanting to speak, he put his right hand on Stafford's. They stayed like that, silent and still, until Gibson closed his eyes and drifted off to sleep. Stafford had no idea how long he'd been there when he withdrew his hand and walked silently back to the nurses' station. The same nurse was there; he didn't stop, but turned to her and nodded his thanks, she nodded her understanding. Stafford arrived back at his car totally unaware of the walk. He opened the door and sat for a while, until he came back to the moment. He'd promised Gibson he'd get justice for Sophie, and that's exactly what he was going to do.

Slowly he created a strategy in his mind, a blueprint he thought would work. They had little hard evidence on the top men in this ruthless organisation, so well had they covered their tracks. But having spilt so much blood, the syndicate bosses would have turned some of their troops against them. Amos and Miller's statements could be vital in bringing these people down. But Cooper, that was different, he'd plotted and planned with Edwards to douse Sophie Gibson in acid. Cooper hadn't thrown the acid, but he'd agreed on the course of action and now she was dead. As he thought about her suicide, he thought about his people hurt and killed for the sake of illegal profit. He cared about them all. Sometimes they could be such a burden, but they also made him feel so proud. Then there was Nicole flaming Martin – why could he not get her out of his head?

Settling back into the driving seat, he took out his mobile phone. As he set it in it's cradle, he noticed it was switched off. He'd forgotten to turn it back on after the phone call from Salisbury District Hospital. Immediately the phone rang; the desk sergeant at Eastleigh Police Station.

'Major Stafford, gotta tell you, Cooper's been bailed and has left the station as you requested…Uh, and I also thought you should know, Major, the DCI has apparently given him your number, to arrange a new interview. But the lads who—'

Stafford interrupted him, 'He did *what*?'

'Yeah, I know, I figured you must have upset him,' said the sergeant. Stafford shook his head in disbelief, but it was done, no point dwelling on it. The sergeant continued, 'The lads who did the forensic search on his truck mentioned they'd found an active tracking device, so his boss, or whoever owns the motor, can track it in real time. Just thought it might come in useful to know.' Stafford thanked him and ended the call.

We pulled in a few of those trucks from Weyhill, I wonder if they all have trackers? Got to be a way of using that knowledge to our advantage, surely?

About to put the phone away he saw he had several missed calls and a voicemail; it was from Cooper. He listened to it. Stunned with disbelief, he raised the phone in anger, but managed to resist smashing it on his steering wheel. He listened again, then a third time.

'*Hung out to dry*? I'll give you hung out to fucking dry.'

As he navigated the screens to call him, he received another call, this time from the head of the bomb disposal boys who had collected the grenade from Ryan Peters. He pressed the speaker button.

'Ah, is that Major Stafford?'

'Speaking.'

'Guess I should say *Rehashed* to start this conversation on the right note, so to speak.'

Stafford thought, *just get the fuck on with* it, but said, 'Good, well, in your own time.'

'Ah, yes, it's about the grenade we took from Captain Peters earlier.'

Stafford hoped his sigh hadn't sounded too obvious.

'I'm the Second Lieutenant in charge of this little band of brothers. We thought it imperative you should know, when we examined the grenade, while the outside shell was absolutely genuine – a beautiful vintage American pineapple World War Two grenade – its innards had been replaced totally and expertly.' He paused for breath, then continued, 'Well, long story short, pull the pin and *bosh*, up in bloody smoke! Deceased, expired, bereft of life. This little beauty was designed to kill the thrower.'

Both men remained silent for a protracted moment. Stafford started to speak, then realised he was speaking to a dead connection. Knowing Peters would be wondering where he'd got to, he called him.

'Hi, boss, thought you'd be up here by now.'

'Yeah, sorry about that, but after I left, I had a call from the Salisbury Burns Unit. There's no easy way of saying this, Ry – Sophie Gibson killed herself earlier today.'

'Oh, for Christ's sake, Staf... Poor kid, poor Lee.'

'Yeah, I know, so I went to see Lee in Winchester, sat with him for a while.'

'I hate to say it, but maybe—'

Stafford cut him short. 'Don't go there, Ry, it'll drive you mad.'

'So how did she do it?'

'I don't know, the doctor seemed evasive, desperate to get off the line, but believe me, there will be a bloody investigation.'

'But wasn't she in ICU?'

'Yes she was, I'm just telling you what I know, but we'll talk about it later. I'm also calling to let you know that the grenade Cooper had was booby-trapped. If he'd pulled the pin, he'd be long gone. And serve him bloody right.'

'Jesus! His masters really are nasty bastards, but I guess we knew that all along.'

'And the people down at Eastleigh found a real-time tracker on his motor, so his bosses can see where it is at any time.'

'Interesting. But odd we didn't get any feedback off the ones they took from Weyhill. Guess I need to follow up on that, boss,' said Peters. 'So where are you now?'

'I'm about to leave the hospital car park in Winchester and head up to you in Aldershot.'

'OK, so how would you feel about doing a detour first, while you're sort of down that way?'

'Yeah, course, what do you need?'

'Well, we've determined that the Porsche 718 Cayman was taken to our old friend Frank Healey at Southampton Metal Recycling. It'd be good if you could bend his ear about it. You know; see who organised it, and where it went.'

Stafford didn't answer immediately as he thought through the implications.

'Now that is useful. It means we've got a definite link between the earlier operation and Mr bloody Aksanov's hotel…and that's great, but at this stage I think it's another red herring. They're still playing head games with us. OK, Ry, I'll do a lightning visit to Frank Healey, then get up to you soonest and we'll take the fight to them,' he said. 'So what I need you to do now is get everyone who's been working on the investigation, including Nicole, the two agents who were looking after Marva and all the forensic techs, up in Aldershot nick for a briefing tomorrow morning at eight thirty. OK?'

'Yes, will do, boss, but there's another thing, while I've got you; the families of the two Asian blokes are coming down for three o'clock today to do the formal ID. We need to cover it, one way or another.'

'Yes, we do, Ry… I reckon I could do that on my way back from Healey's place. Consider it done.'

CHAPTER 38

Aksanov's Russian guests had spent most of the day on their phones, setting up the transfer of huge quantities of crack cocaine, MDMA and marijuana in its various forms. And heroin, cut with anything that came to hand: Fentanyl, paracetamol, flour, chalk and even talc. Enough gear to keep Aksanov's business afloat and his customers happy for the immediate future.

They had spoken to Aksanov's storemen at the World Citizen Hotel, and they'd chuckled at the Southern Washroom Services bins being used to store and transfer various drugs. The storemen told them how they used a plain van with stick-on-peel-off vinyl decals and signs showing *Southern Washroom Services* and listing all the services a company of that sort would offer: collection of ladies' sanitary products, sharps and clinical wastes… A vehicle with this kind of signage would be unlikely to be stopped and searched by police; it appeared totally convincing. For this alone, the Russians considered their time in Basingstoke had been well spent. Their London-based County Line couriers were always being stopped and searched by police. Or stopped and robbed by police and crooks alike. This happened because these bottom-feeders, their end-user dealers, liked to show off their newfound, and often short-lived wealth by driving around in pimped-up motors. Convincing them to use such a low-key vehicle could be a very painful business. The two men laughed as they discussed how many fingers would be lost on the way to introducing this change in working practices. They had spoken to Jamie Sweetman earlier about undertaking training sessions and knew a little of his working practices.

A visit to Whitelines nightclub was next on their itinerary. They wouldn't be accepting money as payment for this first shipment of drugs.

Aksanov, not wanting to confront Sheila, had arranged for one of his security guards to meet his guests at the club later that evening. The guard was under strict instructions to make sure the guests enjoyed all the club had to offer. Aksanov had arranged a private showing of the merchandise on offer as payment for the drugs. Having set the postcode into the sat nav, they arrived just after ten and were surprised to see a queue maybe sixty metres long and two or three people deep waiting to get in. A sight not seen often at London clubs, unless an A-list celebrity was about to make an entrance. Aksanov, anticipating the queue, had given them directions to the rear doors. Parking up, they walked across to the double doors, pressed the button on the keyless entry system and were met by a security guard. As they walked into the storage area, motion sensor lights lit up the space. The two Russians exchanged smiles as they spotted Southern Washroom Services bins stacked ready for collection. They nodded approvingly at each other; judging by the number of bins, the quantities would be even higher than Aksanov had suggested.

The older man laughed at his colleague's jest: 'It would take a brave policeman to open any of those bins.'

The Russian pair had wasted no time. Over the next few months their London organisation would be shuttling contraband goods up and down the M3 corridor. Any advantage they could gain to escape detection would be important. They realised that using Southern Washroom Services as cover might just give them that edge. Deliveries of the vast array of the drugs Aksanov required would start as soon as vans and signs were in place. Hygiene & Washroom Services (London) Ltd would start to operate when Aksanov made his first payment. Initially, they had been sceptical about the financial rewards, in what they considered to be nothing more than an urban backwater. But having seen the operation close up, they knew that, alongside the two clubs and hotel, Aksanov had granted numerous franchises to club and pub owners to discourage them from setting up in competition. They bought exclusively from him … or suffered severe consequences. This made the whole deal worthwhile, and gave them a sneaking admiration for Aksanov's business savvy. All they needed now was to collect their first payment.

The security guard took them up in the lift. They got out on the third floor and, by following a discreet corridor, avoided the areas used by the club's punters. The guard knocked once, then opened the door to TFS's office and ushered the visitors in. Sheila rose from behind her desk, leaned across and offered her hand, then waved them to sit in the two padded armchairs in front of the desk. Introductions out of the way, they took stock of each other. Sheila had a slight advantage, she had seen CCTV footage of the men as they moved around the hotel and she'd observed them making their way through the nightclub to her office. They had no information about her at all, but assumed she was Aksanov's most trusted and influential business partner, and this made her someone to be wary of.

But she didn't look dangerous; quite the opposite, in fact. Thirty-three years ago she came to the UK from Albania and was now sixty years old, and looked it. She wore little make-up, had thick salt-and-pepper hair cut into a neat bob that framed her pale, pleasant, motherly face. Unremarkable, she would be invisible to most people, most of the time. It was a look she aimed for. Her eyes; sharp, clear and almost black, gave a hint of an inner strength. The Russians were not used to dealing with women at the top, but they were astute enough to realise that this ordinary-looking *mamushka* must have extraordinary strength of character to achieve such an elevated position in a male-dominated, testosterone-driven business.

'So,' she said, turning the large computer monitor around to face them, 'your first shipment here is valued at sixty K net? Correct?'

The older man nodded, trying to place her accent. The younger one said, '*Da* – yes.'

'And Pavel has agreed to pay with merchandise instead of cash?' she continued in heavily accented English. She said this in her usual calm manner, but inside she was seething. Not with these two men, who she planned to do much more business with, but with Aksanov who had ridden roughshod over her and simply assumed she would agree to let her top girls go at ten grand a time. He hadn't even had the courage to discuss it. For her, this was the final straw. Not only had Aksanov been basking in the success of her innovations via the dark web, he had, against her advice, been trying to play with Stafford as a cat does a mouse. She had told him on more than one occasion it would be the undoing of them all. She was determined this would not happen.

'Yes,' the Russian said, 'we have agreed a value of ten thousand for each unit.'

Sheila bit her tongue. *We have agreed a value* – who the fuck did Aksanov think he was to agree a value without consulting her?

'OK, so first we have twenty-four images for you to look at. These are pictures from our online services. Where you see a flashing red light in the bottom right-hand corner, this means the girl is working tonight in one of the third-floor bedrooms. Click on the light and you will see her working, live. Press the stack of paper icon on the left and you will see a brief bio and a copy of her passport with any other identification documents we have provided for her. When you see a girl you are interested in, make a note of the number in the top-left corner. OK? Any questions?' she said as she slid a notepad, pen and a Wi-Fi mouse across the desktop to them.

The men looked at each other. The more she spoke, the easier it became to understand her. The older one opened his mouth, then slowly shook his head and looked back at Sheila, his mouth still open. Her brow furrowed as she anticipated his question. 'No, no, you have made things very clear,' he said.

The screen split into six pictures, two of them with flashing red lights. The older man clicked on one and the picture changed, showing the interior of a bedroom. On the bed, with his back up against the headboard, sat an elderly, overweight man, still wearing a vest and socks. His eyes were closed, and his pudgy hands gripped the shoulders of a woman lying alongside him. Naked, apart from a pair of extremely high-heeled black shoes, she was giving him a blow job, expertly and with some enthusiasm. The Russian changed back to the woman's profile picture. He studied it, then smiled and jotted down her number.

His colleague leaned close to the screen and said, 'Can we enlarge profile picture?'

'Yes,' said Sheila, 'just double-click the icon, top right.' He did as instructed and clicked through a few more profiles, examining each girl carefully.

'Do you guarantee the women are clean? Free from disease?' he said.

'The same guarantee you give that your merchandise is pure,' said Sheila, with a what-a-stupid-question look on her face. Leaning back in her chair, she looked from one to the other and said, using the only Russian swearword she knew, '*Blyad*, you'll be wanting virgins next.' As she finished speaking it occurred to her they could achieve that, for the right price. Then she thought, another time, for sure. Neither Russian could disguise his smile.

'I understand that you are no longer able to bring people across the Channel. How long before you run out of suitable women?' said the senior man.

Sheila let the silence stretch before answering. 'I'm not sure you grasp the full size of our operation. Since I persuaded Pavel to run this area, we have brought people across week in, week out. Those looking from outside, think we can't keep doing it – that we're going to get full up or some such bloody nonsense. Gentlemen, our network is huge. They pay to come here, then they earn their keep somewhere in our organisation, but – trust me on this, gentlemen – we have systems in place to ensure that the numbers coming in are balanced by, ah, how shall I put it? Hmm, balanced by the numbers going out one way or another will suffice.'

The visitors exchanged glances. By now they almost didn't notice her accent.

The older man said, 'Yes, we have heard about some of your, ah, outgoing methods. It may be another area we can explore to our mutual advantage, but Pavel seemed reluctant to show us the special operational suites you have at the hotel and here for this purpose.'

'Yes, Pavel said this was an area you were interested in, but I think he wants to move forward one step at a time. However, when and if we get that far, for your peace of mind, we do offer a guarantee that any donor we use will be disease-free, healthy and selected with great care. But that's further down the line, so let's finish here and get this up and running. Yes?' she said.

The two men nodded. It took a further twenty minutes to finalise their selection of merchandise. As they stood up to leave, the older man said, 'Excellent, thank you for your courtesy, Sheila, we will deliver your first consignment in two days. Please have the women ready, and prepare your staff to help offload Hygiene & Washroom Services stock.'

Sheila picked up her desk phone and called for the security guard to escort the Russians back to their car.

'We'll be ready, gentlemen, never fear,' she said, her accent more pronounced than ever as she shook each man's hand.

CHAPTER 39

It was clear to Anne Borley that Tony Amos was scared almost out of his wits. His police record, though extensive, was for petty stuff and now he was being questioned about the murder of one of his mates. Borley knew if he hadn't killed Winstone then he too must be on the hitman's list and had every reason to be scared. She was here to defend him, to make any charges against him disappear. Or at least, to negotiate a deal. Yet she knew his best and probably only chance of walking away from this unscathed – except maybe for a year or two in jail – was to tell Stafford and Co all he knew about the whole set-up. She had to convince him to give the investigating team anything and everything he knew about the criminal operation. But she knew if she did that, her chances of a successful defence were reduced to a plea of mitigation. She decided to give it to him straight.

'OK. Sit back, Tony, try to relax, take a few deep breaths and we'll start again.'

Amos shook his head forlornly, took a deep breath and blew out his cheeks. It took all of Borley's resolve not to wince as the blast of stale cigarettes hit her full in the face.

'Now, listen to me. Ordinarily, I would be advising you not to volunteer any information, but simply answer any questions they ask you. If you did that today, you would either be charged with some fairly minor offences and released on bail, or you would be released with no charge, free to go home.

'Christ, lady, never thought I'd be praying to get put away, but they still managed to get Matis, even when he was banged up in Winchester Prison. Seems they can get you, inside or out.'

'Come on, let's not look at the negatives, let's see what we can do to keep you safe.' Amos slumped further down in his chair as Borley continued, 'I think your best course of action is to look beyond the jobs you were paid or told to do and to think about what you've seen at the scrapyard in Southampton, then at the boat used for people and drug smuggling. Then think about the Weyhill site and what went on there, the weapons, immigrants and so on. Think about where you and other people fitted into the whole organisation. Name names, Tony, name names.'

When at last he responded, it was almost a whisper. Struggling to hold it together, his bottom lip trembled as he spoke.

'If I do that, I'm fucked.'

'Trouble is, Tony, if you don't, then, as you've said yourself, they're cleaning house, killing anyone who they think will grass them up.'

'But, woman, you're supposed to be defending me, not throwing me to the dogs.'

Borley shook her head and glared at him. 'You were asked to come here to talk about what happened when you took Winstone to the Aldershot flat. You haven't been arrested, you're free to go. If you tell the police and security services what you know, they will either place you under arrest or put you in a safe house, out of harm's way. Do you hear me, do you understand what I'm saying?'

'Yeah, I hear you – whatever I do, I'm dead in the fuckin' water.'

Borley realised that in his present state of mind, she was unlikely to get him to think straight.

'I'll get us something to eat, then talk to Major Stafford about how best to keep you safe. OK?'

His eyes were downcast, his shrug half-hearted as he said, 'Whatever.' Then, as she stood to go, he said, 'Maybe if I went to see Aksanov, talk to him. What do you think?'

'I think, Tony, that would be like walking into the lion's den.'

He slumped back in his chair, hands thrust in his pockets.

She stepped out of the room, went to the downstairs restroom. There were still a few packs of sandwiches in the vending machine and a couple of packs of cheese and onion crisps. She pressed a few buttons and fed in a tenner. Gathering up the food and change, she sat at the nearest table, called Stafford and outlined the situation.

'Look, Anne, I'm in Southampton at the moment on other business… I need time to get things sorted here, but from what you've told me, I think you should see DCI Talbot; get his officers to interview him. If you advise him to put his hands up to various criminal activities, enough for them to charge him, then he'll be safe for a while, at least. They might put him in the safe house with Miller. But make it clear that unless he starts naming names, they'll simply send him on his way. Oh, and while you're there, is Cooper still around?'

'Yes, he's still sitting here, patiently waiting to be interviewed. He's in much the same boat as Amos.'

Stafford deliberated a moment before saying, 'These cowardly bastards have been taking us for fools – it's time we took control, made something happen. Sophie Gibson, the woman who we're convinced Cooper and his buddy Edwards doused in acid, jumped off a building and killed herself because of her injuries. I don't care if Cooper and Amos are cut loose. Tell Cooper, we'll reschedule the interview for later in the week. His car will be in the compound; I know forensics have finished with it. And Amos, well, see if Talbot wants to charge him, then get them both bailed and turf them out.'

'Do you think that's wise, Major? They'll both be in danger.'

Borley reverting to calling him by his title didn't escape his notice, but he ignored it and said, 'Yes, I know they will. D'you think it's all right when they're being a danger to others, then? And now you want us to babysit?'

'Of course I don't think that, but I don't want to throw them to the lions either, and Amos is now saying he might try talking to Aksanov.'

'The choice is theirs, Anne; name names, put their hands up and get charged or leave, it's that simple, and I don't care which they choose. But when you see Cooper, tell him he can't go home, his flat's now a crime scene.'

'What? What the hell are you trying to do here, Major? You said he was handing himself in because he didn't want to blow up the safe house, and you know they're both going to be hunted down by their masters.'

'Justice, Anne, justice.'

'Major, that sounds like rough justice to me.'

'Ms Borley, these are big men when they're dishing it out to others. I'm only interested in justice for the likes of Sophie Gibson, Garfield Lewis and those poor sods brought across the Channel for slave labour and worse.'

'So why can't he go home?'

'Because it's crawling with cops trying to find out who killed his buddy, Edwards,' he said, resisting the urge to say, *try to keep up Ms Borley*. He ended the call.

She sat for a long moment staring at the blank screen of her phone. That, she thought, with a shiver, was a side to Major Stafford she had not seen before. But somehow she knew she couldn't and wouldn't hold it against him, she decided if the police bailed Cooper, then it wasn't down to her to tell him not to go back to his flat; or the reason why. It was a moment or two before she started to walk back to the interview room and Amos.

Once Amos had been released on bail, he knew he couldn't spend the rest of his life waiting for Aksanov's axe to fall. He needed an ally, someone well in with Aksanov. Amos had done a few jobs for and alongside Jamie Sweetman in the past, including most recently collecting the Porsche Cayman. And they'd got on OK, never a problem between them. He decided to call him.

Sweetman answered almost instantly and Amos, briefly tongue-tied, hesitated, then said, 'Listen, Jamie, it's Tony Amos. I hear Edwards is dead, so that's him, Winstone and the Polish kid. I reckon Aksanov's getting rid of the people the law's been talking to. And I've just been bloody bailed again so I need to talk to Aksanov – and I need someone to back me up, tell him I'm gold, you know? Could you tell him we've worked together, tell him it was me that pulled out the Porsche. Yeah?' There was silence on the phone. Amos took it away from his ear, looked at it; there was still a connection. Then, finally, Sweetman's voice was heard.

'OK, Tone, tell you what, come over to Sheila's office in Whitelines and we'll suss something out. Mind you, it's always best to talk to him at casino chuck-out time, because he's knackered, but happy, having taken plenty of money!'

'Brill, thanks Jamie, that's fucking great, mate. When shall I get up there?'

A silence, shorter this time, as Sweetman worked out a suitable timescale.

CHAPTER 40

Ray Cooper was well pissed off. He'd been kept hanging around Eastleigh Police Station for hours. Now he'd been bailed and told he could go, he'd chewed a couple of his fingernails down to the quick, had been outside smoking more cigarettes than even he was used to. One bit of unexpected good fortune; that arrogant fucker, the DCI, had only gone and given him Stafford's number.

He'd had enough and, marching up to the desk sergeant, he said, 'For Christ's sake how long does it take your lot to get my motor? Haven't they finished mucking about with it yet?' The desk sergeant asked him for the vehicle's registration number.

'I told you before, it's a bloody pool car, mate, I've got no bloody idea, but it's not likely you've got too many Mercedes X-Class pickups being torn apart by your forensic boys, is it?'

The officer gave him a hard stare, 'As it happens we've got a bunch of 'em from your Andover lot.' He picked up the desk phone.

'Have you finished with Mr Cooper's Mercedes pickup?... Yep, the last one in... good. All clear to go? Right, thanks.' He replaced the receiver and said to Cooper,

'Yep, they're bringing it round to the car park now.' Cooper nodded a curt thank you and left. As he drove out of the police compound, he pondered his next move. Aksanov would know by now he hadn't carried out the job; he knew he was a marked man.

'Fuck you, Stafford, fuck you,' he said, as he bashed the steering wheel with his palms. He found his mobile, punched Stafford's name. It went to voicemail. He left a message. 'Stafford, you arsehole, what d'you think you're playing at? Fucking hung me out to dry here. When I'm tryin' to do you lot a favour.'

He made his way to the M3 and headed towards Basingstoke. He knew he couldn't stay at the flat; Aksanov would surely have that in his sights. But he needed a weapon, clothes, money and a few bags of poke for dealing, and maybe just a hit or two for himself, purely for medicinal purposes, he reasoned. Then he remembered Kurt. *Oh what a flamin' shambles, how the hell can I take him with me?* Then, *How can I not take him with me? I can't just leave him there. Jesus, he's gonna bring us both down.* Though the day was cool, he wiped sweat from his eyes. Cold streams were running down his back. He powered up the air conditioning, came off the motorway at Junction 6 and made his way to the old town. As he drove, excitement surged within; he was on the edge of something. Maybe a trap? Maybe a spur to action? The hairs on the back of his neck and arms prickled as he steered into his road. No sweat now, just ice-cold calm. *Well, wasn't this what it was all about – survival; them and us? But here, not like Iraq or Afghanistan, there were no IEDs, no 40 degree heat, no rag-heads, but maybe highly trained killers in air-conditioned motors.*

The ice-cold calm didn't last long. As he got closer, he could see a massive police presence. He almost stood the car on end, braking heavily as he pulled into the nearside kerb. Fighting the adrenalin rush and the urge to flee, he jumped out of the vehicle and crossed to the far side of the road. Unsure which house was demanding so much police attention, he wandered slowly towards the action. Police vehicles, some plain, some with the distinctive blue and yellow Battenberg pattern, blocked the road completely. Uniformed police officers were trying to control a crowd of onlookers and the usual media melee of photographers, newspaper journalists, radio and TV crews. Leaning against a garden wall some fifty metres from the flat, he watched techs in forensic suits and plainclothes police officers walk in and out of the front door to his building. He pushed off the wall, jogged back to his car. He sat for a moment, gathering his thoughts, steadying his breathing. This level of police presence meant it had to be a death, a violent death. He slumped in the seat, pulled out his cigarettes, lit one, took a deep drag. His immediate thought was one of relief. If it was Edwards, he couldn't bring them both down now. He fired up the ignition, did a careful three-point turn, checked his mirrors and drove back the way he came. He was almost at the M3 when the wave of guilt hit. Like the ice-cold calm, it didn't last long. He rolled down the window and threw his cigarette out.

Cooper drove on for half a mile or so, pulled into a side road and rolled to a halt, took out another cigarette and lit it. He pulled heavily on it, and drew the smoke slowly down. Leaning back, he blew it out in a slow stream.

Fucking Paul Stafford, he thought, I should be safely banged up in a prison cell now, not running for my life. He couldn't help but smile at the irony. As he contemplated his situation, he realised that Aksanov must have set the whole thing up. Getting him out of the flat, supposedly on a mission to blow Brandon Miller to kingdom come, had left Edwards alone and helpless in an unlocked flat. He realised that two violent deaths miles apart would have stretched Stafford's investigators even further. *Fuck*, he thought, *I could do with a drink*. He knew the area well. Finishing his cigarette, he flicked the butt out of the window and headed towards the railway station. Cruising past, he entered Bunnian Place and parked next to the Queens Arms. It looked out of place here, stuck right on the corner, an olde worlde white-painted pub dwarfed by the surrounding commercial and industrial buildings and terraced housing. It looked like it should be out in the country, surrounded by fields and grass and trees. Inside, there were a number of rooms, each small, warm and cosy. Black wooden beams were everywhere, walls and ceiling. Cooper had been here a few times, but wasn't a regular. He liked that, dressed as he normally was – suit, white shirt and tie – he blended in.

It was now early evening and the pub was quiet, midway between end of lunch and the dinner crowd. Only five or six people were drinking alone. Three or four couples, probably co-workers from the nearby offices, leaning in close. Whispered conversations, a hand on a knee, maybe on the verge of developing relationships. He strolled up to the L-shaped bar, he sat on one of the stools running down one side, leaned forward and examined the range of spirits on offer. A short, overweight, blonde-haired barmaid walked over, polishing a glass. The red dress she wore was too high at the bottom, too low at the top.

'What'll you have?' she said.

'I'll have a pint of Doom Bar and a whisky chaser from that bottle with the bird on the front,' he said, pointing to a bottle of whisky on the shelf behind her.

She finished polishing the glass and put it on the bar, turned, looked at the bottle.

'Ah, yes. The Famous Grouse.'

'Yeah, yeah, that's the one.' He smiled, and said, 'I don't ask for it by name, because I usually get, "Well, I like the job, but I don't get paid enough."'

She stared at him for a second, frowned and said with a sour face, 'Well, I don't.' With that, she poured his drinks, took the offered money and slammed his change down on the bar. Nonplussed, he gazed down at her ample bosom, shuddered a little, picked up the change and carried his drinks to a small vacant table, away from the window. He sat back against the wall. It was automatic, and sometimes he couldn't remember why he did it – back to the wall, facing the door, away from windows – just second nature. He shrugged, picked up his Famous Grouse, then smiled inwardly as he put it back on the table and downed half his pint instead. Once a rebel always a rebel, he thought.

CHAPTER 41

Aksanov keyed 014 into his laptop, the tracker number to the car Cooper had been driving. The map displayed on the screen navigated its way from Browndown to Eastleigh. The flashing green arrow showed *Eastleigh Police Station*. In disbelief, he enlarged the image on the monitor and checked again. No doubt about it, the motor was at Eastleigh nick.

'Where do we find these people?' he said out loud. 'Bloody idiot, how could he get picked up before he'd even done the job?' He smirked, realising it would have been much harder to pick him up if he had completed his task. But his humour didn't last; he assumed that by now, Cooper would be spilling his guts, bargaining for leniency. He slammed the laptop closed, took out a cigarette. He hadn't been too worried about Brandon Miller. Miller had only been involved at the Weyhill operation and in a small number of deliveries. Aksanov reasoned Miller must have done a deal with the law, hence his incarceration in one of their safe houses. Offering Cooper the bogus chance to redeem himself after the hotel car park fiasco and his various other cock-ups looked to be a way of getting rid of another weak link. Now that had backfired, he realised

Cooper had plenty of ammunition for a leniency deal. He lit his cigarette and took a long drag. Should he get Howard Neilson to go down to Eastleigh to try and get Cooper to ditch the duty solicitor, Anne something-or-other? Then he realised, as soon as Cooper knew he'd been on a suicide mission, he wouldn't go near anyone Aksanov sent. So who did Neilson use to shut up the Polish kid in Winchester Prison? Perhaps he could be brought into play again? But that would depend on too many coincidences. However, Cooper needed to be stopped, as a warning to others – fuck up, step out of line, get pulled in, you suffer the consequences, he reasoned.

He shook his head, shrugged, opened the laptop and again keyed in 014. Surprisingly the green arrow was still flashing, but moving now, heading for the M3 and Winchester. He watched for five or six minutes. The flashing green arrow cruised past Junction 9 for Winchester, and on towards Basingstoke.

'And that, my friend, will do you no fucking good at all,' said Aksanov quietly as he stubbed out his cigarette. He watched as the green arrow flashed its way from the M3 onto the slip road at Junction 6. He realised with some amusement that Cooper was heading back to his flat. Now definitely interested in seeing Cooper's reaction, he opened the bottom drawer in his desk and took out a bottle of Jack Daniel's, fished around to find a tumbler and poured himself a good measure Then with another cigarette in hand, he settled down to watch the flashing green arrow. It snaked its way into Basingstoke old town and, after navigating through narrow side streets, it stopped. Aksanov leaned in towards the screen and, with two fingers, enlarged the image; Cooper had stopped some way short of his flat. Aksanov smirked again, he knew there was only one reason Cooper hadn't continued to the house itself; the presence of the law. Leaning back in his chair, he took a swig of whiskey and savoured the warm, slow burn. His eyes were fixed on the arrow, urging it on, keen to see Cooper's next move. The arrow was still. Leaning forward, bouncing on the edge of his seat, he mentally pushed it on, and the arrow moved again; this time, pointing in the opposite direction. Realising he'd been holding his breath, he let out a sigh.

'Sensible move, Ray, sensible move,' his voice was almost a whisper.

For fifteen or twenty minutes the arrow appeared to move randomly. Aksanov laughed out loud and said, 'Yeah, Ray, come on, Ray, it's decision time. Your life could depend on your next choice.' Face now close to the screen, his cigarette smouldering in the half-full ashtray, he watched as the green arrow changed direction again. It was now moving slowly on the Alencon Link road then took a left into Bunnian Place. Fascinated, he shook his head in disbelief, laughed out loud and sneered, 'Fucking idiot.' Slamming both palms on the desk he shouted, 'Wrong move, Ray my man, wrong fucking move.' The flashing green arrow was now stationary in the car park of the Queens Arms public house.

Aksanov picked up his mobile phone, made a call; it went to voicemail. He left no message, but redialled; Jamie Sweetman answered on the third ring.

——————————— ‖ ———————————

Cooper downed the whisky and, finishing his pint, walked back to the bar with both glasses. The barmaid sauntered across, this time with a smile on her face.

'Yeah, very good, I get it now, famous grouse, good. Same again?'

Cooper managed to resist the urge to say *duh*, nodded and returned the smile half-heartedly.

Back at his table, he contemplated his next move. The adrenalin he'd felt as he saw the police swarming around his flat was now working against him, and he felt shattered. He just wanted to sleep, but knew sleep wasn't an option. This time, downing the whisky, he pulled out his mobile and selected Stafford's number. Thoughtfully he laid the phone down next to his pint. What will it be? he mused, Doom Bar or Stafford? Stafford or Doom Bar? Doom Bar won hands down and he drank half of it in one swallow. Now he was ready for Stafford. He picked up the mobile, touched the screen and held it to his ear, laying into Stafford as soon as he answered.

'What the fuck are you lot playing at, Stafford? What's going on at my flat? It's swarming. I was ready to answer your questions hours ago. I was gonna spill it all, turn Queen's evidence or whatever it's called. I've even got DVDs I was gonna give you.'

He picked up his pint and took another swig. As he did, he noticed some of the other drinkers were staring at him. He was talking too loudly. He stood and walked through the bar to the half-glazed door that led to the smoking area at the rear of the pub. Leaning up against one of the wooden roof supports, he took out another cigarette and lit it. 'Cooper, are you still there?' Stafford said through the phone's speaker.

'Yeah, I'm still here, you—'

'For Christ's sake Cooper, shut up and listen – where are you now?'

'Why the fuck should I tell you that?'

'Just shut up and answer the bloody question.'

'For what it's got to do with anything, I'm in the Queens Arms in Basingstoke.'

'OK, how did you get there? Did you drive in the motor we brought into Eastleigh nick?'

Cooper had calmed down but was starting to feel nervous, he answered, 'Yeah, why?'

'Listen to me, you need to get away from there fast. And not in that motor, it's got a tracker on it.'

'What?' You sneaky bastards!'

'Not us, you fool, your bosses.'

Cooper froze, stock still. He felt the hairs on his arms and the back of his neck stand up.

'Shit,' he said, stuffing the phone into his jacket pocket and picking up his three-quarter-empty pint glass. Moving quickly, but slightly unsteadily, to the rear of the pub, he peered cautiously around the corner that led onto the car park. In the growing evening gloom he was relieved at first to see a black Mercedes pickup truck still there – just not where he'd parked it. Looking further around the parking area, his stomach lurched as he realised his truck was precisely where he'd left it. 'Fuck,' he said, almost a whisper. He knew straight away it would be Sweetman.

He walked back inside and into the Gents lavatory; no one was there. He selected a cubicle and emptied the remaining beer into the pan then, holding the glass upside down, he swung it gently from side to side, hitting it against the toilet. With scarcely a sound, the top edge and more of the glass fell away, leaving three uneven, vicious, jagged edges. Walking cautiously out of the loo, glass in his right hand down by his thigh, he risked a look around the door jamb. Nothing had changed and there was no sign of Sweetman. He moved back, heading for the smoking area.

Outside, in the dusk, he looked across to the car park; he could see only the outlines of the cars and reflections from the lights in the smoking area. He needed somewhere to stand out of sight, somewhere he could see who was coming through the door, before they saw him. The only cover of any sort was the nine-inch square wooden roof supports to the smoking area. Not ideal, but he only needed cover for a split second to identify friend or foe. A split second to make his move. He didn't have much choice. As he propped himself against the wooden support, he felt the buzz of excitement he always got during a call to action.

CHAPTER 42

Jamie Sweetman had been in the middle of fifty one-arm push-ups when his mobile phone chimed. Annoyed, he sank face first to the floor and contemplated not answering it. It stopped, but before he could continue with his routine, it chimed again. Using both arms, he pushed himself off the floor and grabbed the phone.

'Cooper failed,' Aksanov's voice said on speaker. 'He got pulled into Eastleigh Police HQ, but they've bailed him. Stupid sod's still driving the Merc pickup. He's in the Queens Arms in Bunnian Place. He needs sorting, Jamie, and fast.'

Sweetman chuckled to himself at the *Jamie* and thought, *crawling bastard*, but said, 'I can be there in fifteen minutes. I'll bung the phone on Bluetooth, so shout if he moves on.' Pushing the mobile into his jeans pocket, he pulled on a black hoody, walked through to his bedroom and took his Glock 26 from the bedside cabinet. Unwrapping it from the lint-free cloth, he wiped the gun clean of any traces of oil or grease. Every time he took the gun out on a job, whether he had fired it or not, he cleaned it, oiled it and carried out various checks. It wasn't a chore; in his line of work it was essential. He rubbed his index finger along the cartridge-loaded indicator; there was one in the chamber. He slid out the magazine: fully loaded with ten nine-millimetre rounds. Satisfied, he slipped the magazine back. Pushing the weapon into his waistband and pulling down the hem of his hoody, he picked up his wallet and keys, and left the house.

He knew the pub; it would take him less than ten minutes to drive there. As he got close, he kept a watchful eye on the vehicles coming towards him, knowing that anyone leaving the pub would have to drive back down Bunnian Place. Heading the opposite way led to a dead end in the station car park. Though a couple of vehicles passed him, neither were Mercedes pickups. He cruised around the far corner of the public house and slowed, taking in the half dozen or so vehicles parked there. He smiled thinly as he saw a black Mercedes truck, identical to the one he was driving. He reversed into a space at right angles to Cooper's motor. He killed the engine and sat for a while, trying to remember the pub's layout. Strangely, the pub had two doors along the front, but he couldn't recall if it had a rear door. Picking up his mobile, he found a street view, which showed a small rear garden with wooden decking and a covered paved area for smokers.

Getting out of the car, he pulled up his hood and walked across the car park. Though it was dark he could clearly see the little wicket gate in the low wall surrounding the garden. Lights in the smoking area created an eerie mix of movement and shadows as moths battered themselves against the glass.

Sweetman knew Cooper was a smoker, but seeing no one in the smoking area, he walked around the pub and in through the main front door. Inside the doorway, he only needed milliseconds to take in the half dozen or so drinkers in the bar. Cooper wasn't among them. The barmaid was looking at him expectantly; making what seemed to be an attempt to push his hood down, he rushed forward pointing at the toilet sign, indicating an urgent need before ordering. She caught on, smiled and nodded. Sweetman sped through the bar to the Gents. As he rounded the corner and pushed the door open, he pulled up his hood and slipped his right hand under his hoody on to his gun. No one was using the urinals or the wash basins. He walked forward two or three paces and pushed each of the four cubicle doors open. They were empty. He turned, walked out into the little hallway between the Gents and the half-glazed door to the garden. With a sweep of his head he took in the lit-up smoking area and the darkness beyond. It appeared empty. He gripped the handle, and slowly opened the door. Right hand still on his hidden gun, he moved forward a pace, then another.

II

Cooper froze when he saw Sweetman move past the half-glazed door and pause. He watched with dismay as Sweetman pulled up his hood and disappeared into the Gents toilet. Cooper's first instinct was to retreat, to run, but he knew if he ran now, he'd likely never stop. He tried to make himself smaller behind the timber pillar, aware he'd have a fraction of a second to react. He cursed inwardly as Sweetman came back out of the toilet, hood still up. His only chance of hurting Sweetman with the glass now was limited to smashing it directly into his face. Christ, he thought, what a mistake getting here with no weapon. Shit, if only he'd been able to get back to his flat for a knife, or even brass fucking knuckles, anything. But here he was, about to fight for his life with a broken beer glass. Even though his thoughts were dire, he couldn't stop an edgy grin, a grin of resignation.

Sweetman stood behind the door for a second before pushing it open. Now Cooper could see he had his right hand under the waistband of his hoody. Christ, he thought, he's got a fucking gun. He can't be gonna use that in a pub garden, can he? Jesus, I heard he was a psycho, but he should come with a fuckin' health warning. Rule nothing out, mate, you know what you need to do; get your retaliation in first.

In the blink of an eye, Sweetman took a pace through the doorway. Cooper tensed, ready to act. Sweetman hesitated, his left hand came up to his face, he slid the hood back a shade, as if to give him better peripheral vision.

Cooper, with left hand gripping the pillar for purchase, right hand gripping the jagged glass, swung in front of the pillar. Yelling at the top of his voice, he thrust the glass directly at Sweetman's face. With lightning speed, Sweetman's right hand shot out, trying to ward off the blow, gun still in hand. He managed to cover most of his face, but left the inside of his wrist and palm exposed. The jagged glass smashed into pieces as it cut deep into the exposed flesh. Blood spurted from the wounds and the Glock crashed to the floor as Sweetman raised his left hand. Cooper ducked back, but, realising Sweetman was trying to staunch the flow of blood, grabbed the pistol and crashed it into the side of Sweetman's head. The hood softened the blow, but Sweetman was still brought to his knees. With adrenalin pumping at a rate of knots, Cooper was about to make his escape, then realised he may never get another chance like this, and took half a pace back, aiming the pistol at Sweetman's head. His finger tightened on the trigger, his hand began to tremble, and he used his left hand to steady it. Shaking his head in exasperation, he lowered the gun.

'Fuck you,' he said, 'I don't want to get life for killing a piece of shit like you.' Instead he swung a kick at Sweetman's groin. Sweetman groaned as he crashed face first onto the decking. Cooper hesitated, contemplating sticking the boot in again. He took a pace back, and said with a sneer, 'Don't get up, I can find my own way out.'

A flurry of movement behind the half-glazed door helped make up his mind. He ran through the little garden into the car park. Reaching the front of Sweetman's motor, he raised the pistol and fired a shot into the nearside tyre, swung right and shot out the offside one. Rushing towards the back of the Mercedes he fired into the offside rear. Stuffing the gun into his waistband as he ran, he fumbled in his pockets until he found the key to his vehicle. He clicked the fob and almost cheered as the orange lights flashed the car open. He scrambled in, and with a squeal of tyres, smell of smoke and burning rubber, drove out onto Bunnian Place. Driving towards the station, his mind was racing.

He couldn't go back to his flat and he couldn't stay in the truck for long as both Aksanov and the police would soon track him down. There was bound to be CCTV and ANPR cameras around the station area. He needed a different motor, and fast. Approaching the roundabout entrance to the station, vehicles were busy going in and out of the dropping-off zone, slowing his progress. The car immediately in front of him, a blue VW Polo, had no passengers, just a lone driver. It stopped at the roundabout to allow traffic from his right to pass. Cooper slowed, but didn't stop. As he hit the rear end of the Polo, it lurched forward a few feet. Cooper leapt from his truck and ran towards the Polo driver's door, arms outstretched in a conciliatory manner.

The Polo driver clambered out and dashed to the rear of his car, shouting, 'You stupid bugger, are you pissed?' That was as far as he got. Cooper crashed his right fist into the Polo driver's left temple and the unexpected blow knocked him spark out; he hit the deck unconscious. Cooper squeezed himself into the Polo and roared away, heading for the M3, adjusting the seat as he went. As he drove, he began to think of Sweetman; he must have been to their flat and had almost certainly been responsible for the massive police presence there. *Sweetman killed Edwards under orders from Aksanov, and now he's gunning for me. Christ, I should have killed the bastard.* Taking the next exit off the ring road, he headed towards the old town.

CHAPTER 43

It had taken Stafford less than half an hour to get to Southampton Metal Recycling's yard. Parking up outside the blue corrugated metal fence surrounding the compound, he got out of the car and walked towards the main gates. The yard was heaving with men on fork-lift trucks and in JCB and CAT excavators, all shifting scrap metal and lifting scrapped cars to the crusher. Deciding to use the little wicket gate in the blue, ten-foot-high metal double gates, he slid the bolt back and walked across the compound to the Portakabin office.

Parked alongside was the recovery vehicle used to remove the Porsche Cayman from the World Citizen Hotel. Stafford pulled out his phone and took a picture of it for proof of the connection between the hotel and Frank Healey. There was no sign of the sports car. Reaching the office, he banged on the metal door, pulled it open and stepped inside. The office, though small, was surprisingly modern, clean and well appointed. Healey was sitting behind a contemporary workstation, tapping the keys of a top-of-the-range laptop. As Stafford walked towards him, he stood and reached his hand across the desk. He wasn't a big man, maybe five feet nine inches, maybe 185 pounds, but with the shoulders of a light heavyweight boxer. He had a rugged, weather-beaten complexion, a number two buzz cut, and exuded the confidence of a man used to getting his own way.

Stafford ignoring the outstretched hand said, 'What? You want to be my friend now, Frank?'

'Well, Major Stafford, you found fuck all to charge us with last time you were here, so I'm just showing there's no hard feelings,' said Healey.

'Ah, so that's how you see it? From our point of view, there were plenty of problems here, unfortunately the CPS decided we didn't have enough evidence to guarantee a conviction. But that doesn't mean we've stopped trying.'

'That's bollocks. All you had on me was allowing a couple of dodgy dinlos to park their vehicles here and I didn't check two of my drivers' CVs well enough. But soon as I saw the error of my ways, I sacked 'em both,' he said, smiling broadly. Spreading his hands wide he continued, 'So what is it you want now?'

'The recovery truck in the yard, whose is it?' said Stafford

'It's registered, as you well know, to this yard and me. Why?'

'What happened to the Porsche Cayman you pulled out of the World Citizen Hotel with it?' Healey's eyes widened almost imperceptibly. Stafford said, 'No point in lying, Frank. Ask yourself how would I know about the car if I hadn't seen it?'

'Lying? Me? Why would I lie?' There was silence in the room for a moment, before Healey broke it.

'Maybe it was a figment of your imagination? Or maybe you don't like people who drive decent motors? You still driving that ancient piece of shite Volvo?'

Stafford couldn't help smile, he said, 'Yes, Frank, and it's called low profile.'

'Low profile? Low profile? That's a stupid name for a car. It's a piece of crap, that's what it's called.' Again there was silence in the room, and again Healey broke it.

'Well, that's one thing about us, Stafford, we can disagree, but it doesn't affect our strong and lasting relationship.'

'The only relationship I'm interested in is your relationship with that Porsche.'

'OK, I gets a call from a client, he tells me he's staying at a hotel in Basingstoke, and he's going back to Pakistan. Meanwhile he's flogged his motor – the aforementioned Porsche – to a fella in Bosnia, and could we ship it out if he emails us the details? We organised a price, he paid, we picked up his motor and the documents; simple as.'

'So where's the motor now? I didn't see it in the yard.'

'We don't muck about here, Major; it's in a container, and likely halfway across the English Channel by now.'

'That sounds highly efficient.'

'One of the advantages of working on the River Itchen and close to the docks.'

'And of course you've got all the documents to prove this?'

'If I need to. And if you've got a warrant.'

Stafford shrugged. 'So what's this customer's name and how did he get to know about you?'

'Told me his name was Ravani. Never could get on with his first name, Abduk or some such. Me? I called him My-duck, but he never understood the joke. He lives up in the Midlands, but he likes to buy and sell nice motors. We've done a bit of business over the years.'

'So he's a friend, then?' Healey hesitated, screwed up his face. 'Nah, I wouldn't call him a friend, more like a business acquaintance.'

'Well, Frank, the bad news is you won't be doing any more business with him; he and another Asian gentleman were both found dead, in a flat used by some of your dodgy employees in Aldershot.'

Healey looked directly at Stafford. 'It comes to us all in the end, Major. And like I said, soon as I realised they were dodgy, I sacked 'em. Anyone living there now is nothing to do with me.'

'So, if you sacked them, who was driving the truck when it picked up the Porsche?'

Healey began to look through desk drawers, hunting around in each.

'That doesn't look quite so efficient, Frank. It wasn't that long ago, I'd have thought the name would be on the tip of your tongue.'

Healey's eyes bored into Stafford.

'But don't worry, we can always check it on the hotel CCTV.'

'I thought that it had—' said Healey, stopping mid-spiel.

'Thought it had what, Frank? Been destroyed? Well yes, it had, but we were lucky, one of our lads drove in using his dash cam. Got it all down on film.'

'Then you'll know it was Tony Amos.'

Bonus, thought Stafford, who said, 'So if there was nothing dodgy going on, why was that so hard to remember?'

Healey folded his arms across his chest, did the staring thing again, but said nothing.

'How well do you know Floyd Winstone?' asked Stafford, changing tack. He could see Healey was thrown for a second.

'Floydy? I don't really know him. He worked out of Weyhill, so he occasionally came over here in a truck either dumping scrap or collecting electronic waste for their cleaning operation over there.'

Stafford's mobile vibrated in his pocket. He flinched, not wanting to take the call. It continued to vibrate. Reluctantly he pulled it out and checked the caller ID.

'I need to get this, Frank,' he said standing, accepting the call as he walked out into the yard. It was Ryan Peters.

'Sorry to interrupt yet again, boss, but we haven't talked about Nicole and PC Whitley's discovery in Cooper and Edwards' flat.'

'So come on, tell me.'

'It's bloody brilliant. They found the two dead Asian guys' wallets and bank cards. But best of all, they found their mobile phones.'

'Christ, that is brilliant,' said Stafford, not wanting to say Hawkins had already told him. Then he remembered what Healey had said only a few moments before. 'Hang on, Ry, Frank Healey said he'd had a call from Ravani, saying he was staying in a hotel in Basingstoke. We need to find out if they did in fact register there.'

'Trouble is, we're going to need a warrant for that,' said Peters.

'Yes, maybe. But don't worry, I'll find a way. So did you get anything from the phones?'

'No, not yet. They're password-protected, but the technical boys have them – they're trying to get round the encryption system, so it might take a while.'

'Regardless, it'll be useful to get some info on what those two likely lads were doing down here. Ry, that's good work, so say well done to, uh, Whitley and Nicole for me, yeah?'

'Certainly will, boss.'

Stafford terminated the call, walked the few paces back to Healey's office and stepped inside. Healey hadn't moved.

'So,' he said, 'are we done here?'

'For now, Frank. For now.'

CHAPTER 44

Stafford stepped out of the office and walked to his car, feeling hungrier than he had for days. Next stop lunch, he thought. He drove out of Southampton and got on to the M3. He stuffed Jack Bruce's album *Songs For A Tailor* into the CD player. The music swept over him and he almost overshot Junction 9, the slip road that led to the services.

Parked up, he walked across to the burger bar, joined a short queue and ordered a cheeseburger, fries and a regular coffee. Collecting his meal and adding a stirring stick and three sachets of milk, he found himself a tall stool; one of many lined up against a narrow, Formica-topped counter facing a window. As he unwrapped the burger, he found himself thinking about his three o'clock meeting with the families of the two dead Asian men.

He understood from the officer at West Midlands Police that these two were not innocent victims, but out-and-out bad lads. Gangsters, involved in some pretty heavy shit. Drugs, prostitution, extortion, protection, money lending, money laundering. Stafford did not relish this meeting. He'd been told their wives were coming and were being driven by Buzdar's younger brother. On one level,

Stafford felt sorry for the women and any children, but in the scheme of things he knew they'd have been happy to accept the rewards of their husbands' criminality. Stafford's attitude was: if you choose to stand close to the fire, don't cry when you get burned.

Noting with surprise that he'd finished his cheeseburger, he took the lid off his coffee and added the three sachets of milk, stirring it as he picked off the few remaining fries. Lunch finished, he headed out to the car and Basingstoke and North Hants Hospital. He knew he was going to be early, but though he was aware of where the hospital was, he'd never been there. He followed the signposts and eventually came off the A340 and into the hospital grounds.

Having no idea where the mortuary was, he followed the one-way system until he spotted an entrance into a building called the Overton Unit. He parked and walked across to it. He asked at the reception desk for directions. Back outside, he turned left and continued walking; he saw a single-storey red-brick building, with dark green double doors and a window on the left-hand side. The mirror and opaque striped window, matched the description he'd been given. There was no sign on the front of the unit. Each door had a small window in the top half and a battered metal panel protected the bottom two and a half feet. He pushed the doors, they were locked. Looking around he noticed the audio entry pad on the wall to the left of the doors. Pushing the green button, it crackled into life; Stafford leaned in close.

A woman's voice said, 'How can I help?'

'I'm Major Stafford, ah, for Mr Ravani and Mr Buzdar.'

'Ah, yes, we're expecting you. Come on through, we're the first door on the left.'

This time the doors opened at his push. Inside, he was in a corridor decorated in typical institutional style: shiny concrete floor painted mid-green, walls painted light green, all lit by a row of fluorescent tubes running dead centre down the corridor ceiling. He tapped the first door on the left and walked in.

The office was small, maybe twelve feet square. It housed two desks, both at right angles to the window, which Stafford could now see was one-way security glass. There were two gun-metal grey filing cabinets behind each desk. Against the right-hand wall was a row of four chairs, black woollen upholstery on the seats and backrests. A woman wearing green scrubs came out from behind a desk holding out her hand. As she moved towards him, Stafford registered dark eyes, dark hair, pale complexion, attractive and slender; age? Not important, he decided.

'Good afternoon, Major Stafford, I'm Doctor Vivian Ford, the pathologist. I'm afraid the wives aren't here yet. Can I get you a coffee or something while we wait?'

Stafford released her hand and said, 'No. But thanks all the same.' He continued, 'I haven't heard anything to the contrary, so I'm guessing you've found nothing to override our original thoughts as to the cause of death?'

She picked up two buff folders from her desk. 'No, both men were extremely fit and healthy. It looks like they both worked out. So in one instance the stab wound was the cause of death, and the other was without doubt a skillful severing of the brainstem, in other words, a broken neck.' She replaced the folders on her desk unopened.

'The third man to be brought in to you on that day, Floyd Winstone; I'm afraid you're stuck with him for a little while longer as we've not been able to find any next of kin.'

'That happens from time to time, so we're quite used to it,' she said. Going back to her desk, she indicated towards the window, 'Ah, this looks like it could be them now. If you'll take a seat, I'll go and open the door for them. I'll bring them in here first. We have to do identity checks and stuff, well, you know, don't you?' she said as she hurried out.

Stafford remained standing, watching as the two women approached the building. Both women were slim, walking elegantly and assuredly in black high-heeled shoes. It was difficult to see their faces or assess their ages as they both wore the traditional Muslim shayla wrapped around the head and neck. The woman on the left was an inch or two smaller than her companion at maybe five feet four inches. She was wearing a mid-grey shayla over a dark grey ankle-length full-skirted dress. This had a white floral design across the right breast, repeated larger on the bottom left half of the skirt. Her right hand was tucked into a pocket at just below waist level. In her left hand she carried a black handbag; the double Gs intertwined and obvious.

The second woman wore a maroon shayla over a plain black ankle-length flowing dress. In her right hand the LV logo on her brown handbag was prominent. Stafford moved away from the window and sat on one of the padded chairs furthest from the door. Moments later the door opened and the two women came in with the doctor... Stafford rose, and faced them. The pathologist made the introductions.

'This is Major Stafford, he's the senior investigating officer. Major Stafford, this is Mrs Ravani.' The woman with the Gucci bag nodded once, and then looked at the floor. The doctor continued, 'And this is Mrs Buzdar.' The woman with the Louis Vuitton bag also bowed her head, but Stafford was already aware these were extremely attractive women. The shorter woman's heart-shaped face was slightly fairer than her companion's. Neither woman wore make-up and neither woman offered their hand to Stafford. He estimated their age as late twenties or early thirties.

'Now, if we can all take a seat for a moment. As I mentioned when we first contacted you, I need some ID. Have you brought some photo ID with you?' Both women opened their handbags and found their passports. The doctor checked the pictures, and then looked at the women in turn. Satisfied, she returned to the passports and noted the details in the two buff folders on her desk. After putting the folders into a drawer she stood up and handed the passports back. 'Good, thank you. Now I'll take you through to the viewing room.'

They followed her into the corridor, turned left and walked to a door on the right-hand side a few metres further down, the Asian women's heels echoing in the empty space as they walked. Stafford walked to the front and opened the door, then stood aside to let the women into the tiny room. The room was probably less than twelve by ten feet, but the white paint made it feel light and airy. Four chairs against the right-hand wall were the only furniture. In the middle of the left-hand wall hung a pair of beige curtains, a pull-cord to the right-hand side. Next to that was an intercom unit. The doctor pushed a button on the intercom, leaned towards it and said, 'Mrs Ravani and Mrs Buzdar are ready now.' She stood upright and pulled the curtain cord; the curtains slid back across a window, revealing a much larger, brightly lit room. Both sides of the room were lined with ten stainless steel doors. Each door was divided by four equally spaced brass label holders.

Stafford and the Asian women stood in front of the viewing window. From the right-hand side, a porter wearing a green skull cap, face mask and scrubs pushed a gurney with a body covered in a white sheet close to the window. The porter carefully gripped the sheet, drew it back to uncover the face and held it there. The woman wearing the maroon shayla caught hold of Mrs Ravani's arm. It was obvious they had both recognised Abduk Ravani. Doctor Ford said to Mrs Ravani, 'Can you confirm that this is your husband, Abduk Ravani?'

Mrs Ravani nodded, and then said in a whisper, 'Yes, it is Abduk.'

The doctor pressed the intercom again, 'Thank you,' she said. The porter replaced the sheet and wheeled the gurney away. Mrs Ravani, tears running down her cheeks, scrabbled about in her handbag, and took out a pack of tissues. The doctor took her arm and guided her to the chairs.

'Sit here for a while, Mrs Ravani. Can I get you a glass of water?' Mrs Ravani shook her head as she sobbed quietly into her tissues.

Doctor Ford returned to the viewing screen and pressed the intercom. 'Thank you, we're ready now.' The porter returned and repeated the procedure with a second gurney. Mrs Buzdar seemed to shrink as her knees buckled and her forehead hit the window. With her right hand to the glass, she pushed herself upright.

'Is this your husband, Hakim Buzdar?' said Doctor Ford, gently placing an arm around Mrs Buzdar for support.

'Yes, it is he. It is Hakim,' she said.

Pressing the intercom, the doctor said, 'Thank you,' and closed the curtains.

As Mrs Buzdar moved away from the viewing window, she narrowed her eyes and glared at Stafford. He could see there were no tears; just anger.

'Someone will pay for this.'

Stafford nodded. 'Mrs Buzdar, Mrs Ravani, I'm sorry for your loss. And we will find who did this.' Stafford was aware of a fleeting look of defiance as Mrs Buzdar took her friend's arm and helped her to her feet.

Doctor Ford moved towards the door and said as she held it open, 'Mrs Ravani, Mrs Buzdar, if you'll come back to the office with me, there are one or two formalities we need to complete in order for you to make the funeral arrangements.'

As they reached the office door, Stafford thanked the doctor, then to the Asian women said, 'Thank you for your time. I'm sorry you had to make this long journey.' This time the look he saw in Mrs Buzdar's eyes was scepticism.

'I assure you both, we will do everything in our power to bring these killers to justice.'

The three women, hesitated a second, said nothing, then went into the office.

Stafford walked out to his car. He lowered himself into the driver's seat and slid down as far as his six-foot-two-inch frame would allow.

He kept watch on the mortuary doors. It was almost ten minutes later when they came out. They stopped a few paces outside; Mrs Buzdar took out a mobile, tapped the screen and raised it to her face, she said a few words then ended the call. They didn't walk away, and were obviously waiting for their transport. Moments later a black Porsche Macan SUV pulled up alongside them. What is it that crooks like about black motors, thought Stafford as he made a note of the registration number. A slim Asian man wearing jeans, a white shirt and white trainers jumped out of the car and rushed round to open the rear passenger door. He held it open until the women got in. When the Porsche had passed his Volvo, Stafford followed it back to the A340. He watched as they reached the roundabout leading to the A339. Stafford knew it would take them to Oxford and the M40. He watched as they indicated, and saw them pull out into the heavy Midlands-bound traffic. Satisfied they were heading home, he completed the circuit of the roundabout and headed to Farnborough. He parked up close to his front door, dashed inside and switched on his computer. Within minutes he had found the registered keeper of the Porsche Macan. Logging in to the Police National Database, he discovered that the owner was a West Midlands Pakistani gangster with a string of criminal convictions. It also mentioned among known associates Messrs Ravani and Buzdar. He sent a couple of mugshots to his printer along with his crime sheet and the gangster's last-known home address.

He switched off the computer. Feeling hungry, he walked across to the fridge and checked the contents. It was almost empty, but was saved a phone call to the takeaway when he spotted a cottage pie ping meal. Noting it was only out of date by a day or so, he put it in the microwave, then grabbed a tray and a fork. Twenty minutes later, he was fast asleep on one of his mismatched sofas. It was some hours later when his buzzing and vibrating mobile phone woke him up. Wearily, he looked at the screen: *No Caller ID*. He took the call regardless.

CHAPTER 45

The barmaid was first through the door. She hesitated as she watched Sweetman push himself into a sitting position. He grimaced and groaned in agony as he realised there was more broken glass now pushed even deeper into his right palm.

Clamping his left hand around his damaged wrist, he said calmly, 'Sorry about this, love, but have you got a first-aid kit?' She nodded and squeezed her way through the small group of customers who had gathered behind her in the smoking area.

Sweetman managed to get to his feet, and then sat down heavily on one of the wooden benches. As the group of onlookers began to talk among themselves, a shot rang out from the car park, then two more shots. As one, the group ducked and screamed, fighting each other to get back to the safety of the bar-room, and Sweetman was left alone.

The barmaid came back with a first-aid kit, followed by a rotund, red-faced, balding man, who'd been quietly enjoying his dinner in the landlord's quarters above the bar.

He saw the blood and, white as a sheet, said in a breathless voice, 'Look, mate, I dunno what's goin' on here, but we don't want any trouble.'

Sweetman said, 'What? Do you think I did this to myself? It was one of your customers, mate. Came at me with a glass, and he's obviously got a gun as he's shot at something out in the car park. So don't give me that "I don't want any trouble" shit. What sort of a place are you running here?'

The landlord hesitated for a mere fraction before saying, 'When I heard the first shot, I looked out of my window and saw this guy stood next to a Merc pickup truck shooting its tyres out. So I phoned the police, and before anybody even answered he's jumped into another Mercedes truck and buggered off like the proverbial bat.'

While he was recounting this the barmaid had knelt down and was trying to clean up Sweetman's injuries.

'Christ,' she said, 'you still got loads of bits of glass in here. I called the ambulance when I got the first-aid box, because you're going to need loads of stitches and someone to make sure all the glass is out.'

Sweetman pulled his eyes away from her cleavage, smiled at her and said, 'Well, thanks for that, darlin'. And landlord, seeing it was your bloody customer that did this, and then shot my tyres out, I reckon you owe me at least a double Scotch or two.'

The landlord spluttered, 'He was obviously looking for you.'

The barmaid answered, 'I'll tie off this bandage then I'll get you one… Famous Grouse OK?' Sweetman said nothing, just smiled and nodded his thanks. He reached in his pocket, took out a packet of Benson & Hedges and lit one.

A few minutes later, sirens blaring and blue lights flashing, an ambulance rolled to a halt alongside the front door. Having been given the basic details by the landlord, barmaid and a few cursory comments from Sweetman, one of the two paramedics began to unwrap Sweetman's bandage to check the damage. Slighted, the barmaid stomped off. Taking up a position behind the bar, she began polishing glasses aggressively. Now she definitely had something to grouse about.

II

Sweetman's mind was in overdrive – he knew he had only a few minutes to make the decision: stay and bluff it out, or run. Cooper had fired the shots that would bring not only the usual posse of police, but an armed response unit to the scene. He could even now hear the sirens wailing in the distance. One of the paramedics was sitting on the bench alongside him. Having pulled out as much of the broken glass as he could see, he was putting on a piece of sticking plaster to hold the end of the new bandage in place. The other paramedic was preoccupied putting unused bandages and various medical items back into their work bags.

Decision made, Sweetman shook his head, ground out his cigarette, looked directly at the first paramedic, and as he said, 'Sorry mate,' raised his good left hand and stabbed with straightened fingers into the side of the man's neck. The medic's eyes rolled to the back of their sockets, he crumpled sideways across the wooden garden table, and crashed to the floor. Sweetman's moves were instinctive. On his feet he spun around and backhanded the second paramedic, who was halfway to standing up, across the bridge of his nose. The force was enough to discourage retaliation. He slumped back to the bench, hands clutching his nose, blood and snot oozing between his fingers, tears streaming down his cheeks. Sweetman ran through the bar, out of the front door, the barmaid watching, mouth agape. Outside, the ambulance's blue lights were still flashing. Sweetman ran to the driver's door. It was unlocked. Clambering in, he wasn't surprised to see the ignition key still in place. As he struggled with his left hand to turn the key, he thought, maybe they'll see I've taught them a valuable lesson here? The motor roared into life. He could hear sirens now, much closer than before. If he could just get a few streets away from the pub, he guessed the police crews would assume the ambulance was rushing to or from a callout and wouldn't attempt to intercept it. As he approached the station roundabout, traffic began to build. It was a second or two before he realised he was in the perfect vehicle to clear the road ahead. He found the switch and hit the sirens. He couldn't stop a thin smile as the traffic parted to let him through. To complete the illusion, at the roundabout he followed the signs for Basingstoke and North Hants Hospital.

Inside the Queens Arms, the barmaid was tempted to use her first-aid training again, then remembering the paramedic's slight of her skills, she dialled 999 for another ambulance instead. Meanwhile, the landlord watched in dismay as the last of his customers drove out of the car park.

CHAPTER 46

Stafford's unknown number turned out to be a particularly astute call handler in the emergency services control centre. He'd taken the details of the 999 call from the Queens Arms pub then, once he'd organised the dispatch of Scenes of Crime Officers and two armed response vehicles, he carried out intelligence checks on his database. He discovered the incident involved the shooting out of the tyres on a black Mercedes pickup truck and a similar vehicle had been driven away at high speed by the perpetrator. He also discovered a Major Paul Stafford was lead investigator on attachment to Hampshire Police, and had been making enquiries about black Mercedes pickups linked to various criminal activities in Basingstoke and Weyhill, near Andover. As the call handler detailed the incident, Stafford knew that with Cooper there earlier, this had to be part of his investigation.

He ended the conversation and phoned Ryan Peters. After telling him about the incident, Stafford said, 'So can you and Nicole and whoever else you can get make your way to the Queens Arms pub, in Basingstoke? Take a picture of Cooper with you. It seems that he and another of their hit squad have had a bit of a shootout down there. Both parties have fled the pub, but it's not clear if one is chasing the other. You should find local police, forensic techs and two ARVs in attendance. I'll get up there as soon as I can, but I'll try and locate Cooper first.'

Peters on it, he ended the call. Stafford sat in the gloom of his living room and shook his head; again, he thought, we're being pulled around by this bunch of lawless thugs. He walked into the kitchen, splashed cold water on his face and ran his fingers through his hair before going out to the car. Prior to turning on the ignition he determined a course of action. His priority was to locate and apprehend Ray Cooper. He knew if whoever had followed him to the pub caught up with him first, Cooper's life expectancy would be zero. Stafford didn't feel strongly about saving Cooper's life, but he did want to interview him about the attack on Sophie Gibson. He also realised that Cooper's other option to stay alive was to hand himself in to the police, and, if that happened, the sort of interview Stafford had in mind would never happen. He called Cooper's number. It rang and rang, then clicked into voicemail. Stafford switched on the ignition and headlights. Heading towards the M3, he tried Cooper's number; again it went to voicemail.

'For Christ's sake, Cooper, what the hell's going on now?' he said. 'If you're driving, pull over somewhere and call me. Gunshots have been reported, there'll be any number of armed response units out there looking for you. What with CCTV and ANPR out there, you don't stand a chance – your best bet to stay alive right now is with me.' He ended the call.

Traffic was light and Stafford was soon on the M3 heading towards Basingstoke. He settled back and tried to take stock. It was incidents like this that ate away at his calm. This attack on Cooper, the killings of Edwards, Winstone, Ravani and Buzdar; all these violent events – however tragic they were to the individuals and no doubt their mums and girlfriends – were smokescreens hiding the core, the root of the evil. They had to be investigated as a matter of course. And though it was obviously a cleaning-house operation ordered by the criminal hierarchy, the perpetrators still needed to be brought to justice. But working so close to front-line action meant Stafford and his team were not able to get to grips with the bigger picture. He had to find a way to take a pace or two back and work the entire ballpark and not just these peripheral crimes.

Mulling this over, his concentration was shattered as Bluetooth kicked in and a local Hampshire TV reporter announced himself.

'How the hell did you get this number?' Stafford asked.

'Major, look,' the hack said, 'I don't know if this is important or not, but have you seen the online versions of the headlines in one of tomorrow's red-tops?'

Stafford continued calmly, 'No, I've been a tad busy. So fill me in – relevant details only, though, eh?'

'OK, it seems that someone has found pictures of Marva Lewis, Nicole Martin and Sophie Gibson, and they've put all three pictures together under the headline, *What attracts beautiful women to dangerous men?* Then the story tells about Sophie's acid attack and suicide, goes on to talk about Marva and Garfield Lewis's murder, and asks, *Who's next?* beside a picture of DS Martin. I thought you should know, maybe warn DS Martin that the press are likely to be hounding her.'

Stafford was silent for a long moment.

'OK, look, thanks for keeping me up to speed. Not sure what I can do about it, but at least I'm forearmed.'

Call ended, he began to think about the incident at the Queens Arms pub. Although he thought it was going to be another distraction from the main investigation, he had to admit, this time he didn't mind; this time he would see Nicole again. Though it would be difficult and not a little awkward, he was feeling excited at the prospect.

It was getting on for ten o'clock in the evening when Ryan Peters, Nicole Martin and Harry Whitley left Aldershot police station. Nicole left a text message for her new boss, DI Thomas Masterson, telling him about the incident and informing him that she was responding with her two colleagues. She had yet to meet him in person, but he was scheduled to attend the briefing in the Aldershot nick at eight thirty the following morning. They piled into the SRi, Peters taking the driver's seat. Nicole strapped herself into the front passenger seat and put the pub details into the sat nav on her mobile. Whitley had just about sorted out the rear seatbelt when Peters hit the throttle and roared out of the car park in a plume of smoke and a squeal of rubber.

Looking in the rear-view mirror, he said with a straight face, 'All right in the back there?'

'Never better, Ry, never better,' came back the curt response.

Nicole smiled to herself. *Nice one, Harry.* As they accessed the slip road to the M3 she couldn't help thinking about Stafford, knowing he would be leaving home, and might be just behind them on the same road. She felt the colour rise to her cheeks; one second she knew she wanted to see him, the next she was unsure. She began to take deep breaths; surreptitiously, she hoped.

Ryan Peters looked at her and after a second said, 'My driving bothering you, Sergeant?'

'No more than usual,' she said.

The roads were quiet until they got to within a couple of streets from Bunnian Place. Coming to the station roundabout, traffic started to back up, so Peters hit the blues and twos. As the traffic parted, the cause for the build-up became obvious. On the far side of the roundabout a police car was half on the pavement in front of an ambulance, lights flashing on both, and uniformed police officers were examining a black Mercedes pickup truck. Peters pulled on to the nearside pavement and stopped; killing the sirens, he left the blue lights flashing.

'Just hang on here for a moment, Harry boy, me and the sergeant will see what they know about the Mercedes driver.'

They clambered out; dashing across the road and taking out their ID, Martin offered hers to the cops and said, 'Have you managed to nick the driver of this Mercedes?'

The policeman looked at Nicole's warrant card and said, 'No, Sergeant, he crashed into the rear of a blue Volkswagen Polo, jumped out and assaulted the driver, knocking him out. Then he hijacked the car. We've notified ANPR and CCTV operations rooms of the registration details. We're hoping we'll get lucky.'

'Is that the Polo driver the paramedics are attending to?' asked Martin.

'Yep, that's him. Says he doesn't want to go to hospital and he's called his wife to pick him up.'

'So he's pretty compos then?'

'Seems so, more angry than hurt I think, but he'll have a corker of a headache and a massive lump come morning,' said the copper with a grin.

'OK, thanks. We've got a picture of the guy we think did this, so we'll check with him, see if he recognises his attacker.'

'So you know the perpetrator, then?'

'We've certainly got a good idea who it might be,' said Martin as she walked towards the victim, not wanting to be drawn into a conversation of how the perp was freed from custody earlier that day.

Peters waved his ID at the paramedics, Martin did likewise.

'We need to ask him some questions, do you think he'll be up to it?'

'Reckon so… He's steaming angry about the whole thing, wants to get his hands on whoever did it, so yes, I think he'll want to get the ball rolling.'

'Fair enough. So, you heading back to the hospital now?'

'No, we'll wait till his missus arrives, then we've got a call to pick up a couple of our chaps from the pub up there. They apparently lost their ambulance,' said the paramedic, unable to smother her amusement.

'See you soon, then. We're heading there when we've chatted to your patient,' said Martin. The paramedics walked away leaving Martin and Peters to show their credentials to the Polo driver alone.

'Do you feel up to answering a few questions?'

The Polo driver nodded. 'Yes, I'm all right. I'd like to catch the bastard and get my car back.'

'Good,' said Nicole taking out her notebook. Writing down the details from his proffered driving licence, she added the information about his stolen car. 'What happened?' she asked him. 'Did he threaten you with a gun?'

His eyes widened and without hesitation said, 'God, no, no way, he came at me looking kind of sheepish, you know, arms out like this.' He acted out the events leading up to his getting thumped. He finished, 'Next I know, I'm waking up on the road with a bleeding great headache, me car's gone and there's traffic piling up all around me.'

'So did you get a decent look at him as he came towards you?' asked Peters.

'I suppose so. I remember thinking, he looks a reasonable sort, you know, smart. Dark suit, collar and tie, that sort of thing. I thought he was a businessman… Perhaps I shouldn't tell you this,' he said, looking sheepish, 'but I thought, I can make a buck or two out of him off his insurance.'

Peters shrugged and said, 'But he didn't threaten you with a gun?'

'No, never said a word, just bloody whacked me,' he said touching his bandaged head carefully.

'Would you recognise him again?' asked Peters as he took out the print of Cooper.

The Polo driver looked at the picture and, without hesitation, said, 'Yes, that's him, that's the one – how do you know who it was?'

'We were called out to another incident just up the road; the Mercedes pickup gave us a clue as to who it was and you've just confirmed it,' said Martin. 'Now we've got to go, but here's my details, if you think of anything that might help. All right?'

The Polo driver nodded; then realising his mistake, touched his head gently, his face twisted in pain. He said, 'I'm fine, the missus will be here soon. Just hope the bastard hasn't wrecked my car.'

'Oh, I doubt that, he'll have driven a few streets away and dumped it; too many CCTV cameras around this area. Don't worry, we'll be in touch as soon as we locate it, and we'll need to come round to get a formal statement from you.'

Again the driver nodded, more gently this time.

CHAPTER 47

Martin and Peters returned to their car and made their way to the pub. From twenty-five metres away, the road to the pub and right through to the car park was blocked with emergency services vehicles and all manner of estate cars, vans and trucks with the names for this or that newspaper or television outlet emblazoned on their sides.

Peters pulled up as close as he could to the barrier created by the vehicles and they got out, Peters saying, 'See, all it takes is gunshots and a bit of violence to make ordinary places come alive; people every-bloody-where.'

There were rubberneckers, uniformed police, some with helmets and Kevlar vests, some carrying weapons. There were people in plain clothes carrying cameras, mobile phones or video recorders; some climbing on their vehicles. Experienced reporters had brought step ladders with them to get a better view. A steady stream of comments rose from twenty-four-hour news channel reporters.

'*...reports of three gun shots*'.

'*...talk of a car chase and a stolen ambulance*'.

'*...injured man attacked medics, took off in an ambulance*'.

Making their way slowly through the mass of vehicles and people, their progress was halted by police tape used to cordon off the road ahead. Half a dozen police constables, one complete with clipboard, stood guard. Peters showed his ID.

'Good evening, Constable, can you tell me who's in charge?'

'Currently, it's the Operational Firearms Commander from the lead AR unit.'

'Can you give him a shout, tell him it's Captain Peters from Major Stafford's team?'

The constable took another look at Peters' ID, this time harder.

'Security Service? Why? What's this got to do with the Security Service?'

'It's a long story, Constable, but suffice it to say, a Major Stafford is on his way and he will take charge when he gets—'

Martin pulled out her ID, waved it under the constable's nose and said, 'Just do it, eh, Constable?'

The copper took a pace back so he could see her warrant card clearly, then said, 'Yes of course, Sarge, sorry, Sergeant,' and ran off through the now floodlit car park to the smoking area and into the pub.

Martin said to Peters, 'I wonder if it's one of the AR guys who was at Weyhill?'

Moments later, the constable returned with the Armed Response team leader. On seeing Martin and Peters, he broke into a smile, reached out his hand and said, 'Good to see you again, Captain Peters.' As he shook Nicole's hand there was a slight hesitation before he said, 'And pleased to see you looking none the worse for wear, ah… I understand it's *Sergeant* Martin now.'

Nicole felt the colour rising to her cheeks and was grateful for the cover of darkness. The AR man lifted up the police tape and said, 'So is this still part of the same investigation?'

'Yes,' said Peters as he, Martin and PC Whitley ducked under the tape, 'we're pretty sure this involves someone we've been looking for in connection with an assault or two and possibly a murder.'

Before they moved away, Martin held out her hand to the uniformed constable, who just looked at her.

'Log,' she said.

The constable managed to stutter, 'Oh God, sorry, Sarge, and thrust his clipboard at her. She signed it, handed it to Peters. As she waited for the other two, a newspaper reporter recognised her and shouted over.

'Hey, that's Nicole, Sergeant Nicole Martin! Hey Nicole, have you seen the morning papers? Aren't you frightened – could be you next?'

The assembled media crowd surged forward, desperate to see her, to get a word from her or a picture of her.

Martin hurried ahead and shouted for Whitley to catch up and they followed the armed response officer into the pub. She was used to men cat-calling and whistling at her, but she didn't understand why this reporter had shouted about the morning papers. She hesitated, screwing up her face trying to think what the guy had meant – she gave up.

'So what's the story here, then?'

'From what I'm told, this involves two men driving identical Mercedes pickup trucks – made me think they were both working for the same organisation. It appears one attacked the other with a glass, then ran out and shot the other guy's tyres out before escaping in his own vehicle.'

'Odd,' said Peters, frowning. 'I wonder why he glassed him if he had a gun?'

'That's a damn good question, but sadly I have no answer,' said the AR man, going on to explain about the injuries to the paramedics and the hijacking of their ambulance.

'We think,' said Nicole, 'that these two men are working out of a five-star hotel just outside Basingstoke and maybe the Whitelines nightclub. Which all ties in with the Weyhill and Southampton operations.'

'Christ almighty, it gets bigger and bigger,' said the AR man.

As they approached the bar, Martin said to Whitley, 'Go back to the car park and check with the forensic boys, see what they've got. See if they've managed to retrieve any of the bullets and any other info they may have. OK?' As Whitley nodded and turned to go, she said, 'And if there's any customers in the smoking area, ask them to come in and look at the picture, will you?'

'Ha!' said the landlord, 'Customers? They all buggered off before your lot arrived.'

Martin shrugged. 'Do the best you can, 173.' Whitley raised a hand.

The barmaid and landlord were behind the bar, leaning on its highly polished top. The two paramedics were on the near side, sitting on bar stools, each with a small glass of beer. Martin introduced herself and Peters; as she showed her ID, the AR man walked back out to the beer garden.

Peters pulled his eyes away from the barmaid's chest and placed the picture of Cooper on the bar facing her. She confirmed it was the man who had sat and had a couple of drinks, then smashed the glass into the unknown man's hand.

'So can you give us a description of the injured man?' asked Peters.

They were silent for a moment. The landlord, nodding at the barmaid, said, 'She saw him more than I did, she sat there and cleaned up his hand. And put a bandage on it. So she was right up close to him. I only saw him from the back.'

The barmaid shrugged and said, 'I know, but like, I didn't sit there looking at his face, I was too busy pulling the glass out of his hand.'

Nicole put a hand on the woman's arm. 'Just take your time, think back to when you first became aware of him. Try to recall your first thoughts. Was he tall? Short? Fat? Thin?'

'I seem to remember thinking I couldn't see his face because he had his hood up, like, and he dashed across the room pointing, so I thought, OK, he's rushing to the loo before ordering. Then I thought, sod it, I bet he pees all over the floor,' she said, with a little snigger.

Nicole smiled back and said, 'So how tall did you think he was?'

'I s'pose not really tall, maybe under six feet, five feet ten or so. But he looked well built, y'know, able to look after himself. But I s'pose that could've been just the clothes.'

'So, can you describe the clothes?'

'I only saw the black hoody really. Oh, and, yeah, black trousers with lots of pockets, like, where he stuffed his fags and lighter."

The landlord said, 'Yeah, that's right, that's about what I saw.'

'So when you bandaged his hand, did he have his hood up or down?' Again silence for a while. Martin, feeling this was going nowhere said, 'OK, tell you what, can you get some paper and a pen and just sit here for five or ten minutes. Think about this guy, and jot down anything you remember?' Turning to the paramedics, she said, 'And please, anything you can add will be a great help too.'

'Yeah, OK, good idea,' said the landlord opening a cupboard beneath the rows of spirits. Hunting inside he found the pad and pen they used for noting stock requirements.

Martin said, 'Anything that comes to mind. You know, hair colour and length, eye colour and so on. OK?' Getting nods of assent, Martin and Peters walked out into the smoking area. Forensic techs were still searching. One of them asked her, 'Do you know if the guy who hit the paramedics was smoking?'

'Yes, I think so – the barmaid mentioned fags and lighter. Why?' The tech held up a little plastic bag. Inside was a crushed half-smoked cigarette butt – they could just make out the word *Benson*. 'That may be the only clue to who this guy is,' she said. Looking at Peters, she continued, 'It's no good, Ry – even if we get a DNA match off this fag butt, this is just another effin' waste of time. OK, we're looking for some nasty bastards, but they're stopping us getting to the main players, the men pulling the strings.'

'Yep, not going to argue with you there, but Stafford's on his way. We'll hang on till he gets here; see what he wants to do.'

Nicole had all but forgotten Stafford was due to meet

them there and she felt a little shiver of excitement. Again, she was thankful that the evening darkness hid the colour rising to her cheeks. It seemed like ages since she'd seen or even spoken to him. She didn't know if she was angry, happy or sad at the thought of his imminent arrival. She did, however, realise she needed the loo.

CHAPTER 48

As Stafford approached the station roundabout, traffic had all but dispersed, but it was impossible to miss the melee at the end of Bunnian Place. Stafford parked near Peters' Vectra and walked across to the tape barrier. He showed the constable his ID.

'Ah, yes, Major Stafford, been expecting you. Your colleagues have gone into the pub via the smoking area.' He lifted the tape and gave Stafford the log to sign.

As he walked, Stafford could feel his heart beating faster. He wasn't worried about the shooting incident; it was the realisation he would shortly be confronted by Nicole.

With no warning, she walked into the smoking area. He stopped and watched as she moved, her head cast down, looking carefully at the decking floor, moving slowly around the wooden tables and benches. Once again he was struck by how beautiful she was, though she never seemed aware of it. After a second or two he started towards her – she must have seen or noticed a movement, as she raised her head and looked directly at him. With the floodlights in the car park behind him, he realised she could only see him in silhouette. She raised a hand to shield her eyes from the glare.

'Stafford?' she said.

Stafford nodded and walked towards her, stopping just a pace in front.

'Hi, Nicole,' was all he could think of to say. She moved a pace towards him, stretched up and kissed his cheek. She stood back a pace. He wasn't sure where to look as he said, 'Uh, ah – but it's good to see you. I've—'

'Yes, I know,' she said, her voice a little breathless.

A half-smile crossed her face and she shook her head. Coming back to the moment, she took hold of his arm, and said, 'Come on, this way, Ryan's in here. Let's get you up to speed.' As she opened the door to the bar, she let go of his arm.

'Look who I just found,' she said to the group of people gathered there. Ryan Peters ambled across and shook his friend's hand.

'Good to see you, boss. Come and meet the stray PC Nicole's managed to extract from Aldershot nick.' Peters looked towards the uniformed Whitley and beckoned him over. 'PC Harry Whitley, AKA PC 173, meet your new, but only temporary governor Major Paul Stafford.'

They shook hands and Whitley said, 'Good to meet you, sir. Sergeant Martin has told me a bit about you, so I've been looking forward to working with you.'

'Good to meet you too, Harry. I trust the sergeant didn't go into too much detail… So what's the situation here?'

Peters and Martin walked him through the events as told by the barmaid and landlord.

The four of them went out into the car park and spoke to the forensic techs. They hadn't managed to retrieve the bullets. But as only entry holes were visible in the tyres, they were confident that once they'd recovered the vehicle to their Eastleigh HQ, they would find them. Stafford asked if they could hazard a guess at the size of ammunition used. Their best guess, judging by the entry holes, was that they were nine-millimetre rounds.

The lead tech said they had retrieved numerous usable fingerprints from the truck's steering wheel, but they hadn't had a hit on their mobile fingerprint scanner. They hoped for more from IDENT1, the National Fingerprint Database. They also anticipated the blood samples would throw up a decent DNA result, good enough to find a match.

Stafford pulled his people to one side.

'Here we go again. There's nothing we can do here. It's yet another annoying incident to get us to take our eyes off the main prize, so we'll leave these guys to it. I suggest we go home, get a good night's rest and start again at the briefing in Aldershot tomorrow morning. OK?'

Peters, Nicole and Whitley murmured their assent. They said their goodbyes to the AR man and the forensic teams, and signed out. As they made their way to their cars, they were besieged by the media scrum, shouting questions aimed mainly at Stafford and Martin. Stafford held up his hand for quiet; it didn't happen.

As they squeezed into their cars, he shouted, 'We'll hold a press conference in Aldershot tomorrow, late morning.' Stafford had wanted to ask Nicole to join him, but knew this was not the time or place. Besides, he thought as he switched on the ignition, she might say no. As he reversed the car to drive away, he noticed that she was standing with the Vectra's passenger door open, watching him depart. He wasn't sure if she could see into his car, but he smiled and nodded regardless.

Half an hour later, back at home in Farnborough, he walked through to his kitchen-cum-office and made a cup of tea and a cheese sandwich. As he settled down at the kitchen table, he began to ponder the evening's events. It took a while to get Nicole out of his head. Nursing his tea, he began to think about Cooper and the man he had injured at the pub. He wasn't too worried about Cooper; he was playing him like a fish. Stafford knew he would eventually reel him in, preferably alive. Failing that, he guessed that Cooper, fearing the syndicate's wrath, would give up the fight and hand himself in. No, it was the other man he was interested in. He knew Cooper couldn't have had a gun with him when he drove out of Eastleigh Police HQ. So he must have taken it from the second man, the man he'd cut, then used it to shoot out his tyres so he couldn't be followed. If the techs could retrieve the ammo and test it against the bullets taken from Winstone and Edwards, they might find a match. A link to the weapon for those two killings at least, if not to the shooter himself. OK, it wasn't the main prize, but it would help get another vicious killer off the streets.

It was strange, too, that the fingerprints they'd found tonight from someone who may have killed at least two people were not on the police databases. They hadn't even shown up on the IABS database for non-EU citizens. This man was either excellent at avoiding detection or extremely lucky. But no one is that lucky, surely? He took a sip of tea – then almost spat it out.

'Jesus H Christ,' he said out loud. 'He's ex-forces.'

Excited, and ignoring the late hour, he pulled out his mobile and called the lead forensic tech. He got no response.

He tried again, it went to voicemail. He ended the call and tried again. The tech picked up.

'Sorry to disturb you so late, it's Stafford, Paul Stafford, I need you to do me a favour or two. I need some info for the morning briefing. The blood sample you took at the pub, and anything else you found in the Mercedes truck, will you rush them through this new DNA four-hour lab-on-a-chip testing system that I keep hearing about? Also, when your lads retrieve the bullets from the tyres, get them to do ballistic tests against the bullets pulled from the recently departed Winstone and Edwards, could you, please? Thanks for that, sorry to...' The connection was dead.

Putting the mobile on the table, he opened his laptop and found the scanned fingerprints from the Mercedes truck. Using his entry code, he opened up the military equivalent of the police fingerprint and DNA databases. Various covert ops that Stafford had undertaken required him to track and find service personnel. Since 2008, he knew the British Army had given their soldiers the right to choose to have their DNA and fingerprints on record. So when unidentifiable bodies, or limbs were found in war zones, DNA samples and maybe fingerprints could be taken, then matched against the database. The aim was to reduce the number of graves around the world with headstones bearing the legend *Unknown Soldier* and the number of families not knowing what had become of their loved ones. The military did not share this database with the police.

Within seconds, he had a result; a staff sergeant called Jamie Sweetman. Digging into Sweetman's history showed that he had risen to the rank of warrant officer, but had been busted back to staff sergeant just before leaving the army six years ago. His last known address was shown as Herefordshire. Digging for more information, he found he was locked out – information apparently too sensitive for his pay grade. He would have to talk to the Colonel to get more details, if they needed them. Stafford printed off half a dozen pictures of Sweetman, logged out, closed his laptop and finished his sandwich and now lukewarm tea.

He sat quietly contemplating the evening's events. Nicole flashed into his mind; he pictured her standing by the Vectra car door. Was he making it up, he wondered, or had she looked … maybe wistful at his departure? Regardless, he was pleased they had made their first moves to – to what? He stood, walked around the table and added his mug to the pile of crocks in the sink, promising himself he'd wash up in the morning. He switched off the kitchen light and made his way through the hall to the stairs.

He sensed rather than heard movement outside in the front garden. He stopped and stood stock still for half a minute. Hearing nothing, sensing nothing, he continued up the stairs. Yet again something stopped him mid-step. He closed his eyes and concentrated his mind, trying to eliminate the ambient house noises. He pushed his mind, his instincts, his hearing. Something was out of kilter. He moved quietly back down the stairs. His eyes grew accustomed to the darkness as he walked through the kitchen, negotiating the furniture, to the half-glazed back door. Peering out into the gloom of the back garden, nothing was moving. He could see the outlines of bushes and the few mature trees silhouetted against the dark orange glow where the low cloud reflected the lights of the nearby town. He opened the back door silently and, keeping close to the rear wall, moved right. Stealthily and slowly, he inched his way to the corner of the house. From there he crept along the side wall to where the front garden began. Leaning his back against the wall, he listened intently. Above the sounds of the night, he was certain he could hear the clicking sounds of a car engine cooling down.

CHAPTER 49

He knew it wasn't his Volvo; that had been standing long enough to be cool by now. Risking a glance around the corner, he could make out the outline of another car parked just inside his driveway, alongside the garage. He realised the driver must have cruised in slowly and quietly, and stopped as soon as the car was behind the front hedge; out of sight from the road. Bent low and moving slowly across the driveway, Stafford could see an eerie glow inside the car, emanating from below the driver's door window. The glow was enough to show the outline of a man in the driver's seat, preoccupied, using a mobile phone. Stafford recognised the man's profile, and his heartbeat quickened. Crouching low, he ran the few paces to the car, ripped open the driver's door and smashed his fist into the side of the man's face. The phone flew out of the man's hand and on to the driveway. The driver, not quite unconscious, fell across the passenger side, cracking his head against the seat. While the driver was scrabbling to recover, Stafford picked up the mobile phone and put it in the pocket of his jeans, reached into the car, grabbed the man's hair and right arm, and dragged him out. Now starting to recover, the driver tried to speak, but Stafford hit him full in the face, breaking and splitting his nose messily and noisily. The driver clutched his hands to his face and Stafford hit him with a left and a right to the midriff. He doubled over, crashed to his knees and sprawled face first on the ground. Slowly he rolled on to his side.

'Fuck's sake, Stafford, you prick. It's me, Cooper, Ray Cooper,' he said, spraying out blood and snot at the same time.

'Yeah, I know,' said Stafford as he pulled him up and propped him against the front wing of the car, 'I thought it was time we got our interview started.'

As Cooper groped in his pocket for a handkerchief, Stafford said, 'Now give me the gun.'

Cooper began to gently dab his face with the handkerchief. 'What gun?' he said, 'I haven't got a gun.'

Stafford sighed, shook his head, took a pace back and kicked him in the nuts. Cooper screamed and retched in anguish as he crashed face first to the ground. His hands to his genitals, he made no attempt to protect his face.

'You don't fucking learn, do you?' said Stafford as he patted Cooper down. He found the Glock 26 stuffed into the rear of Cooper's waistband. Stafford put the gun to Cooper's head.

'This gun, Cooper. You remember it now, do you?'

'Christ's sake, Stafford, I came here to help you,' came the mumbled response.

'You mean like you helped Edwards to kill Sophie Gibson?'

'We didn't kill her. We just wanted to—'

Stafford had heard enough. 'I should shoot you now like the vermin you are, but I think I'll leave that to Aksanov, now get into your motor and fuck off, you cowardly piece of shit.'

'But the cops are looking for this motor, and Sweetman is out to kill me.'

'Do I look like I give a toss? I'm giving you a better chance than you gave Sophie… But what's this, anyway, Cooper? A name at last? Tell me, where does Sweetman fit in, and where does he live?'

Cooper struggled to his feet and slumped back into the driver's seat. He looked up at Stafford.

'I don't know. Honest, I don't fuckin' know. All I know is, he's freelance. Does the wet work for Aksanov and a few others.' He sparked the ignition, then wiped more blood and snot from his face.

Stafford held the door open, leaned into the car and said, 'So who else does he work for?'

'I hear he does stuff for the Russians, but these guys, they're way out of my league.'

Stafford looked at Cooper's smashed nose. He pursed his lips, sucked air noisily. 'So are you willing to stand up in court and testify against these guys?'

Cooper looked down at the ground and said in a whisper, 'It's more than my life's worth.'

Stafford looked at him with disgust and said, 'Fuck off, Cooper, you're no use to me. You should go to the hospital, get that looked at; this interview is over.'

He slammed the car door and walked away a few paces. He watched as Cooper slowly turned the car round and headed out on to the road. He waited until the engine noise disappeared, then walked back to the kitchen door. He put the gun on the table, sat down and took out Cooper's mobile. The screen was cracked from the fall, but it still worked. Stafford was amazed to find no password protection and Cooper was obviously not thought important enough to have the EncroChat system the other operatives they'd encountered had. He found *Contacts*, scrolled past *Aksanov* and on to the S's. *Sweetman* was the last of five. Stafford made the call. It was answered almost immediately.

'Sweetman? You might want to know that Ray Cooper is now driving a blue Volkswagen Polo, registration number RT04NBX and he's heading to the Frimley Park Hospital just outside Farnborough. Afterwards, he'll likely head for Aldershot Police Station.' Stafford ended the call.

He guessed Sweetman wouldn't waste time calling back, so continued to search through the phone. Annoyingly, it was almost out of charge and sod's law meant his own charger didn't fit. It would have to wait, along with the gun, for the technical people at the eight thirty briefing. With the remainder of the charge, he put Aksanov's, Sweetman's and a few other numbers into his own phone contacts, then called Ryan Peters.

'Sorry if I woke you, Ry, but can you meet me at Frimley Park Hospital, soonest? I'll fill you in when we meet up, but I've emailed you a picture of a guy called Sweetman – he's the one Cooper hurt at the Queens Arms. Don't approach him if you see him, wait for me, OK?'

Call ended, Stafford selected Nicole's number and dialled. He tried two or three times before she answered, but finally her voice came over the speaker.

'This is an unexpected surprise,' she said.

Stafford hesitated, unsure how to respond. 'Ah, er – sorry, Nicole, it's not a social call. I wondered if you were up for a bit of action.

'And there's me thinking you'd gone off me, but it's the second best offer I've had all day,' she said.

He was silent for longer this time. 'Come on, boss, I'm only teasing you!' Half wishing she wasn't.

Stafford pulled himself together. 'Things have moved on a bit tonight, and there's a chance Cooper will hand himself in at your nick in the next hour or so. It could be he's being tailed by a guy called Jamie Sweetman – he's the bloke Cooper cut up at the pub.'

Nicole jumped in and said, 'Brilliant, boss, you have been busy.'

'Yeah, well... Now listen, this might not happen, but I've sent you a picture of this guy Sweetman. What I need you to do is get your new PC and Sergeant Hawkins, and any other spare bods you can find, and set up surveillance around the Aldershot nick. If Cooper turns up alone, try and get him safely inside, but if you catch sight of Sweetman, do not approach him, he's fucking dangerous. Just keep him under surveillance. Understood?'

'Yes, Staf. Are you coming over?'

'Not yet. That's Plan B. Plan A is... I think Cooper will go to A&E in Frimley Park first to get patched up, and I think Sweetman will attempt to get to him there, but—'

'Did Sweetman damage him, then?' Nicole interrupted. 'You're not going over there alone, are you?'

'No, Cooper got, um, damaged during our interview... I subjected him to my enhanced interrogation technique.

And Ryan's on his way to the hospital, so it'll be like I've got another four people,' said Stafford and laughed.

Nicole was silent for a long moment before she said, 'Take care, Staf.' Stafford ended the call, but sat for a moment thinking, *second best offer?*

But Sweetman did call back. Stafford had just put on his leather bomber jacket and was preparing to leave for the hospital when Cooper's phone chirped. Stafford was puzzled, not recognising the sound. After a second or two he twigged, picked up the damaged phone and found a text message apparently from Sweetman. It was short and to the point: *Think I'm that fucking stupid.*

Mildly disappointed, Stafford left the house and headed for the hospital, calling Nicole again on the way.

'Sorry to muck you about,' he said, 'but I don't think Sweetman will be around your way any time soon. He left me a message saying he ain't that stupid! So I think you're OK to stand down tonight and I'll see you at the briefing at eight thirty.'

'OK, well, you're the boss, so I'll see you later. And look, it was good to see you earlier; if you want to come over later when you finish…do you hear me?' But she was talking to a dead connection.

CHAPTER 50

As Sweetman drove, he cursed under his breath. Cooper had no idea of the amount of hurt coming his way. Not only had he brought Sweetman to the attention of the law, he'd managed to cut him badly *and* steal his Glock. Sweetman vowed that Cooper would pay for these transgressions in the severest way. But first he needed weapons. The police had no information on him, and no idea where he lived. It didn't matter if they did a trace on the Mercedes pickup, it was registered to the Whitelines Entertainment group and a trace on his encrypted phone would prove useless too. And being self-employed, he was damn sure he hadn't given his address to anyone, including Cooper. It was at times like this he was pleased he'd put his married sister's name on the deeds when he'd purchased the house. It would be safe enough to go home for the next hour or so.

Sweetman had left fingerprints all over the Mercedes and a bucketful of blood in the pub; certainly enough to get a DNA sample and result. But he couldn't resist a chuckle as he imagined their annoyance when the fingerprints and DNA samples registered zilch, no hits at all on the Police National Database. He'd managed to keep his identity, if not his various activities, well under the radar. Now though, thanks to Cooper, he'd have to be more canny than ever. Sweetman knew that as soon as the police caught up with Cooper, he'd spill his guts about everyone and everything Aksanov, the World Citizen Hotel and the two nightclubs were involved in. Maybe now was the time to call in a few favours from the Brotherhood.

Turning off the siren and flashing lights, he headed in the direction of his home. He parked up a little way from where he left his Audi A3 and killed the engine. He left the keys in the ignition and stepped out of the ambulance. The street was well lit and crammed with parked cars, but there was no one about so, pulling up his hood, he jogged the short distance to his car.

Parking outside his house, he let himself in and, though he was almost 100 per cent certain that neither Cooper nor Aksanov knew where he lived, he decided to grab what he needed and clear out. He needed cash and weapons, and, as a well-trained soldier, he always had an exit strategy. His rucksack and cricket bag were packed and ready for such an eventuality. The effort of loading the bags into the Audi, opened up the cuts on his right hand, and blood started seeping through the bandage. Carefully he unwrapped his damaged hand, washed the blood off under the cold tap and dried it. Looking through the cupboard under the sink, he found a tube of superglue and his first aid kit. Taking out a new bandage, he put it to one side and picked up the superglue. With his left hand he squeezed out the glue onto his palm, effectively sealing the cuts. His face screwed up in pain as he spat *fuck fuck fuck* through gritted teeth. It was excruciating – he knew it would be, he'd done it before. As the glue solidified, the pain gradually lessened.

He threw the empty tube into the bin, lit a cigarette and waited for the glue to cure enough for him to re-bandage his hand. As he smoked, his mobile rang and when he saw *Coop* on the screen, he snatched up the phone.

'Cooper you cu—' was as far as he got. He listened to the caller for some seconds then said, 'So who the fuck are you?' But the connection was dead. He sat for a moment contemplating the call.

'Fuckin' clever bastard, worked it out then,' he said out loud. He knew this was the start of a whole different ballgame. Fucking Aksanov, he thought, this guy Stafford should have been dealt with permanently, weeks ago, but I'll take that up with him later. As he pondered his next move, he sent a text back to Cooper's phone. He was vulnerable, no two ways about it. It was time to call in favours from Third Floor Sheila before his meet with Amos.

CHAPTER 51

At 05:30 hours, Stafford parked in the Aldershot police station car park, dragged his briefcase off the passenger seat and got out. He and Ryan Peters had spent two fruitless hours, in the dark, wandering around Frimley Park Hospital. Cooper was nowhere to be seen, and according to a triage nurse, no one had presented with the sort of facial injuries Stafford described. They'd gone home, but Stafford had been unable to sleep. Frustrated by the night's debacle, he decided to get to the briefing room early and try to make sense of this ever-expanding investigation. He walked into the reception area and signed in at the desk, receiving a visitor's ID card on a blue and white striped lanyard, and a comment about the briefing not being till eight thirty.

He climbed the stairs and entered the incident room. His mood was always lifted when he entered an incident room like this and saw the array of top-notch IT equipment in use. The irony never failed to amuse him. Since the introduction of the Proceeds of Crime Act 2002, criminal assets could be seized by police and auctioned off, and the proceeds used for various community projects. Much of the top-of-the-range computer equipment found its way into incident rooms like this, utilised in the ongoing fight against crime.

Stafford had called this briefing and knew the whole group would be looking to him for leadership. The events of the last few days had stretched their resources and pulled them away from their main goal. He needed to refocus the investigation. Ryan Peters and Nicole Martin had been contacting everyone involved with the investigation so far. They had included the forensic teams, the officers who had searched the Weyhill compound, police photographers; anyone who they thought could make a sensible contribution.

Of course the attack on Sophie Gibson and the killings of Floyd Winstone, Kurt Edwards, Abduk Ravani and Hakim Buzdar needed to be investigated further. But Stafford was sure these events had been coordinated by the head of the criminal syndicate to deflect the investigation from their door, a way to muddy the waters, giving them time to regroup. By hurting people involved in the investigation, they hoped Stafford would lose his grip. Stafford needed his crew to focus on whoever was coordinating these happenings. It seemed obvious that the World Citizen Hotel was central to much of the criminal activity. Pavel Aksanov, Howard Neilson and now Jamie Sweetman had to be the main focus of the investigation.

But the whole point of coming in so early was to use the whiteboards and photographs of the people who'd been killed and try to link them in a way that would move the investigation forward. He opened up his briefcase and pulled out a stack of brown folders. He selected a range of photographs and a couple of marker pens. On the left-hand side of the first whiteboard, he put photos of those who had been killed while operation *Trashed* was ongoing. On the right-hand side he put up pictures of the criminals thought to have been involved in these deaths. People like Aksanov, Kapusniak, Runihura, Winstone, Amos, Miller and Matis Bockus, the Polish lad who had died in Winchester Prison. Using a black marker, he linked the dead on the left to those on the right suspected of being involved in their deaths. Then, using a red marker, he linked the Weyhill criminals to the World Citizen Hotel via the criminals' lawyer, Howard Neilson, and the use of Mercedes X-Class pickups registered to the umbrella group Whitelines Entertainments Ltd and therefore to Whitelines nightclub.

While Stafford needed to show this progression at the briefing, the CPS and DCI Talbot were currently pursuing further charges and the possible deportation of Kapusniak. On the left-hand side of the second board, he put photos of the two dead Asian men, Floyd Winstone, Kurt Edwards and Sophie Gibson. On the right-hand side he put pictures of Aksanov, Neilson, Sweetman, Cooper and the Queens Arms Pub. Using his marker pens, he showed links to Aksanov and his hotel. And to Neilson via his knowledge of the hotel and the fact he was the Weyhill crew's legal representative. He included links to Whitelines via Edwards and Cooper working there and driving Mercedes pickup trucks, and a link to their involvement in the attack on Sophie Gibson. Finally he showed links to Sweetman via the attack at the pub and the Merc truck.

He stood back and contemplated his efforts. Picking up the red marker, he drew a cross on the faces of all those who were now dead. After a moment or two he put the empty folders and marker pens back into his briefcase and decided it was time for a coffee. Waiting for the kettle to boil, he could hear footsteps and chatter as the investigating team began to gather.

Joining him in the kitchen, Sergeant Hawkins said, 'I hear you've come to your senses and brought Sergeant Martin back into the fold.'

Stafford hesitated a moment, hunted for a clean mug and waved it at the sergeant. 'You want a coffee?' he said.

'You can't dodge the question that easily, Major,' said the sergeant, smiling.

'I wasn't trying to dodge the question, I was merely being pleasant. And yes, Sergeant Martin will be working alongside us again. And I'm sure you know I didn't get a lot of choice in the matter. But I'm pretty sure we can keep her out of harm's way.'

Stafford finished making their coffees and they walked back to the incident room together. Though the room now heaved with people, many of them milling around and pointing at various parts of the whiteboards, it was unusually quiet. Stafford saw why – the presence of DCI Talbot from Police HQ. Stafford groaned inwardly and hoped the DCI wouldn't try to commandeer the briefing. He was standing at the front of the room looking at the whiteboards while talking to a tall, slim man of about forty-five. The man had cropped brown hair and was wearing a light grey suit, white shirt and striped blue tie. Stafford hadn't met him before and the relative silence in the room indicated many of the others hadn't either. DCI Talbot, noticing Stafford and Hawkins' arrival, waved them over.

'Ah, there you are, Major. I thought I would come along and introduce Aldershot's new detective inspector. Major Stafford, this is DI Thomas Masterson.'

Sergeant Hawkins, who'd met the DI earlier, nodded and made his way into the body of the room.

Masterson reached out his hand to Stafford.

'Good to meet you, Major. DCI Talbot has explained your attachment to the Hampshire Force and though I'm still in the process of getting settled in, you can be assured of my support and help as and when you need it.'

Stafford asked if the DI was staying around for the duration of the briefing; Talbot answered for him.

'Yes, I want him to get up to speed with this investigation as soon as possible, it seems to be dragging on... Thomas, er, DI Masterson has a rep for getting things done, so the quicker he gets involved the better. So get stuck in, Thomas... Good, that's all, I look forward to talking to you later.' As an afterthought, he nodded to Stafford, said *Major*, then turned and walked away.

'Yes, sir, thank you, sir,' said Masterson, but Talbot was already halfway out of the door.

Stafford gave a sigh of relief. It was his experience that the more the top brass got involved, the more things slowed down as the levels of bureaucracy and paper increased. That was why the E Squadron had been so successful – normally there was only one senior officer involved and he would let his men get on with the job.

Stafford looked at Masterson and said, 'Right, Tom, we're still waiting for a few more people to arrive, so find yourself a seat or grab a coffee, and when the crew are all here I'll start off the briefing by introducing you to the assembled masses. OK?'

A few moments passed and Stafford was just about to call the meeting to order when a uniformed officer poked his head around the doorframe, leaned in and called over. 'Major Stafford, there's a call for you.'

Stafford screwed up his face and said, 'Can't you get someone else to deal with it?'

'Well, sir, it's the DI at Basingstoke, says he was trying to reach DCI Talbot, but can't get any reply. He thinks you should take the call instead, says it's important.'

'OK, patch it through then, constable,' said Stafford and seconds later a phone on the nearest desk to him rang. Before it could ring a second time Stafford had the receiver to his ear; he said nothing, listening. The room was eerily quiet as those assembled tried to tune into the conversation. Moments later, chairs were being scraped on the floor as the group began to get fidgety, murmuring to each other and trying to ascertain the subject of the call. At last Stafford was heard to say, 'OK, will you get back to the lead officer at the hotel, and get them to separate staff into one room, guests into another. No one, repeat, no one should be allowed to leave. Get as many coppers as you can with mobiles to photograph all the guests, and prepare to start taking statements. Make sure the lead has my mobile number and get them to ring me when that's done. Got that? Good, thank you.'

Slowly Stafford put the receiver in its cradle, placed both hands on the desk, leaned forward and appeared to be looking thoughtfully out of the nearest window. It was ten seconds before he stood up and moved to the front of the room. By now the room was buzzing, everyone speculating on what they'd overheard. Stafford faced the group, the silence immediate, and said, 'This briefing is adjourned.'

As a group, they all started with questions. Stafford raised his hand to silence them, and continued, 'But all of you involved in this investigation are to reconvene as soon as possible at the World Citizen Hotel near Basingstoke. Pavel Aksanov is dead.'

CHAPTER 52

Cooper had no intention of going to hospital; he had his own private nurse. Knowing the police would be looking out for the Polo, he drove carefully, using as many side roads as he could, determined to avoid ANPR and CCTV cameras. From Farnborough, he aimed for the old Fleet Road, which took him under the M3 and on to Hartley Wintney. From there it was a straight run in to his sister's on the other side of Basingstoke, using the old London Road. Although it was a longer route than across town, traffic was sparse and he made good time. He parked up three streets from his sister's flat. Hunched over, he limped slowly and painfully towards it.

Charlotte lived in a rented first-floor, two-bedroom flat on one of the major council estates. He knew she'd gone to work after leaving his flat. Even allowing for a twelve-hour shift he guessed she would be home or at least on her way, but her car wasn't outside. He cursed himself for losing his phone. Mumbling away to himself, he pushed open the street door. The hallway was spacious and clean-smelling, serving just two flats in the building. He rang Charlotte's doorbell and could hear the chimes, managing a smile as he recognised the *banjo on my knee* refrain from 'Oh Susanna'.

He rang three, four times, not because he liked the tune, but to wake her up. Getting no response, he leaned against the wall and slowly slid to the floor. Exhaustion had taken over, the adrenalin dissipated. He fell asleep.

Half an hour later he was startled awake when his sister screamed as she stumbled over his legs in the dark of the hallway. Cooper struggled to his feet, disorientated, and then the pain kicked in, reminding him just how badly he'd been beaten. With a grunt of realisation he leaned against the rear wall.

Finding the light switch and recognising her brother, Charlotte looked at him in despair. Fumbling her key in the door, she said, 'Ray, you arsehole, what the fuck have you done now?'

Wincing, Cooper hauled himself after her into the kitchen where he slumped on to a chair. Leaning both elbows on the table, he said, 'Sorry about this, sis. I just need a couple of paracetamol and a quick wipe down with a damp cloth and I'll be on my way.'

Charlotte stared at him as the kettle came to a boil but, despite being furious, couldn't help but smile at his attempt at humour. She shook her head in sorrow, then handed him a mug of tea.

'Drink this,' she said, 'then I'll clean you up a bit.' Mug in hand, she sat down opposite him. 'So what happened this time?'

Cooper hesitated for a moment, and then decided she deserved an explanation. 'This bloke we work for asked me to do a job… Well, not that I had a choice.' As they drank their tea, Cooper told her about the day's events. While he talked, Charlotte got a bowl of warm water, placed it on the table and began to bathe his wounds. The worst injury was to his nose – it was split and badly swollen, obviously broken, but he refused to go to hospital to get it set. He told her he'd gone to Stafford's house, hoping to be taken into custody, but instead he'd got a beating. Charlotte finished tidying him up as best she could, but when she'd poured away the bloody water, she studied him. His eyes were distended, his nose split, his cheeks red and bloated.

'Christ, Ray, you're going to have a couple of right bloody shiners in the morning.' She grabbed a clean towel and, sitting down beside him, dabbed his face and hands dry. She sat quietly for a moment, and then asked, 'So these two men, Sweetman and what was the other one's name? Aksy-something?'

'Yeah, Aksanov.'

'Well those two; you say they're out to kill you?'

'Reckon so. They've already done for Kurt, I think.'

'*What*? When did that happen? Bloody hell, Ray, what the fuck have you got yourself into? What the fuck have you done?'

Her anger was such that Cooper couldn't look at her. Elbows on the table, he cupped his head in his hands. 'They must have got to him earlier today. I went to go back home, but the whole street was full of cops. That's when I went to the pub. Turns out Aksanov's got a tracker on the motor, must've sent Sweetman after me.' Again there was silence between them.

It was Charlotte who broke it. 'Christ almighty, you do get yourself in some shit. Look, you can kip in the spare bedroom tonight, but listen to me, Ray. You've done some pretty bad stuff, but you haven't killed anyone, have you?...

Have you?' When he shook his head, she continued, 'So tomorrow morning you need to get yourself down to the police station and hand yourself in. OK, you may end up in prison for a few years, but at least you'll still be alive.'

'I gotta tell you, sis, I handed myself in, down in Eastleigh. And I sat there for bloody hours waiting to be interviewed by that bastard Stafford. There was another geezer there. You know, one of the mob that got busted down in Weyhill. Waiting for ages we were, and then they reckoned they had too much going on. They just chucked the pair of us out. Bailed us with a *we'll need to talk to you again – don't leave the country* threat. Bloody wankers. The other geezer said he thought he was fucked. He reckoned the guy we work for already put down two of his mates, and one of them was banged up at the time. So this fella we been working for – Pavel fucking Aksanov – he's been cleaning house, seems to me. So, sis, nowhere's fucking safe.'

'Least you'll be OK, tonight, Ray. Then see what tomorrow brings, eh?'

Cooper couldn't rest, though. He had around six hours of fitful sleep before he decided to get up. His sister was still in bed when he dressed and moved quietly into the kitchen. As he sat drinking a cup of tea, he switched on the little radio. It was tuned to the local station and playing a stream of eighties music. Cooper wandered over to the kitchen window and opened it. He stood there for a moment and lit a cigarette. He wasn't actually listening to the music, but to the sounds of the rush-hour traffic as it began to build. He returned to the chair, quietly singing along with Spandau Ballet's 'True', when it came to an abrupt end as the radio presenter said: *Sorry to break into that song, but we're getting reports of a shooting at the well-known five-star World Citizen Hotel.* Cooper grabbed the radio and turned up the volume just as Charlotte came into the kitchen. Using the still warm water in the kettle, she made a cup of coffee and sat at the table with her brother. He put a finger to his bruised lips and mouthed *listen*.

The presenter continued: *The hotel is in lockdown, with a massive police presence since around eight o'clock this morning. Though no details have been formally issued, our source at the hotel tells us that a senior member of the management team was found shot dead in his office earlier this morning. Police have issued no details and are asking for people to stay away. A police spokesman at the site said a press conference would be held later, once next of kin have been informed – don't worry, we'll keep you up to date as we get more details. So now folks, it's back to the music…*

Cooper didn't sing along this time, he just sat there stunned; unsure if this was good or bad news. After a moment's thought he perked up considerably, and said out loud, 'If it's Aksanov that's dead, why would Sweetman still want to kill me?' It was a rhetorical question. To his sister, he said, 'Hey, Charlie, can I borrow your phone for a minute? I might be able to get myself out of the shit here.'

She stared at him, grim-faced, then softened and slid her phone across the table to him. He sat looking at it for a moment or two, and slowly tapped the screen. 'I think I can still remember his number,' he said, putting the mobile to his ear. It went to voicemail. He hesitated a fraction, then said, 'It's Coop… I guess you heard about the hotel. Listen, after the pub last night, Stafford jumped me and gave me a fuckin' good hiding. Believe me, I ain't going to spill to them, mate. Can we meet up and talk? Stafford took my phone, I've borrowed this one. I'll contact you again when I've sorted a new one.'

He ended the call and passed the phone back to his sister. She looked at him, trying and failing to catch his eye.

'Are you sure you're doing the right thing, here? I still think you should hand yourself in to the nearest police station.'

'Nah. This is best. Bloody Stafford wanted me running scared of Aksanov. Now if he's dead, I might be OK.'

She still couldn't catch his eye.

CHAPTER 53

It was a split second before the group found their voice and responded. Then everyone had questions. This time Stafford had to raise both arms and shout to quieten the room.

'He was found in his office this morning. Basingstoke are in attendance and have effectively locked the place down. Apparently it looks like murder, one bullet to the head, but he'd been badly beaten prior to being shot. So, ladies and gentlemen, before we set out, I want two of you uniformed boys to take over the gate duties from the Basingstoke lads, and the rest of uniform to help out photographing and interviewing the hotel guests.'

He turned to the new DI. 'Are you going to be joining us, Detective Inspector?' DI Masterson, eyes wide, looked like a cornered animal, but managed a nodded yes as Stafford turned to Nicole and said, 'DS Martin, you're with PC Whitley in the lead squad car – this time of the morning blues and twos all the way. Tom, jump in with me. You forensics guys know what to do. And Sergeant Hawkins, do me a favour, see if you've got a charger to fit this, it'll be good to see who Cooper's been talking to.' He handed the sergeant an evidence bag containing Cooper's phone. A second bag held the gun he'd taken from Cooper. 'And best put that somewhere safe too.'

The sergeant nodded and took the bags. 'Anything interesting I'll get back to you.'

'OK, let's go and do this,' said Stafford.

As he sped through the corridors and down the stairs with Masterson at his side, Stafford couldn't help but think, *Jeez, where do they get 'em from? Another one, supposedly on the fast track – but to where? Disaster?*

Out in the car park, Masterson pulled up short and screwed up his face in disbelief as Stafford led him to his ancient Volvo. 'You're kidding?' he said.

'Don't worry about how it looks, it's called low-key,' said Stafford with a grin.

'I can think of another name for it,' said Masterson.

Stafford grinned again as he jumped in, fired up the motor and said, 'Wait till you see how she performs, you may well change your opinion. She's got all the gizmos you can think of. Rebuilt to my spec just recently, so get strapped in and hold on tight.' He put his mobile in it's cradle and set it to voice control, and as they joined the line of vehicles heading out of the police station car park he received message.

'Major Stafford? I'm a forensic technician. I didn't get chance to talk to you this morning, but I swept the house where Kurt Edwards was killed. Sergeant Martin pointed out a cigarette butt, different to all the others, in an ashtray there and asked us to run a DNA test on it. I was discussing it with one of my colleagues from last night's crime scene before we set off for this morning's meeting… Anyway, he showed me the results of the tests he rushed through at your request for this morning, and the DNA matches up. The injured man at the pub last night – the one who stole the ambulance – had also been in the flat where Edwards was killed.'

Stafford took a moment to digest the information.

'Bloody good work, thanks for letting me know. I take it you're on your way to the World Citizen, so I'll catch up with you there. Great work – and pass the message on to your colleague.' Stafford slumped back in his seat, whistled, looked at his passenger and said, 'Well, well, well. At last a decent lead… looks like our "victim" from the pub last night had an extremely good reason to flee the scene.'

While Stafford appreciated the usefulness of forensic evidence in gaining a conviction, he also understood that forensics such as this simply helped to put the suspect at or near the crime scene. Real detective work would be needed to prove a suspect had indeed committed the offence, but it would surely help. *God knows we could do with it.*

The morning rush-hour traffic was slow to part. The convoy, all using their blues and twos, managed to pass at high speed by dodging right and left, finding the clearest lanes. They completed the twenty-three-mile journey in around eighteen minutes. The final cars in the convoy parked across the hotel's open gateway to block it. Everyone disembarked and began to assemble at the foot of the faux Grecian portico entrance to the hotel.

The forensic techs opened up their vans and took out various bits of equipment, handing out forensic gloves, suits and booties to those who needed them. Stafford and Masterson were met by a uniformed police sergeant from the Basingstoke unit.

'Ah, good; Sergeant, if you'll show this lot where they need to be, then meet me in reception in five minutes, OK?'

The sergeant nodded and called for the assembled crew to follow him. Stafford walked over to the two Basingstoke police constables at the front gateway.

'I'm Major Paul Stafford, on attachment to Hampshire Police – thanks for what you've done here. Two of my lads are coming across to relieve you, so have yourselves a break, then join the crew interviewing and photographing the hotel guests. OK?' Both men responded with nods.

Stafford and Masterson walked to the steps leading to the two huge glass front doors, and spotted the Basingstoke sergeant waiting in the luxurious reception area. Stafford reached out his hand.

'I'm Stafford, Major Paul Stafford – you're probably aware by now that me and my oppo Captain Ryan Peters are on attachment to Hampshire Police until further notice to try and clear up this and other ongoing investigations.'

'Yeah, good to meet you, Major. I've been following the details on the PND; great results down in Southampton and Andover, by the way.'

'Well, we did put some bad bastards away and pulled a few immigrants out of the firing line, but we've not been able to get at the main men and now it looks as though one of the key players has been taken out. Annoying – we were just starting to get close. Anyway, thanks for keeping things together here.'

'No worries, Major. Where do you want to start?'

'Well, best start with the end of Aksanov and whoever found the body, I guess.'

The sergeant looked amused, and started to walk away. 'Best follow me, then, Major,' he said as they walked past the reception desk, where the same receptionist as before was holding a wad of tissues to her red and puffy eyes. 'It was one of the cleaners who found him. She's in their rest room having a cup of tea.'

'OK, we'll catch up with her later,' said Stafford, as they took the stairs to the first floor and turned left. Some twenty-five metres along the corridor he could see a door marked *Staff Only*. Immediately to their left was an open door leading into a large office suite. A police constable stood outside holding an entry log. As Stafford moved forward to sign it, he could see Aksanov's massive body lying alongside the equally massive desk. Vivian Ford, the pathologist, was kneeling beside him still in the process of examining the corpse. Aksanov was flat on his back, fully clothed: dark grey trousers, black leather shoes and what would have been a white shirt. The long-sleeved shirt was saturated with dried blood.

Stafford tapped his knuckles on the doorframe and the pathologist looked up, smiled, stood up, took off her latex gloves, walked towards the door and dropped the gloves into a brown paper sack. Offering her hand to Stafford she said, 'I have to say, Major Stafford, the bullet to his head was the killer, but the way this poor bastard had been beaten earlier, it was an act of kindness.'

Stafford took a pace or two into the room and could see how badly damaged Aksanov's face and head were. It was difficult when looking at the face to understand where the obvious identifying features were, or had been. Yes, the bullet hole in the centre of the forehead was obvious, but it was difficult to make out which was the actual left eye socket. Or where the left eye was. It was difficult too, to see precisely where the mouth started; but the bloody and gaping hole was definitely a mouth, identified by the one or two shattered teeth still protruding from broken gums. A strip of bloody gaffer tape hung from his left cheek, bits of flesh and broken teeth sticking to it. The thick beige carpet was dark brown from the amount of blood he had lost, starting around his waist and including an eighteen-inch halo around his head. Stafford noticed too, that Aksanov's hands were bloody and broken, with fingers and thumbs in unnatural angles and shapes. Wounds he'd likely received while trying to defend himself from the frenzied attack.

Stafford fought to eliminate his immediate compassionate thoughts, remembering instead how many lives this man had ruined, saying, 'Looks like someone got fed up with him cleaning house, and totally lost their rag. This looks like the work of someone out of control. So, doc, what the hell was he beaten with?'

'Best guess,' said the doctor, 'is a Cobra King.'

'A what?'

'A Cobra King – a brand, spanking new golf driver. A bloody great big golf club,' she said, indicating the golf bag in the corner.

'*What?*'

'Yes, you said that already,' said the doc with a grin. 'Look, I can't tell you any more until I get him on my table. I've done all I can here.'

'So can you give us any idea of time? And is there an exit wound?'

'I hope to be able to tell you more later, but best guess time-wise, I reckon somewhere between eleven p.m. and four a.m., and no, no exit wound.' As she was talking she'd stepped out into the corridor and removed her forensic suit and booties and stuffed them into the brown paper sack. She signed out, then said, 'We'll get him out of your way in five.'

'We OK to go in now?'

'Yes, all the real detective work's been done now.'

Stafford gave her a sideways glance and said, 'I'll need that bullet soon as possible, doc.'

As he walked over to the body with Masterson and the Basingstoke sergeant, Stafford said to no one in particular, 'To think I've been fretting over catching this bastard for weeks and now some scumbag has scuppered our chance of getting him in front of a jury. But I won't let the fucker rest in peace. I'll make sure all his assets are seized and put to helping the lives of people he's destroyed.'

Stafford looked around, hoping to locate the forensic tech who'd phoned him on the way here. The white-suited tech spotted him, pulled off his latex gloves and walked across. As they shook hands, Stafford said, 'Can I leave you to get the bullet when it's retrieved at the PM and ship it to the National Ballistic Intelligence Service, then get them to do some comparison tests alongside the other bullets we've sent them?'

'Yep, we'd do that anyway where we haven't got the firearm used in the shooting.'

'Great, I appreciate that, but can you follow it up for me, and keep chasing it? Could do with a speedy result here. The media are going to go apeshit over this one.'

The tech looked at Stafford, and said, 'Don't worry, Major, we're on it.'

Stafford smiled and said, 'Yeah, yeah, course you are

– sorry, you know how it is.' He hesitated a moment, then said, 'Have you finished with Aksanov's laptop?' He indicated it on the desk.

'Yes, we've checked it for prints, but we do need to take it away and get one of our boffins to check it out, see what secrets it can tell us. But no problem if you want to check something now.'

'That's great, shouldn't take me too long – but talking about secrets, have you found Aksanov's mobile phone?'

'No, we've been through his pockets and desk drawers, but haven't found one yet. Which we thought was odd.'

Stafford pulled a face; disappointment, not surprise. He slid into Aksanov's deluxe leather office chair and scooted across to the desk. He opened the laptop and, as he waited for it to boot up, took out his mobile and called Sergeant Hawkins at the Aldershot nick.

'It's Stafford. Listen, Tony, that Mercedes with the shot-out tyres, has that been removed from the pub yet?'

'Not yet, we're putting the wheels in motion now, if you'll pardon the pun. But the one left on the roundabout, we brought back here.'

'Good, do me a favour – get one of your lads to find the tracking devices on them and get hold of the numbers. The vehicle we checked in Eastleigh earlier had it located on the left side looking into the engine compartment.'

'Will do. It'll only take minutes to do the one parked up here, but I'll phone the recovery truck people as well. They should be on their way to pick it up. I'll give them your number because they'll be taking it down to Eastleigh. OK?'

'Yes that's great, thanks.' Stafford ended the call and left his phone on the desk. The laptop screensaver was a picture of the hotel's golf course clubhouse. With a click of the mouse, it was replaced with a desktop showing thirty or so apps, not even password-protected. He found the vehicle tracking app and logged straight in. Aksanov, he thought, was either very arrogant or had very little patience, and couldn't be arsed with PINs and passwords.

CHAPTER 54

Twenty minutes later, Hawkins rang back. Stafford had meanwhile navigated his way into the tracker app website and found out how to use its various functions. He was mainly interested in the one that showed any vehicle's historical movements. He was so involved, it was a second or two before he realised his mobile was vibrating and rattling around the desk. Grabbing it, he accepted the call; hit speaker so he could take notes.

'OK, Staf, nice and easy for you: the Mercedes used by Cooper is zero-one-four; the one with the shot-out tyres is zero-one-one. Hope that's going to help?'

'Yes, cheers, Tony, I'll let you know how I get on.'

Call ended, Stafford put the phone back on the desk, rubbed his hands together, interlaced his fingers and cracked his knuckles. It was only while doing this that he realised the new DI was no longer in the room. He shrugged, and then typed 0-1-4 into the system, requesting details of its movements since it was driven away from Eastleigh Police HQ. It showed that Cooper had driven close to his own flat, but stopped some distance away, stayed for five or so minutes, then U-turned and driven off. Stafford knew the grim truth, of course, but try as he might, he couldn't help being amused as he watched this about-turn in the opposite direction. To some, it might seem unfeeling finding humour while investigating a brutal murder; to Stafford, however – and to murder squads and soldiers the world over – finding laughs in the darkest places helped keep them sane. Stafford's check showed Cooper had noted the police presence and decided to stay well clear.

He keyed in the date and time of Sophie Gibson's assault and cursed out loud when it showed the vehicle had spent a considerable amount of time in the car park of the Royal Hampshire County Hospital. It also showed that car 014 hadn't been near Flat 10a in Aldershot's North Lane. Keying in 0-1-1, Stafford began tracing Sweetman's movements. He wanted to see where the vehicle was the day Winstone, Ravani and Buzdar were killed and, more recently, Kurt Edwards. Keying in the first date, the tracker showed conclusively that car 011 had been at both the Aldershot and Basingstoke addresses. The timescale the pathologist had given for the deaths tallied with the new onscreen data.

Stafford called over one of the forensic techs and said, 'Not sure how to do this, so could you take screenshots for me and ship them to my email address?'

'Yeah, course – no problem,' said the tech, sitting down at the desk. Stafford showed him what he needed and, after just a couple of minutes, the tech stood up, saying, 'There you go, all done.'

Stafford sank back onto the leather chair, thinking the evidence against Sweetman was growing. But if he was just the hitman, who would he be taking orders from now? Or could it be that Sweetman was moving up the chain of command? As Stafford pondered, he was joined in the office by Ryan Peters and Nicole Martin. Bringing up the rear was PC Whitley.

Stafford explained what he'd discovered, then said, 'So folks, let's look for motives. I can see how Sweetman would benefit from Aksanov's death, but if he's responsible for the Aldershot and Basingstoke killings, what's with all the rage here?' said Stafford.

'Right,' said Peters. 'Everything else he's done has been calm and calculated. Then he loses his rag with his paymaster? I don't see it, but can you two think of a better motive or suspect for Aksanov's murder?'

PC Whitley, his face red with the embarrassment of feeling out of his depth, said, 'What about Amos or Cooper? They must have known they'd been targeted – maybe one of them decided to go on the attack?'

'Good thought, Harry,' said Martin, 'but knowing them as we do, I don't think they have it in them... Staf, why don't we use the tracker app to see where Sweetman goes at night? He's the only lead that's not cold and we don't even know where he lives.'

Everyone was silent for a moment. Stafford looked up at her. 'Good point, Nicole, bloody good point,' he said, turning back to the laptop and opening the tracker app. 'Let's see where the bugger parks 011 at night.'

Whitley whistled and said, 'Good call, Sarge.'

They crowded round the laptop and watched Stafford pinpoint the street and then the house where Vehicle No. 011 had recently been parked up for five nights in a row.

'OK, Nicole, will you find the sergeant from Basingstoke – get him to call the station and get an unmarked car and a couple of bods to keep the house under surveillance? Meanwhile, I'll get on to DCI Talbot – get a couple of armed response vehicles there asap. We also need warrants, including one to freeze and search any bank accounts.' As Nicole nodded and went to find the sergeant, Stafford turned to Peters and Whitley, and said, 'Right, you two find the hotel's head of security – he should be in with the staff for interviews – get him to trawl through last night's CCTV pictures from, say, twenty-one hundred hours onwards. I want to see what vehicles were coming and going.'

Stafford called DCI Talbot and outlined what he needed, then left the office and wandered slowly along the corridor noting a number of what he guessed were CCTV cameras built into the ceiling lights. He made a mental note to talk to the Guv about them – and there he was, talking to Peters and Whitley, as Stafford walked back down the stairs. He caught up with them and the guy led them to the security office. Stafford was stunned at the size of the room and the number of workstations.

'Jesus,' he said, 'you do take your work seriously, don't you?'

Guv puffed out his chest, 'I always say, if a job's worth doing—'

Peters interrupted him. 'Right, so let's hope the system doesn't collapse, as it did on our first, uh, imaginary meeting.'

Red faced and frowning, Guv rushed to the nearest workstation and switched on the monitor.

'No, no, we don't often have glitches like that, it's all sorted and hunky-dory now.'

'That's good to hear, because as you well know, this is a murder enquiry – any lack of cooperation and you will be arrested for attempting to pervert the course of justice. Is that understood?'

'Yeah, yes, of course. So where do you want to start?'

Stafford said, 'In the car park at around nine o'clock last night.'

The Governor tapped a few keys and the screen divided into six pictures. The car park was fairly full – mostly with vehicles, according to the security guy, belonging to hotel guests, rather than casual punters in the casino or bar. At that moment, Nicole Martin rejoined the group, catching Stafford's eye and giving a thumbs-up. Stafford nodded his thanks.

On screen, there was little movement. Peters asked if there was a camera aimed specifically at the front entrance. The Governor looked at Stafford, who nodded. The Guv tapped the keyboard and the screen filled with a long shot of the gateway. Stafford asked him to fast-forward to around ten thirty, then to fast-forward again. The Guv hit a key and the timestamp at the bottom showed *23:02*, then *00:34*. Nothing had moved in or out. Stafford indicated for the Guv to continue. *00:45, 01:15, 01:34…* Nothing.

'OK,' said Stafford, 'fast-forward to zero-one-fifty hours.'

The Governor held his finger down for a few seconds. The clock whizzed forward. For several seconds nothing moved. The lighting went up and down as unseen clouds skittered across the sky. At *02:02*, Guv hit stop and shifted the image back, and back, and back again. He hit the key for normal play speed. The time now showed *02:00*, the gateway was empty. The group watching seemed to hunch in closer. It seemed no one dared breathe. A beam of light crossed the threshold as a vehicle swung into the opening. Headlights blazed into the camera, making it difficult to see more than just a silhouette of a truck. As it moved slowly into the car park proper, the picture showed quite clearly that it was a battered white pickup truck.

The stunned silence was broken by Peters. 'That's the truck used to pick up Winstone from hospital. Amos was the driver, then. Flamin' truck's registered to him.'

The room was silent again, until Stafford said, 'Right, mate, can you get that on a DVD for us, please? And Nicole, Harry, will you check out the car park, see if it's still there. If it is, get the forensic team to check it out pronto.'

'OK, let's see if we can't make out who gets out of it.'

Stafford and Peters watched as the truck made its way further into the car park. Guv tapped more keys, changing the picture to a different camera, still with a view of the battered truck as it moved past a gap between two cars and started to reverse into the space.

Nicole came back into the room, sauntered across to the group huddled around the monitor, and tapped Stafford on the shoulder, saying, 'Yep, the pickup's still there. I've left Harry guarding it and asked the forensic crew to check it over. Oh, and I've also checked out the two rooms where the interviews are taking place – Amos isn't with either group.'

Stafford nodded his understanding and they both went back to watching the screen. She was so close, Stafford couldn't help but close his eyes for a split second as he drew in a pleasurable waft of her floral perfume.

As the truck reversed on screen, the glare of the headlights once again reduced the image to just a shimmering outline. A split second later, the vehicle lights went off. The internal cab light came on but was extinguished too quickly to allow any meaningful image of the occupants. The auto-exposure camera struggled to adjust to the change of the lighting conditions, but righted itself to give a reasonably good picture of the truck.

Everything remained still for two minutes, then the passenger door opened and a hooded figure stepped out. The door initially blocked the view of the passenger, but his build and the way he moved made it fairly obvious it was a man. As he moved round to close the door with his left hand, a bandage could clearly be seen on his right hand: Jamie Sweetman.

Stafford had been concentrating so hard on the right-hand side of the vehicle that he had to ask the Governor to backtrack to see who had been driving it. The image on screen shot back too far and they had to watch again as the vehicle reversed in and the headlights corrupted the image. He stared at the driver's door in absolute silence, breathing subdued, controlled. As the door swung open, the driver, head down, swiftly slammed it shut and ran towards the wall on which the camera was mounted. Despite playing it back three or four times, it was impossible to identify the driver. Unable to see his face – and they all agreed it was a he – the only hope of identifying him would be by the clothes he was wearing. With a modicum of luck, the hoody, jeans and trainers he had on would match the image on the CCTV footage from the Royal Hampshire County Hospital or from Anne Borley's interviews at Eastleigh HQ.

Stafford held up his hand up for quiet. To the Governor

he said, 'That's great so far. Now can you please continue to search the footage and see if you can spot these two guys trying to leave. Coming back into the car park, whatever.'

'Bloody hell, Major, that'll take forever.'

'Don't worry, I'll get a couple of lads to help you when they're finished with their interviews. And I see you have internal CCTV cameras – check those as well. Please.'

Stafford left the head of security sitting there and pulled his team over to a workstation about twenty feet away. As the three of them sat around the table, he leaned in and spoke quietly. 'So, Nic, I guess you didn't see Sweetman in the rooms when you checked for Amos?'

Nicole grinned. 'I wish,' she said.

'OK. Look, give PC Whitley a buzz, get him to pull in a couple of the Guv's lads once they've finished their interviews, to give a hand going through the footage.'

As she wandered away to make the call, Stafford said to Peters, 'This presents us with a bit of a conundrum, doesn't it? Two blokes turn up in an old truck, then what? They can't just disappear, leaving the wheels – so how did they get away from the hotel?'

'Maybe,' said Peters, 'they're still here.'

'Unlikely,' said Stafford. 'The first police lads and lassies on the scene checked out all the rooms. *Nada*, apparently.'

'OK, so, playing devil's advocate here, they made their way across the golf course?' said Peters.

'Unlikely again, not in the dead of night. Not unless they'd done a previous recce,' said Stafford.

'So Sweetman could have arrived in a separate vehicle, parked close by and been picked up by Amos – assuming the Ford's driver is Amos – meaning they had another getaway vehicle in the vicinity,' chipped in Nicole, having finished her call and rejoined them.

'And that also assumes both Sweetman and Amos were involved in the murder, but, from what I've seen of Amos, I don't think he's a killer,' said Stafford.

At that moment Whitley returned with two of the hotel's security team. Stafford called over to the Governor. 'OK, now set up PC Whitley with your lads and show him how to check out the internal cameras... Ryan, if you would check out all the reg numbers of the staff cars in the car park, see if they tally. Nicole, I want you to go down to reception and get the girl on the desk to help you go through the guest register and link everyone staying to the cars in the car park. See if they tally. OK?' She was nodding and beginning to walk away, when Stafford clapped his hand to his forehead.

'Wait! Christ, how could I have missed that?' Nicole stopped in her tracks – looked a question at him.

'While you're talking to her, find out if the Porsche Cayman registration's there and if those guys, Ravani and Buzdar were booked into the hotel.'

Nicole was quiet for a second then her eyes widened. 'Wow! Good thought, Staf.'

'Good, this could be really interesting,' said Stafford to her back as she made her way through the room, gracefully sashaying around the workstations. He swiftly turned back to the monitor in a desperate attempt to stay on track.

CHAPTER 55

Stafford wandered out of the security office and into the luxurious hotel lobby, where he sat on one of the banquettes in the waiting area. Something was gnawing away at his brain. After three or four moments deep in thought, he got up and walked into the room where staff were being interviewed, looking for the Basingstoke police sergeant. He wasn't there. He found him in the large ante room where the guest interviews were being carried out. Staying in the doorway, Stafford signalled to the sergeant, who walked across to him. As they stepped out into the corridor, Stafford said, 'So how's it going in there?'

The sergeant shrugged and said, 'We're getting nothing useful at all from this lot. It's a struggle to get their bloody names and, when you do, you realise they've all got something to hide. They're all a bunch of scumbags, but I don't think any of 'em are mixed up with this killing.'

'Yes, I'm getting the feeling that the perpetrators are long gone.'

'Your new DI chappie, I reckon he's ready to let the whole bunch of 'em get back to whatever they were doing.'

Amused, Stafford said with a straight face, 'Can't imagine any of them staying around for too long with all you coppers about… Anyway, something else you might be able to help me with – do you know if the ambulance stolen from the pub has been located yet?'

'Yeah, I heard it's been found,' said the sergeant quizzically.

'Good. Will you do me a favour? Get a couple of constables to knock on doors in that area, see if anyone remembers any cars being parked there before the ambulance turned up?'

'I'm on it. I'll get back to you asap.'

Stafford returned to the seating area, pulled out his mobile and called DCI Talbot. The call went to voicemail. He left a message explaining about the parked ambulance hoping it would help pinpoint Sweetman's current mode of transport.

Forty minutes later, Stafford's mobile rang, it was DCI Talbot, he confirmed they had pinpointed the house and continued, 'We had a couple of detective constables in unmarked cars watching the house. There was no movement in or out. We got two armed response vehicles out there …'

'I'm guessing he wasn't home,' said Stafford.

'No. But they confirmed it is Sweetman's place. We've put in a forensic team and they've found a few weapons, taser, knives, no fire arms, a small amount of cash and a small bag of what appears to be Class A drugs; looks like heroin, I'm told.'

'What about vehicles? Did they find any registration documents or insurance details?' Stafford didn't get an immediate response and could hear pages being turned.

DCI Talbot, he realised, was reading from a report. A report, typed up from notes, reread, edited, printed out, handed to him in person. Stafford couldn't help thinking what a waste of time it all was.

Talbot came back.

'Yes,' he said, 'they found registration documents for a four-year-old Audi A3 TDI, sports saloon. I've been on to the ANPR data centre at Hendon, they're searching as we speak.'

Stafford whistled.

'Nice motor,' he said. Talbot ignored him and continued, 'The registration, if you want it, is…' Another hesitation.

Of course I bloody want it, thought Stafford.

'VP17PPR,' came the response.

'And the colour?'

Another delay, paper rustling. Then, in a voice Stafford thought sounded almost petulant, the DCI said, 'Metallic Mythos Black, whatever that is.'

Stafford started to thank the DCI before realising he was talking to dead air. He stayed in the seating area, elbows on knees, looking at the floor, tapping the phone against his left palm. It was all beginning to point to Sweetman. But what was it Peters had said – *why all this rage?* OK, so the Aldershot killing had been staged, set up like a gruesome tableau, but that surely showed confidence, not rage or panic. And Edwards' death was simply cold and calculated, no rage evident at all. So if those killings were Sweetman's work, this new one, by anyone's standards, was messy in comparison. This was the work of someone who wanted Aksanov to suffer. Or to talk. The perpetrator or perpetrators wanted to prolong the agony. This, Stafford thought, was not a bid for the top job, this was vengeance. And if Stafford had read it right, Sweetman was now a target. Stafford went to find the sergeant from the Basingstoke nick. As he walked, he searched through his phone contacts, stopped on Sweetman's number and called it. It went to voicemail.

'Do me a favour,' Stafford said when he found the sergeant, 'contact your base and get them to put out a message to all coppers on patrol. We need them to be on the look-out for a metallic black Audi A3 TDI Sports Saloon.'

The sergeant pulled out his notebook and began to jot down the details. Stafford gave him the full details of the car and then continued, 'There may be two people on board. Jamie Sweetman and Tony Amos. These men should be regarded as armed and dangerous, and should not be approached. Report their position immediately when spotted, and try to keep them under discreet surveillance.'

'Consider it done, Stafford. What about ANPR?'

'DCI Talbot has sorted that with the national data centre, so it's in progress.'

The sergeant nodded and walked away, talking into his radio.

Stafford went back to the security office. Seconds later, Nicole Martin came charging in, notebook in hand, looking for him. Not able to see him immediately, she stopped in the doorway, bouncing with excitement. She couldn't stand still as she hunted him out. When she spotted him in the far corner, she rushed towards him.

Getting close, waving her notebook, she said in a loud whisper, 'Staf, Stafford, you'll never believe this. This is the break – look, when I checked with the girl on reception, neither of the Asian men were registered, nor was the car. She said she hadn't seen anyone matching their description come through to the restaurant or bar. In fact she knew nothing about them.'

'Yet according to Frank Healey, they were staying here.'

'I know. Also interesting, I noticed two unusual names in the register, and it turns out they're Russian, they arrived in a white Range Rover and its registration number was logged in the system. They don't seem to have checked out, so I tried the room where they're interviewing the guests, but they're not in there. I also checked the car park – their car's gone.'

'Does the receptionist think they've done a runner?'

'No, she seems to think they were friends of Aksanov's and she thinks they went for a night out at his Whitelines nightclub. But they haven't returned here, for sure, she says.'

'Excellent work, Nic,' he said. 'Mind you, it's bloody worrying. We might just have found ourselves in the middle of a three-way turf war. Now, will you press on in here while I do a bit of checking outside?'... *Christ, she looks more excited than worried.*

Walking through the foyer, he stood for a second as the huge glass front doors hissed and slid smoothly open. He took the entrance steps two at a time, then strode across the car park to his Volvo. He lowered himself into the driving seat and sat still for a while, putting all thoughts of the investigation out of his mind. In the quiet of his old car, he felt cocooned, comforted, at peace.

Some ten minutes later, he got out of the car and walked deeper into the car park then round to the rear of the hotel. At the edge of the golf course, he looked at the vast sea of green; with hotel guests in lockdown and the police controlling the gateway, no one was playing. He looked back towards the hotel and nodded to himself; back in the moment. He noticed a pair of black wooden doors in one section of the rear wall – presumably the deliveries entrance. As he walked towards them he could see a keyless entry pad on the right-hand door. But the small gap between showed considerable damage to both doors; they had been jemmied apart. Small slivers of wood still littered the ground – a sign, he thought, that this had happened recently.

He hesitated, then returned to his car and opened the boot. Removing the cover from his go-bag, he opened it and took out his hand gun. He slipped out the magazine, fully loaded, then pushing it back in, he checked the chamber indicator with his thumb. It was raised; one in the chamber. Satisfied, he slipped it in to his jacket's inside pocket, then took out his Scorpion clasp knife, closed and covered the bag again, locked up the car and, knife in hand, returned to the doors.

Pulling out the knife's marlin spike, he eased it into the gap and began to apply pressure; the right-hand door began to open. Folding the spike away he slipped the knife into the pocket of his jeans and took out his gun. Putting his left hand into the gap he flung the right-hand door open. Staying behind the other door and moving carefully backwards, he opened the doors completely. Leaning close to the jamb, he half-closed his eyes and concentrated his mind on what he could hear in the open space. Hearing nothing, he inched sideways to the edge of the door and peered into a large storage area. To his right he could see aluminium beer barrels, stacked boxes of wine – all the things you would expect to see in a hotel storeroom. With the gun down at his right-hand side, he moved silently inside. The whole area was lit by banks of ceiling-mounted fluorescent tubes. Rows of eight-foot tall metal storage racks filled most of the left-hand side. He walked up and down the aisles, saw no one. He guessed that any store men arriving for work would have been taken directly for interviews.

As he came back towards the doors, he noted with amusement a number of different-sized *Southern Washroom Services* bins each labelled with what should be placed inside for disposal. Stafford pushed a few with his foot, some moved easily. The first two he opened were empty, but the next was a quarter full with hundreds of paper wraps. Stafford opened up a few, and recognised the contents as MDMA crystals. Other bins held similar quantities of what appeared to be wraps of heroin, cocaine and poly bags of marijuana. In a smaller bin labelled "sharps", after carefully prizing off it's lid, Stafford could see dozens of small transparent bags each with circular tablets of various colours each with a smiley face emblem pressed into them. Ecstasy tablets, no doubt.

As he moved past the last of the *Southern Washroom Services* bins, he saw four larger black household-style wheelie bins and, on the dark concrete floor some eighteen inches away from the bins, a dark cloying stain. It looked like spilt red wine, drying. But, thought Stafford, why would they clear up the bottle without mopping up the wine? As he looked, he could see three or four similar patches up to ten or twelve feet away. It looked like something leaking had been dragged across the floor to the bins. Stafford kicked the first wheelie bin, it moved easily – empty. The second one didn't move, and using his knife's marlin spike, he lifted the lid. It was full of rubbish. He pushed the third bin with his foot. Again it stayed where it was; again he used the marlin spike to lift the lid. Again it was full.

At first he thought it was rags or soiled laundry, but as he looked closer he recognised the clothes from the CCTV film earlier. The bin contained the body of Tony Amos. He lowered the lid, lifted the lid on the fourth bin; empty. *So where is Jamie Sweetman?* He dropped the lid back, folded the knife and slipped it into his jeans. With his gun back in his inside pocket, he marched back to the delivery bay's external double doors and phoned the pathologist. He pulled the doors together then walked back through the storage area to an identical set of black doors at the rear. These opened inwardly, but before he stepped out into the corridor, he called Ryan Peters.

'Listen, Ry, can you get Aksanov's office taped off – presumably the forensic boys are close to finishing up there? Get a constable on the door, then you and all the crew wait for me in the corridor outside, OK?'

Exiting the store, he closed the doors, looked around and was somewhat disoriented. To his left was a door with a *Staff Only* sign; to his right, a corridor that he guessed would lead to the bars, restaurant and reception. He tried the *Staff Only* door, which opened directly on to a narrow staircase. Closing the door behind him, he started to climb, realising with grim satisfaction that not only had he now found Amos, he'd also solved the riddle of Southern Washroom Services, and he'd found out how Howard Neilson had been able to get out of the hotel without passing through reception – the *tradesmen's entrance* as the copper at the time had said. He'd also discovered that if you didn't drive into the car park, but parked outside, and walked in keeping close to the walls, you could get to the goods-inward doors without being seen by the CCTV cameras. Stafford guessed there'd be a number of gateways into fields on the approach road where you could park up, cross a couple of fields, then access the hotel from the golf course.

He anticipated another door at the top of the stairs; reaching it, he leaned his head against it and listened. He could hear voices. Gently, he levered the handle down and opened the door an inch or two. Peering through the gap, he could see Ryan Peters, the forensic crew and a few uniformed constables standing in the corridor outside Aksanov's office.

Pushing open the door, he said, 'Good, glad you're all here.'

CHAPTER 56

Sweetman had escaped death by luck and quick thinking. He had arranged to meet Amos close to the World Citizen Hotel. They were to see Aksanov in his office at around 2 a.m. when his guests and punters had left the casino and had gone to bed.

At around 1.45 a.m., Sweetman parked in a gateway close to the hotel. Moments later, Amos pulled up alongside in his battered white truck, and Sweetman climbed in. Amos stared out of the window at Sweetman's car.

'A Mini Clubman? Bit of a comedown after the Audi, innit?'

'Just being careful, mate. Anyway, it's a Clubman Cooper S,' said Sweetman with a thin smile. 'Aksanov thinks I always drive his Merc pickups, but I parked the Audi at Whitelines and borrowed this off Sheila.'

Amos opened his mouth to speak, and then thought better of it as he drove into the hotel car park. Getting out, they stayed close to the walls and walked around to the goods-inward doors. Sweetman, about to use the keyless entry pad, stopped as Amos said, 'Fuckin' door's been jemmied.' Prising the doors apart, Amos, with Sweetman a pace or two behind, walked cautiously in, all the lights were on. Nothing appeared untoward. The racks were well stocked, the bins to hold drugs neatly aligned. The intruders weren't interested in the stock; at this time of night they're probably after the casino cash, thought Sweetman.

He was still a pace or two behind when Amos reached the double doors at the far side. Hearing the sound of onrushing footsteps and muffled but excited voices, he hung back then dived headlong behind the storage racks as the doors flung wide open; the noise of the intruders masking his movements. Amos, too late to move, stood there, eyes bulging, mouth open, staring at four Asian men, wired and jittery. One silenced Amos with a straight right to the face. Two more grabbed his arms. Without a word, the fourth man swung at Amos with a massive golf club. Though not a classically executed swing, it connected perfectly with Amos's balls. His mouth opened to scream, milliseconds before the pain hit. He sagged, unconscious. The two men holding him let go and he crashed face first onto the concrete floor; the signal for them to lay into him with feet and fists. After a moment, the golfer intervened, pushing the others aside. With feet spread thirty inches apart and toes pointing slightly out, to the delight of the others, he took a few practice swings, then with a wiggle of the hips, and an almost perfect swing, he crashed the golf club into Amos's head. He wasn't able to complete the follow-through, the club stopping not quite dead as it ploughed its way into Amos's brain. The golfer dropped the club and shook the pain from his hands. One of the other men ran forward, lifted the lids on the larger wheelie bins, found an empty one, and waved to the others. Two grabbed

Amos's feet and dragged him to the bins, lifted him up and somehow managed to fold him inside. The golfer picked up the club, wiped the head on Amos's shirt and flipped the lid closed. They turned out the lights, walked out of the store, closed the doors behind them, strode across the car park and onto the golf course, and disappeared into the dark.

Sweetman stayed hidden for a further ten minutes before walking to the front doors and peering out. Seeing nothing threatening, he jogged back to the Mini. Lowering himself into the seat, he took out a cigarette, switched on the ignition, and stuffed the gearstick into first. Nought to sixty in six point eight second, he took off down the road before lighting the cigarette.

What the fuck has Aksanov got us into now? He pointed the car towards Whitelines. It was now well after 2 a.m., and as any car on the road at this time of night was always an easy target for police, he stayed within the speed limit and made his way through all the back doubles avoiding CCTV cameras as best he could. The club had turned out when he got there, the whole place in darkness. He left the Mini in the car park and, as he walked up to the double rear doors, motion sensor lights kicked in, enabling him to see the keypad numbers and tap in the entry code. Inside, he closed and leaned up against the doors. Breathing more easily now, he eased past his Audi parked in the goods bay and made his way to Sheila's third-floor office.

Sitting behind her desk, Sheila looked up as Sweetman walked in. One look at his face told her things hadn't gone as planned. He put her car keys on the desk and slumped into a two-seater settee. She waited patiently while he calmed down.

'Fuckin' Aksanov – Christ knows what he's brought down on us now.'

She said nothing.

He continued, 'So I met up with Amos – you know he wanted to talk to him. Well, he thought he was on Aksanov's hit list, and I planned to have a go at about him pratting about with Stafford. We didn't even make it to his office.'

Sheila picked up a packet of cigarettes, took one out and threw the pack to him. There was silence as they both lit up.

'Back doors had been jemmied. We'd just gone in when these four Asian geezers burst in through the inner doors. Amos was just bloody stood there; poor little fucker. They beat the shit out of him. Course, we'd gone not expecting trouble. You know, late night, skeleton staff. Left my tools in the Audi, for fuck's sake. Anyhows, I waited a while, then came back here.'

Sheila stood and walked to a cupboard behind her, took out a bottle of brandy and poured a couple of glasses. Handing one to Sweetman, she said, 'Pratting about? What is pratting about?'

Sweetman gave her a thin smile and explained.

'Ah, yes. But I guessed something like this would happen. You cannot kill two top bosses and not expect punishment,' she said in her heavily accented English. 'He has done well until now, so he thinks he is God. I tried to tell him, but he wouldn't listen.' They sat quietly for a moment, savouring the brandy, and then she said, 'So, did you check on Pavel?'

'No way. Having seen what they did to Amos, it was obvious what they'd already done to him. And I didn't want to hang around in case one of the night staff raised the alarm.'

'Hmm, wise move, Jamie. I am pleased I told the two Russians to head for the West Midlands. It will be easier there now, I think. No?'

'Yeah, maybe, but down here it means Stafford will be all over us like a fuckin' virus. Time for some serious clean-up, Sheila.'

Sheila nodded thoughtfully, picked up her car keys and left. Sweetman made his way to her en suite bedroom and settled down for the night.

The two Russians had long since settled down for the night. Not in the West Midlands, but in a four-star hotel, some two and a half miles away. They could, it seemed, smell the blood.'

CHAPTER 57

The group turned as one, surprised, anticipating Stafford would arrive from the other direction.

He held up his hand to stop the chatter and said, 'I'm guessing that when the Basingstoke contingent first arrived, you all went in through the front entrance? Yeah?' He got a few nods from the uniformed cops. 'Yeah, no reason not to. Then when we all arrived, we also came through the front entrance and straight up to Aksanov's office. Now, a few minutes ago, I took a time-out and wandered around outside. Follow me and I'll show you where I ended up.'

They walked through the *Staff Only* doorway and down the narrow stairs to the corridor with the double doors to the store room. Stopping outside, Stafford addressed them again.

'Now, before we go in, I have to tell you that I've found Tony Amos…' – a murmur went up from the assembled crew – '…and, sadly, he's dead. Murdered.' Again a murmur, but louder this time, so Stafford held up his hand for quiet. 'I don't know how he was killed because his body is in a black wheelie bin, but I do want you forensic boys to do your stuff before we go any further.'

Stafford pushed open the doors and the forensic crew entered the store. He gave instructions for securing the area.

'Now you, Ry, can see what's what in the store, and I'll join you shortly. I've notified the pathologist and she's on her way back.'

Stafford walked through to the reception area and came across DI Masterson, who told him, 'We've just about finished interviewing the guests and, while there's a lot of stuff I'm going to follow up on, I don't think any of them are involved in this murder. So, what do you think? Are we ready to let them go?'

'Yes, I'm thinking much the same. We'll need to let the staff go back to work as well. But I think that's fair enough, even though we've found another body.'

'What? Who and where was this?'

'One of their foot soldiers, I think. We've come across him before, name of Tony Amos. Found him in a wheelie bin in the storeroom, alongside bins used for transporting drugs.'

'Bloody hell, Stafford, I heard you attract dead people; perhaps I should start believing the stories.'

Stafford made eye contact and held it, but the DI dropped his gaze.

'Good job it's just the scumbags then. Anyway, I'm on my way to find the sergeant from the local nick – I want him to take all the security staff and storemen down to the station for further discussions. Most, if not all must have known about the drugs and, I suspect, blackmail.'

'Blackmail? How do you reckon that?' the DI asked.

'Too many monitors in their security office and too

many staff for just keeping watch on the car park and hotel security. We'll probably find hidden cameras in most of the bedrooms, and obviously in the casino.'

'Interesting thought, Major, interesting thought.'

Stafford left the DI to organise things in the hotel and rounded up DS Martin, Ryan Peters and PC Whitley.

'OK, you lot, we're going to pay a visit to Mrs Aksanov. Nic, here's the Volvo keys – you can drive, as you probably know the way,' he said, a look of amusement on his face. 'But first,' he continued, ignoring the little red patches that had crept up her neck, 'find our friend DI Masterson and give him the keys to your patrol car, then meet us in the car park in five for a quick briefing.'

It was rather longer than five minutes before Nicole reappeared, trying hard to hide a smile as she walked across to them.

'I see you've been using your winning formula on our new DI then, Staf.'

Stafford looked a question at her. 'Why? What did he say?'

'Ah, he was somewhat annoyed that he's not coming with us, so I told him you needed someone in authority to clear up here,' she said, trying not to laugh.

It was a fraction of a second before Stafford said, 'Precisely– anyway, when we get to their house, I'm guessing Mrs Aksanov doesn't know her husband's dead, so Nicole and Harry, you go in first; you know the drill, kid-glove stuff.' He thought for a moment, then said, 'And Ryan, I think you and I should go in, ah, prepared.'

'You got it, Staf, just like the Boy Scouts,' Peters said, then threw the SRi's keys to PC Whitley and asked, 'I take it you've passed your test, Harry?'

'Yes, Ry, first time too. How many attempts did you need?'

Peters looked up and laughed as he opened the boot. He took off his bomber jacket and, opening his go-bag, took out a Kevlar vest and slipped it on. Putting his jacket over the top, he selected his machine pistol, took out the magazine and checked it was fully loaded, then slid it back in and tucked the gun inside his jacket.

Stafford having also put on his protective vest, selected a similar weapon from his bag in the Volvo, and eased himself into the passenger seat. Nicole drove out first and told the gate cop to book all four of them out. A gaggle of reporters and news media crowded round both cars, shouting questions.

'How many are dead?'

'How were they killed?'

'Is it Pavel Aksanov himself?'

'Hey, look, that's Nicky driving – hey Nicky, you back for good?'

As Nicole drove carefully through the crowd, Stafford said, 'Just as well they couldn't park close by. We should be able to lose them before they can get to their cars and turn around.'

For the first half mile or so, the hedgerows and gateways were littered with badly parked media vehicles. It was only ten miles or so to Dummer, but on the narrow country lanes it would take fifteen minutes before they reached the Dummer village sign.

'So why the firearms?' Nicole asked.

'I just have a suspicion you won't need to tell Mrs A her old man's dead.'

'Why? Do you think she knows? Do you think somebody from the hotel phoned her?'

'I think if someone had phoned her, she'd be at the hotel by now, playing the grieving widow.'

They were silent for a mile or two, but as they passed the *Dummer 1 1/2 miles* signpost, Stafford shot forward in his seat, the seatbelt snapped tight as he tried to peer over the hedgerow. 'What the fuck…?' he said.

Nicole could see it now too – a pillar of black smoke rising in the near distance. 'Farmer burning crops?' she said.

'No, they stopped all that, didn't they? Besides, it's too narrow a plume.'

'Their house is just round the next right bend, the fire looks to be damn close.'

'OK, Nic, so slow down to walking pace when we get close to the gate.'

'This next gateway coming up is theirs, there's another one fifty metres further down. Should be able to see most of the front drive.' She slowed the car and gently eased past the gap.

'Jesus,' she said, 'a bloody car's on fire in their driveway.'

'Drive on, Nic, find somewhere to park,' said Stafford, pulling out his mobile and dialling 999.

Nicole pulled into the gateway to the field she'd used the other evening and rolled the car forward, leaving space for the SRi to park up behind. They piled out of the vehicles and huddled by Stafford, but Nicole spoke first.

'If we go back to the first gateway we passed, and turn immediately right, you'll see there's round paving slabs, same colour as the gravel. I think it's a way in or out without being seen by the CCTV cameras. It takes you behind the garage, then it's just a short dash to the front or rear doors.'

'Good one, Nic,' said Stafford.

They ran back to the nearest gate, then bending at the waist they ran one by one past the opening to the other gate. Stafford peered around the tall hedge.

'Christ,' he said, 'there's a man's body lying in front of the car. Can't tell who it is from here, but it looks like the car is a white Mercedes.' Stafford took out his mobile, got Nicole's number up on the contacts and then put the phone back in his pocket. 'Keep your phone handy, Nic, and stay here with Harry. Wait for my call – when the fire brigade turn up, don't let them in the drive until I've given the all-clear. Understood?'

'Yes, boss,' said Nicole.

Harry nodded, 'Yes, Staf.'

Stafford and Peters ran through the gateway and saw the paving slab route to the house. Stafford didn't stop until he reached the corner of the garage nearest to the house. He took out his gun.

'You take the far side of the front door, Ry, I'll cover you and come across to the near side on your signal.'

Peters nodded and, machine pistol in hand, ran the thirty metres, dodging and weaving, to the house. He reached the doorway, paused for a second, then dashed to the far side. Another pause, then index finger to thumb, he gave Stafford the universal OK sign. Stafford, bent at the waist, ran across to join him. The door was hinged to the right – Stafford inched forward and pushed it. It moved, it was unlocked. He pushed it all the way.

Peters dived through the open doorway in a combat

forward roll, came up in the classic crouched firing position, yelling, 'Police, police, come out now! Hands where I can see them!'

Stafford, also now inside, moved past Peters and checked out the room to his left. 'Clear!' he shouted. They did the same to all the downstairs rooms and met up again in the hallway. The sound of sirens in the distance came through the open front door.

'We need to clear upstairs before we let them in, but I'll get Nicole to call Talbot and set the forensic teams and pathologist wheels in motion.'

That done, Peters inched his way up the wide staircase to a landing and return. He peered around the corner, turned and nodded to Stafford, then went on up to the wide first-floor corridor. Stafford made his way to the landing Peters had vacated; another signal from Peters, and Stafford joined him at the top of the stairs. Ahead were three doors, all open to the left, and a single closed door then a turning into another shorter corridor on the right. The house was deathly silent. It took no effort to move stealthily, every footstep cushioned by thick pile carpet. Stafford pushed the door to his right. It opened into a large bathroom, black marbled tiles on three walls and white marbled tiles and a large mirror on the fourth. It was empty.

Peters started looking into the rooms on the left. All were bedrooms, all were doubles, with luxuriously carpeted floors and fitted wardrobes. All were unoccupied. They walked together down the right-hand corridor to the only door – it was half-open. Stafford pushed it fully open; with a two-handed grip on the gun and crouching, he moved around the door. He stopped, stood upright, put his gun back in his jacket and took out his phone, pressing Nicole's number.

'OK, Nic, you can let the fire engine in and come in yourself. Gotta tell you, we've found Mrs A, she dead, and it's not nice. Get Harry to close the far gate and control entry on the first one. Check out the body by the car if you can get close enough, if not, we'll have to wait until the fire crew's finished.'

Ryan Peters was now at his side, shaking his head in disbelief at what he was seeing.

'Fucking hell, Staf, I thought they were brutal with Aksanov. But this, to his wife, to a woman, whatever he'd done, this is absolute madness. Sheer fucking madness.'

They backed out of the room.

'I've got a nasty feeling about this, Ry. Look, phone Talbot, get him to set up a couple of ARVs, one to the back and one to the front gates of Southampton Metal Recycling – I think they're going to be attacked. I'll phone Healey now.'

Healey answered after the third ring.

'Christ, Staf, twice in two—'

Stafford cut in. 'Shut up, Frank, and listen. Get your men off site now, any way they can.'

'Why? What the fuck...?'

'Frank, this is for your own good. Either get them off site or lock both gates. Shutter your office window and lock yourselves in there. Do it, Frank, and do it now!'

Ten minutes later, Healey called back; Stafford put it on speaker.

'Bleeding hell, Staf! What's all this about? I managed to get all my lads away and both gates shut. But as I'm doing up the shutter on the Portakabin, these mad bastards crash into my front fuckin' gates. Bastards are still doing it, trying to get in.'

'So you're in the cabin?'

'Fuckin' right. Soon as I heard them crashing the gates, I was in, mate. Can't see fuck all because of the shutter, but I can hear the bastards revving and smashing the gates. What's this all about? What do they think I've done, for Christ's sake?'

'Hang in there, Frank, we're just minutes away. There's two Armed Response Vehicles on their way to you… Just don't go anywhere, Frank.'

Stafford heard him say, 'Where the f—' as he terminated the call. Peters stared at him with an *are you for real* look but Stafford looked straight ahead. They made their way outside, to the front of the house. Black smoke swirled around, trapped inside the tall hedges, their eyes began to stream and sting. They put hands to mouth and nose; stench and smoke affecting their breathing.

The fire engine was in the driveway and had the fire under control. Stafford asked Peters to get the SRi, then walked over to Nicole, who was kneeling by the side of the body. Stafford could see that the dead man was white, naked from the waist up, and had light brown hair. He was wearing a pair of grey trousers and brown slip-on shoes; it was the solicitor Howard Neilson. Nicole stood up as Stafford approached, she opened her mouth to speak. Stafford held up his hand and said with a rasping voice, 'Sorry, Nic, me and Ryan need to get to Southampton asap. Stay here for now, see if you can find the CCTV set-up. It may give us a clue to what happened here. But their next attack will be on Frank Healey. We'll take the SRi, you come down when the forensic guys have done their stuff.'

As Stafford was speaking, they were hurrying towards the first gate. He continued, 'Apologise to the fire crew for us dashing off, and when you go into the main bedroom – warn Harry, will you? It's pretty bad.'

The SRi screeched to a halt outside the gate, Stafford lowered himself into the passenger seat, and within minutes they were on the M3 heading south. Peters hit the blues and twos and carved his way through the afternoon traffic, dodging from lane to lane.

'I'm guessing you're thinking this is not Sweetman?' said Peters.

'No, this is something else entirely. I'm thinking Sweetman for Winstone, the two Asian guys and Edwards. All neat and tidy, no rage. This, my friend, is the lethal response. This is what happens when someone like Aksanov thinks they're unstoppable – all powerful.'

Peters began to reply, but Stafford's phone cut him short. Stafford checked the screen – *No Caller ID*. He took the call anyway, putting it on speaker.

'What the hell are you playing at, Stafford?' DI Masterson's voice shouted. 'Where in God's name have you disappeared to now? What's the DCI going to think when I tell him you've buggered off again?'

'Don't worry if you have trouble keeping up, Tom. You can catch up when you read the report he'll undoubtedly be writing as we speak,' said Stafford and cut the call.

Peters shook his head, burst out laughing and said, 'What's the matter with the guy? Why couldn't he just have asked for an update?'

'I think he's a bit fed up that we're in the driving seat. Talbot keeps saying he's a man who gets results, so I guess he likes to run things.'

'I think the whole bunch of 'em thought they were dealing with a few local bad lads and didn't realise it was an international criminal organisation until too bloody late.'

'And now it looks like we're dealing with at least two powerful criminal syndicates. But what really pisses me off is that they got to Aksanov before we pinned the bastard down. But then, these guys aren't for following rules, that's for sure.'

CHAPTER 58

Dummer to Southampton is around twenty-six miles, give or take. Stafford looked at the SRi's speedo, it read 112 miles per hour. He started to calculate journey time, but before he could finish, the phone rang again. It was Frank Healey.

'Jesus Christ, Stafford, who are these guys? What the fuck have I done to upset them? And where's this armed response you promised? The only shots I can hear are pinging off this fucking cabin.'

'Hang in there, Frank, we're only minutes away.'

'Wasn't that what you said—' The phone went dead – no connection.

'Shit,' said Peters, as Stafford's mobile rang again, this time the commander of the armed response team, who they knew from an earlier investigation.

'Major Stafford? I'm with the AR unit, we've arrived at the site; one team back and front as you requested.'

'Good, we're just a few minutes away; we'll meet you near the front gates. What's the situation at the moment?'

'Looks like there are four of them, Asian lads, seems they came in two cars. They used one to ram the gates until there was enough of a gap to gain entry. That vehicle is now disabled. They were attacking the Portakabin when we arrived, then they spotted our guys at the far gate, which is nearer the office, and initiated contact.'

'So have they breached the Portakabin?'

'Not so far as we can see – we've managed to keep them away from it. How many people are in there?'

'Fortunately, only the one, the rest of the workers got clear before the attack started, but the one still there is the bloke they want.'

'Right. After incoming fire, my lads engaged them in suppressive fire. Three of the enemy have taken cover, the fourth we haven't spotted for a few minutes. The local police have cordoned off the area and all traffic has been stopped.'

'Excellent,' said Stafford. 'We're just coming up to the second cordon now, so be with you in two minutes.'

Peters pulled up behind the AR vehicle. As they got out of the car, they could tell by the noise coming from behind the blue ten-foot fence surrounding the yard that the situation had escalated since the phone call. It was impossible to see into the compound, but it sounded as though it was operational, with the roar of a huge diesel engine and the loud banging and crunching of metal.

Approaching the front gates they could see a grubby white Ford Mondeo, the front half of which was embedded in the gate. The force of the multiple attempts to smash a way in had sprung the small wicket gate open. Peering around the frame of the little gate, it was obvious that the workers had downed tools and left in a hurry. Bulldozers, excavators and fork-lift trucks had been abandoned haphazardly around the yard, some, it seemed, in mid-operation. One of the CAT excavators was still in use, battering the office with the lip of its huge bucket, pushing it underneath the Portakabin, lifting the front edge some two or three feet, then reversing at speed, to drop it back down on the concrete floor. Stafford winced visibly as he thought of what Frank Healey was enduring inside. Peters climbed onto the boot of the Mondeo and up onto its roof. Moving slowly forward, he leaned against the top of the fence and peered over. Looking carefully around, it took him seconds to assess the scene. He jumped down from the car and using his finger began to draw a rough layout of the site on the dusty boot lid.

'The guy in the CAT has pushed the Portakabin about a bit. It's ripped out all its electrics. That's here now,' he said pointing to the image he'd drawn. 'There are metal cages that we could use for cover, here, here and here. The bulldozer is here and there are two other excavators, here and here. The other three men are taking cover behind full metal stillages over here, just twelve or fifteen metres from the rear gates,' he said stabbing his finger on the boot as he spoke.

'These guys have obviously got more balls than brains,' said the commander, who'd joined them. 'I don't see how they expected to get out.'

'They didn't need an escape strategy; they thought they'd just drive in, do the business and drive out again, much as they've done in Basingstoke and Dummer. They didn't expect any repercussions down here either,' said Stafford.

'So who are these guys?' asked the commander.

'It's a long story, so let's get this done,' said Stafford, 'then I'll tell all.'

All the time they were talking, the digger driver had been relentlessly battering the shutter over the Portakabin's window. The whole thing was looking ready to break open.

'The CAT driver is so focused on what he's doing, we should be able to blindside him if your lads at the far gate keep those three occupied,' said Peters.

They all looked at the layout on the boot lid. Pinpointing the digger, Stafford said, 'I can get close to the digger from the right, using those stillages for cover. If you, Ryan, came in from the left, and with your AR lads covering us from the rear, we should be able to nullify the driver fairly easily.' He looked to the commander.

Who nodded. 'Unless he has a death wish. They must realise by now that there's no way out.' He switched on his personal comms and spoke to the other unit. 'We're coming in for the CAT driver. Keep the other three in lockdown; and try not to shoot us... Start firing on my count of ten.' He gave Stafford the thumbs-up.

Stafford and Peters, guns at the ready, took up positions either side of the twisted frame to the open gate, and waited for the commander's count. On the count of ten they ran, crouched, weaving from side to side, and reached their objectives, the protective cover of the stillages. Kneeling down, they could hear gunfire coming from the far side of the compound. The AR unit with Stafford, moved in behind them and took cover.

The excavator driver had tipped the Portakabin on to its side, the door and shuttered window now facing upwards. He had crumpled the shutter inwards and was trying to rip it off by getting the lip of the bucket under one of the corners sticking out.

Stafford came from behind cover and, aiming above the driver's head, fired a burst of three shots into the cab. The glass on the door to the right shattered and the bullets ripped through the cab's roof. The driver dived to his left, and Ryan put a burst of three through that side. Alerted by the noise, one of the other gunmen turned, and seeing Stafford in the open, fired at him. The shot was wide. Stafford's wasn't and the man went down, two bullets high in the body mass. As Stafford returned to cover, the CAT driver realised he was a sitting target. Not understanding his assailants had spared his life, with gun in hand he leaped on to the excavator tracks and, firing in Stafford's general direction, made a run for cover to his mate's position. He didn't make three paces; Stafford shook his head in disbelief and put him down with a single shot to his right thigh. The man crashed to the ground screaming, his gun spiralling away as his hand hit the concrete. He lay there howling, holding his leg, rocking from side to side, trying desperately to stop the blood gushing. After a few seconds, Stafford's compassion waned and he was tempted to put a bullet in his brain, just to shut him up.

Peters had moved to the side of the Portakabin and shouted to the remaining gunmen, 'That's two-nil now, lads, you don't want to go down four-nil, do you? Just throw your guns out, and walk forward with your hands where we can see them.'

The silence in the yard seemed to stretch for ages, but then the men threw out their guns and, arms raised, stepped out into the open. The AR commander shouted for them to lie down on the ground with their hands behind their backs. They complied instantly and the AR men handcuffed them both. Stafford, meanwhile, had found a length of domestic electrical cable and fashioned a tourniquet around the leg of the man he'd injured; he could do nothing to help the other man.

Stafford said to the AR commander, 'I think we can let the troops in now.'

The commander nodded assent, switched on his personal comms and said, 'OK, lads, come in through the back gates and leave them open for the ambulance –one of you control entry until you get a uniformed constable there.'

Ryan Peters had climbed up on to the Portakabin and peered in under the bent-up corner of the shutter. He could see very little inside, and could hear nothing.

'Hey, Frank, you OK in there? Can you move, can you hear me?' There was no answer. The gap in the shutter was too narrow to gain entry, so he lay flat on the cabin and reached in as far as he could with his left arm, trying to find the winding screws that locked the shutter in place. He managed to grab one, but try as he might, it was so damaged and bent out of shape he was unable to shift it. He climbed down, walked to the CAT excavator, jumped on to the tracks and settled into the cab. The engine was still running. Peters, like many recycling centre operatives, had a licence to drive the thing – he selected a lever and manoeuvred the bucket, putting the lip underneath the buckled corner of the shutter. He pulled the lever back sharply, the bucket ripped into the shutter and the whole cabin rose a foot into the air. Peters lowered it gently and pulled the lever again; the result was the same. The bucket lip was well and truly wedged under the shutter now, so he pulled on the lever and raised the angle of the bucket. Again it lifted the cabin nine inches off the ground. There was a loud crack, then three more in quick succession as the shutter flew open. Ripped clear of its broken hinges and fasteners, it landed some six feet clear of the cabin. This was greeted with a loud cheer from Stafford and the assembled AR crews. Peters raised the bucket, reversed the machine and dropped the bucket safely on the ground. He switched off the engine, jumped out and took a bow to the small round of applause that followed.

Stafford and the AR crews ran to the Portakabin. Stafford climbed on it, knelt down and peered in through the gap. He could see Frank Healey in the far corner, almost totally covered by his desk and a filing cabinet, which had spewed out its contents. The window glass, office chairs, PC and monitor were scattered around him. Stafford jumped in, cleared the stuff from around Healey, who was unmoving, obviously unconscious. Stafford poked his head out of the window and asked the AR guys to get the paramedics. Stretching his arms up out of the gap, asked the men to haul him out. As the paramedics jumped inside and began to tend to Healey, Stafford checked his phone. There was one missed call from DI Masterson; no message.

Stafford looked around the compound. The Mondeo had been pulled out of the front gates, and a constable controlled entry. There were two ambulances, a forensic team and a pathologist, who was examining the dead man. Two paramedics were attending to the man with the leg wound. All in all, he thought, DCI Talbot had pulled out all the stops, on the flimsiest of a Stafford hunch. Stafford gave him a call to update him.

'I just wanted to say thanks for the prompt back-up. Everything went well, and the situation is now under control. All the workers and customers managed to clear the site before the trouble started. The boss, Frank Healey, was their target. We've arrested three Asian suspects; one of them is injured, and a fourth was shot and killed. There were no casualties on our side. Healey is being treated by paramedics on site now.'

'So a good result all round, Staf; uh, well done. What were the four Asians about then?' Stafford's mind registered the DCI reverting to Staf, but couldn't believe that the man hadn't worked it out yet.

'It was retribution for Aksanov setting up the killing of their brothers in arms, Ravani and Buzdar. It'll all go into the report, Detective Chief Inspector,' he said and ended the call. Almost immediately, his phone pinged with a text from Nicole: *Word of warning, Masterson on his way – we're on our way too. xx*

Stafford groaned, but stopped as he noted the kisses.

CHAPTER 59

Stafford walked to the Portakabin where the paramedics were bringing out a semiconscious Frank Healey, strapped to a stretcher. Stafford asked one of them what the damage was.

'He was hit on the head, and has a huge lump – that rendered him unconscious. And from what we can see, he's got a couple of broken ribs, a cracked ankle and his left radius is broken; can't tell if he has internal injuries, though.'

'But he'll survive?'

'Oh, yeah. Should make a full recovery,' said the medic as they loaded him into the back of the ambulance.

As he walked with Peters to the front gates and ducked through the opening, Stafford said, 'Well done, Ry, with that digger; it would have taken forever with an angle grinder. Nicole texted, she'll be down in the Volvo shortly, and DI Masterson is on his way too.'

Strolling towards the SRi, he could see his green Volvo coming through the second police cordon. It pulled up alongside them; Nicole and PC Whitley stepped out and joined them on the pavement.

'So,' said Martin, 'mission accomplished?'

'Down here, yes. I mean, Healey's a bit battered, but he'll survive. All his workers are safe, though – he managed to get them off site before it all kicked off.'

'That's got to be down to your quick thinking, Staf,' said Martin.

Stafford could feel the blush coming, but was saved when Whitley said, 'It was the four Asian lads, then?'

'Yes… So you must have found CCTV footage at the house,' said Stafford, smiling broadly.

'Yeah. It showed a black Porsche Macan parking up in the drive, four Asian blokes got out. They smashed the Mercedes' window, poured petrol inside and set fire to it. Minutes later, Neilson, poor sod, comes running out waving his arms around and they just shot him. All on bloody camera. Then we lost sight of them as they went into the house.' Whitley hesitated, bottom jaw trembling, unable to speak for a moment. He shook his head, as if to clear the thoughts. 'They were in the house for about half an hour, then they all came out bouncing around, laughing like kids. Looking as though they'd had a great time. The fire had gone out, so one of them doused it in petrol again and re-lit it. Then they got into the Macan and drove away.'

'They were all in one motor?' asked Stafford.

'Yeah, like I said, a Porsche Macan.'

'They turned up here in two cars, the white Mondeo you can see down there and the silver car behind it,' said Stafford.

'Christ, they must have stopped off and nicked those from somewhere. If they'd have come straight here in the Macan, God knows what we'd be doing now. Clearing up more dead people, I guess,' said Peters.

'Did you put out a call for the motor?' said Stafford.

'Yes,' said Martin, 'we put out a call and a trace. Trace came back, a little while ago...' She stopped and dug the phone out of her jeans pocket; Stafford fought hard to tear his eyes away as she wriggled her hips to get her hand into the pocket. 'It's registered to Fahad Buzdar, brother of the deceased man we found earlier. Known associates include Abduk Ravani. So I'm thinking the guys here, one's bound to be Fahad, the others known associates too.' As she put the phone back, a movement caught her eye. 'Uh oh, here comes the DI now.'

'Oh, great. Right, we'll bring him up to speed here. But we need to sort out Sweetman and Cooper before they create more mayhem,' said Stafford.

Masterson pulled the squad car up behind the Volvo, jumped out and, leaving the engine running, ran over. Red-faced and pausing to catch his breath, he said, 'What the bloody hell's going on? What's the situation here, then?'

'I know Sergeant Martin will have explained our reason for leaving Dummer. And the situation here, well, three Asian men have been arrested. Two are on their way to Eastleigh nick. One is on his way to hospital and a fourth is on his way to the morgue,' said Stafford.

'I guessed there'd be a body somewhere, Major.'

'Between the four of them, they're responsible for at least four brutal murders and, as we can't trace Sweetman or Cooper, there may be more,' said Peters.

'Allegedly, you mean; allegedly responsible for four murders,' said the DI.

Peters glared at him and said, 'And if we'd got here any later, who knows how many customers and workers they would have added to the list – allegedly.'

'You'll be pleased to know, Tom, it'll be in our report, but here's the short version,' said Stafford. 'Earlier, we smashed Aksanov's criminal activities in Southampton and Weyhill. Looking to rebuild, we think he invited syndicate bosses from the West Midlands and maybe a London-based Russian group to help him out. It's likely the Asian syndicate turned him down, so they were killed, and their very expensive motor turned up here, delivered by the now deceased, Tony Amos. The boss here, the would-be deceased Frank Healey, shipped said car to Bosnia…with me so far?' Masterson, colour rising, said nothing. Stafford continued. 'The remaining Asian syndicate members retaliate, possibly aiming to take over Aksanov's territory. First they beat the shit out of him, to get information, then top him. Amos and Sweetman turn up hoping to talk to their governor, Amos gets caught as the four Asians are leaving, but Sweetman escapes. They do what they do to Aksanov's wife for fun, and as a warning. Neilson would still be alive if he hadn't been boffing Mrs A. Then they nick a couple of motors and come down here to sort out Mr Healey. My guess is they wouldn't have stopped until they'd found and killed Sweetman. And that, DI Masterson, brings you right up to date. Now, if you'll excuse us, we need to find Sweetman and Cooper.'

Masterson glared at them, turned and marched back to his car, then motor revving, clutch spinning, he drove away.

Stafford's crew watched the departing car in stunned silence. Stafford brought them back to the moment.

'You realise this is not over? Once the West Midlands crew find out they've lost another four brothers in arms, there's going to be bloody mayhem, up there and down here.

I suggest we adjourn to Winchester Services and discuss, first, how we're going to find Sweetman and Cooper, and then, how we stop the mayhem.'

They piled into the cars and set off. The nearest police cordon caused them no trouble. At the next cordon, they battled through a teeming media scrum. TV crews and newspaper reporters waved around mobile phones, microphones and cameras, all pointing towards a parked police patrol car. Alongside the car, smiling wide, arms waving, talking to the excited media throng, stood DI Thomas Masterson.

CHAPTER 60

Forty minutes later, sitting in a booth, four coffees, taco wraps, cheeseburgers and fries spread out on the tabletop, Stafford said, 'I've caused a problem with Cooper I'm afraid. Instead of tying the bastard down when I had the chance, I've let him get away – twice. Bloody stupid, I know, but I wanted him out there, running scared. I wanted him looking over his shoulder, watching for Aksanov, Sweetman and us. And now, we really do have to find him. Sweetman too, of course. Any ideas?'

The other three, eyes cast down, attacked their food.

'I take it that's a no, then,' said Stafford, an amused expression on his face.

Whitley looked up. 'Last we knew, Cooper was driving the VW Polo he nicked. Have we heard if it's been found?'

Nicole perked up and, taking out her mobile phone, said, 'Good thought, Harry, I'll check with Hawkins.' She did so.

'Yep,' she said as she ended the call, 'it's been found on one of the big council estates in Basingstoke.'

'So why would he dump it there?' said Stafford.

'He's got to know someone in the area, surely? Someone who'd put him up for a while,' said Peters.

'Bloody annoying; I took his phone off him, so we can't even give him a bell to ask him,' said Stafford. 'But we can get his phone contacts from the forensic techs.'

'And we could get a few PCs with pictures of him to go door-to-door round there, see if anyone spotted him dumping it,' said Nicole, reaching for her phone again.

'Hang fire a sec, Nic... I never saw the Edwards crime scene live, if you see what I mean, but I did see the video you sent,' said Stafford, taking out his phone. It took him a moment to find the video. He watched it and said, 'If Edwards didn't go to hospital, who plastered his arms and patched him up?'

Peters, Nicole and Whitley glanced at each other, blank looks on their faces. Eventually, Peters said, 'When I picked him up, I asked him about it and he said, "Oh, some bird we know who's a nurse." I didn't question it.'

They were silent while they finished their meals. Stafford said, 'So we need Cooper's mobile contacts, and to search his and Edwards' known associates. Nic, you phone the Basingstoke sergeant, and ask him to set up door-to-door using Cooper's picture off the PND. Then we'll call it quits today and meet up at eight tomorrow morning in Aldershot nick. OK?'

Buoyed up from their success the day before, the four of them turned up at Aldershot Police Station at much the same time, keen to get stuck in again. After grabbing coffees, they gathered in the incident room.

Stafford started things off. 'Our priority is to find, and hold on to, Cooper and Sweetman. Nicole, you have some decent contacts with the tech boys – as well as the list of contacts in Ray Cooper's phone can you get them to check who he phoned after the battle of the World Citizen Hotel car park. If they can't find the details, go to the service provider. OK?'

She nodded and moved to a quieter workstation.

Stafford turned to PC Whitley. 'Harry, will you check Cooper and Sweetman's info on the PND? I know we've done it before, but we weren't looking specifically for female known associates. This time, concentrate on associates and relatives; it could be a partner, ex-wife, girlfriend, whatever. And go back to their time in Slough, and before, if need be. Any questions?'

Harry stopped his note-taking, raised his head and said, 'No. All clear.'

'Good. Now, Ryan; I'm almost too nervous to suggest this, but will you go and shake a few trees at Whitelines nightclub?' said Stafford, an amused look on his face.

'We managed to shake a few nuts loose last time,' said Ryan, smiling.

'Yeah, but try not to crack too many this time, yeah?'

'Do you want me to start now?' asked Peters.

'Yes, I think it'll be good to start at the back end, you know, the storage areas, behind-the-scenes stuff. Maybe suggest we could cut some deals here, that sort of thing.'

'Good thinking, boss. I'll keep you updated,' said Peters as he left the room.

Stafford sat at a workstation and took out his mobile. For sheer devilment, not expecting a result, he called Aksanov's number. To his surprise, it was answered.

'Either I'm talking to a dead man, or I'm talking to someone who's nicked a dead man's phone,' said Stafford.

'It's neither, Major Stafford, you're talking to a tech in Eastleigh,' said an amused voice.

'Ah, sorry about that,' said Stafford, trying, but failing, to stop a laugh.

'Yes, we found the phone on one of the blokes arrested at the scrapyard.'

'Anything useful on it?'

'Nah, we've got sod all. Damn thing's protected with this EncroChat system, but we'll crack it sooner or later.'

'Shame – but let me know if you find anything interesting.'

'Will do, Major, will do; we've already updated Sergeant Martin with some of our findings; I trust you'll find it useful.'

Stafford walked over to Nicole. 'Heard you have some news.'

'Yeah, and it's good stuff.' She looked at her notes. 'About ninety minutes after the bust-up at the hotel, Cooper made a call to someone called Charlie. The call lasted around four minutes. They got the phone's ID number and, using triangulation, they've sent me the coordinates where the signals cross. It gives us an indication to within two or three hundred metres of where the phone was last used. I'm printing off the map now. It's three streets away from where the Polo was found.'

Stafford shot across the room to the printer and returned to Nicole's desk, where the pair of them studied the map. It pinpointed a long street on a major council estate. Though still quite large, it did narrow the search area considerably. Stafford thought for a moment, then called the Basingstoke sergeant and asked him to call off the door-to-door with immediate effect.

'Did I hear you say Cooper phoned a Charlie?' asked Whitley, wandering over. Nicole nodded.

'Then this may well tie in… according to his bio, a few years back, Edwards had a partner, name of Charlotte Frances Lesney. Doesn't give any more details; she hasn't got a police record. But this is the good bit; Cooper's bio shows he has a sister called Charlotte, so I'm guessing Lesney is her married name, I checked Facebook, and there's a few Charlotte Lesneys round here – and one is a nurse. There's even a profile picture of her in uniform. Got to be this Charlie, hasn't it?'

'Good work, the pair of you. Now, I stopped the door-to-door because I don't want to risk alerting them. What I want is for you two to set up surveillance there,' said Stafford. 'I want you to stake out the street. You, Nicole, in your motor, Harry in a plain patrol car. You OK being in civvies, Harry?'

'No problem,' said Harry, 'I've got street clothes in my locker.'

Stafford nodded and said, 'Go and get yourself changed,' then logged in at the nearest computer and searched the Basingstoke Electoral Register.

Five minutes later, Harry, wearing jeans, checked shirt and trainers, walked back in to the incident room.

'When you're ready,' said Stafford, 'I pulled Charlie's address from the electoral roll; it's twenty-six B Spindle Street, the street shown on the map here. So that ties in OK. We could go straight in and arrest her with, I don't know, something like attempting to pervert the course of justice, or aiding and abetting, but we need him; Cooper, not her, so I want you to keep a watch on the property, see who comes and goes.'

'But he could be in there and not move out for days, specially since you busted his nose,' said Martin, suppressing a chuckle.

'Yes, I agree, and we may end up barging in. But for what I have in mind, I'd prefer to find out what car she drives, then pick her up straight from work and have a chat about where brother Ray is.'

'OK, Staf, you're the boss. Come on then, Harry, let's go and surveil,' said Martin.

'Meanwhile,' said Stafford, 'back at the ranch, I'll be trying to track down Jamie bloody Sweetman. I will of course come and relieve either one of you in a day or so – ah, scrub that, maybe a couple of hours.'

CHAPTER 61

Nicole Martin and Harry Whitley had been watching the address in Spindle Street for little over an hour when Charlotte Lesney left the house.

Martin called Whitley. 'Stay put, Harry, and phone in the reg number. I'll follow her.'

Charlotte, not in uniform, walked along the pavement, passing half a dozen or so cars. Nicole Martin started to get out of her own car, ready to follow on foot, but Charlotte stopped alongside a dark blue Ford Ka and got in. Martin waited; then pulled out behind the Ka, leaving some two hundred metres between them. Ten minutes later the nurse parked up in a supermarket car park. Martin pulled into a spot a few cars away and waited. Now unsure what to do, she phoned Stafford.

'She's in a supermarket, shopping, do you want me to stop and talk to her, arrest her or what?'

'No, don't arrest her. See how much shopping she comes out with. If it's more than, say, three bags, he's probably staying with her. For now, follow her home, then give me a bell.'

Slumping further down in her seat, Martin waited. More than half an hour later, Charlotte came back to her car pushing a shopping trolley. Nicole counted four full bags and one half full. Hmm, she thought, she's either stocking up for the winter, or she's got guests. She decided to phone Stafford.

'I'm on my way, and Ryan'll be with you in a minute, too,' he said. 'He phoned to say he's hung around the nightclub, and there are no cars in the car park and no signs of life.'

---------- II ----------

Ryan Peters arrived before any of them and Whitley almost had a heart attack when he opened the passenger door of the patrol car, sliding into the seat and saying, 'Any movement?'

A red-faced Harry looked straight ahead as he said, 'Almost a bowel bloody movement when you opened that door.'

'Not in this confined space, Harry, please,' said Peters.

'Charlotte Lesney left the flat about forty-five minutes ago. Sergeant Martin tailed her. But there's been no movement at the house since,' said Harry.

'Ah well, best settle back down again,' said Peters.

Stafford cruised past in his old green Volvo estate and parked up some hundred metres away. He stayed in the car. Two or three moments later, Charlotte Lesney drove up and parked as near as she could to her home. As she struggled to the front door with her shopping, Martin parked behind Peters' SRi. Stafford texted Ryan and Nicole the same message: *Meet up outside number 26.*

As the four of them gathered at the front of the house, Stafford said, 'Nicole, you and Harry go first, show your ID and we'll follow you in.'

They made their way quietly up the stairs. Martin took out her warrant card and nodded at Whitley to do the same. She rapped on the door a couple of times. The silence stretched to thirty seconds; she rapped again.

A female voice inside said, 'Who is it?'

'It's the police, Ms Lesney, you need to open up or we will force entry,' said Martin, and held out her warrant card as the door opened a few inches.

'What is it? What do you want?' said Charlotte.

'I think you know full well, Ms Lesney. It really will be best if you let us in.' The door opened wider and Martin, followed by Whitley, walked through into a neat, pleasantly decorated hallway, and then into the living room. Stafford and Peters brought up the rear.

Ray Cooper was sitting on the edge of a light grey, two-seater settee. He looked at Martin, grimaced and said through swollen, scabby lips, 'Bugger – just looking at you makes my nuts ache.'

'Shut up, Ray. Let's hear what they've got to say,' said Charlotte.

With six of them in the room it was feeling crowded, and Stafford said, 'I'm sorry, Ms Lesney, we have to search your flat. It'll be easier if you let my colleagues do it while Sergeant Martin and I talk to you and Ray.'

Charlotte glared at him. 'Do I have choice?'

Stafford nodded at Whitley and Peters and they moved off into other rooms to begin the search. Charlotte sat on the settee beside her brother.

'Is this going to take long? Because I have to be at work later,' she said.

'That may not be possible, Ms Lesney – is it OK if we

call you Charlotte? That depends on this conversation,' said Stafford.

'But I haven't done anything.'

Stafford stared at her, and she lowered her eyes as he said, 'At this moment we could arrest you for aiding and abetting a fugitive, and for attempting to pervert the course of justice—'

'Hang on a bit, Stafford,' Cooper interrupted, 'it's me you're after, it's me who's dragged her into all this. She's just been trying to patch me up a bit, is all. She is my sister – what d'you expect her to do?'

'You're right, we're not interested in dragging Charlotte into this, but we will if we have to. Now, one way or another you're going to pay for what you did to Sophie Gibson. So that's a definite – where we go from there is down to you and how much you're willing to cooperate.'

'I'm fucking fed up with this, Stafford. I want to get it over and done with.'

'Good, it'll save you both a lot of heartache in the future. So first off, I want you to make a phone call,' said Stafford.

CHAPTER 62

Sweetman couldn't settle. He knew this was the end game for Aksanov's syndicate. He'd throw his lot in with the Russians, tell his sister to put his house on the market and move to the West Midlands or London, wherever they could use him. Bastard Stafford thought he was being clever, putting a block on his bank account, but with the best part of ten grand in his pocket and a slab each of H and C, he could last for a few months, no problem.

But he needed a new motor; they'd have all the info on his Audi by now. And he wanted a replacement for the Glock 26 Cooper had nicked off him. OK, he still had the Berretta machine pistol, and it was a great weapon, but the Glock was neat, easier to conceal. He guessed Sheila would have a weapon stashed away somewhere and he began to search. Three floors and a basement was a hell of a search area and after an hour he gave up, and tried to settle down again. The staff didn't start work until around 2 p.m. and he'd be long gone by then. He slept fitfully; eventually time crept round to a reasonable hour to start making phone calls.

He found his mobile, tapped in a number.

'It's Jamie. I wanna do a deal on a motor, needs to be fairly new and nimble. And I need you to take the Audi off me, and I don't want to spend more than three grand.' He listened for a moment or two, and said, 'Yeah, sounds OK. Get it ready to go, I'll be round about midday. This better be kosher, mate, I don't need any hassle, savvy?' As he put the phone down, it rang again. He checked the screen; not a number he recognised, but he accepted the call. Silence.

Sweetman, about to click off, heard, 'Jamie? Is that you, Jamie?'

'Who's askin'?'

'It's me, Cooper, Ray Cooper, I thought we—'

'You thought fucking wrong, Cooper, whatever it is, you thought wrong.'

'No, listen, Jamie, listen to me. You know Aksanov's dead, you got no reason to kill me now, have you? I mean, surely to Christ, mate—'

'Don't fucking "mate" me.'

'Jamie, listen to me, we can work this out together. Look, I'll even bring your gun back… I didn't fuckin' shoot when I had the chance did I, so, Jamie, mate, listen to me a sec. I'll meet you wherever you want; you name it, I'll get there. Even bloody Neilson's been killed. And Aksanov's missus."

'I thought Stafford had caught up with you?'

'Yeah, he did, gave me a bloody good hiding, then fucked me off. I think he thought you or Aksanov would get to me. So I want to get even with him, and maybe even shag that bird he's with.' He tried a feeble laugh.

Sweetman didn't laugh back. 'Last I heard, you'd gone to hospital.'

'No, that was Stafford, making up stuff to try and trap us – but I didn't. Me sister's a nurse, she patched me up some.'

'So you're still in the wind then?'

'Yeah. Borrowed her little car, got me this phone, emptied me account, all hunky-dory, mate. Listen, I'm sorry I hurt you, but fuck me, you were trying to kill me.'

They were both silent for a while. Smart bad guys adapt, and Sweetman was smart. He made up his mind. 'OK, Cooper, meet me at Whitelines in an hour. Bring my Glock and come alone. Anything else and you're dead. Savvy?'

'Thanks, Jamie, that's great. I'll be there, I won't let you down.'

Sweetman killed the call and, sitting on the edge of the bed, pondered what had been said. He wasn't sure Cooper could be trusted. Christ, he had every reason to hurt me; tables turned, I'd have killed him, he thought. But Cooper had his chance and didn't shoot, so perhaps he was on the level and wanted to work together. Best to be prepared, though. He got off the bed and wandered down to the ground floor. Opening the boot to the Audi and his go-bag, he took out his Beretta 93 machine pistol. It was brilliant when up against a mob, a rapid fire spray, accurate over short distances, but one on one he preferred the Glock; neat, easy to carry and to conceal. So if Cooper was out for trouble, up close he'd have a slight advantage, but it had the standard ten-shot magazine and Cooper had used three shooting out tyres at the pub, so max there were seven shots left.

He finished his checks and returned the gun to the bag. He'd swap the bags over when he collected the new motor. Walking back to Sheila's suite, his mobile chimed. It was Sheila. Her voice; strident, shrill.

'Jamie, Jamie, where are you? You still at the club?'

'Yeah, got to organise a new motor; be off in about—' She interrupted him.

'Jamie, I've been trying to get to the club, all streets, back, front, everywhere, all police everywhere. I can't get to, all police stopping every one.' Her English was failing. 'Some got guns, and bullet vest.'

Sweetman was stunned, and fell silent for a very long moment. 'Jesus, that bastard Cooper, he's fucking set me up.' He dashed to the storeroom exit doors, unlocked them and pushed one side open a fraction. Slamming it shut, he leaned against them, assimilating what he'd seen; half a dozen police cars and two armed response vehicles, all posted around the low perimeter wall of the car park. He ran to the front of the building where the doors opened on to the main street. He risked a glimpse through the small, wired-glass windows in the double entrance. Police cars and an ARV were setting up positions and he could see an ambulance parked up. The street had been blocked off at both ends. He moved back, leaning against the wall. Above him he heard a muffled *boom*, then the walls vibrated and the floor shook. He remembered his phone and put it to his ear.

'Sheila, what can you see? Sounds like they're fucking bombing the place.'

'No, Jamie, sorry, Jamie, that is me, I can't let police find stuff there, I have firebombs in place. You need get out Jamie, I remote one on top floor. Now soon, I remote one on middle, the basement, you must go!'

'Fucking hell, Sheila, you as well? How the fuck do you suggest I get out of here? Give myself up, and spend thirty years in fucking jail?'

Another *boom* from above, this one louder. The building shook again.

'For Christ's sake, Sheila, you mad bitch, you can't fucking blow me up as well!'

The phone was quiet for ten or twelve seconds before Sheila spoke. 'Jamie, there is chance – in ground floor, see metal cabinet in corner, behind your car, you find things to help. Sorry, Jamie – *paç fat*,' said Sheila, her voice, thin, reedy, so nervous she'd lost the English for good luck.

Sweetman looked at the cabinet; it was padlocked. Returning to the car he retrieved the Beretta and fired a burst of three shots at it, the padlock fell apart. He ran to the cabinet and ripped the doors open. In the base was a grey-painted, wooden box with Chinese lettering on the top and sides. Sweetman lifted the lid; it was divided into six sections. One section was empty, the others packed with wood wool. Pulling it out, he saw what Sheila had meant. And as he took out the black pineapple hand grenade, he thanked her silently. He took out three; *that should be enough, one way or another.*

Rivers of sweat ran down his back, down his arms. Sweat ran down his forehead into his eyes and he wiped it away. All around him, chunks of plaster fell from the ceiling. He looked up to see the paint bubbling. The whole storage area was heating up like an oven. He opened the doors to the car park and could see Stafford standing behind a green car. A low brick wall surrounded the parking area; two ARVs were parked across the entrance. The AR crews were taking cover behind the low wall. Sweetman could see their weapons and tops of their helmets as they moved into position.

His mind was made up; Sheila must be ready to detonate the incendiary device in the basement, he knew she wouldn't wait forever. He had to get out fast. He watched as Stafford put a mobile to his face. Milliseconds later, Sweetman's mobile vibrated; he took the call.

'Make it easy on yourself, Sweetman, walk out with your hands in the air. We're not going to shoot.'

'Is that prick Cooper with you?'

'No, once we knew where you were, his job was done, but you, you're not going to die in the fire, are you? The whole place looks about ready to fall in on you.'

Sweetman stepped back inside, threw his mobile onto the passenger seat of the Audi. Grabbing the Beretta, he fired it obliquely into the centre of the steering wheel, disabling the airbag. He fired again into the right-hand windscreen pillar. That's fucked my PX value, he thought with a grimace. He jumped in, fired up the engine and strapped himself in. In his mind's eye, he could visualise where Stafford was standing. He picked up a grenade, pushed it between his thighs; he didn't want to be scrabbling around the floor to find one. He opened his window, slammed the gearstick into first, then with Beretta in his right hand, left hand on the steering wheel, engine screaming, he lifted his foot high off the clutch. The bonnet rose about four inches as it smashed its way through the doors. As the Audi surged across the car park, a ball of fire shot out from the doors behind him and the storeroom doors were engulfed in flames. Sheila's clear-up.

CHAPTER 63

Spraying the ARVs with a hail of bullets, the Audi crashed through the low wall and slammed into the side of Stafford's car. The force of the impact threw Stafford to the ground. Sweetman's passenger airbag deployed, but it didn't impede him. Once the Beretta's magazine was empty he threw the gun into the car park, and grabbed the grenade. He waved it out of the window.

Stafford, climbing to his feet, yelled, 'Sweetman, don't pull the bloody pin.'

Sweetman grinned and said, 'Move the car, Stafford, get the road cleared, or I'll do it for you.'

'How can I move it? You've wrecked it.'

'You had your chance, Stafford,' said Sweetman, pulling his hand back inside. Seconds later he held up the pin in his left hand, grenade in his right, outside the window again.

'Last fuckin' chance, Stafford,' he shouted.

Stafford, eyes wide, arms waving frantically, shouted, 'Don't throw it, Jamie, the bloody thing's rigged.'

Sweetman hesitated, pulled his hand back in to the car. All was silent for a second or two, then Stafford, machine pistol in hand, edged slowly to the back of his car. Sweetman saw the movement, stuck his right hand out again, and said, 'So what the fuck's up–'

Sweetman's head exploded. A mass of blood, hair and grey matter splattered across the inside of the car. It was a millisecond before anyone heard the shot.

Stafford yelled, 'Everybody down, *now*!'

Stafford saw the AR man who fired the shot start to move towards Sweetman's car and dived headlong towards him, yelling, '*Down*!' As he piled on to the AR man, the Audi erupted, sending a fireball through the windscreen, ripping the roof apart, like a volcano blowing. The front doors blew out, ripped into lethal shards that flew across the street. The blast hit Stafford mid-flight; he slammed head first down the side of the ARV, blood spewing out, pooling in the gutter. Split seconds later, the sound of the blast ricocheted from building to building across the street. Somehow Stafford managed to push the shooter to the relative safety of the pavement.

The AR unit commander ordered the two vehicles across the entrance to move, just as a fire tender screeched to a halt – the driver had seen Stafford lying there. Paramedics from waiting ambulances ran to move him out of harm's way. As they loaded him, unconscious, onto a stretcher, the AR man struggled to his feet, suffering little more than cuts and bruises. The fire tender rolled into the car park; fuel leaking from the Volvo's ruptured petrol lines caught fire. Within seconds it reached the petrol tank. The fire crew saw it and shouted a warning to the coppers and AR men moving in to help. As they aimed their hoses, the back end of the Volvo lifted a foot into the air and blew apart, sending a shower of blazing petrol and shrapnel over the backs of the retreating officers. Again the noise from the deafening explosion ricocheted from building to building.

Stafford hadn't worn his Kevlar ballistic helmet as he'd wanted to make sure Sweetman would see him and recognise him. He'd wanted to talk Sweetman out of a battle. His Kevlar vest, though, had been a godsend; the paramedics left it in place as they tended to the massive gash, from his left temple, up into his hairline. Blood flowed copiously. One paramedic wiped the blood from Stafford's face and eyes. He could see no further damage to his head or face. Pressing a cotton swab on to the torn area, he taped it securely in place. They began to peel off his Kevlar vest – the right-hand side and back were deeply scored by metal shards and grenade shrapnel, some embedded in the vest. The shards hadn't been able to penetrate the Kevlar, but the medics knew Stafford would suffer from many bruises caused by blunt-force trauma. Stafford was wearing a polo shirt under the vest. His right arm was lacerated and grazed from shoulder to wrist, and some of the skin was burnt and blistered, doubtless caused by red-hot metal shards. They had to unclench his fingers to remove the Beretta machine pistol.

--- || ---

The clear-up now in the hands of the professionals, Martin, Peters and Whitley ran towards the ambulance, hotly followed by DI Masterson. The paramedics had put Stafford on board.

Nicole ripped off her Kevlar helmet and vest and climbed into the back. 'How is he?' she asked.

'Worst bit is the head wound; don't know how much damage there is. And can't see any life-threatening injuries or broken limbs. But he's gonna need a shitload of stitches in his head and arm. We'll know more about the head wound when we get him to hospital. Are you going with him?'

'Yes, I'll come and—'

DI Masterson interrupted her and said, 'Hang on, Sergeant, you're needed here, taking statements, doing interviews.'

She glared at him, red rising up her neck. She paused for a second, then said, 'Can you walk on water as well as raise the dead, because there's no one here alive to fu— flaming interview.' She stopped, looked at her watch, and said, 'Besides, I've been on the go since seven thirty this morning, now I'm on Code 4. Give me a shout when you find someone for me to interview.'

A red-faced Masterson had already walked away when Peters said, 'Harry, you started the same time, you're Code 4 too. Jump in with me – you OK with hospital food?'

Five minutes earlier, standing by the police cordon overlooking the blazing cars and nightclub, Shpresa Berisha made the sign of the cross.

'*Pushoni në paqe,* Jamie,' she said. Turning away, she realised Jamie wouldn't understand, so she said it in English, 'Rest in peace, Jamie, rest in peace.'

Reaching her Mini Clubman, she took out her mobile, made a call. After a short wait she said, 'Ah, can you please make delivery to Hurricanes; Whitelines is no more.' She listened to the men talking, muffled tones, then *Da* came the response. She threw the mobile onto the passenger seat, turned the car round and, with a satisfied smile, headed for Hurricanes.

Watch out for the third book in the series:

THIRD FLOOR SHEILA
(current working title)

Coming towards the end of 2021.

Follow the author at:
http://www.facebook.com/NormanTownsendwriter

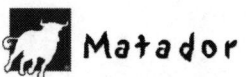

For exclusive discounts on Matador titles,
sign up to our occasional newsletter at
troubador.co.uk/bookshop